The Build

"*The Build-a-Boyfriend* [...] of swoons, and, most importantly, full of things to say about life, love, and becoming who we want to be. Mason Deaver has built a winner!"

—Adib Khorram, *USA Today* bestselling author of *I'll Have What He's Having*

"Sweet and sexy, *The Build-a-Boyfriend Project* is a delightful romance about taking chances and embracing the unexpected. Disastrous first date to possible true love . . . what could be more delicious?"

—Ashley Herring Blake, *USA Today* bestselling author of *Iris Kelly Doesn't Date*

"*The Build-a-Boyfriend Project* is an addicting story full of hard-hitting emotions, balanced perfectly by a whip-smart and hilarious voice. An adorable love interest will have you rooting for a well-earned happily-ever-after until the very end. The trans masculine representation was glorious, and it was so exciting to see Eli's experience as a trans man on the page. Mason bravely does not shy away from difficult topics, and it's validating and gratifying to see Eli's realistic struggles. Mason has knocked it out of the park with this heartwarming romance."

—Kacen Callender, National Book Award–winning author

"From the frustration of feeling creatively stagnant to the anxiety of exploring romance and love for the first time as a queer adult, Deaver captures the awkwardness and vulnerability of your late twenties in a fake-dating romance that's full of charm, authenticity, and so much yearning. Eli and Peter's messy, tender love story speaks to anyone who's ever felt like an outsider, capturing at once the heartbreak and joy of finding yourself and your people."

—Emma R. Alban, *USA Today* bestselling author of *Don't Want You Like a Best Friend*

the
build-a-
boyfriend
project

Also by Mason Deaver

I Wish You All the Best
The Ghosts We Keep
The Feeling of Falling in Love
Okay, Cupid

the build-a-boyfriend project

A NOVEL

Mason Deaver

AVON

An Imprint of HarperCollins*Publishers*

THE BUILD-A-BOYFRIEND PROJECT. Copyright © 2025 by Mason Deaver. All rights reserved. Printed in the United States of America. No part of this book may be used or reproduced in any manner whatsoever without written permission except in the case of brief quotations embodied in critical articles and reviews. For information, address HarperCollins Publishers, 195 Broadway, New York, NY 10007.

HarperCollins books may be purchased for educational, business, or sales promotional use. For information, please email the Special Markets Department at SPsales@harpercollins.com.

Avon, Avon & logo, and Avon Books & logo are registered trademarks of HarperCollins Publishers in the United States of America and other countries.

FIRST EDITION

Interior text design by Diahann Sturge-Campbell

Library of Congress Cataloging-in-Publication Data has been applied for.

ISBN 978-0-06-339430-8

25 26 27 28 29 LBC 5 4 3 2 1

For the lovers, the dreamers, and me

Dear Reader,

While The Build-a-Boyfriend Project *is a rom-com that features a happy ending, it's a story that touches on heavy topics from time to time. Inside, you'll find conversations between characters about the racism, homophobia, and transphobia they've faced. You'll also find discussions about conversion therapy, outing, and the grief of losing a parent.*

Please exercise care while reading this book if any of those topics may affect you personally.

I believe there's a hero in all of us that keeps us honest, gives us strength, makes us noble, and finally allows us to die with pride, even though sometimes we have to be steady and give up the thing we want the most. Even our dreams.

—*SPIDER-MAN 2*

Chapter One

Sorry to Bother You, dir. by Boots Riley

All Eli Francis can think as he shuffles into the elevator of the *Vent* offices is how much he hates Frappuccinos. Frappuccinos *specifically*. He's not a coffee snob by any means, feed him whatever flavors, brands, temperatures. Black, oat milk, no sugar, even tea! He likes to think he's not a hard man to please.

But having spent every single Tuesday for the last five years going to the local café down the block where he orders five different Frappuccinos—alongside the macchiatos, the matchas, and the mochas—has led to a certain level of hatred that even he knows is inexplicable. Maybe it's the way the cups are always too full, or how the whipped cream on top of the early morning sugar bombs is always melted by the time he makes it back to the building, leaving it to leak out under the lids and down the cups to the sleeves of his sweater.

Or how there's this odd stickiness that seems to follow him for the rest of the day no matter how rose red he might scrub his hands in the bathroom afterward.

He watches the numbers on the elevator screen rising floor by floor, the floor underneath him shifting as it moves as slowly as possible.

And of course, because it's *so* early in the morning, there are stops at every floor, employees at the other publications and sites that share the building with *Vent* joining him along his journey, making small talk, offering quiet greetings to Eli as he tries to balance the drinks and food in his arms before the elevator creaks to life again.

They crawl to the eleventh floor, the doors seeming to take as much time as they possibly can to open, not that Eli likes who he sees.

The list of people Eli doesn't want to perceive before nine a.m. isn't a very long one. There's Gwen, head of IT, whom he adores but who spends her mornings fielding "Can I upload a PDF to Instagram?"–type questions, so it's best not to bother her unless it's life or death. There's the one barista who always gets at least half of Eli's orders wrong. There's Adam, from the mailroom, who's disliked Eli ever since he accidentally tipped over an entire mail cart and was in such a rush to deliver a last-minute contract that he hadn't been able to stay and help clean it up.

To be fair, Eli fully understands *why* Adam dislikes him. Not even a yearly Christmas card with an apologetic gift certificate included has repaired that relationship.

But above almost everyone else on the list sits the name Michael Clay, his boss, senior editor at *Vent*, head of content and whatever the vagueness of that title includes. Eli thinks his inclusion on the list is fair; after all, who ever wants to see their boss until it's absolutely necessary?

And if that wasn't bad enough, standing right next to Michael is number one on Eli's list.

Keith Harper.

San José graduate from their journalism program, former assistant and staff writer at *Vent*, current editor. Hater of grilled-cheese sandwiches, enjoyer of classical music, and lover of wine with an "oaky" aftertaste.

And Eli's ex-boyfriend.

His spot on the list is probably self-explanatory.

Eli's eyes dart away, but not before Keith's meet his for the briefest of moments, and Eli wishes that he didn't feel that twinge in his stomach as he desperately hopes he hasn't caught their attention.

But he's never been all that lucky.

"Oh! Eli, great, we caught you on your way up!" Michael smiles, tucking his iPad under his arm as they try to find space in the already cramped elevator.

Neither man makes an effort to relieve Eli of the load he carries. "Yep."

"Do you think you could make twenty copies of our pitches before the meeting? I'll email you."

"Sure thing." Eli bites back the rest of his words.

"So, anyway." Michael turns toward Keith, both of them forgetting Eli in an instant. "I was thinking that we could up the amount of those Marvel listicles with that new movie coming out. Those always boost our numbers."

"I've got the team working on a few ideas," Keith tells Michael.

Eli has to stop himself from rolling his eyes at Keith, wondering just how many of those lists he'll have to suffer through, double-checking the details and making sure the barrage of GIFs that serve as an excuse for actual journalism are embedded correctly in the page before they're put in front of Michael.

"Also, I had some ideas about the *Delish* posts for the meeting. I was thinking uploading videos to Spotify as podcasts might bump up the views if we could include listens. Most people just turn it on as background noise anyway."

Michael nods his head excitedly, like he's ready to agree with anything that Keith might say. "I like it. It could be a lot of fun, plus it'll keep people in the brand."

"It's a video series, though . . ." Eli can't help himself.

He'd think after years of suffering through working at *Vent*, being parked in front of Michael's office, fielding emails and calls, reading through articles, fact-checking sources, and editing stories line by line when Michael didn't "feel like doing the work" he's paid to do—which was *far* more often than not—he'd have learned to keep his mouth shut.

"What was that, Eli?" Keith asks, his eyes focusing on Eli as he struggles to balance everything. There's annoyance in his tone, which Eli finds so funny since Keith used to *love* listening to Eli. Especially when he could take the ideas that Eli gave him and pass them off as his own, or when Eli corrected his grammar.

"*Delish* is a video series," Eli repeats. And one of their more popular ones at that. Sped-up videos that showed homemade recipes that were way more complicated than they had any right to be. "It's kind of key that they stay videos, or at the very least GIFs. A podcast doesn't make any sense."

Michael looks at Keith, not saying anything.

Keith pokes the inside of his cheek with his tongue, staring at Eli. An expression Eli is familiar with. One he used to find cute.

"Our podcast numbers are strong," Keith insists. "Our audience is always looking for new content from us. If we can get some of the staff to just sit and talk about the recipes for fifteen minutes or something quick, it'll work."

"Well, we've got to give the people what they want!" Michael says, beaming, looking to Eli as if he's searching for permission. "That's why Keith's leading this meeting."

The elevator door *dings* and the rush of people eager to escape the tension inside is nearly enough to knock Eli over. It's certainly enough to spill Gwen from IT's chai latte all over the front of his sweater.

"Motherfucker . . ." Eli stares down at the mess. He sets the drinks down and fishes the handful of napkins he grabbed from the café out of his shoulder bag, soaking up as much as he can, trying not to feel guilty at the way the leftover stickiness of the floor rips into the soles of his shoes when he balances his feet.

"I need to pay rent," he mutters to himself, hoping that the jani-torial crew of the building won't be angry with him. "I need to pay rent, I need to pay rent, I need to pay rent."

"Eli?"

Eli dares to look up, the elevator door moving to close before Keith reaches out with a strong arm and holds it back.

It's hard enough for him to believe that this is the man he gave seven years of his life to. Seven years of going to the movies, laugh-ing over dinner, taking the bus to Ocean Beach where they spent the day reading or watching one of the local volleyball leagues practice while they sat on the sea wall, eating too-greasy breakfast sandwiches and enjoying the breeze.

This is the man that Eli practiced saying "I love you" to for six months before he finally said the words out loud, and Keith smiled at him like he was the only person in the world who mattered. This is the man whom Eli pictured spending the rest of his life with, no matter how cheesy that might sound, maybe getting mar-ried even though neither of them was the marriage type, adopting a cat because they both disliked dogs, moving into a new apart-ment, one they'd pick out together; they'd never leave the city, but Eli thought maybe they'd settle down in the Inner Sunset, or the Richmond. One of the quieter neighborhoods.

This is the man Eli thinks he still might be in love with, despite how Keith looked him in the eye, his lips forming carefully around the words "I think it's time we ended things."

He'd planned an entire life with Keith Harper. Even through Keith's promotions, when Eli transformed from a peer to a sub-ordinate who had to take Keith's lunch orders every morning at 11:30 a.m. He'd never considered any part of his life "traditional," but he felt lucky to have Keith, someone who clearly loved Eli for himself.

And then Keith broke up with him on a Saturday morning. It

was 8:30, foggy outside. Eli was making French toast that burnt to
a crisp in the ten minutes it took for the relationship to end.

Seven years, gone in ten minutes.

Six hundred seconds.

The worst part is that he knows part of himself is still there, in
that apartment. Sometimes he was still there in bed with Keith,
tracing the Sylvia Plath quote tattoo in typewriter font on his bicep
that Keith had gotten just to feel that rush of college rebellion he
was so desperate for; sometimes he still smelled the burning egg
and bread, the salt of a piece of bacon he'd snuck for himself still
fresh on his tongue.

Keith walks forward, hitting the button to hold the door open
before squatting down next to Eli to take a bundle of napkins, their
fingers touching for the briefest of moments before Keith goes to
clean up the spilled drink.

"You okay?" he asks, and Eli hates how he can tell that Keith
means it. That he genuinely cares.

There's still a piece of Eli that misses that.

A piece that's larger than Eli would ever care to admit.

Keith's green eyes meet his, that perpetual five-o'clock shadow
ghosting Keith's jawline, the slight chap of his lips.

"I think you might've gotten a bit on your sweater," Keith says
when Eli doesn't reply to his question.

"It's fine, it's wool." He can't even see any potential stains forming.

"You always did love a good sweater." The past-tense words are
doing their best to sound familiar, comforting, but Eli doesn't want
them. "I'll see you at the meeting, I guess . . ." Keith says to him.

He doesn't say anything, just watches as Keith takes the sopping-
wet mess in his hand and tosses the napkins into the nearby trash bin.

The elevator doors go to close again, and Eli rushes back to his
feet, rearranging the drinks in his arms. He nearly collides with

Jackson, one of their accountants, almost ruining more drinks as he speed-walks toward the conference room.

Michelle, another writer at *Vent*, holds the door open for Eli, taking one of the drinks from him.

Coworkers murmur their thanks as he rounds the table, setting out the drinks and food in their familiar spots, grateful that everyone has their preferred seating, and even more grateful that he and Gwen drink the same thing, so he can simply offer his iced chai to her.

"You didn't get anything?" she asks him.

"I'm cutting caffeine," he says, digging his iPad out of his bag.

Eli might just be an assistant, but with how forgetful Michael tends to be, and the man's resistance to taking notes of any kind, Eli carries more responsibility than he's compensated for.

Keith walks by, rolling up the sleeves of the button-up that Eli gave him three Christmases ago as he heads to the front of the conference room, his eyes meeting Eli's, his gaze sticking as he reaches for his drink where Eli left it.

Even now, a part of Eli's brain that he desperately wants to ignore is sending signals to his heart, urging his blood to pump faster, his pulse to leap wildly.

"Thanks for the coffee," Keith says, slurping from the paper straw that's already disintegrating in the cup. "Okay! Everyone, thank you for coming in, let's go ahead and get into it."

Eli remembers they'd had three meetings about their relationship with HR. The first one promised that their dating wouldn't interfere with the day-to-day at the site, that the two of them were more than capable of doing their jobs, of remaining focused even though they were working alongside one another.

The second came when Keith got his promotion, and they'd had to sign some paperwork where Keith promised he wouldn't use his position on the staff to unfairly reward Eli.

The last assured the exact same thing as the first, the only difference being the promise that their breakup wouldn't make things harder for either of them. Or, more importantly, the company.

Eli stares down at the blank document on his screen, unable to resist the oral fixation to put the end of his Apple Pencil between his teeth before he remembers just *how* expensive the accessory was, even if it is technically the property of the website. He takes notes when he deems it appropriate, which means that he exits the meeting with just two.

Make sure Michael reads article proposals!

And *Read comments for Workplace Drama List story.*

Truly gripping journalism.

* * *

Hours later, Eli has exchanged the mundanity of the meeting for the boredom of reading through one of the listicles that *Vent* has become known for: bite-size bits of "news" that combine written and visual elements in order to tell "a gripping story."

At least, that's how Michael once described them to him. So now, instead of taking notes that Michael won't read over, Eli is instead forced to type out: *Clint Eastwood says "Do I feel lucky?" not "Do you feel lucky?" He's speaking from the perspective of the bank robber,* in an email to a staff writer for an article titled "Movie Quotes We Use Every Single Day and We Didn't Even Know It!"

He's already had to correct the writer on Darth Vader's famous "No, I am your father" when the writer wrote "Luke, I am your father," and he's sure that it won't be the last misattributed line of dialogue that he has to look at.

For the time being, though, his growling stomach is enough to force him to save the draft after noting a reminder to send another list of edits to Keith before the end of the day so that he can approve the "buzziness" of the article. He's so focused on his computer screen that the blue light feels like it's burning his eyes. The only thing that pulls him away from his work is the container full of lettuce that's dropped onto his keyboard.

He can't help the yelp. An instant shot of adrenaline hits his heart before he realizes that Patricia is the Tupperware tosser in question.

"You scared me," he says, picking up the plastic container with his lunch and setting it off to the side.

"You shouldn't be sitting that close to your monitor," she tells him, grabbing the back of a nearby chair at an empty desk and wheeling it over toward Eli. "You'll hurt your eyes."

"My doctor says my eyesight hasn't changed," Eli replies, pushing his thin metal frames further up his nose. Never mind that his last eye doctor appointment was three years ago, back when he was still on his mother's insurance.

"Eat, it's lunchtime." Patricia picks up her own salad, made fresh that morning in their shared kitchen because—unlike Eli—she actually wakes up when her alarm goes off, and doesn't hit the snooze button ten times before rushing to get dressed.

She's also all too aware that Eli's breakfast was nothing other than a KIND bar, and knows that it's long gone by now.

"One second, I need to finish something." Eli opens up his email, remembering that Michael is waiting for his suggested edits on another piece. This one about readers' "Favorite Skin Care Must Haves!" with hyperlinks that just so happen to link to the product's Target page, a tiny little disclaimer at the end saying that *Vent* makes a commission from any items bought through the links.

"Nope." Patricia leans over, stealing Eli's wireless mouse and dropping it right into her corduroy tote bag. "It's lunchtime."

"Pat . . ."

"I have an hour to eat with you," Patricia lectures. "You've already wasted five of my sixty minutes. Now eat."

"Fine," Eli grumbles, taking the metal fork Patricia supplied and snapping the Tupperware lid off. "It's not like you're not going to see me tonight."

"So?" Patricia spears another piece of lettuce and tomato onto her fork, making sure to add a black olive to the combo. "What if I want to see you now?"

It was a group assignment in college that brought Patricia and Eli to each other, featuring a third classmate who refused to do any of the work. Patricia and Eli spent nearly every night together for the following two weeks and became best friends in the way that only bonding over shared contempt for a person can do.

They decided to move in with each other post-graduation to ease the cost of living in the city, both of them even managing to get jobs in the same building. Eli at *Vent*, and Patricia at fashion magazine *InVogue*, spending her day poring over pieces, predicting trends, and interviewing models and designers alike. It only made sense, what with how her love of clothing informed nearly every decision she made, how she selected outfits and pieces to write about, how she pored over three-hundred-page books about specific shades of red and their historical context, using her position at *InVogue* to put Black fashion at the forefront of the magazine.

Eli had even gotten the chance to pull her into *Vent* last year to film a video dissecting the Met Gala looks. A video that still happens to be one of the most viewed on *Vent*'s YouTube channel.

And Eli's name appears nowhere in the description. Not even as a special thanks.

"Oh, come on . . ." Patricia reaches into her bag, pulls out the small bottle of vinaigrette, and hands it to Eli. "Where's that smile?"

"I'm not really feeling it today," he tells her, pouring the dressing over his lunch.

"Keith?"

Eli doesn't have to say yes; his silence is enough of an answer.

He looks ahead, past his computer monitor, at the glass enclosure that Keith gets to call his office.

"Did he do anything specific?" Patricia asks quietly.

He was nice to me, Eli thinks to himself. Which might just be the most heinous crime of all. "Does he ever have to?"

"Nope," she says, her mouth turning into a grin. Like they've ever needed *actual* reasons to be haters. "But legitimate reasons help me paint a broader picture."

"He's just being . . . himself," Eli admits.

"I don't think I love you anymore."

He tried to tell himself there were worse seven-word sentences to start your day to.

"You're pregnant and I'm not the father."

"The cat was hit by a car."

"Ayo Edebiri decided to retire from acting."

He tells himself that he should feel lucky, that not everyone gets to experience that great love of their life, even if this one didn't last.

"I'm offering again," Patricia says. "Let me set you up. One of my friends, she knows this guy who—"

Eli stops her then and there. "Nope. Not interested."

"You barely tried the apps for a month."

"And you saw the responses I got," he reminds her. Patricia and Rose—their other roommate—were sent every single cringe-worthy response and opener that Eli had been subjected to. From guys looking for the "Pam to my Jim" to dudes with bare-bones profiles with no profile picture to criminal offenders who thought a hike through the entire length of the Presidio or the Valley Trailhead was an appropriate first date.

Those didn't even include the people he matched with who couldn't be bothered to reply back to him, who left Eli hanging after the always-awkward introduction message that was apparently enough to turn them off from him completely.

Then there were the guys from Grindr and Scruff. The men who saw the "trans-guy" Eli put in his profile to try to avoid the exact kind of people he wound up running into. He'd deleted both profiles after a full two days of "What guy wants to fuck a dude with a vag?" and "Grow a pair before I fuck you."

Or the ever-delightful users who wanted to "taste Eli's boy pussy so bad."

He still hadn't decided which was worse.

That was all it took. The very same day, Eli swore off men and dating entirely, deleting the apps, the accounts, their conversations.

Just like that, it was over.

He'd had the one true love of his life in Keith, and that had been lost. And even if he didn't want to, Eli was prepared to spend the rest of his life alone.

It just wasn't worth it.

"I'm done dating," he says, reminding her of the proud proclamation he'd made. "Done. D-O-N-E!"

"But you could meet *the* one, that guy that'll totally sweep you off your feet." Patricia goes all starry-eyed. "And you won't know unless you try!"

"I've tried. Been there, done that, got the T-shirt. Not worth it." Eli stabs at his lettuce violently, accidentally spraying his glasses with dressing.

"Says the guy who sobs over rom-coms any chance he gets."

"Those are movies." He cleans his glasses with a spare napkin, leaving them streakier than before. "And they're not even accurate." If they were, he and Keith would've had their big reunion: running into each other's arms, Keith coming to his senses, and Eli forgiving him in that big third-act climax as the music swells and everything turns out okay. The credits roll, and the audience gets to imagine what their perfect future looks like, all complete with a montage that shows their life *just* after the end of the movie.

Eli's eyes drift across the office to Keith's office, Patricia's following him.

"I'd love to squish his stupid little head . . ." Patricia murmurs, setting her empty Tupperware down.

He wasn't even doing anything, just typing something on his keyboard.

"I just think we're different people," Keith explained when Eli had asked him what went wrong. He hadn't been brave enough to ask Keith in the moment after the breakup. He'd only gotten the courage when he'd collected his things from Keith's apartment.

He'd gone home and cried after that, much like he had in the days that came before. Rose and Patricia had found Eli in the dark apartment after they turned on the lights, Rose yelping when Eli scared her.

They'd done their best to help cheer him up; alcohol from the liquor store downstairs was purchased at some point, which led to the two of them opening their individual Notes apps to do dramatic readings of every issue either of them had with Keith.

Selections included:

- Never posting a single picture of Eli on Instagram because Instagram is "for networking, not relationships."
- His terrible choice of cologne that made their apartment reek for days.
- When he tried to explain a Vietnamese dish to Rose even though she's literally Vietnamese.
- He talks through every single movie and TV show and reads the TV Tropes page for spoilers so he can act like he figured out every twist before it happens.
- That time he liked the wine Patricia bought and when he asked where it came from and Patricia said "I don't know, it's

just from Target," he went on a twenty-minute rant about how important it is to "know where your wine comes from."

• Never introducing Eli to his parents or family.

Eli's ashamed to admit he never even noticed some of these things until it was too late. Of course, the Instagram thing hurt, but he tried to be understanding when Keith explained himself. And Eli had once thought the smell of Keith's cologne was nice; he even sprayed some of it on his clothes while Keith showered just so he could smell him throughout the day.

And his family . . . Eli told himself that he understood. His own family was a little out there as well, always wanting to tell the most embarrassing stories from Eli's childhood, even though he hadn't been the person they were talking about in a decade. But it always struck him as odd that Keith's mother never seemed to know that her son was in a committed relationship. Eli almost asked him multiple times if Keith was out, if their relationship was a secret. Not that he'd mind—it was Keith's business if or when he came out, and who he was out to—but Eli would've liked to know, just so he could help, or at least lend an ear to Keith's anxieties. They were *boyfriends*, after all.

And isn't that what boyfriends are supposed to do?

"Do I have anything in my teeth?" Eli flashes Patricia a forced grimace.

"You're changing the subject," she tells him.

"Help me out here."

"You're clear," she relents. "Special occasion?"

"Meeting with Michael when he's back from lunch."

"Wait, like *meeting* with Michael, or meeting with Michael?"

Eli stares at her for a moment. "I don't hear the difference."

She raises her shoulders a bit, leaning in. "Is it what we've been discussing for the last three weeks?"

Eli's nerves seem to jump in an instant as he reaches for the computer mouse that isn't there. "Yep . . ."

Patricia's reaction is immediate. "You're doing it?"

Eli can't resist the infectious nature of her smile. "Yeah, I am."

"Ah!" She squeals, wheeling closer toward Eli to wrap him in an awkward hug. "I'm so proud of you!"

"Relax, relax. He hasn't even interviewed me yet," Eli tells her, deciding that he's done eating too. "And it wouldn't be the first time he's told me we'll 'revisit' my position at the site."

"Okay, but he promised you last year," she reminds him. "If a staff job opened up, you'd be the first person interviewed for it."

"He promised the year before that too, and the year before that. And the year before that I interviewed for the *same* job, and was made his secretary instead."

"Executive assistant," Patricia corrects him.

"We both know that's horseshit."

"Well . . ." Patricia takes the Tupperware containers and slips them back into her bag, digging around further so she can give Eli back his mouse. "It's going to go great. You just have to walk in there believing it. You've got the experience, and without you this entire office falls apart."

"That's not true."

"You're literally the only one here who knows how to replace the toner in the printer," she reminds him.

"Which is *so* essential to the office."

"And how many times has payroll had to come to *you* about checks?"

Eli can count seven times in the last month alone.

"Stop doubting yourself. We're manifesting!"

"I hope so . . ." Eli takes the mouse and pulls his emails back up. Five whole years of working at *Vent*. Of getting coffee for meetings, and finishing Michael's read-throughs when he found an article "too long." Half a decade spent sitting in on meetings for Michael when he didn't want to attend them, calling cars to and from SFO, arranging lunch dates and meetings and flights and conference talks. Five whole years of Eli writing his own articles, doing his own research, all for his proposals to be turned down with no hope of going the freelance route because Michael thought it would "confuse the brand" or "distract" Eli, and he had made him sign a noncompete when he took the job.

There'd been a time, years ago, when *Vent* was at the forefront of guerrilla journalism. It wasn't hard for Eli to remember the scathing articles they wrote: outing politicians and the arms companies that funded their campaigns, the insider trading that happened in DC, the actors and executives who abused their power in Hollywood; *Vent* had put their voice behind every strike and union movement happening all over the world.

And Michael had been right there with them for nearly two decades. He'd been someone to push boundaries, someone Eli used to look up to.

Now? Now *Vent* published listicles. Now they were more concerned with which Chipotle order aligned with readers' zodiac signs, or tweets that had gotten celebrities canceled. Articles that drive their ad revenue.

There have been many times when Eli's wondered exactly what he's doing at *Vent*, if this is a place that's even worth his time and energy. But he remembers the old *Vent* so vividly, their pieces that made a difference, that helped expose corruption and hold people accountable for their actions.

And he knows he can bring that back. He can help to make *Vent* a reliable source again. For everyone.

"You're going to kill it, Eli." Patricia stands and leans over to kiss Eli on the forehead.

"Thanks, Pat."

"I'll text Rose—we'll celebrate tonight, okay? I'll make brownies." Patricia starts to wheel the chair she borrowed back to the desk just as Michael steps out of the elevator, his phone in hand as he types something. Eli likes to think that after five years of watching Michael every single weekday, he's learned the minutiae of how Michael acts. He's smiling, which is an obvious good sign, there's a slight pep in his step, and there are no visible stains on his shirt despite eating Italian for lunch, so there's nothing for him to be frustrated over.

All signals point to a good mood, including the greeting he gives to Eli before he strides into his office.

Eli still waits for his time, watching as the clock ticks toward 2:00 before he grabs his iPad, packed with his digital portfolio and notes, and tip-toes to Michael's office door, knocking gently on the glass.

"Michael?" Eli ducks his head in, catching Michael mid–phone call.

"Yeah, no. We can definitely do that," he says to the other person on the line, which is odd because every call Michael gets is filtered through Eli.

Well, *almost* every call.

Michael's eyes meet Eli's, and he urges him in to take a seat. "Of course! Of course, yeah. That'll work out for us. So, I can expect it by tomorrow end of day? Good! I'll let my assistant know, ask him to keep a lookout. Good, talk to you later, then." Michael laughs again before he sets the phone down on the receiver.

"What should I keep an eye out for?" Eli dares to ask.

"A friend of mine is applying for the staff position that opened up. I wanted to make sure we got his résumé."

"Oh . . ." Eli feels his stomach sink to the floor. No, no. He's not going to catastrophize, not yet. There's still hope here.

"So, what's up?" Michael leans back in his desk chair, the hinges creaking loudly, sending a shiver down Eli's spine.

"We had a meeting scheduled," Eli says, knowing that he shouldn't be at all surprised that Michael forgot. "About my articles. And the . . . the staff position."

Realization hits Michael. "Right, right! Yes, yes. I totally forgot." He rests his elbows on the desk, clasping his hands together. "Let's talk about it! Interviewer mode on!" He laughs, and Eli forces a similar sound out.

Not that Michael would know anything about interviewing—he usually forces Eli to take his place during the process.

"So, it's not like I need to ask you about your credentials," Michael jokes, reaching over toward his computer mouse and clicking to pull *something* up, though Eli isn't sure exactly what he's looking at; it could be anything.

Eli once caught him watching Instagram Reels on mute during a meeting.

"You've been a valuable employee these last few years, Eli. I seriously think that I couldn't go a day without you here."

"I appreciate that, Michael. I've really enjoyed my time working at *Vent*. And you know how much I'd like to start making a name for myself."

"Well, I don't have to give you the spiel about hard work, determination, doing whatever you can to move up in the world. You know that better than anyone here. I feel like you've been my apprentice, learning and growing along with me. You're the Yoda to my Anakin."

"Right." Eli nods, ignoring his urge to correct Michael. "Absolutely. And I think that I'm ready to be taken more seriously."

Michael raises an eyebrow. "You *think*? Or you *know*?"

"I *know*." Eli tries to make his voice firm, but there's no denying the slight tear that comes from experiencing puberty twice in a lifetime.

"Good." Michael nods. "Show me what you've got. What do you think has earned you a spot as a staff writer?"

Eli opens his iPad, finding the downloaded portfolio filled with PDFs of the articles and essays that he's written, some of which he's submitted to Michael before, only to have them rejected as "not right for the brand of *Vent*."

"I've also sent you an email with everything," Eli tells him, watching as Michael clicks away on his computer. He can only hope that he's actually opened up the file, but Michael's attention is a hard thing to vie for. "But I have several ideas for more hard-hitting articles for *Vent*, really giving us that voice that I feel like we've steered away from. We could really work to reestablish ourselves as a trustworthy news site."

"Right, right. I've read all of your pitches."

"Really?" Eli doesn't want to admit he's surprised, but . . . well . . . he is.

"Of course I did!" Michael tells him. "I read everything you submit. Your judgment is one that I put quite a bit of faith in, Eli."

"Oh, well . . . thank you, Michael. That really means a lot to me." Suddenly he feels a twinge of guilt for every snide comment whispered under his breath.

If only that goodwill could last a moment longer, before it all comes crashing back down.

"But I just don't think that those are the types of articles our audience goes to *Vent* to read," Michael says to him, his words slow. "They're too heavy. Our readers want something more relaxing; they want something funny, they want something that'll make them laugh and brighten their day."

Eli sits there in shock for a moment, registering exactly what Michael is saying. Until he eventually stammers out the reminder that *Vent* broke the story about the Republican legislator who sent bomb threats to San Francisco's mayor for vowing to make the city a haven for trans people.

Or the Democratic party member who claimed protests against gun violence wouldn't solve anything, and then *Vent* revealed he'd received thousands upon thousands of dollars from the NRA.

"Yes, but . . . that was the old *Vent*." Michael leans back further in his chair. He continues, "The new *Vent* is about entertaining our readers. No one wants those downers of a story. No one wants to know about how"—Michael turns to his screen—"how homelessness is being criminalized? Is that real?"

Eli nods.

"Jesus . . ."

"We also first reported on the test records of those self-driving taxis that were prone to hitting pedestrians. And how that billionaire CEO funneled money out of the city infrastructure fund to build his ugly tech buildings only for the buildings to be left halffinished so he could ditch us and move to Seattle."

"More bummer stories. No one wants those, Eli. The world sucks enough these days—don't you think people need a break from the dire news cycle? They can get that stuff anywhere."

"I *think* that people should be informed." That was what *Vent* used to be. An independent source of news that never had to worry about being "advertiser friendly" or whether or not they'd pissed off some politician.

It used to be the place that Eli dreamed of working for.

And Michael used to be someone Eli respected. Someone who stood for the truth. He still remembers finding *Vent* in college, reading an article that exposed a local sheriff taking bribes from the socialites of the city. And right under the article title was the name Michael Clay.

By the time he'd graduated from college, there were announcements naming Michael as the newest editor in chief at *Vent* and talking about the changes he wanted to make, keeping the integrity of *Vent* while taking strides to grow their reader base.

"These are stories *about* our city, though. These are things that people should care about; they just need someone to tell them what's going on."

"Well, they don't care now," Michael says bluntly. "Our numbers spike when we post about actors and musicians getting canceled, viral moments on X or TikTok, celebrities being hilarious, things like that."

"So you're saying that we can't write about the things that matter? That impact the citizens of San Francisco? Don't they have a right to know what's happening?" Eli's aware this argument is fruitless.

Working at *Vent* is fighting one losing battle after another.

"I think you have the wrong idea of what *Vent* is here to do. Those hard-hitting pieces? That's the past, Eli. Our viewers want to feel good when they visit our website; we want to bait them with a little nostalgia, get them riled up, keep them scrolling while they're stuck at work or on the toilet. The longer they scroll, the more they read, the more ads they see, the higher our revenue gets. Those are the basics."

"So, we're supposed to be fine as toilet paper?"

"Well, I wouldn't put it that way. But your ideas, they're too highbrow for us."

"But you've promised me a position for the last—"

Michael stops him. "I know what I promised. But I'm not seeing the growth that I want from you."

"The growth?" Eli repeats.

"You're not willing to adapt, Eli. You're not willing to bend to the course, to give me what I want. You have a strong voice, it's just . . . misguided for the website." Michael sighs. "It's a different era, Eli. Leave this serious stuff to the big swingers. I promise you; it'll be fine."

And just like that, Eli is left sitting there, staring at the meta-phorical remains of his entire life. For years, he's worked tirelessly to make sure Michael's day goes off without a hitch. He arrives early in the morning and is usually one of the last to leave at night. He's covered for Michael when he was sick, or didn't have the right info, or just when Michael completely forgot to do something. He's thrown together events, fundraisers, parties, he's argued with ca-terers, sent out thousands of emails, letters, and cards. He's kept track of the important names and faces of people Michael is sup-posed to know but never bothered to learn.

He's worked on countless articles, reaching out to various sources, poring over old articles in the archives at the head branch of the city library. He's spent thousands of hours editing, perfect-ing every single word, pulling in Patricia and Rose and asking them to read his work, watching them as he sat on the edge of his seat, wanting, *waiting* to know what they thought.

He's given years of his life to *Vent* in the hopes that it might lead *somewhere. Anywhere.* That he might make a difference, not just at the publication by bringing *Vent* back to its roots, but in the mis-guided effort to make actual change.

He should've known better. He knows that.

Hope always won, somehow . . .

Now look at where that's gotten him.

"But hey!" Michael says. "If you show me what I want to see, I'll reconsider your spot here. Deal?"

Eli sits there, his hands feeling numb from being balled up on his lap.

"Yeah, sure . . . Thanks, Michael."

"You're welcome, kid, and don't take it personally, okay? You're young, you've got plenty of time to accomplish your goals."

"Right, yeah." Eli stands, holding the iPad loosely, his fingers tingling. Nothing ever makes him feel as small as these meetings do. Eli steps toward the door, praying silently that maybe, just *maybe* it'll be a moment like in the movies. In this split second, Michael will come to his senses, or feel pity for Eli and offer him something.

Anything at all.

"Oh, and Eli?"

Eli pauses, his hand on the handle of the door. He barely turns, hopeful despite it all, a lesson he never really learns.

"Yeah?"

"Keep an eye out for that application from my friend? His name is Owen."

He hesitates, feeling like he's just been punched in the gut, like all the air has been sucked out of his lungs.

"Of course, Michael. Anything else?"

"Nah, you're good. Thanks, Eli!"

Eli steps out of the office, dumps his iPad on the desk, and sinks into his desk chair. Maybe it's not the smartest move to have a reaction in a public spot. Michael is *right* there, just fifteen feet away, a single glass wall separating the two of them.

But he doesn't care. It's not like Michael will fire him, that much is obvious. He just lets his head drop back, eyes focused on the ceiling. Only one word comes to mind, a word that perfectly encapsulates just how trapped he is, how frustrated he feels, how his insides keep twisting and twisting.

Eli buries his face in his hands, trying to come down from the panic, trying to relax, trying to feel like his world isn't coming to some overly dramatic end. But only that one word comes to mind, just one word, whispered under his breath.

"Fuck."

Chapter Two

Idle Hands, dir. by Rodman Flender

"You could just kill him," Rose says from the kitchen, shuffling around in the cabinets until she lets out a satisfied "Aha!" and pulls free the unopened bag of Cool Ranch Doritos.

"Keith or Michael?" Eli asks her, setting down the remote and picking up another still-warm brownie from the tin on the coffee table.

After the disaster of the informal interview, he'd texted the group chat with Patricia and Rose, telling them to disregard any and all celebrations they'd planned. Rose still stopped by the liquor store on her way home from the school where she teaches, and Patricia set about making her weed brownies the moment she set her bag down at the front door, despite Eli's protests.

They even gave him the remote, begging him to throw on whatever movie he wanted, promising to sit through it without complaining. He couldn't even bring himself to pick from the digital catalog on his TV; he ended up throwing on cycle six of *Top Model* to have something to focus on.

A pitiful way to end a pitiful day, as far as Eli is concerned.

"Why not both?" Rose prompts, crunching loudly.

"I'll help you hide the body," Patricia offers, her focus shifting toward the television as one of the contestants burns their caramel sauce. "My cringe true-crime podcast phase has to pay off somehow."

"You have a spare woodchipper?" Eli asks, resting his head on the pillow in her lap.

"No, but I know a guy." Her hands find his hair, slowly playing with the curls. Her long nails just *barely* scratch at his scalp, and he's convinced he could fall asleep.

He feels that specific combination of being so light yet so heavy at the same time that comes with eating the cannabis butter that Patricia bakes with. He almost wishes that he'd stayed sober, preferring to avoid any substances Sunday through Thursday, but tonight called for it.

That, and he can never turn down Patricia's brownies. And it helps that she packs them with enough chocolate to avoid the nasty weed taste edibles tend to have.

"What if you deleted the other guy's application?" Patricia asks, taking a sip of her beer. "You have access to Michael's emails. And he never remembers a thing."

"He's expecting it. Besides, his friend will just check in."

"I'm sorry, babe . . ." Rose flops onto the other end of the couch, taking just enough time to lift Eli's legs before she plants them on her own lap.

"It's fine!" he tells himself. Two words he's been repeating for hours now. "I shouldn't have expected anything."

He should be grateful for what he has.

But there's still that emptiness he feels. Like he's fallen behind. He's twenty-eight, he hates the job he's stuck at, and there's no possibility of moving upward. He's buried under a mountain of student debt that only seems to grow larger the more of it he pays off. He has zero prospects beyond his writing, and thus far that's gotten him nowhere. And the only person to ever break his heart works twenty feet away from him.

Maybe it's the weed, and maybe that's enough of a reason for Eli to swear off substances while his heart is still healing. Eli knows all too well what it's like to miss Keith.

The smell of Keith's shampoo on his pillows, that lingering

scent of Keith's cologne on the clothes that Eli stole. Early morning walks down to Amoeba Music where Keith would spend too much money on records and Eli would spend too much on Vinegar Syndrome Blu-rays. They'd get a coffee at the café nearby and walk the length of the Panhandle, stopping at the playground if it was empty and just swinging next to one another.

From the moment he laid eyes on Keith, Eli knew he was the person he wanted to spend the rest of his life with. Which was hilarious given that their relationship began with an argument.

It wasn't anything dramatic— Eli and Patricia had accepted an invitation to one of their friends' parties, and Eli just so happened to overhear Keith say *Mad Max: Fury Road* was "overrated and boring."

Eli couldn't keep his mouth shut and spent the following hour explaining how it's a perfect movie from beginning to end: the acting, the directing, the sets and locations, the cinematography and color choices, the costuming, the action sequences and stunts.

Apparently, it only took three shots for Eli to decide that he *had* to defend George Miller with his life.

Keith just stood there, his mouth painted in this confused expression that transformed into a smile over the next sixty minutes, like he couldn't believe this guy was lecturing him about a movie.

And when Eli was done, slightly out of breath and more than a little heated, Keith asked a simple question.

"Do you want to get out of here?"

He could feel it, at that very moment: Keith was the man he was destined to spend the rest of his life with. There was just a . . . a something about the moment, he couldn't explain it, not even really to himself.

Keith defined it as best he could, though. When Eli woke up next to him in the mornings, Keith was still asleep, his eyes closed, soft snores slipping past his lips. Or on lazy Saturday afternoons when Eli made dinner while Keith did his crossword puzzles. Or those bus rides in the morning when Eli was still half asleep, laying his head on Keith's shoulder and breathing in his citrus smell.

That was before things became . . . not bad, but indifferent. When Eli could feel that there was something gone from their relationship. What was worse was that it wasn't a fight or an argument—no one burned dinner, their jobs didn't interfere, no one cheated.

Nothing happened.

It was just the slow, gradual death of a relationship, neither one of them admitting that there was a problem until Keith mercifully ended things.

It was one thing to feel so deeply for someone that it hurt to think about them, to have feelings that were so impossible to explain. But to have *had* that love, to have felt the connection with another person, to have accepted what they had to offer and to give back what you had, only for them to decide that you were no longer worth it.

That bled worse than any wound.

And now there's just this dull ache. A discomfort.

Eli despises how much his heart still lingers there with Keith, and he hates himself for just how much it still bothers him.

"How long does it take to get over a person?" Eli dares to ask.

"I think it's supposed to be like double the length of the relationship," Rose says, digging further into the chip bag, leaving her fingers coated in fine Cool Ranch dust.

Eli feels his stomach twist.

"Really?" Patricia sounds confused. "I thought it was half?"

"Is it?" Rose asks. "No, no, I think it's double. So, what's that, Eli? Fourteen years?"

"I meant for the two of you," he clarifies. "Like how long did it take the two of you to get over your past relationships?"

"Two months, two weeks, and three days. It was a Friday; or, technically, a Saturday morning, one thirty a.m."

Eli and Patricia both stare at her.

"You know it to the hour?" Patricia asks.

Rose nods. "It was ladies' night at Kelly's. I met this girl, we were talking. Turns out Alecia had cheated on *her* too, so we hooked up in the bathroom."

Patricia nods her head in respect. "Huh . . . Was it good?"

"Not really," Rose says. "I mean the sex was; we met up later that week too. But the floor was sticky. She was hot, though." She steals Patricia's beer. "But my example is an isolated incident. You can't really *predict* when you're over someone, Eli. You just kind of . . . get there."

"But *how*?"

"Well, meeting someone else does wonders for you," Patricia adds, sprinkling a little salt on the wound. Eli can't roll his eyes fast enough. "Don't do that."

"Do what?"

"Roll your eyes. You haven't gone out with us in months, let alone on a date with someone."

He huffs. "I haven't felt like it." He hasn't felt like much lately.

"But you've felt like going to the theater down the street to watch some weird black-and-white Swedish movies from the fifties?" Patricia gives Eli a look that's supposed to make Eli feel ashamed, but that sounds like a perfect night to him.

Eli turns defensive. "I only have four more Bergman movies to watch before I've seen all of them in my Criterion set."

"God . . . That is the saddest thing I've ever heard." Patricia sighs, finally pushing Eli off her lap to walk to the kitchen and grab another beer since Rose had snatched hers. "The point is that, like Rose said, it's different for everyone. And you're not going to get over these feelings just sitting alone and doing nothing all day except going to a job you hate and watching movies a hundred years older than you."

"But I *like* staying inside and watching movies," he says. "And the job is . . . the job is the job. There's nothing I can do about that."

Patricia stops her sip short. "We're not even going to touch on *Vent* right now."

"You could at least *try* to date. It seems like all the guys you showed us were perfectly fine," Rose says. "But you always found some imaginary problem with them."

"I don't *want* to date," Eli tells them both. "I'm done with that part of my life."

"You're twenty-eight," Patricia reminds him. "Stop being so dramatic."

"I had my soulmate," Eli says, his words slurring softly. "And he broke up with me. So, it's done. I'm done. No more guys for ol' Eli."

"Jesus." Patricia throws her head back. "You're far too young to be so jaded about love, Eli."

"Doesn't matter. It's my choice."

Out of the corner of his eye, Eli can see Patricia's and Rose's eyes meet from across the apartment. Patricia crosses the living room in just a few strides, walking back over to where Eli rested his head, nudging him to sit up straight, but he doesn't budge.

"What?"

"I want to sit here and your head is in the way," she says, trying to take the arm of the couch.

"You can't make me move," he tells her. Except Patricia's day includes regular exercise and weight lifting, meaning that she *absolutely* can make Eli move if she wants to.

And she does, pulling him into an upright position and sliding in behind him.

"What's going on?" he asks, aware that he's now surrounded.

"We've needed to talk to you," Rose says bluntly. "Pat, you wanna go first?"

"What's going on?" Eli repeats, slower this time.

"Think of this as . . . an intervention—" Patricia starts to say.

And Rose hops right on the ride. "A *You have no life and it's getting pretty sad* intervention."

"Jeez, don't spare my feelings." Eli brushes his hair away from his face, thinking about how badly he needs a haircut, but also how Keith loved the shaggier look of his curls. How Keith would play with the strands, twirling them with his finger, or even washing Eli's hair for him in the shower because he found it relaxing.

"Rose and I have been talking, and we really think it'd be good for you to get back out there for yourself." Eli feels Patricia's hand on his knee.

It's in this moment that he realizes this is a serious conversation. Not the half-baked kind where Patricia and Rose would drop the topic after a minute or two. "I told you *I'm fine*."

Rose snorts. "You really aren't, dude. Only people who aren't fine say 'I'm fine.'"

"Rose!" Patricia hisses.

"What? What's the point in lying to him?"

Eli knows that she's right, that he isn't okay, no matter how often he tells himself he is. "I've tried," he admits to them both. "I've been trying! Guys just . . . they fucking suck."

Despite living in one of the queerest cities on the planet, Eli feels lucky to get a single-word response to most of the messages he sends. He could count on one hand how many conversations went past the introduction. And he could count on two hands how many of those messages ended up being from couples looking for a third, or a group trying to get him to join their polycule.

And while he doesn't see anything wrong with that, Eli strongly prefers monogamy. A concept that—seemingly—most of the men in San Francisco consider strange and foreign.

"We understand that you're still hurting from Keith. It'd be stupid to think that a few months would be enough to get over a relationship that lasted more than half a decade," Patricia continues. "But we don't think that you're doing yourself any favors by isolating yourself in the apartment and smoking weed on the weekends."

"You know I prefer edibles," he tells them. No smell from edibles.

"Not the point. You're hurting now, but it'll get better," Rose replies. "Day by day, it might seem slow, but it does get better. You don't ever get rid of the pain, you just learn to live with it, to tolerate it." Her voice goes quiet. "That's what I had to tell one of my kids when her dad died."

Patricia and Eli both turn toward her slowly, concern vibrant in their expressions.

"Jesus, Rose . . ." Patricia whispers.

"Or maybe it was a dog . . ." She seems to think for a moment. "I can't really remember."

"Either way . . ." Patricia says, dragging out her words, like she's trying to brush past whatever it was that just happened. "Rose is right. You just get used to it."

"It was a guinea pig!" Rose finally reveals. "Her guinea pig died. Her mom didn't see it and sucked it right up with the vacuum cleaner."

"Okay . . . that's enough talking from Rose for the night, I think," Patricia jumps back in, then stands and offers a hand to Rose to help her up from the couch.

"What did I do?"

"Nothing, sweetie. Nothing at all. Go down to Orphan Andy's and get some milkshakes. I'll handle talking to Eli."

"Two chocolate and a peanut butter?" Rose slips on her teal Crocs at the door before she grabs her phone and keys.

"Please and thank you!"

"I'll be back!" Rose heads to the door. "Oh, and Patricia!"

"Yes?"

"Convince Eli that he needs to get back out there again and it's really sad that he just wants to sit on the couch and watch old Swedish movies."

"Will do, sweet cheeks."

"Eli!"

Eli braces himself for whatever it is she's about to say. "Yes?"

"Realize you're a treasure and that you just need to get over yourself to find a guy who you will fall madly in love with."

"Thanks, Rose." He appreciates the enthusiastic truthfulness that Rose loves to hand out when she's even *slightly* intoxicated. Both Patricia and Eli watch as she disappears out the front door, and then listen to her footsteps as she marches down the stairs, the silence of the apartment juxtaposed with Tyra Banks giving girls a lesson on smizing.

"So, you're saying that I like . . . need a rebound or something?" Eli asks, pulling a throw pillow from the couch close to his chest, his fingers playing with the strands that dangle from the edges.

"Well . . . it might not hurt? But I think you need something a little stronger than just a rebound," Patricia says. "You need to get out there, go on a date with *someone* other than the toys in your nightstand."

"Okay, but how do I do that when people don't seem interested in me at all?"

"I think that maybe you're reading the situation wrong, Eli. Maybe it's not that these people aren't interested, but maybe you're putting out the wrong energy."

"So, what's the *right* energy?"

"Well, the dating apps are your first mistake." Patricia picks up Eli's phone from the coffee table, plugging in the passcode with ease. Being friends for as long as they have, there aren't many secrets between the two of them. They've popped each other's zits in awkward places and had full conversations with one sitting on the toilet while the other showered. Patricia helped administer Eli's testosterone shots before he made the switch to the gel; Eli showed up at Patricia's terrible dates pretending to be a scorned ex-boyfriend. They've even walked in on the other masturbating. Accidentally, of course, but there are certain walls around a friendship you can never put back up when you've seen your roommate having sex with themselves.

"You need to meet someone face-to-face," Patricia says. "I think that'll be good for you. Though, knowing your interests, I don't think I can recommend you meet a guy at some *Persona* showing."

"You say that like meeting people is *so* easy." At least the dating apps had no stakes. If it fizzled out, it fizzled out.

"True." Patricia nods. "But I know that you're desperate enough, and if I have to suffer through one more of your depressive episodes where all you do is watch Wong Kar-Wai movies, then I'm going to put a bullet in my brain."

"You liked *Chungking Express.*"

"Yes, that's what I told you. But none of that matters right now."

"So, what does?" Eli asks warily.

Patricia smiles at him slyly. "I'm glad you asked."

"Oh no . . ."

Eli watches as she readjusts her position, scooting closer and leaving Eli's phone to fall between the couch cushions.

"No, no. It's not bad. I swear."

"I feel like you saying that means it's going to be bad."

"Remember that guy I mentioned? The coworker of my friend of a friend?"

"Do you have a flowchart for me to follow?" he asks. "Maybe a PowerPoint presentation?"

"It's not *that* complicated," Patricia reassures him. "His name is Peter, he's fresh to the city, doesn't have many friends, and is *very* gay."

"Pfft, well, then, sign me up!" Eli spouts sarcastically, trying to pick himself up off the couch, but none of his limbs really seem to be cooperating with him.

"Come on, you're judging him before you've even met him."

"Have you? Met him?"

Patricia hesitates.

"Okay, then." Eli nods.

"He works at Zelus. The tech start-up."

"And that's a positive thing?" A tech bro? Eli can name about a thousand other professions he'd rather date before braving the tech world for dating options. "Anything else? If he drives a Tesla—"

"I know that he's Korean. And his first name."

"Do you have a picture? What's his Instagram?" Eli digs in the couch for his phone, then pulls up the app, ignoring how Keith's profile waits for him in Recently Searched.

"He doesn't have one," Patricia admits. "And I have no pictures."

"You know nothing about this guy? Even what he looks like? He could be a murderer for all you know!"

"He's not, I swear. Francine—the coworker—just thinks that he needs to get out more. Like you! He works totally remote, he's pretty much logged on all day, declines all her invites out for drinks, never shows up at company outings."

"So, it's a pity project?"

"Eli . . ." Patricia whines, tossing her head back. "Work with me here. I'm trying to help."

"By setting me up with a complete stranger who is afraid to leave his house? Has Francine ever considered that he's agoraphobic? Maybe he doesn't want to leave his house—maybe he's happy?"

"Francine said nice things! And he's told her that he wants to date, explore the city. He just doesn't know how."

"I've never even met Francine. How can I trust their opinion in men?"

"You could trust mine?" Patricia says to him.

Eli stares at his friend, gnawing softly on his bottom lip.

This isn't what he wants. He's spent the last few months coming to terms with his love life being over, the idea of finding someone new an impossible task that has kept him up until three in the morning, staring at his ceiling in a rolling fit of anxiety. Unless by some miracle Keith wanted to take him back.

And he thinks for a moment, considering all the possibilities. He hadn't expected to fall in love at that party; how could he have? But deep down he knows that Patricia and Rose are right, no matter how badly he doesn't want to admit it. If his job isn't going anywhere, why shouldn't his love life? At least this he can control. At least he can *try*.

He just wants to love French toast again.

"It's just one date, and you don't even have to like the guy," Patricia tells him. "I just think it'll be good for you to—"

"I'll do it," Eli says.

Maybe it's the brownies talking, maybe it's the hurt in his heart. More likely, it's some weird chemical imbalance of both. But he weighs his options carefully. Even if he doesn't like this Peter guy, he tried, and Patricia and Rose can't lecture him about getting back out there. And if he does like him . . . maybe he'll have made a friend?

Patricia seems surprised at the complete one-eighty. Eli doesn't tell her that he is as well. "You . . . you will?"

Eli nods. "Set it up. Send me his number."

"Oh . . . okay!" She smiles. "Okay, yeah. Let's do it."

It's a bit anticlimactic; Patricia can't exactly text Francine at ten o'clock at night to get a guy's number. Leaving him with nothing to do except devour the milkshake that Rose brings back. Eventually, a movie is decided on, Rose and Patricia relaxing their "No Muppets" house rule because of Eli's heartbreak. Not that it matters since Rose has to leave for the bathroom halfway in because she's never properly taken care of her lactose intolerance.

The night goes on, and Patricia and Rose both eventually fall asleep on the couch, draped over each other while Eli stretches out on the ottoman, laughing to himself as the TV auto-plays *The Great Muppet Caper* after the original movie finishes.

He sees his phone out of the corner of his eye, the mustard-yellow case nearly glowing in the darkness of the apartment. He picks it up, opening Instagram again and going to Keith's profile. He ignores the urge to watch Keith's stories, knowing that his name would appear right at the top of Keith's viewers. And there's no way he would give Keith the satisfaction.

He scrolls past the rows of photos to just before they ended things, and even further than that. There are no photos of Eli; Keith always promised it was because of networking, which means nothing ever stopped him from tagging Michael, or their coworkers, or the celebrities that Keith got to meet.

It's almost like Eli never existed.

He wants to imagine that Keith's smile was brighter in the photos from last year, two years ago, back during his final year of college. He wants to claim that gleam in Keith's eye for himself. But there's truly no way of knowing.

Eli deletes Keith's username from the search bar and sets his phone down, turning his attention back to the movie. He's spent the last seven months convinced that romance isn't for him, that he doesn't want to date if it isn't to win Keith back, even if he doesn't believe in romance anymore, even if he thinks that his love life is done, that he lost the chance with the man he thought was *the one*.

At the very least, maybe he can get a free meal out of it.

Chapter Three

How to Lose a Guy in 10 Days, dir. by Donald Petrie

Even after wrestling with his hair for an hour, Eli still isn't happy with the results.

Maybe it's a sign that this night is over before it even begins. How can a date possibly go right if he can't even get his hair to cooperate?

"You're making excuses." He can hear his mother's voice in his head. Well, it's more a twisted combination of his mother, Patricia, Rose, and a little bit of Keith thrown in there for good measure. As if he couldn't feel worse about himself.

And it annoys him to no end knowing that they're all right.

He's trying to achieve that *perfect* balance of looking both messy and neat all at once. Patricia calls it his Timothée Chal-ification. The curls had been one of the more unexpected changes from the testosterone; his once-wavy hair began to grow in tighter curls that he actually had to take care of and maintain if he wanted them to stay healthy. He'd listened to Patricia talk for hours about her own hair care, wrapping it at night, watching every video she sent his way about the proper shampoos, conditioners, masks, silk pillowcases.

"Dammit . . ." he whispers to himself as his hair continues to fall flat across his forehead.

He doesn't have time for this. The day has been stressful enough already, fielding Michael's potential cronyism hire and sitting in to conduct the interview for the job *Eli* had been promised. There'd been a moment halfway through when he considered sabotaging the entire thing, but he knew that wouldn't get him anywhere he wanted to be.

Then countless meetings followed about IT issues and a few budget discussions, during which Eli was fairly certain Michael admitted to committing tax fraud. And it was all capped off by Eli having to explain to one of his older coworkers what Ctrl+F does. Needless to say, by the time five came around, he was ready for the day to be over.

But it couldn't be. Not until tonight was done and he'd proven Patricia and Rose wrong.

The entire bus ride home was spent doing math in his head to figure out if he had enough time to shower, brush his teeth, do his hair, and pick out an outfit he'd actually want to wear tonight.

Despite it all, there's this desire to impress. Eli's mother had instilled in him the belief that you only get one first impression, and while he tended to disagree with just *how* often she considered other people's opinions of her, he was inclined to agree.

It'll be fine, Eli tells himself. He can't even explain the anxiety; it's not like he's worried about impressing Peter, not at *all*. He keeps telling himself that it doesn't matter, that tonight doesn't mean anything, that he's just doing it to get Rose and Patricia off his back.

Even if he does want it to go well.

He doesn't like how often his eyes have drifted to his phone over the past few days, silently hoping to see a notification from the newest addition to his contacts. Just standing here trying to tame his hair, he's stopped every time the screen lit up, only to be disappointed.

The first time, it was Rose in their apartment group chat, asking Patricia what their dinner plans were. The next three times were all emails from Michael about things that certainly could've waited until Monday.

He'd talked to Peter *just* long enough to decide on a place to eat and something to do. After that? Radio silence.

Eli wants to text Peter. Ask him about his day, his family, his interests. Though he supposes that would defeat the purpose of the blind part of this blind date. Not that it matters anyway. But Eli's last message is the one that hangs there, unanswered.

> **ELI:** have you seen knives out?

The AMC Kabuki in Japantown decided to bring the movie back as a Fall Vibes celebration, complete with $5 tickets, and Eli's been dying to see it on the big screen again. He figures it's funny enough to be a good first date movie.

But there was no answer. The text had been read. Because Peter is apparently masochistic enough to leave on his read receipts. He just didn't bother to answer it.

It's okay, he repeats to himself. *That's the point of the blind date. To get to know each other. To start from zero and work our way up. Why am I worried?*

Tonight's going to be okay, he's just catastrophizing.

It's going to be fun, dammit.

Which Eli would feel *so* much more confident about if he could just get his hair to cooperate. Frustrated, Eli yanks on the cord of the hair dryer so quickly that the plug comes free of the outlet, flying right into his face.

"Shit!" he hisses, almost dropping the hair dryer on the floor and then going to the mirror to make sure he isn't bleeding. Thankfully, only the plastic part seems to have struck him, which causes a pink mark to appear right in the middle of his forehead, but his hair is long enough to hide it.

"What's wrong? Are you okay?" Patricia rushes over, bracing her hands on either side of the doorframe.

"It's fine, it's fine," Eli promises her. "I just can't get my hair right."

"You've been in here for like an hour. I thought you didn't care about tonight."

"I don't," he promises. Eli picks up the hair dryer and plugs it back in. "I just want to make a good first impression. Plus you and Rose seem to want this to go well, so . . ."

"*Just* me and Rose?" she asks with an eyebrow raised curiously.

"Shut up."

It's been years since he felt those first-date jitters, that weird fluttering in his stomach that makes him cough to the point that he wants to vomit. Like his body is searching for an excuse to not go out. For all he knows, Peter is a serial killer, and this is all some elaborate scheme to kidnap and butcher Eli.

It was easier with Keith because their relationship began with a hook-up first, and nerves couldn't be *as* bad after they'd already seen each other naked. What else is there to hide at that point? Keith knew what he was getting into; he'd seen the faded scars on Eli's chest, Eli's vagina, the bottom growth that had resulted from being on testosterone.

There was a moment, shedding his clothing that first night, where he considered being ashamed of his body, worried that Keith might be grossed out.

But Eli had spent too much time as a teen hating every photo of himself. After he'd spent all of his own savings paired (generously) with help from his mother and stepfather, and their insurance, he knew he should never look at his body as anything other than a work of art. Because it was, because he'd gotten the chance to make it himself.

Of course, he could do without the body hair that sprouted along his stomach, chest, and ass. God, the ass hair. But he liked it, in an odd way. It made him feel more . . .

More like Eli.

And he'd felt so proud of himself.

So was Keith, because he'd called Eli every name he'd ever wanted to hear from another man's mouth. To Keith, Eli was beautiful, perfect, good, handsome, gorgeous. Even if Keith didn't think it now, it was true then, and that was enough to make Eli's stomach twist.

Shit. He can't think of that right now, he can't get all worked up over one man right before he's literally about to go out with another.

"What are you going to wear?" Patricia asks him, taking the nail file she's been holding and going back to shaping the acrylics she'll spend her night painting and applying. "Picked out an outfit yet?"

"I had some ideas," Eli replies. "But I hate all of them now." He huffs when his hair falls flat. Again.

"Okay, I've had enough of this." Patricia sets the nails and her file on the back of the toilet before she steps out into the hallway. "Rose! You're needed!"

"Where are you going?" Eli asks.

"To rummage through your clothes," she tells him with a sly smile.

"I've been summoned?" Rose appears, dressed down for her Friday night in. She's already dedicated most of her evening to lesson planning in an effort to get ahead of the weekend, hair mask and under-eye strips already on for the night.

Eli takes the curl serum and the hair dryer and presents them to her. "Help me?"

"Sit." She motions to the toilet, and Eli does just that, closing his eyes as Rose blasts his hair again, then uses her fingers to work through to the roots before she turns the hair dryer back on. Patricia might've *taught* him about taking care of his hair, but Rose worked at her mom's hair salon all through high school and college, so she has the experience. Despite all of her searching across the city, Patricia has yet to find anyone else she trusts to braid her hair other than Rose.

When Eli opens his eyes again, he sees Rose mouthing something, but over the sound of the hair dryer, she's totally inaudible.

"What?" he shouts.

The hair dryer cuts off. "I said, are you excited for tonight?"

"Oh . . ." Eli pauses, wondering the answer to that question himself. "I don't know, actually."

"What has—" Rose begins to ask before the hair dryer is flipped back on, and the rest of her words are totally lost.

"What are you saying?" Eli shouts again.

The hair dryer shuts off again. "Worried!"

"What?" Eli doesn't like repeating himself, but he has zero clue what Rose just said.

"I asked, what has you so worried?"

He probably should've figured that out. "I don't actually know, I just feel—"

Rose kicks the hair dryer back on, and this time, Eli just reaches up and switches it off for her.

She winces. "Sorry."

"I guess I just feel anxious. It's been a long time since I went on a first date."

"It's a lot of pressure, huh?" Rose sets the hair dryer down, teasing Eli's hair again.

"Yeah . . ."

"You never dated anyone before Keith?" she asks.

"No. Between the gender dysphoria and trying to pass geometry, it wasn't exactly my highest priority." Eli hangs his head. "What about you?"

"Oh, you know. You're away from your parents for the first time, you start doing all these crazy things because you can. I wanted all these lesbian experiences that I'd never gotten as a teen," Rose explains. "God, there was this one girl I dated, literally she brought a whole box of her stuff to my dorm on our *second* date. Like I understand there's some truth to stereotypes, but I thought we were better than that."

Eli laughs, his heart feeling lighter.

"But there were other girls, nicer girls, worse girls."

"And you were never scared?"

"At first. It's weird, you know? Hard to explain. Like if aliens landed tomorrow and we had to explain how we as a society go through a whole courting process that involves apps and how shallow we are, and how we have sex without the desire to procreate, you'd realize how weird all of this is."

"You're imagining very rigid aliens," Eli tells her. "You don't think they'd be more relaxed?"

"Depends on what aliens we encounter first."

"True."

"I think being nervous is a good thing, though."

"Really?" Eli can't think of a time he's ever been nervous in a helpful way. Even the days leading up to the best ones of his life, his first appointment with his gynecologist about going on HRT, his first day of college, his first consultation for his top surgery, his final exams, his graduation. All of those core memories had been preceded by weeks of anxiety and fear.

"Mm-hmm." Rose tugs on a strand of hair, twirling it with her finger before she releases it. "I think it shows that you care. That you're afraid to mess things up. If you were some uber-confident guy who went into every interaction expecting everyone to love you just for breathing, then you'd be pretty insufferable."

"But those guys never have to worry about what people think of them."

"Trust me, Eli. Those guys worry *too* much about what people think of them. More than either of us ever have." Rose stands back, and Eli peers up at her through the short curtain of hair that shrouds his forehead now.

"How's it look?" Eli asks, feeling relief for the first time all day.

"You tell me." She takes Eli by the shoulders, leading him to stand in front of the mirror where his hair is curled to *perfection*. Fluffy with plenty of body, the acceptable frizz that Eli walks around with totally gone.

"You're a miracle worker, Rose," he tells her, leaning further toward the mirror to see every single curl perfectly in place.

"I know. Just buy me dinner this weekend."

"Done."

"Eli!" Patricia calls for him from his attached bedroom.

A Mario Kart tournament had decided who got the master bedroom with the en suite, and Eli had pulled through with his usual Yoshi build. Patricia had contested the win, citing that Eli had spent more time than the rest of them practicing the shortcuts of the track, but the argument died when Eli reminded her that she'd picked the game.

Besides, having the extra square footage meant paying $300 more in rent than the other two, so she wasn't *that* upset.

"Get in here!"

Patricia has three sweaters on Eli's bed, all from what she's labeled his Grandpa Collection. Jacquard and wool sweaters with all kinds of wild patterns that he'd procured from thrift stores all over the city. Eli would have argued against the grandpa allegations, but the sweaters *had* most likely come from someone's grandfather's wardrobe.

Though Eli preferred not to think about who his thrifted clothing came from, especially when he stumbled upon a large collection, all the same size, donated all at once.

Those poor—probably dead—grandpas.

"No pants?" he asks, picking the cerulean with accents of gold and white with diamonds and stripes. The *perfect* amount of hideously tacky, and just to Eli's taste.

"You're wearing these." Patricia reaches into Eli's dresser, pulling out what Eli calls his sweatjeans. Which just means they're Uniqlo jeans with drawstrings, but God they're comfortable. "Cuff them. And wear your white Filas."

"Filas?" Eli stares at her. "You don't think I'm going too casual?"

Patricia scoffs, falling back onto the bed. "You're getting tofu soup and going to the movies. Besides, casual fashion will set the mood just fine."

"You think he'll like me?" Eli asks, pulling his white undershirt on, tucking it into his pants before he ties the drawstring. He asks the question quietly, not wanting Rose to hear him. Hell, he doesn't want to ask Patricia the question, but she's the only one he wants to talk to right now.

"I thought you didn't care?" Patricia eyes him with a satisfied smirk.

"And I don't. I don't care about dating, it's stupid."

But it's not a crime to want to be liked by someone.

"I think you're pretty neurotic," Patricia says. "And that you need a haircut, that your taste in movies *and* music is pretty pretentious. And that you have skin so perfect I'd kill my grandmother for it even though you literally just wash it with warm water and some over-the-counter nonsense you buy from Target." Patricia lets out a long huff. "But yes. I think that he's going to like you."

"I get zits sometimes," he jokes. "You're just saying all of that because you're my friend."

"No, I'm saying that *despite* being your best friend. I know you better than anyone else, so I know that he's going to like you."

"It'd be nice if this went well."

"I know, babe. I think it will. And even if it doesn't, hey, it's a date, you're getting back out there. And that's enough of a win for right now."

Eli tries to take her words to heart, because he does want this to go well, despite his assurances that it doesn't matter, the lie he keeps telling himself that he doesn't care.

Because he does.

"It's going to be fun, you'll see." Patricia stands, hanging up the leftover sweaters Eli hadn't picked on the clothes rack that sits next to Eli's dresser. The true exchange for the en suite bathroom was the pantry of a closet that barely contains Eli's heavier winter coats, so a freestanding clothes rack is a necessity.

Patricia offers him a kiss on the forehead before she walks out of the bedroom, leaving Eli to himself. He can't resist a smile, finally feeling reassured for once. He goes to his dresser, grabbing the rounded bottle of Orphéon—one of the few luxuries he affords himself—that he dabs on his wrists and behind his ears, letting the earthy smell of jasmine and cedar relax him before he grabs his phone, double-checking that he has the right address for the restaurant.

It's a short walk and a thirty-minute bus ride up to Geary on the 22 from Eighteenth and Church, which means there's a whole half hour where Eli gets to try and talk himself down from the ledge he's climbed up on.

He picks the single seat by the very back door, opening his phone to tell Peter that he's on the way to the restaurant.

He doesn't even realize that his leg is shaking, but instead of nerves, it feels like excitement. Eli can't help but smile at the idea of what tonight could be, where it could lead. Because it's nice, despite how terrifying the idea is, despite how worried he's been about tonight. He takes Patricia's words to heart, thinking of them the entire bus ride to Japantown.

He wants to believe in tonight. He really does.

So, Eli makes the decision. And instead of making it to spite Keith, he makes it for himself.

Because tonight is going to be good.

He's going to have *fun*.

* * *

An hour.

That's how long Eli sits at the table in Doobu alone. An hour and fifteen minutes actually, but who's *really* counting?

At the ten-minute mark, he figured it didn't have to mean anything. He'd managed to get to the restaurant a few minutes early and ordered waters for Peter and himself.

People are late all the time. Twenty minutes in, he figured that Peter must be a bus rider like him, and there's really no accounting for what might happen on Muni on a Friday night. There's even an art festival a few blocks over, so maybe Peter's just running late?

There have been mornings where Eli's been late for work because someone wanted to argue with the driver, or the wheelchair ramp broke just as someone was getting on.

People are late all the time. There's no need to worry.

At thirty minutes, Eli orders a bottle of strawberry soju, the ice in his water long since melted. It's a poor combination, a mostly empty stomach mixed with the *too*-tasty alcohol. He pulls out his phone, texting Peter again to let him know that he's here, waiting for him. But the read receipt never appears.

At forty minutes, he orders a second bottle of soju, the sinking feeling that he's been ghosted settling into his stomach. The older waitress seems to take pity on him too, bringing him a plate of kimchi pancakes that she promises are on the house. Or maybe she just doesn't want an obviously drunk man who was—even more obviously—stood up to make a scene.

He isn't going to cry, because he's an adult; and he tells himself that the alcohol is making things better, even if that's not really true and Eli hasn't gotten drunk since college, so his tolerance is in the garbage.

It's then that he maps out the rest of his night, deciding that he's not going to let Peter ruin his plans. Technically, Patricia and Rose only wanted him to get out, and going out doesn't mean he *has* to be on a date. He can date himself! He can eat the delicious soup he's been craving all week, go see a movie he loves on the big screen with a crowd that enjoys it just as much. He might even treat himself to the gourmet caramel-and-cheddar popcorn at the AMC.

He calls the waitress back, ordering his usual soon tofu soup and another plate of kimchi pancakes so that way he can try and sober up before the movie begins.

At the hour mark, Eli's food arrives.

And at an hour and fifteen minutes, a large Korean man stumbles through the front door of the restaurant. People have been coming in and out all night, so Eli doesn't think anything of the guy at first.

Dressed for the colder night in a dark gray hoodie and matching sweatpants, and very obviously not for a date, there's a wild look in the man's eyes, his cheeks flushed, like he's running from something. Or *to* someone. Eli has no reason to suspect that this man is Peter, but something in his rumbling gut tells him that this is the man who just stood him up.

Though now he has to wonder what constitutes actual *standing up*, and if it can still be considered being stood up if Peter still showed, no matter how late.

From a simple glance across the restaurant, Eli can tell that Peter's taller than him, much broader too, with strong shoulders and a rounder face with thick black hair that almost shines a maroon color in the reflection of the warm lights of the restaurant.

Eli looks away, his cheeks hot, before he dares to look up again, catching Peter talking to the waitress, who motions to Eli's table.

So that's it.

This is Peter.

Eli has to figure out how he wants to handle this. In the half hour since he decided Peter had ghosted him, he's thought of a hundred different things to text to Peter afterward, even drafted a few choice words chosen under the influence of the strawberry soju, leaving them unsent in his Notes app.

Any thoughts of anger or vindication are lost, though, when it hits him just how handsome Peter is.

"Are you Elijah?" Peter asks as he tiptoes up to the table, like Eli's a caged animal and Peter's afraid of him.

"It's Eli," he corrects, suddenly pulled deep in his feelings again. "You're late." As if Peter didn't already know that, based on the expression on his face.

"I know, I know. I'm *extremely* sorry," he says quickly. So quickly that his words almost come out as one singular sound, just like the explanation that follows. "I lost track of time and I missed your texts and I hadn't showered and I didn't know what to wear so I changed outfits like five times, and I had to take the bus because my car didn't have a charge. And . . ." Peter looks at him, taking several deep breaths. "I'm sorry."

Eli doesn't really know what to say at first. He's spent the last thirty minutes of his life angry at this man he'd never met. And now that Peter is finally in front of him, he doesn't really know what to feel.

"It's okay," he says eventually, unable to hide *all* of the impatience in his voice. "Have you eaten?"

Peter shakes his head fervently. "I was too nervous."

"Okay, well, you can just order something. I'm pretty much done." Eli stares at the nearly empty bowl.

"Sorry," Peter says again as the waitress comes by, leaving a menu and a fresh glass of water since Eli drained both of theirs. Suddenly he feels self-conscious about the state he's left the table. The two empty water glasses, the half-filled soju bottle next to the empty one, and the shot glass he'd been drinking from, empty plates.

"Uh, do you want something to drink?" Eli slowly pushes the second bottle of soju toward Peter.

"No." Peter says, his voice still hurried. Eli wants to tell him to relax, but he's not sure that would do much good. Then Peter's phone begins to buzz in his pocket, and he searches for a bit before he finds it in the pocket of his hoodie. "Hello?"

Eli sits silently, listening to the Korean folk song that plays through the speakers, tapping his foot impatiently along to the rhythm.

"Yeah. No. You need to run the tests. I left the program running. It should be done by the morning. So check in a few hours your time and it should be okay. If it doesn't run, I can work on it over the weekend. Okay. Yes. Yes. No. Yes. I'll message him on Slack. Okay. Yes. Yeah. Bye."

Eli perks up at the phone call finally ending.

"I'm sorry," Peter says again. Eli's quickly realizing that this phrase is a familiar one in Peter's vocabulary.

"It's okay. Was that work?"

"Yes."

"Patricia said you work in tech."

"Patricia?"

"My friend. Your coworker Francine's friend? Or friend of a friend, I can't keep track."

"Oh, yes. I like Francine." Peter says these words just as he takes a sip of water, almost seeming to forget that he's doing two things at once. Which wouldn't be so bad if these two things weren't at odds with each other.

Peter's water spills right out, dribbling on his shirt.

"Ah, Jesus . . ." Peter yanks some napkins free of the dispenser, pulling with such force that he nearly takes the entire hunk of plastic with him as he cleans up his mess. Eli doesn't want to laugh, because it's not funny, it's more like he's in shock. Like he can't believe whatever slapstick routine is playing out in front of him is actually happening.

"So . . . Francine?"

"Yeah. Yes." Peter straightens, still cleaning up his mess. Eli can't help but notice a slight twang to his voice, like a Southern accent he's trying to hide. "I work with her."

Eli waits for Peter to elaborate. He imagined the answer following an explanation of some kind. There are a lot of jobs in tech, especially in one of the—if not *the*—most tech-oriented cities in the country. But Peter doesn't say another word, just turns his attention back to the menu, reading over the dishes silently. Eli stares down at his half-empty soup bowl, pushing it away from him.

"I've never eaten here before," Peter says.

"You haven't?" Eli can't think quickly enough to hide his confusion. "But you picked it?"

Peter nods. "I thought it'd be good, and I scoped out the Yelp page for like two hours reading reviews and looking at pictures."

Eli isn't really sure what to say to that. "Well, the soup is good," Eli tells him. He eats here pretty regularly when he comes to Japantown, the irony of a Korean restaurant in the middle of Japantown not lost on him. "They've got all kinds of tofu options, but soon is their specialty."

"I don't like soup," Peter says bluntly.

"But you picked a soup place?" Eli cocks his head. "How do you not like soup?"

"The spicy pork looked *really* good." Peter lowers the menu, finally giving Eli his face again. Up close he can make out the fine straight line of his nose and the thickness of Peter's lips. "I don't like that it's a liquid you're expected to eat, the soup."

"I . . . Huh?" Eli has to consider if he just didn't hear Peter correctly, or if the alcohol is doing *that* much of a number on his systems.

But no, he heard exactly what Peter said.

"It's a liquid. You can't eat liquid. You can *drink* it."

"But soup has other things in it." Eli tips his bowl in Peter's direction, where leftover pieces of tofu float around other vegetables and shreds of beef. "The soup isn't just the broth."

Peter shakes his head slowly. "It doesn't make sense to me."

"Are you ready to order?" The older waitress comes by again, this time with a smile on her face, as if she's happy that Eli isn't alone anymore.

"I'd like the spicy pork. Does that come with rice?"

The waitress nods.

"I'll have that, thank you." He hands the waitress the menu, and Eli considers asking her to stay, to sit with them, just so he'll have someone else to talk to. He can almost picture a wall around Peter, one that he's expected to climb despite being given no equipment at all. Just a prayer and a "Hope you make it!"

"So, what do you do at Zelus? Exactly?" Eli asks, sipping more of Peter's first water glass, desperate to sober up a bit before the night continues.

"I code."

"Is that fun?"

"No. Not really."

"Oh . . ." Eli doesn't really know what to say to that. So instead, he just sits there, Peter looking anxious, like he *wants* to say something but can't. Their eyes even meet at one point, and Eli smiles at him, but Peter turns red as a beet and looks away, clearing his throat.

Like he's afraid.

Eli wants to ask what's wrong, if there's something going on, or if Peter's just nervous, but he has a feeling that might only make things worse.

"What do you code?" he asks instead, after a silence far too long to be considered anything other than uncomfortable.

"For stock."

"You code stocks? Like for Wall Street? How does that work?"

"No," Peter says. And that's all he says.

"Okay," Eli prompts. "So what *do* you mean by you code stock?"

"For warehouses? And companies."

Eli can't help but feel that Peter's own answer comes out more like a question.

"What does that mean?" Eli doesn't want to sound frustrated, but the talking in circles is starting to get to him. The nervous act might be cute to someone else, but he's already sick of it.

"I help design systems for warehouses, and how they stock well . . . their . . . stock."

"You're killing me here, Peter."

"I run tests for customers and their databases." Eli's astounded that Peter actually managed to string together an answer longer than three words.

He *does* have a nice voice; it's very smooth, almost like he's singing.

"That sounds pretty interesting?" Eli says, still pretty unsure of what it *is* Peter does.

"It's not," Peter says. "My day is mostly running tests, figuring out what went wrong, running them again. Hoping my computer doesn't crash while it does them."

"What kind of tests?"

"Code tests."

"Yeah, I figured that." Eli doesn't mean to snap, but his patience is wearing thin. "But what *kind* of tests are you running on the code?"

"Oh, I . . ." Peter blushes again. "Sorry."

"Don't apologize again, dude. I'm begging you."

"Sor—" Peter stops himself, his reflexes clear. "I have to run tests to make sure everything works. So, it's just a lot of sitting around in front of my computer. We have team members all over the world, people who rely on me knowing what to do if something goes wrong."

"Ah, I see." Eli doesn't, actually. But he figures it's best to get the spotlight off the poor man. He watches as Peter tugs at the collar of his shirt before he pulls his arms through the sleeves of his hoodie, and Eli feels his tongue go dry. He's wearing a black compression shirt underneath, one that perfectly wraps around his muscles as if it were painted on him, the fabric stretching as he moves. And there's no missing the plump shape of Peter's pecs.

Of course, that's what they're actually called, but Eli's brain goes right to calling them boobs.

They look soft, squishy even. And Eli feels his face light up at the thought, but it's true. It's also been too long since he had any- one other than the silicone toys that sit in his nightstand.

Peter has the kind of body where it's clear that he works out, but in the bulking sense, in a way where Peter still has a belly and fat. Eli could so easily picture himself taking a nap on Peter's chest. He never realized he has a thing for men like Peter, men who never sacrificed their softness.

"Are you okay?"

"Yeah, yeah . . . I'm fine." Eli has to recover, feeling that warmth in his stomach. Peter might be a mess, but he's an *incredibly* attrac- tive mess.

"Can I have a pancake?" Peter asks him.

Eli scoots the plate toward him. He wants to call the night off. Being late was one thing, but it's clear that he and Peter just aren't a match for each other. It's like pulling teeth to get a simple answer out of him.

Sure, the man is hot. *Awooga* hot, as Rose might say. But it's clear that there's nothing here. Peter might be fine for a good lay, if Eli thought that he could actually get him into bed without Peter apologizing, but would it really be worth it?

Peter pushes the empty kimchi pancake plate back toward Eli, not looking where it's going or thinking about how Eli's half-empty soup bowl is in its path. The plate collides with the bowl with a *clink* and *just* enough force to send it careening over the edge of the table.

And right into Eli's lap.

"Ah, fuck!" Eli nearly stands in the booth, unable to react before Peter is squatted before him, a pile of napkins in his hand as he tries to soak up as much of the mess as he can.

"I'm so sorry!" Peter throws his arm out, as if he can prevent what's already happened. Instead, he knocks over his own glass of water right in Eli's direction, giving it just enough of a hit to spill onto Eli's pants.

Again.

"Oh, God . . ." Peter reaches for the napkins once again, this time picking up the entire dispenser with the force of his pull, leaving it to fall over on the table.

There are more than a few eyes focused on the both of them now, which only seems to make Peter more nervous as he attempts to clean up the table, handing more napkins to Eli. "I didn't mean for that to happen," he says, the panic clear and present in his voice.

"Well, I'd be more worried if you *did* mean it," Eli tells him, taking the napkins from Peter and mopping up.

"God, I'm sorry." Peter ducks under the table, picking up the empty soup bowl and doing his best to pile the napkins onto Eli's lap, not even paying attention to how he palms Eli's crotch in an effort to clean up the disaster.

"Whoa there, cowboy!" Eli recoils from the sudden touch.

"Oh, God!" Peter shoots up, his head colliding with the underside of the table. "Crap! Ow!"

"Are you okay?" Eli can't help but laugh at the absurdity of it all. *And* hearing a grown man say the word *crap*. He can't remember the last time he heard that out loud.

"Yeah, yeah. I'm fine, I didn't mean to— Jesus."

"Peter?" Eli peers under the table, and Peter refuses to look back at him.

"Yeah?" His voice sounds so quiet, like he's ashamed.

"Please get out from under there," Eli pleads.

Looking like a child caught in a fib, Peter crawls out and sits back in his spot. His hair is mussed and out of place, his cheeks burning a bright red. And yet there's still something so intriguing about him.

"I'm going to the bathroom," Eli tells him, leaving the stained napkins on the table. "I'll try and clean up."

"Okay." Peter still won't meet his gaze.

Eli stands, grateful that the soup was room temperature. In the bathroom mirror, he can see that the sweater is fine, and after some scrubbing with soap and water, his pants are okay, even if it looks like he's wet himself if he stands in the wrong light.

His shoes, however? They're done for.

The orange spray of the soup has colored them, leaving stains with no hope of coming out. Eli knew the risks of buying all-white shoes and wearing them pretty much anywhere.

He just *had* to listen to Patricia.

When he steps back out into the restaurant, he takes a moment to spy on Peter, still sitting there. His hands cover his face, but the way his shoulders are slumped tells Eli everything he needs to know.

He wants to end it here, go back home, hang out with Patricia and Rose and watch a terrible movie. But there's something that tugs at his heart when he looks at Peter. It was an accident, after all. And the shock of the groping was enough to pull him free of any lingering drunkenness that his food hadn't solved.

He sees Peter's phone light up again, this time with a message that he can reply to easily via text versus a full phone call. He types for a bit before he lets the phone fall to the table with a *clack*, raking his hands along his hair and letting out an exasperated, and clearly frustrated, huff.

"Okay, I'm back," Eli says, scooting into the booth, noticing that Peter asked the waitress for a cloth to clean things up himself.

"I'm so sorry, Eli. I can . . . pay for your dry cleaning or something." There's a desperation to Peter's voice that almost makes Eli feel like the guilty party.

"It's fine, Peter. Just forget that it happened."

"I—" Eli can almost hear the second "I'm sorry" on his tongue before he gives Peter a look, and Peter closes his mouth.

"We have the spicy pork." The waitress sets down the sizzling cast-iron plate in front of Peter. "And your rice. Careful, they're both hot."

"Thank you." Peter nods.

"Let's hope that doesn't end up in my lap next." Eli chuckles.

The waitress laughs, taking some of the empty dishes, but Peter just stares at Eli.

"I wouldn't do that on purpose," he says, almost sounding offended.

Eli tries to laugh off the blooming awkwardness. "It was a joke."

"Oh . . . right, yeah." Peter doesn't seem entertained. He just takes the spoon from his silverware set and opens the metal lid of the rice bowl.

Eli closes his eyes and lets out a quiet sigh, wondering when it'd be appropriate to call this date over. He can't help but think of the horror movies he's watched where people find themselves trapped by the psychopath killer simply because they decided they couldn't possibly be rude.

Of course, that's an exaggeration. Now that Eli can look at Peter, he's not sure exactly what he was worried about. Peter doesn't look like the kind of person capable of hurting others; at least, not on purpose.

Eli traces his finger around the rim of his glass. He's not sure where the night could possibly go from here, but he can't just leave in the middle of Peter eating, right? He decides to give it until the bill is paid, then they can go their separate ways. "Did Francine mention what I do?" he asks, since Peter doesn't seem interested in asking himself.

"No," he says plainly, chewing his food.

"Well . . . do you want to ask me?"

"Oh, uh . . . what do you do for work, Eli?" Peter wipes his mouth with one of the few unused napkins remaining.

"Thanks for asking, Peter." Eli tries to keep the sarcasm from his voice as he straightens in the booth. "I work at *Vent*."

"Like the website?"

"Yeah, the website."

"You're a writer?"

"Well . . . not exactly." Eli shuffles his feet under the table. "I'm an executive assistant to the head editor."

"Oh, so a secretary?" Peter asks, and to his credit, Eli doesn't think there's anything malicious about how he asks it, but it sure doesn't sound as kind as it could have.

"*Executive assistant*," Eli corrects him. Even if he knows that's bullshit, the last thing he needs is for a near stranger to talk down to him.

"Right, sorry."

"How long have you been in the city?" Eli asks, desperate to skip past any more awkwardness.

"Four years," Peter says, taking another bite of his still-sizzling food.

Four years? When Eli heard that Peter was new and he wanted to meet people, he thought that Peter must've been in the city four *months* at the most.

And suddenly he feels like such an asshole for thinking that about Peter. He isn't a douchebag or a jerk, he's just . . . Eli doesn't really know exactly. He doesn't want to be an armchair psychiatrist, so he isn't going to diagnose Peter with anything, especially after only knowing him for thirty minutes, but the guy seems more than anxious.

A sensation Eli is all too familiar with.

"Where are you from originally?" Eli asks, hoping that questions about Peter's home might relax him a bit.

"Incheon."

Okay, now we're getting somewhere. "Was it nice there?"

Peter looks up, nodding in agreement while he chews for a moment before he admits, "I don't know."

"Oh. You don't know?"

"My family left when I was two. So, I don't remember it."

"You said you grew up there."

"No." Peter points hurriedly with his spoon, placing the perfect ratio of meat to rice with his chopsticks. "You asked where I'm from. There's a difference."

Eli opens his mouth to reply before he concedes that Peter's correct. "Okay, so where did you grow up?"

"Comer."

"Huh . . ." Eli searches his brain, wondering if he's ever even heard of this town.

"It's in Georgia. Just outside of Athens."

Well, that explains that slight twang to Peter's voice that Eli picked up on.

"Oh . . . Well, I've also never been to Comer."

"I'd be more surprised if you had." Peter swallows a bite of food.

"Well . . . I grew up in the city," Eli says, since Peter isn't going to ask him anything. "Went to San José for school where I got my journalism degree." Eli doesn't just want to hand out his entire life story, but it's clear that Peter isn't going to ask him anything himself. "But I live down in the Castro now. And I'm hoping to get the chance to move up as a staff writer at *Vent*—that way I can write about things that actually matter—"

Eli stops when Peter yawns.

He *yawns*.

"I'm sorry, I had an early morning meeting," Peter tells him, wiping at his eyes.

Eli doesn't say anything. He just wants to go back home, to call this entire night done and let Peter off easy. But he still wants to see the movie.

"We should go," Eli tells him, spying Peter's empty plate. "If you're finished."

"Oh, yeah. Of course. The movie probably begins soon, huh?"

"Yeah . . ." Eli grabs his phone, desperate to give himself something to do. He rereads the same posts and Instagram captions that he read before Peter arrived, scrolling endlessly until the check is awkwardly delivered.

"I can pay," Peter offers. "Since I was late. And because I spilled soup on you."

"Thanks," Eli huffs. He certainly isn't going to pretend like he's grateful. It's the least that Peter can do.

So maybe chivalry isn't dead? Eli thinks. Not that anything could salvage this night. Eli believes that Peter could take him back to his apartment and give him the best sex of his entire life and he'd still consider the night a loss.

At least then I could've gotten eaten out.

Peter reaches into the chest pocket of his hoodie, then pulls his hand out and goes for the other pocket before he checks his pants pockets. He gropes his entire body, and all Eli can do is sit there and watch as the realization dawns slowly on Peter's face. Well, that and he imagines just what Peter's body would feel like if those were Eli's hands instead.

God, he needs to get laid.

"I think I forgot my wallet at my apartment," he finally admits.

Eli sighs, leaving his credit card in the server book. He's not even mad, he's just . . . he's numb. He has no emotions over having to shell out the eighty dollars for dinner.

He simply doesn't care. That's what he tells himself.

"I'm sorry," Peter apologizes when the check is returned, and Eli leaves a generous tip for the mess left behind. "I can pay for the movie tickets?"

With what money? he thinks without really meaning to. "I've already bought them." Eli stands, grabbing his jacket. "Let's just go."

* * *

Eli's been to enough movies to know they have plenty of time to spare, despite his love for previews and the Nicole Kidman ad that plays at the start of every movie; it's no big deal if they miss them. Peter trails behind Eli as they walk up the street to the theater, and their tickets are scanned before they ride the escalator to the second floor to join the concession line. Not a word is exchanged between them, the lights giving Eli ample time to reassess the damage to his shoes.

At least the wet spot at the front of his pants has dried.

Peter's phone begins to ring again as they approach the front of the line, and Eli can make out the name *Joseph (Zelus)* on the screen before Peter looks around like he's been caught doing something illegal.

"I, uh . . . I have to take this." He shows the screen to Eli.

"Okay?"

He can't even pretend to care anymore. At least during the movie, there's no expectation to talk. It'll be two hours of blissful silence, some laughing at Daniel Craig's terrible Southern accent. So long as Peter doesn't spill soda on Eli, the date can end peacefully.

Peter steps to the side of the line, near where the bathrooms and the soda fountains are, sticking a finger from his free hand in his ear like he can't hear the voice on the other end of the line because of the ruckus of the theater.

Clearly frustrated, Peter waves to Eli, then points toward the door on the first level.

Eli nods in acknowledgment, watching as Peter marches down the stairs and walks out the front door.

Eli finally makes his way through the A-List line, grabbing the gourmet cheddar-and-caramel popcorn that he's rewarding himself with for the awful way the night has gone. He pauses at the drink fountains once his Dr Pepper has been obtained, hoping that Peter will make his way back inside any moment now.

Five minutes pass, then ten, then fifteen, and Eli has to figure that Nicole Kidman has wrapped things up by now.

He takes a screenshot of their tickets and forwards one to Peter, so he'll have the theater and his seat number before he follows the late-comers into the movie, stepping over people to get to his seat. It's almost impressive, just how much this man has managed to ruin Eli's night.

It's like he feels somewhere past frustration and annoyance. Because he isn't actually angry. Though he is annoyed at Peter for ruining his shoes, for being late, for barely saying a word to him.

He's just ready for the night to be over with. For the credits of the movie to roll so he can walk back to the bus stop and go home.

Eli doesn't really notice at first that Peter hasn't made a grand reappearance, stumbling over strangers in the dark to get to his seat. He's distracted for most of the first act, laughing with the rest of the audience. But then he realizes that Peter still hasn't shown up. He pulls out his phone, carefully angling it against his chest and turning the brightness down before he goes to his texts with Peter. There's no reply, no *"Sorry, emergency."* Or *"Give me five more minutes."*

Nothing.

Eli begins to check his phone so frequently—wondering if Peter's safe, if something bad has happened to him, or maybe if he just stumbled into a different theater by accident—that he can tell it's bothering everyone around him, earning a side-eye from the guy sitting by Peter's empty seat.

"Sorry," he whispers, putting his phone down and trying his best to focus on the movie.

But the magic is lost. As everyone around him loses it at the jokes, Eli just sinks deeper and deeper into his seat, unable to enjoy himself. He sighs, grumbling to himself and making a mental note to book another ticket before the movie leaves theaters.

It strikes him just how sad this is. How, despite actually *trying* to get back out there, giving someone a chance, he still wound up watching a movie all on his own.

Pathetic.

Then he does something that he's only ever done once before, when a movie was so horrendously boring that he spent most of the runtime on his phone, not having to worry about bothering any other moviegoers because he was the only one in the theater.

He walks out of the theater before the credits roll.

Not even the popcorn tastes good anymore, the soda long gone.

Eli tucks his phone into his pants pocket, and, after a quick trip to the bathroom to pee and wash his hands, rides the escalators down to the ground floor as he attempts to untangle his headphones from being wrapped around themselves in his pants pocket.

He doesn't even realize that Peter is still outside at first. Not much thought is given to the man on the steps that lead up to the theater, his back hunched, his face hidden from the cold. It's only when he hears his name through the SZA album playing in his ears that Eli freezes and turns, catching Peter as he runs up to him.

"Wait, Eli. Where are you going?" Peter asks him, the breath puffing around his soft-looking lips. "The movie's not over, right?"

"No, it's not," he says. "You would've known that if you were in the theater with me. You know, like you should've been."

"I'm sorry, I didn't mean to—" He shows Eli the phone screen where the call is muted. "There was a situation at work, and I had to—"

"Actually? Don't bother. I'm not interested."

"But I—"

"It's whatever, Peter. It's clear that this night didn't mean that much to you, or else you wouldn't have spent so much of it ignoring me."

"I didn't mean to," he says. "I was actually looking forward to this date."

Eli scoffs. "Could've fooled me."

"Eli, I—"

"How about we cut our losses, huh? It's clear that I'm not your type, you're not interested, and I'd rather go out with a guy who will actually put down his phone and pay attention. So, we can call it a night here."

It's not like he's ever going to see this man again. Not if he has anything to say about the situation.

"So, thanks." Eli doesn't like the wetness behind his eyes.

"Thanks for embarrassing me, for wasting my time, and for ruining my shoes."

He tucks his freezing hands back into his jacket. Maybe that last comment was harsh, but he doesn't care. It's not his responsibility to spare Peter's feelings. At least this way, maybe he'll take the night to heart, and Eli has saved whomever Peter bothers next from a night of being stood up and ignored.

"Have a good night, Peter."

Desperate to leave the situation before he truly loses it, Eli walks as fast as his short legs will carry him, praying that Peter hasn't followed him, that the man isn't suddenly inspired to course correct the entire night by making some passionate plea to forget the movie, to go out drinking, to karaoke, or bowling, or . . . anything at all.

Eli skips getting on the bus right away, choosing to walk down Divisadero to help clear his head. Peter doesn't reappear, doesn't text Eli or try to call him or anything. Eli doesn't even know if he wants Peter to do any of that. But it'd be nice to be fought for.

The bus comes and, as he steps on and scans his phone to pay the fare, his Spotify auto-plays Laufey. He can't resist laughing to himself at the absurdity of the night.

Patricia and Rose are both still awake when he walks through the door to the apartment, the loud sounds of an argument between two women on whatever *Real Housewives* season they've put on to kill time in the background, and the smell of whatever they made for dinner lingers.

"Hey, there he is!" Patricia says with a hopeful smile. "How was it?"

"I don't want to talk about it," Eli says. His instinct is to go right to his bedroom, but he avoids that, knowing that shutting himself off right now might do more harm than good. He falls onto the couch, laying his head on Patricia's lap while Rose pulls his legs over to stretch across her own.

"Want a drink?" Rose offers. "Or ketamine?"

"No." Eli throws his arm over his eyes. "To both."

"Want to talk about it instead?" Patricia asks.

"He was over an hour late."

Rose gasps almost hilariously loudly. "You're joking."

He shakes his head. "I'd already eaten by the time he got to the restaurant. And I was a bottle and a half into the soju."

"Did he call you?" Patricia asks.

Again, Eli shakes his head. "Then he just kept apologizing for everything. Which was annoying as hell. He pretty much only gave one-word answers, never really asked about me, and then got weird when I said I'm an assistant. The vibes were just incredibly off the entire time." Eli pauses. "Oh, then he spilled soup on me."

"I can see that . . ." Patricia glances at Eli's shoes left at the door. "Sorry."

"It's not your fault," Eli continues. "He then proceeded to tell me he forgot his wallet, leaving me to pay for dinner after he offered."

"Huh." Patricia's brows furrow together.

"What?" Eli looks up at her. "Do you know something?"

"No, just . . . my friend said that Peter was such a sweet guy. I'm just surprised."

The way Peter looked at him certainly hadn't helped, that helpless expression, like he was a lost dog. Which was hilarious coming from someone as tall and strong looking as Peter.

In fact, he feels more and more like a total asshole the longer he dwells on it.

"It was like he'd never been on a date before," Eli tells them, trying to laugh off the guilt that has crept up on him. "Like I was his first."

"Well, how do you know you weren't?" Rose asks him.

"There's no way." Eli shakes his head in disbelief. "The dude is hot. Like stupidly attractive. There's no possible way I was his *first* date."

Though when he gives it even another second of thought, the blend of being gay, Korean, and growing up in a small Georgia town is a combination of explosive proportions.

Patricia continues, though. "People have different lives, different experiences. I didn't start dating until college. Neither did Rose. Neither did *you*."

"That's normal," Eli says, digging his hole even deeper. "He can't be any younger than me, and you don't go on your first date when you're nearing thirty."

Patricia shoots him a firm glare. "Okay, *now* I think you're being unfair."

"Even if it was . . ." Eli swallows, trying to assuage that bitter taste on his tongue from putting his foot in his mouth. "He skipped out on basic human decency. Not a single text to tell me he was late. Taking work calls instead of focusing on me?"

Though he realizes what that sounds like out loud, Eli knows he isn't in the wrong. When you go on a date, you expect a certain level of attention to be dedicated to you. And in return, you give your attention to the other person.

"It's Dating 101," he says.

"No, no . . ." Patricia tells him, focusing on the TV. "You're right. I'm just saying a little sympathy might go a long way. You don't know Peter's story."

"Because getting any personal information out of him was like wrestling an alligator."

"An alligator?" Patricia asks. "How would you know what that's like?"

"Well, you know . . . whatever," Eli stammers.

"You know," Rose starts to say, picking a loose thread from Eli's pants, "there *should* be a Dating 101."

Eli glances toward her, trying to focus his attention back on their show. "What do you mean?"

"I mean for people who like haven't gotten the chance to date, or don't know how to, or are scared. You should like . . . I don't know, be able to hire someone to teach you how to date, be a good partner."

"That's just the movie *Hitch*," Eli says.

"Is it? Damn . . . I thought that was original."

"*She's All That* too, kind of?" Patricia's eyes go wide as she turns back to Eli. "You could *She's All That* Peter!"

"That could be fun!" Rose tells him. "Teach him how to communicate, how to stop focusing on work, loosen up, and be less of a nervous wreck."

"You're both joking, right?" Eli groans. "Also, that's not the plot of *She's All That*."

"I said 'kind of,'" Patricia continues. "You can't say that doesn't sound like fun."

"Yeah, let me just spend the next month teaching a grown-ass man how to date. That seems like a great way to spend my time."

"You never know. Maybe under that hard, anxious exterior sits the man of your dreams."

"The exterior is not the problem," Eli promises her. "Trust me."

Peter will join the roster of men, both real and fictional, whom Eli likes to conjure up while he masturbates. And that's where he'll remain.

"You have to admit, it'd be pretty fun. Like a boyfriend rehabilitation kind of thing." Patricia nudges him.

"Yeah, no," Eli promises to both himself and the girls. "I relinquish all responsibility for this man."

He can't be expected to babysit a grown man, to teach him the basics of social etiquette, how to *talk* to someone you go on a date with. It's not his job.

"Peter is *not* my problem."

Chapter Four

When Harry Met Sally . . ., dir. by Rob Reiner

Unfortunately, Peter is indeed Eli's problem.

He doesn't hear a peep from Peter all weekend, not that he's *hoping* to hear from him. But there's that uncertain, fleeting desire that springs to life when his phone screen lights up with a weekend email from Michael or a text from Patricia while she's out grabbing groceries.

Eli hates that he *wants* something, some acknowledgment, or another apology; but by Monday he's promised himself that he's ready to move on, to forget about Peter.

Until Michael pops his head in the door of the break room during Eli's lunch break, just as Gwen from IT is showing Eli the LEGO Rivendell set she spent the weekend building with her wife.

"Eli?" Michael looks weirded out, an unfamiliar expression to Eli in the years he's known him. "There's a man here to see you."

"A man?" Eli can't help his confusion. "Who is it?"

"No idea!" Michael says with a smile before he disappears just as quickly as he appeared.

"Scorned lover?" Gwen asks, sipping her coffee.

"Actually, you might not be that far off," he tells her, throwing away the empty cup of ramen. He can't explain why, but it's like he can *tell* it's Peter before he even walks out into the main office, their eyes meeting far too late for Eli to make a run for it.

Where would that get him, though? Eli already knows that Peter isn't a dangerous guy. He doubts that there's a malicious bone in Peter's body. Besides, Eli's suffered through worse. *Vent* isn't nearly controversial enough of a website anymore to warrant any kind of attack on the building or any of its staff, but there have been occurrences over the years, people needing to be escorted out of the office whether they be ex-employees, people who sent digital threats in their email or from Twitter, the subjects of articles who promise to sue them for slander. And Eli can remind them that in print, it's libel.

That still doesn't knock out the creep factor of Peter *showing up* at the office, though.

"Eli, I was hoping we could talk. I just wanted to—" Peter begins to say before Eli takes him by the hand, dragging him down the length of the office—the attention of a few of his coworkers now focused squarely on the both of them—and pulls Peter into a meeting room.

Not that it gives them *much* privacy—the modern design of the building means that there's an entire wall of glass that leaves them on full display for the rest of his coworkers. But at least no one can hear them.

"You've got a tight grip . . ." Peter holds his wrist when Eli lets go of him.

"What are you doing here? How did you find me?"

"You told me where you work," Peter says. "During the date."

"Yeah, okay." As if that makes this better. "Still, what are you doing here?"

"I . . ." Peter's expression sinks, his gaze refusing to meet Eli's. "I wanted to apologize for . . . for Friday."

"Peter, please look at me," Eli asks of him.

And Peter does just that. In the cool, sterile light of the office's modern design, it almost surprises Eli just how warm Peter's brown eyes are. There's a comfort to the color of them, like a burning fire on a rainy day. Of course, the fireplace in Eli's apartment is closed off, so he's had to manage with those ten-hour-long You-Tube videos of fake fireplaces, but the sentiment is still the same.

"Did you really think that showing up here, in front of everyone that I know, was the best way to go about that?"

"I . . ." Peter trails off, clearly indicating that this is the first time he's ever thought this might be an issue. "I'm sorry, I didn't mean to— I just thought that I—"

"Okay, fine. Peter. I forgive you or whatever, just get out of here." Eli talks with his hands before pinching the bridge of his nose. "Please."

"You didn't give me an actual chance to apologize," he says.

"What?"

"You accepted an apology that I didn't give you," Peter elaborates. "I just said that I *wanted* to apologize."

"Okay, well . . . then apologize."

"Oh, uh . . ." Peter stares down at his feet, his hands gripped together. He's still wearing the same hoodie as the other night, except this time he's got on a crew-neck sweatshirt underneath, and his hair is a little less neat. Yet somehow, he's even cuter than he was on their date night.

"Well?" Eli stares expectantly. "I've got work to do, Peter."

"Sorry, I just . . ." Peter pauses before he apparently decides to go for broke, to let it all out. "I've never really been on a date before."

Eli hesitates. "Like with another guy, or—"

"At all," he spills out, his voice still unsure. "You're the first person I've ever been on a date with. I was really nervous. So nervous that I wanted to throw up, and I almost called you to cancel. But Francine told me what she knew about you from your friends, and I found your Instagram, and I thought that you were cute, and I felt like I had to impress you or something. But that only made you hate me even more, so that didn't really work out."

He thinks I'm cute? Eli has to tell himself that's not important right now. "If it really meant that much to you, you could've been on time. And I don't hate you, Peter. I just . . . don't really care."

There's no way to say that without it sounding harsh, but it's the truth. Eli doesn't care; he only feels an indifference toward Peter.

"I know." Peter nods. "I keep my phone on work mode basically twenty-four seven, just so I can focus, and I just . . . let time get away from me while I was in a meeting. But I didn't mean to, and I'm *incredibly* sorry about it."

"Okay, well . . . apology accepted. So, you can go."

"I wish that you'd say something."

Eli pauses, finally meeting Peter's gaze before Peter breaks eye contact with him. Eli sighs, bracing himself against the conference room table. "I mean, I can't lie, Peter. It was a pretty terrible night."

He doesn't see the need to beat around the bush, especially when Peter *asked* for the truth.

"You were late, you didn't text or call, you spilled food on me, you barely said a word, and you didn't seem all that interested in what I had to say."

"I know," Peter says. Eli almost wishes that he'd fight back instead of sitting there and taking it.

"You couldn't pay, which I don't mind, it's not a huge deal; but it's clear you're a little scatter-brained and that dating isn't your main priority."

"Fair."

"And you left me at the movies."

"I had a work call."

"At eight o'clock at night? You know you can ignore those, right? You don't have to answer the calls if you're not on the clock."

"I know . . ." Peter lets his head hang in shame. "I'm sorry. There was a project one of my team members in Mumbai needed help with, so the day had just started for him because of the time zones and . . ."

His words trail off as Peter realizes there's no excuse. There's this silence that stretches out in front of them, while Eli is left to look anywhere that isn't at Peter.

"Am I seriously the first date you've ever been on?" he dares to ask.

"Comer isn't a big town, and there aren't many out gay people, least of all any out gay people who aren't also racist. And college . . . I don't know. I had a few friends, but it was one of those situations where after I graduated . . . I realized I was just friends with them *because* they were my classmates. I just found it so . . ."

"Hard?" Such a simple word, but it means everything.

"Yeah."

"Huh . . ."

"Is that a surprise?"

"Well, kind of. You're hot, Peter."

"Oh, uh . . ." His golden cheeks go red almost immediately, like someone got a little too eager with blush. "Thanks?" He sounds so unsure of himself.

"It's a compliment, you can take it."

"Sorry."

"You say that a lot."

"Sorry."

"There you go again."

"I don't really know what else to say," he offers. "I told Francine that I wanted to actually get out there, meet someone, finally explore the city after living here for so long. Look at where it got me."

Damn, Eli thinks.

"I'm sorry. Really," Peter tells him.

"Well . . . we all have to start somewhere," Eli says. "If it makes you feel any better, I've only ever had one boyfriend, so I was pretty nervous to meet you."

"Really?"

"Yeah, I mean, I don't think first-date nerves are really something that goes away, you know?" Eli asks before he realizes that no, that's not really something that Peter would be familiar with. "You just get used to it, kind of."

"Yeah, well . . . I just didn't want you to think that I was some huge asshole."

"No," Eli says. "Just a regular asshole." He tries to add a levity to his voice so that Peter knows he's being playful.

And Peter actually does smile at that, and there's a comfort to the expression, like he can tell that Eli is telling a joke. "Do you know how to get better at it?" he asks. "At dating?"

"You sort of just have to do it, learn by experience."

Peter smiles ruefully. "I was afraid you'd say that."

Eli thinks about last night, about the Dating 101 idea that Rose had. He didn't realize just how on the nose she was with that one. It almost comes out, Eli *almost* offers to help teach Peter a thing or two. But this isn't his responsibility.

Eli opens his mouth, unsure of the words that he's about to say, but then Michael makes his grand reappearance at the door to the meeting room. "Hey, Eli. Is everything okay?"

Eli wishes he could pretend that Michael actually cares, but he knows Michael is just *waiting* for the right moment to pounce on the gossip.

"Yeah, Michael. We're fine."

"Oh." Michael pauses. "Then maybe you should get back to work, the phones have been ringing."

"I was just leaving, actually," Peter interjects. "Thanks for everything, Eli. And I'm sorry again, about . . . everything." In an instant, the awkwardness seems to come back to the forefront.

Before Eli can say much else, Peter is stepping past him, Michael opening the door wider to let Peter out into the office where he heads toward the elevators.

"Another breakup?" Michael frowns in such a disingenuous way. "I'm sorry, Eli."

"No, he's just some . . . guy I went on a date with." Maybe he shouldn't tell Michael the truth considering how he apparently goes behind Eli's back, but there's no use in lying.

"Oh?"

"Yeah, it didn't go well. He came to apologize. Wanted dating advice." Eli crosses his arms, stretching out the ache in his neck.

"Did you give it to him?"

"What?"

"The dating advice?" Michael asks.

"What was I supposed to say to him?" Eli's asking himself just as much as he's asking Michael. "Why does everyone think I'm responsible for teaching twunks basic etiquette?"

"Okay, okay, no need to get all hysterical on me. I was just curious."

Eli ignores the "hysterical" comment. He hadn't even raised his voice.

"You know my roommate actually suggested dating rehabilitation," Eli says, unsure of *why* he's sharing this with Michael. The moment just feels open. "She thinks that we need people out there to teach other people how to date or something."

"What, were you, like, his first date ever or something?" Michael snorts.

Eli nods. "That's what he told me."

Michael lets out a low whistle. "That is S-A-D sad."

It is sad, but not for the reasons Michael thinks it is. Eli has to figure it's a feeling familiar to a lot of people. Realizing at a young age that they're different, but not having community or support in a rural and incredibly homophobic part of the country. He thinks back to his formative years, lived in the comfort of knowing that it was always safe for him to come out, having grown up surrounded by supportive parents in a city that celebrated queerness.

Eli had every resource available to him since before he even realized he was trans. He grew up surrounded by queer elders, queer art, queer music and movies, queer books. And his parents fostered those feelings, never giving Eli the space to doubt who he truly was.

Peter might not have had any of that.

Just like countless other queer people like him from a similar area.

Then, the idea hits him. He could write an article, interview Peter about growing up queer in the South, the difficulties that queer people face coming of age in an area of the country with few resources, with no real opportunities to find community.

Eli can't help but smile at the idea. "Actually—"

"One second, I'm not done," Michael interjects. "For the dating concept . . . you'd pretend to date him, teach him how to be a better boyfriend. A 'Build-a-Boyfriend Project' of sorts . . ."

"Yeah . . ." Eli's smile dies as quickly as it appeared.

"I like it."

"What?"

"This idea, you should do it."

"Michael, what if we wrote about—"

But Michael interrupts Eli again before he can get another word out. "Think about it. A long-form article, or maybe an essay or something. Or we could do smaller updates, spread them out. You spend a few weeks with him, teach him to be someone that people would want to date . . ." Michael puts his hand to his chin. "Yeah, yeah. This could be gold. I like it."

"No, no, you don't." Eli resists the urge to pull at his hair. "I'm not going to pretend to date someone just to teach him a lesson. We could write something *important*, how many other people grow up like Peter? Isolated and inexperienced because of where they're born. We could make an actual difference to a lot of people, help them see themselves for once."

Michael seemingly ignores him, though it's a coin toss on whether it's purposeful or accidental. "This is what you want to do, though. Right? You want to be a staff writer."

Eli can't deny how scandalous an article like that could be. He'd certainly give it a read if he stumbled upon the headline somewhere online. But doing that to Peter? He couldn't. Besides, he knows in his gut there's something more interesting here. "No way, this isn't journalism, it's garbage."

"Exactly!" Michael looks at Eli with a wild glee in his eyes. "This is what I've been trying to get you to write about, Eli. This is the kind of stuff our audience *wants*. They want messy, they want drama, they want you to spill the tea!" The words form so awkwardly coming from Michael.

"You're not using that correctly," Eli tells him.

"You know our connections, Eli. This could be at the top of the trending page like *that*!"

"No, absolutely not. I'm not putting myself through that." That's when Eli decides to leave, to cut the conversation short, and put an end to this entire discussion. There's no way he's suffering through weeks of teaching another guy how to date when he could be doing something better.

Like writing articles that no one is going to read, that are just going to sit in his Google Drive while he wastes away as a secretary at a job that he hates. Michael steps out of the way, and while Eli has often wished that his desk isn't *right* in front of Michael's office, he's never wanted that to be true more than right now. Because Michael just follows him.

"Think about it, come on! The readers would *eat* it up."

Eli wakes up his computer. Could he do it, though? Could he teach Peter how to date? No, right? What experience does he have? Just a seven-year relationship that crumbled right before his eyes. But Eli likes to think he knows how to date, the expectations, how to connect with someone.

No. Nope. Never, he tells himself.

He can't do this, because how stupid of an idea is that? *Unless.*

He could treat this as an entry point, getting his foot in the door. Maybe he could lie to Michael, pretend to write the dating article. All the while, he can interview Peter, he can learn about what it was like to grow up so isolated as a queer person. He can shine a spotlight on those experiences. And Michael will *finally* understand, he'll see that the readers of *Vent* are so eager for those human stories that they once prided themselves on.

Sure, it's a long shot to think one article will make a change. But given how high the barrier of entry is into the queer community when it comes to lack of experience, maybe it'll open some eyes, start some conversations.

"Imagine the traffic to the site with something like that, and maybe . . . who knows, you could expand it. Tons of articles lead to full-blown books, or movies even!"

He could do it. Pretend to write one article, hedge all his bets on another in the hopes that Michael will *finally* give him a shot.

"But despite all that, bringing you in *so* much traffic and views, or writing *books* for the company, I'd still be your secretary?" Eli asks him, prodding further, desperate to see how far he might be able to take it.

If the way Michael's face shifts is any indication, he understands exactly where Eli is going with this.

"I could do this," Eli lays it on him. "I could help this guy become a suitable boyfriend, I could teach him to be someone that people will want to date, and I could write your article that'll bring you *all* the clicks you want."

Michael lets out a long, low groan, his head hanging over Eli's desk. "Go ahead and ask."

"I want a staff writer job." There's actual risk here. If this article isn't up to snuff, if Michael catches on too early, then Eli can kiss his career goodbye.

Then again, maybe that could be its own reward.

"That's a tough call, Eli." Michael's voice goes quiet, as if he's afraid that Eli will call him out on his bullshit. There are plenty of empty desks at *Vent*, and he could help train another secretary to do all the things that he's used to doing.

"You think this could be big? If it means that much to you, then you'll give me what I want." Eli crosses his arms.

Michael sighs. "Then yes. It will be considered."

Eli raises a brow. "Considered?"

"I will *seriously* consider you for the staff writing job if you do this. If you do a good job, like I think you will, and if the article meets my expectations as well as the site's. I'll even work with you throughout the entire thing."

Eli doesn't like the sound of that, Michael being so involved in the process. But it's clear that Michael wants this *so* badly. And Eli's the only one who can give it to him.

"I'll have to convince him to be a part of this," Eli says.

"Avoid telling him about the article—you don't want him to know. You don't want the experiment to be compromised. If he knows it's a public performance, he might edit his behavior."

Well, he won't know about one *of the articles*, Eli thinks. "I have to catch him."

"Then go!" Michael exclaims, catching a few eyes from their coworkers, surprised by the sudden outburst.

And Eli does just that.

* * *

"You want to write about me?" Peter asks from across the table, his hands wrapped around themselves, most of his iced coffee long gone now that Eli has finished explaining the pitch for the article.

"Well, not exactly about you. I'd take pieces of your story, interview you. But I'd also reach a bit wider. It's less about *you*, and more about the experience. You're more of like . . . a framing device."

"Huh . . ." Peter looks down at the table, picking at some of the tacky aquamarine paint with his fingernails.

Peter was more than a little confused by Eli's invitation as he caught Peter at the guest checkout. But they'd come across the street to a café that Eli and Patricia both frequented when they needed to escape their respective offices.

"I've never been interviewed before," Peter tells him. "Well, besides for my jobs. And my college-entrance stuff. But never like this."

"Do you think you could do it?"

"I mean, do you really think this is worth writing about?" Peter asks. And it's a fair question.

"Peter, I swear I don't mean this personally when I say that Friday night was a disaster."

Peter can't even lie. "I know."

"And I think that your experience, or lack thereof, speaks to where you grow up. Thousands of queer people share a story similar to yours."

"Yeah, I never really gave it much thought until recently."

"It feels like your peers have passed you by, huh?"

"Yeah. I guess so. Growing up, I never got the chance to date. There was . . ." His words trail off. "There was one other gay person in my school, but he wasn't out. We just happened to know each other. I wasn't kidding when I said you were my first date. I tried to get on apps when I moved out here, but everything was so scary and everyone just wanted sex right away. Or drugs. Then there's the people with 'No Asians' in their bio, and that made me feel . . ." The words slip away from Peter, his last thoughts left unsaid.

Eli wants to say something, but he isn't sure just *what* he can say in this moment. He knows that feeling. Not the exact one, obviously. Eli's white, regardless of his gender identity. He has and always will benefit from a system like the one that shuts Peter out before he even reaches the door. Peter's identities as a gay Korean man intersect in ways that Eli will never truly understand, let alone him growing up in an area of the world that he assumes would hate every part of Peter that he can't change.

But Eli can at least listen. And it *is* a familiar feeling, to be shunned for something you can't change, a core part of your being. It's all too easy to recall the men who rejected him once they saw Eli's private photos, and when he dared to put "trans man" in his bio to keep it from ever getting that far, strangers seemed to take that as an open invitation to give Eli their opinion on his body.

"It's been weird and new and I thought it'd get easier after being here for years. I've read articles and books, watched YouTube videos on making friends, being gay, how to find a place. But it was too much."

"That right there!" Eli exclaims. "That's what I want to write about. How so many queer people grow up without those experiences that most would consider essential."

"And you think people will read that?"

"I hope so." Not that it'll matter if Michael fires Eli the moment he figures out what's going on. But if he can work with Peter, make this the best essay he's written, then maybe, just *maybe*, Michael will give him a shot.

Eli just has to keep him happy while he waits.

"And, in exchange for helping me," Eli begins to say. He can't believe he's going to offer this. But he has to admit that Rose's idea—and, okay, Michael's too—wasn't a bad one. "I'd like to teach you how to date."

He has to have *something* to base the fake article on.

"You want to teach me how to date?" Peter stares with an unsure look.

"Yeah, we'd go on these dates where I'd coach you. Teach you to be a better, more attentive date." Eli spills the words in a single breath, knowing just how ludicrous it sounds; he has to get the idea out before Peter decides to walk away.

Peter's gaze darts to the table, then out the window of the café.

God, how could he ever think this was a good idea? Of course Peter wouldn't agree to this—who would? The last time he and Peter had a real conversation, Eli was telling Peter off and storming away with semi-dry pants and soup-covered shoes. In what world would Peter ever want to pretend to date another person just to—

"I'll do it."

It takes Eli a moment to truly register Peter's reply.

"You will?

"It doesn't sound stupid. I mean, it does. But . . . listen . . . you're not the first person I've talked to since moving here." Peter sighs, his shoulders seemingly lighter, like he's been waiting for the moment when he can finally talk to someone about how he's been feeling. "I've been trying my best, but clearly it isn't enough. I'll accept any help I can get."

"That sounds pretty desperate, Peter." Eli doesn't mean it as an insult, just a simple and plain fact.

"Yeah, I guess you could say I am." Peter smiles awkwardly, his eyes catching his own hands where he's been playing with them nervously. "I don't know how all of this works. Obviously. And I need the experience, but I can't get it because my stupid brain can't get past the part where I have to meet someone new, where I have to like . . . form a connection or something. If you're offering to teach me, help me learn, then I want to do it."

"Well, Peter . . . that's great to hear!"

"So . . . how do we do this?"

"Well, I . . ." Eli has to admit, Peter's got him there. The idea is so new, fresh, he hasn't really had time to consider the details. "I think it'll be easiest to go on these fake dates and get to know one another. And through getting to know more about you and how you grew up, I'll be able to shape my article."

Peter takes a heavy breath, still recovering. "That's going to be weird."

"It is, but I think it'll be good for you," Eli tells him. "Now, I think we should lay some ground rules, before we really make a plan here."

"Like?"

"Nothing can be personal."

Peter stares at him, confused. "In what way?"

"I'm here to help you, to teach you how to be a better boyfriend to someone. And to do that, you're going to have to face some insecurities. Nothing that I'm going to say to you will be personal," Eli promises to him, but then backtracks. "I mean, it *will* be personal. There's really no denying that. But you can't really take it that way."

Peter seems to chew on the words for a bit. "So, honesty is the best policy?"

"In this case, I think yes," Eli agrees. "I have to be honest with you. And that goes both ways. If you have a problem with something I say or what I want you to do, I *need* you to tell me. I'm not trying to change you as a person."

"You literally are, though. Aren't you?"

"There's a difference," Eli attempts to explain. "We're trying to make you into a better dater, which . . . yeah, sure, we're going to have to change some things about how you behave, how you tackle certain situations. But I don't want to fundamentally change who you are."

"That's . . . admirable."

Eli smiles at him. "Chivalry isn't totally dead." Never mind that Eli is lying to both Peter *and* Michael.

"So, with these dates . . . do we pretend that we don't know what's going on? Like do we try to act as natural as possible?"

"I think we should have a safe word."

"A safe word . . ." Peter swallows, the very tips of his ears turning rose red in an instant. "There's not going to be sex, right?" He whispers that last part, almost like he's ashamed. Eli can't stop himself from wondering if Peter's ever had sex before.

Not that it matters in the slightest. Virginity is a social construct, an invention meant to shame people when it literally doesn't matter at all. It's just that he can't get over how Peter seems so quiet about sex, almost as if he's afraid of it.

Of course, that doesn't have to matter either. For all he knows, Peter is asexual. Perhaps he's never considered sex as a thing he wants, maybe he's indifferent about it, or maybe he's entirely repulsed by the act.

It's enough to leave Eli chewing on what that could mean for them both.

"God, no!" Eli assures him. "That's not what this is about."

"Oh, I, um . . ." Peter's nervousness is on full display, his cheeks matching his ears. Eli decides to spare the poor man, skipping right past any and all awkwardness.

"No, this safe word is one that we both can use to break character, talk about what's happening, if we're both comfortable with what's going on. Otherwise, we'll act like complete strangers, getting to know each other, no prior knowledge of . . ." Eli looks around the coffee shop, as if the living example of the mess his life has turned into just strolled right in. "This."

"So, we'll be acting?"

"In a sense." Eli nods. "Yes."

"What's the safe word?"

"It can be anything we want, maybe not something so common it'll come up in conversation often."

"Iced Americano?" Peter offers.

"Iced Americano?" Eli repeats, staring at him.

"I hate them," Peter says, sticking his tongue out. "So, I won't want to talk about them."

Eli can't help but smile. "Yes. Our safe word, or *words*, will be 'iced Americano.' If either of us says that, then we stop what we're doing, talk Eli-to-Peter about the situation."

"I have a question," Peter asks.

"Give it to me."

"What if we develop real feelings?"

"Whoa, okay," Eli sputters. "I think you're getting ahead of your-self there, tiger." Sure, Peter is an attractive man, with his broad shoulders that so easily paint a picture of what lies underneath the sweatshirt he's wearing, but Eli doesn't intend to go there.

"That's not what I was—" he stammers. The blush on Peter's cheeks is *immediate*, and Eli can't deny that there's something cute about how embarrassed he looks. "I didn't mean it like—"

"Relax, Peter." Eli reaches for his hand, hoping to pull Peter back down to Earth. "I was just messing with you."

Peter takes a pregnant pause. "Right . . ."

"But you're correct. A pull-out clause might be useful. Who knows, emotions might be flying high. And we're literally going to pretend to be boyfriends and do boyfriend things. It might be easy to get confused."

"And if I find a date, or I meet a person," Peter begins to say. "I don't want them to think that you're someone to be worried about."

"You're right, you're right." Eli notes the rule. It's a fair one; being the third wheel could scare away any potential suitors that might catch Peter's eye.

"What kind of dates would we go on?"

"Uh, dinner. Movies. We could go to the park, or . . ." Eli thinks, having to remember what actual dates feel like. "A cooking class?"

Peter chuckles. "I actually tried a cooking class, to meet people. I caused a fire."

"Seriously?"

Peter nods. "I forgot that you can't put water on a grease fire. They banned me from any future classes at the center."

"Peter . . ." Eli can't resist the laugh that slips out, which makes Peter laugh too.

"It's not funny!" he argues, still smiling.

"I know, I know. I'm sorry." Eli can't stop himself, though.

"People could've died."

"I'm sorry." Eli hides his face. "See, where was this on Friday?" He can already sense Peter's ease. There's a relaxation that wasn't there Friday night.

"I . . . I don't know. I guess I find it easier to talk to you since you've seen the bad parts of me."

"That's the kind of self-awareness that we're looking for, I think."

"So . . ." Peter starts to say. "Where do we start? With my . . . rehabilitation?"

"Finding a better name for it, for starters." Eli sits back in the booth, crossing his arms across his chest.

This has to be the biggest hurdle to climb over in this entire scheme. Eli isn't a big fan of it either—in all the rom-coms he's watched, fake dating always leads to muddy feelings, people falling in love. Not that Eli has to really worry about that.

Then it comes to him in a sudden burst, so obvious. Eli smiles. "But I have an idea."

Peter stares at Eli, his eyebrows raised. "Which is?"

Chapter Five

13 Going on 30, dir. by Gary Winick

A nd you actually *want* to do this?" Patricia sits on Eli's bed once
again, Eli adjusting the collar of his button-down shirt where
it showed from under the sweater, careful of his hair.

All week, he'd spent his free time organizing his thoughts, writing out the throughlines of the articles that he wants to follow,
questions to ask Peter, where he'd even start with writing two entirely
different stories for Michael.

"He asked me to give him another shot," Eli tells her as he
wrestles with his hair once again. Rose is out, having stayed late at
school to finish up her lesson planning for the next week, meaning
that Eli's been left alone to tame the wild mess that sits on top of
his head.

He has his father to thank for that. Despite balding late in
his thirties, David Francis had sported a nest of thick black hair
through most of his young adult years. Pre-transition, Eli's hair
had been just as thick, but more wavy than curly, and much easier
to control.

Truthfully, he hadn't believed all the things he'd heard from
other trans people about the effects of testosterone. How could
your hair magically become curly? How was it possible for your
body odor to change? How could you magically become gay?

And yet, that hadn't stopped it from happening. At least the
first two; the most drastic change with Eli's sexuality was having

to reckon that his attraction to men was of the homo variety and not the hetero kind, which was its own wild battle.

Even now, in a place where Eli considers himself well into his transition, it's haunted him just *how* much he looks like his father. The same thin frame, the same pasty-white skin that burns after just minutes in the sun, the same sharp angle of the nose and shape of his eyes.

"So, I wanted to give him one." Eli runs his hands along the sweater, flattening it out a bit.

"You must think he's really cute to give him a second chance." Patricia beams, shimmying her shoulders in excitement.

"What does that mean?"

"Considering you've spent the last six months whining about how dating isn't for you, I'm surprised you'd want to go out again so soon. Especially with Peter again."

Eli swallows. All week he considered telling Patricia about everything, just to have someone in his corner for this little scheme of his. But something's stopped him every time he tries to bring it up, like his brain just knew it'd be a bad idea.

Technically he's not doing anything wrong, but that hasn't stopped the odd sense of guilt he feels when he really gives this idea thought. He just keeps telling himself he's doing something important, something worthwhile. *And* helping Peter along the way.

Everyone wins.

"I decided you and Rose are right," he tells her just as much as he's telling himself, tucking his hair behind his ears and straightening his glasses. He could do without the zit that's working its way out from under his nose, the red bump tender when Eli touches it. "I thought a lot about what you both said, about getting back out there, and giving people chances. I decided that Peter was worth the second chance."

He almost believes himself; the lie comes out so naturally.

"Well, that's very big of you, Eli."

"Yeah . . . maybe." He doesn't meet her eyes in the mirror.

"Where are you going?" she asks, the bed frame creaking as she stands and joins Eli in front of the mirror, smoothing out the shoulders of the outfit. As they stumbled into September, Eli's sweaters became a little less appropriate for the weather. As if Northern California operated on its own schedule, their version of summer took place mostly at the start of the fall, finishing a few weeks into October. The sweater might be a bit much in the warmer night air, but he doesn't want to wear anything else.

"Doobu and a movie," Eli says, stepping away and grabbing the cologne from his dresser.

Patricia turns, leaning against the wall with her arms crossed, her mouth open. "You're going on a repeat date?"

"We're calling it First Date 2.0. He wanted a redo, and I thought it was a cute idea," Eli fibs, more than happy to let Peter take credit for his idea.

He'd gone as far as to spend his free time watching the rom-com classics that he felt were applicable to his incredibly weird fake-dating situation that isn't actually fake-dating. *How to Lose a Guy in 10 Days*, *Drive Me Crazy*, *To All the Boys I've Loved Before*, *Anyone But You*.

There were some takeaways, sure, but Eli isn't delusional enough to think he can just apply movie logic to his life.

"Do you have a picture of him?" Patricia asks. "Is he cute?"

"None to speak of," Eli tells her. It was one of the few topics they'd discussed so far, and Eli had to break the news to Peter that having no social media was a huge red flag. And, to his credit, Peter made an Instagram right after that conversation.

So far, Eli is his only follower, but they're building a platform. They spent hours picking the best pictures for Peter to post of himself, the ones that really showed off his personality, ones that could easily fit on a Hinge, Bumble, or Tinder profile as well.

Unfortunately, there weren't that many to pick from. The man is gorgeous, no doubt. But Eli had to make a mental note to teach him about angles in selfies.

And because of that, most of their text thread is taken up by pictures of Peter sent over the course of a single day. Him in North Beach, him sweaty in some gym somewhere, him at his desk.

> **ELI:** are you sending these all as you take them?

He couldn't help but ask, his curiosity getting the best of him.

> **PETER:** Should I not have done that?

Eli had smiled at his phone as the message came in.

> **ELI:** no, keep sending them.

> **ELI:** we need plenty of options.

Eli had liked the ones he thought would make good choices, and the longer he looked at these pictures of Peter, the harder he found it to believe that Peter had never gone out with anyone before Eli.

Then again, wasn't that what he was here to find out? So far, none of their few talks had led to talking about Peter's upbringing, but Eli figured it was best to save those heavier conversations for their in-person dates.

A few articles had broached the subject of what it was like to grow up queer in the South, and a handful of books, mostly fictional. A movie or two. A *lot* of music, almost too much. But by and large, the subject seemed fairly unexplored. What Eli did find was distressing, to say the least. Stories of being kicked out of their home, assault, death, isolation, and fear, being surrounded by people who hate for no reason.

Eli's heart ached.

"Okay!" Patricia sings as she steps out of the bedroom and back toward the kitchen where her dinner for the night simmers on the stove, the warm smell of the chili making Eli's stomach grumble. "But I demand a picture before the night is over with. I want to see this guy."

"Okay, I'll take pictures," he bemoans. Of course, he *could* just show her the dozen or so pictures of Peter that he'd saved to his phone, just so he could remember the ones that he likes, but he doesn't feel like it. Showing Peter to Patricia makes this severely more real than he'd like it to be.

"I'd like to know who's courting my best friend."

Eli snorts. "'Courting'?"

"It's a word."

"That no well-adjusted person has used since the eighteen hundreds."

Patricia follows Eli into the living room, standing behind him at the mirror so she can tug at Eli's neckline, pulling the collar of the shirt free, unbuttoning the top button because the relaxed version of his outfit fits Eli better. "Now you don't look like a schoolboy. Unless Peter's into that?"

"Barf." Eli turns.

"Should I wait up for you?" Patricia asks, wiggling her eyebrows so that Eli gets her meaning. "Or are you gonna go back to his place?"

"Yeah, no. There will be none of that." Eli's voice tenses.

"Why'd you say it *that* way?"

He curses himself. It's going to take some getting used to, keeping this act going even when Peter isn't around. "We're just . . . taking it slow," he explains. "I'm easing him into the whole dating thing, remember?"

"Oh, well." Patricia hops on top of the counter, swinging her feet back and forth. "Don't worry if you come back and the apartment is dark. I'm either having mind-blowing sex or I'm wallowing in my own misery."

"Good, nice to see that you're growing." Eli gives her his best smile, which isn't much of anything at all, and grabs his wallet and keys. And he's out the door.

* * *

The entire bus ride to Japantown, Eli isn't really sure what to feel. There are nerves, of course, and they might even be worse than they were last week. But there's a hopefulness as well, not just for the article, but for helping Peter feel good in a way that he didn't expect.

If only he were more confident in his dating skills. He's had a few moments of panic sprinkled throughout the week, wondering just who he is to try and help Peter. And whether or not this hare-brained scheme will actually work.

Whatever it is that he's feeling, it's doubled as he walks through the front doors of the restaurant and sees that Peter is already there and waiting for him in the very same booth that they sat in last week. It's just that now Peter has their seats reversed, so his eyes meet Eli's from across the restaurant.

Peter stands up too quickly, knocking into the table like a calf just learning to walk, holding his hand out in front of him like he's actually trying to properly greet Eli.

"You're here before me?" Eli double-checks the time on his phone.

"I didn't want to be late . . . again." Peter smiles at him, motioning to the booth like he's waiting for Eli to take a seat before he sits again, sliding into the booth more carefully this time. "I set a ton of alarms, so that way I wouldn't be late."

As if on cue, Peter's phone begins blaring an alarm from its spot on the table, and he scrambles to reach for it to shut it off.

"Sorry, guess I left one on." Peter swipes at something on his phone, and then very obviously goes to his messages to type something quickly before hitting send.

"It's okay," Eli tells him.

For a moment, both of them stare at each other, almost as if they're unsure of how to continue. Eli has to remind himself that he's supposed to be acting, that right now he isn't Eli meeting Peter. He's Eli meeting a man that he's been set up with.

"So . . . how was your day?" Eli asks him, desperate to get the conversation going.

"Iced Americano!" Peter blurts out, almost as if he's been dying to say it for hours now.

"Already?"

"I'm sorry." Peter hides his face. "I'm just . . . I'm nervous, I don't want to mess this up. Are you sure this is the best way to go about all of this?"

"Peter, we can be honest. This situation is weird, very much so. Even all the movies I watched to prepare for this didn't make much sense when you gave them more than three seconds of thought. Why would adults ever agree to fake-date?"

"You watched movies to prepare for this?"

"Yes." Eli dares to reach for Peter's hand, closing the distance between the two of them. "But maybe it'll help to keep in mind that you've already messed up?"

"I have?"

"Yes, last week. You already messed up royally, and it's not like I was perfect either. So, what does it matter if we mess up again?"

"But what if I say the wrong thing? Or spill food on you again? Or miss the movie, or—"

"You already did that," Eli reminds him. It might not sound like the pep talk that he wants it to be, but he has a point to make. "You can mess up around me, Peter. I'm not going to be offended.

That's why I'm here, to help you work through what's going on in that brain of yours."

There's the hint of a smile through the nerves, and Eli can't help but smile back at him.

"So, we're okay, right?"

Peter nods slowly.

"Good, okay. We'll start fresh, right?" Eli takes his hand away, letting it hover in the air above the table. "I'm Eli Francis. It's nice to meet you."

Peter takes his hand gently. "I'm Peter Park."

"Peter Park?" It occurs to Eli that he didn't actually know Peter's last name before now.

"Yes, like *Spider-Man*," Peter says to him before Eli can even complete the thought, like he's been dealing with this for his entire life. "Just without the 'er,' and the webs."

"Color me disappointed."

"Well, my name is Ho-Seok, but when my parents came here, they were told by teachers that no one would be able to pronounce my name. And my dad is a big *Spider-Man* fan, and he thought it was cool, I guess."

"I like Peter, it's a good name. But do you prefer to be called Ho-Seok?" Eli's all too familiar with the idea of being called a name that isn't yours, how it eats away at you slowly.

Not that the experiences are the same. They might be similar, sure, but their reasons are miles apart. Eli never had someone tell him that either of his names was impossible to pronounce.

Peter shrugs. "It's okay. Only my immediate family uses my Korean name, really. And I feel like a Peter."

His ears turn red.

"I feel like I'm *named* Peter. Not that I *am* a Peter."

Eli can't help but laugh through his confusion. "Was that supposed to be a joke?"

"Well, no, but where I'm from 'peter' is another word for . . . you know." Peter looks down at his own crotch. "Dick."

Eli swallows his laughter. "You can say *penis* in front of me, Peter. We're both adults."

"I don't think my mom would appreciate me saying that in front of you."

That's when Peter's phone begins to ring, and he steals a glance at Eli before he grabs it.

"I'm so sorry, this will be quick."

Eli doesn't say a word, just lets the waitress leave his glass of water, refilling Peter's own while she's at the table. Eli tries to make anything out of the conversation that Peter's having, but tech talk has never been his area of expertise.

"So run the test again with the changes I made, watch to see where it stops if it fails. Then send the report to me. I can take a look at it later."

Peter pauses, listening.

"No, I, um . . . I'm out right now, so I can't run them. Sorry."

Eli relaxes back into the booth, still annoyed, but marginally less so given that he already expected this to happen again. Still, it doesn't make the night any less tense.

"Okay, yeah. Yes. Yeah. Okay. I will. Thanks." And finally, he hangs up. "I'm so sorry about that," he apologizes, setting his phone down.

Eli just stares at him.

Peter sighs. "Iced Americano?"

"Didn't realize you were psychic."

Peter hides his face. "I'm sorry."

"What *is* it that you do, exactly?" Eli asks, deciding that brushing past the situation might be for the best.

Peter hesitates before he asks, "Are you asking me that as first-date Eli? Or as real Eli?"

"Real Eli, but explain it to me like I'm first-date Eli."

"This is confusing," Peter says.

"You're telling me." Eli picks up his water again.

"I work at Zelus, the tech company."

"They're not into AI, are they?"

"No, Zelus mostly does UI design. Like the databases I make, and they helped to create the new readers for Muni."

"Oh, right, right." Eli vaguely recalls reading an article about the new card readers making their way throughout the city on the electric buses. "So, what do you do for them? And don't just tell me you code or do stock or whatever."

"I create and test the code for some of their clients, mostly chains who need to keep track of their inventory. But we're taking on new companies all the time, designing all kinds of things for them; there's a project starting in a few months with Lucasfilm." It strikes Eli that none of Peter's words are being said with any enthusiasm at all. Not that he has much room to talk.

"And that requires you to answer the phone during your off time?"

"It's not really that . . ." Peter says.

Eli folds his hands together carefully. "Then what is it?"

"One of my supervisors had a question about a test I ran earlier today."

"Okay, but it's seven o'clock at night on a Friday; they shouldn't be calling you when you're not on the clock."

Peter shrugs. "I don't mind answering their questions."

"Are you getting paid to do that?"

"No, I'm technically off the clock." Guilt hangs heavy in his tone.

"That's not fair, Peter."

"I guess not, but . . . like I said, I don't mind helping out or answering their questions. It's for an important project we have to have done by January."

"Well, they've got enough time to let you have a social life."

"They want the timeline moved up, though."

"That sounds like their problem," Eli says to him. "Do you enjoy doing that free labor during your off time?"

"Well . . . no. Who would?"

"Exactly."

"But it's just one phone call."

"In the middle of *our* date." Eli feels like he's talking to a brick wall. Again.

The phone buzzes, this time just once. Peter looks to Eli, as if asking for the permission he has to know he won't get, picking it up slowly and staring at the message.

"It doesn't make the other person feel good," Eli says, "when you're so caught up in work that you can't even have fun, or get to know them."

"I know."

"It doesn't seem like it." Eli doesn't want to sound mean, but there's really no other way to get it into Peter's head.

"I'm sorry."

"Let me ask you, Peter . . . What is a date?"

"Like the fruit, or the thing that we're on?"

Eli has to resist the exhausted laugh that wants to slip out. "The thing that we're on."

"Two people, or more, I guess, go and spend time together and get to know one another?"

"Yes. And what part of that sentence you just said involves taking work calls and fielding Slack messages?"

Peter pauses, staring at his phone as it buzzes again. "None. I guess I just . . . I guess I'm just so used to working off the clock that it doesn't bother me."

"But if your date told you it bothered them, what would you do?"

"I guess . . . I'd stop answering work calls?"

Eli nods. "So, try and ignore your phone for the rest of the night.

No more calls, no more Slack messages. Just focus on me, on the night we're having."

"Here." Peter picks up the phone and tries to hand it to Eli. "Keep it for me."

"No." Eli leans away from him, his back straight against the cushion of the booth. "You won't learn anything if I do all the work for you."

"Are you sure?"

"Do what you have to, put it on mute, or turn the phone off. But *you've* got to make the choice to not let work bother you."

Eli watches as Peter stares at his phone, another message popping up on the screen. For a brief moment, Eli can see the picture that serves as the background, two older-looking people with their arms wrapped around each other's waists. Eli has to assume these are Peter's parents.

"Let me just respond to this, make sure the test went well." Peter unlocks his phone and types something quickly.

Eli tries to hide his disappointment, but he promises himself that it's fine.

Rome wasn't built in a day, he thinks. *And twunks can't be fixed over just a single date.* Then where would he get his fake article for Michael?

"Okay." Peter shows Eli the screen again, holding down the power button until the Apple logo shines on the screen. "The phone is off. I'm done with work."

"Good!" Eli picks up his menu. "Now are you finally ready to get this date started?"

He watches Peter swallow, his throat bobbing up and down. "Yes, please."

Despite it all, despite his annoyance with Peter, and despite the incredibly odd circumstances that led to this date, he does *like*

Peter. At least what he's seen. He seems like a genuine guy, earnest—maybe to a fault—and despite his addiction to his work, he seems like he *does* care.

And for the rest of the night, without the distraction of his phone, and with more than a little prodding from Eli, Peter manages to open up. Peter even dares to pull out a folded piece of notebook paper where he's written basic facts about himself that he shows to Eli.

"In case I ran out of things to talk about."

He hands Eli the paper, and Eli gives it a quick read.

"Your favorite color is yellow."

"Mustard or goldenrod, no pastels."

"Your favorite vegetables are broccoli and bok choy. Your favorite hot pot broth is tom yum."

Peter nods.

"And you graduated from UC Berkeley?"

Eli looks over the paper once again, smiling at the small details like "allergic to cats" and "hates the smell of citrus." He'll admit, this is the first time he's heard of someone bringing a list of their personality traits to a date, but he doesn't mind.

"Berkeley's far from Georgia," Eli says, supposing now is as good a time as any to start the impromptu interview. "What made you want to come to school here?"

"I figured it was a good school. And, I mean, Comer isn't a huge city." Eli doesn't admit to the research he's done into where Peter is from. "I think . . ." Peter pauses, almost seeming unsure of his words. "I think I wanted to explore more, have some different experiences. I thought about going back to Incheon, a lot of my mom's family is still there. But the moving process was a lot to handle."

"That sounds fair. Would you ever go back to Incheon?" Eli wants to press, to ask Peter what it is he isn't telling him, but Eli resists. At least, for the time being.

"Oh, yeah! We used to go back every few years or so, but money got tighter the closer college got. I think I was fourteen the last time I went."

Eli smiles softly at him, appreciating that information.

"What?" Peter pauses, a spoonful of the purple rice and sizzling pork halfway to his mouth.

"Nothing, it's nothing." Eli wants to dig deeper; something feels off about Peter's tone. But maybe that's too deep for a first date. Even if it isn't their first date. "I went to San José State."

"But you've been in the city your entire life otherwise?" Peter asks, and Eli's proud of him for the follow-up question, even if he already knew the answer.

"Yeah. Moved down just for college. My parents live in Berkeley now."

"Do you see them often?"

Another point in Peter's favor for the night. He's just *narrowly* recovered from answering his phone at the start of the date. "I try to. We're actually having dinner tomorrow night."

"Oh, that's nice."

"Yeah . . ." Eli almost dares to invite Peter, but it's too early to throw him to the wolves like that. Even if Eli's sure his mother would adore Peter and his shyness. "What about you? Do you go back to Georgia often?"

"Not often enough for my dad. Really just to see them. It's not like there's much to do out there." Peter laughs to himself. "I keep trying to get them out here, maybe move so they can be closer, but my parents hate flying and big cities. It's the whole reason they chose Comer, for the 'quiet rural life.'"

Eli's heart warms at the mental image in his head. It's nice to hear that Peter seems to have a good relationship with his parents.

"Mm-hmm!" Peter hums as he scarfs down the rest of his rice. "What time does the movie start?"

"Ah, shit . . ." Eli completely lost track of time. "Fifteen minutes."

Peter waves shyly over toward the waitress, digging in his pocket for his wallet. For a moment, Eli thinks that he might've forgotten it again, but then he pulls out the small leather square, grabbing a blue credit card from one of the pockets.

"I didn't forget this time." Peter beams proudly.

Eli smiles back at him.

Peter then reaches into his pocket again, instinctively pulling out his phone before he remembers that it's off, and he bites at his bottom lip before he hesitates and puts it away. With the phone off, Peter has no choice but to sit there and enjoy the movie that they decide on. Much to Eli's disappointment, *Knives Out* has ended its single-week run, meaning they've had to select a half-baked horror about a doll that comes to life.

It's so bad that even Eli Francis, forever the fan of terribly cheesy horror Z-movies like *Primal Rage* and *The Severed Arm*, is bored to tears; but he still watches every scene, doing his best to follow the nonsensical plot.

Peter, however, seems to have a terrible time, his face hidden in his hoodie as he closes in on himself. During one particularly bad jump scare, he even yelps with the rest of the audience and grabs for Eli's hand, not letting go until the credits are rolling.

"Were you *really* scared?" Eli asks as they ride the escalator down to the lobby. "It was just a doll."

"A *scary* doll. I wanted to pee my pants when it started singing."

"Well, I appreciate you keeping them dry," Eli says to him as they step into the night. It's gotten a little cooler since they walked into the theater, but not considerably so. And right on track, Eli watches as Peter reaches into his pocket to dig his phone out once again before he remembers.

"It's fine," Eli tells him. "You can turn it on."

"You said that—"

"Yeah, but you didn't sneak to the bathroom to check it or reach for it once during the movie. So, consider it a reward for good behavior."

"Am I going to get those often?" Peter dares to ask.

And Eli smirks. "Only if you're a good boy."

Peter pauses, and just like last Friday, the red of the AMC lights paint Peter in a bright red, so Eli isn't sure what is just the neon and what is Peter's cheeks lighting up, but he's sure it's at least a twenty-five/seventy-five split.

He stares down at the phone, and Eli is a little disappointed, but what can he expect, it's only been a few hours.

But just as quickly as he turned it on, Peter is sliding the phone back into his jacket pocket.

"Aren't you going to check it?"

"The date isn't over, is it?" Peter asks him.

"You turned it on."

"I have to pay for the bus somehow."

Eli feels a swell of pride in his chest. Then Peter looks at him . . . well, he looks *above* Eli.

"You have a, uh . . ." Peter reaches toward Eli's hair, tugging on something until it comes free, showing Eli the piece of caramel corn that was lodged in his curls. "Sorry, I think that happened when the body fell out of that cupboard."

"It's okay." Eli takes it, tossing it on the sidewalk for a pigeon to feed on later.

"Which bus stop are you?" Peter asks.

"I'll just walk down to Divisadero." Then Eli promises, "We can leave things here, though, if you want."

"I'm headed that way too," Peter says. "Do you mind the company?"

"Well . . ." Eli smiles. "I won't say no."

Eli watches as Peter marches down the steps of the theater to join him. That's when Eli makes a bold move. He reaches for Peter's hand, wrapping his fingers around Peter's. It's only hitting him now just how much bigger Peter's hands are compared to his. Of course, everything about Peter is bigger than him, except maybe his hair.

Eli might look like his father, but he got his height from his mother.

"What are you . . ." Peter asks, never breaking stride, only looking at Eli. "Um . . . w-what are you doing?" He stammers his way through the sentence.

"Holding your hand."

"Why?"

"Iced Americano?" Eli asks him.

"No, I mean, yes. I guess. But I don't mind it."

"Are you sure?" Eli asks. "You don't have to be okay with it."

"No, it's okay. I promise. It's just . . . unexpected."

"Part of dating, of being in a relationship, is showing affection, whether it be physical or otherwise. But your own boundaries are just as important. That's what that safe word is for."

"Right, right." Peter's hands heat up, his palms sweaty. Eli doesn't mind, though. He's always had cold hands and feet.

"Is it okay? That we're doing this?" Eli pleads with Peter silently. He doesn't want Peter to be uncomfortable, even if a part of this whole experiment is to push Peter's boundaries in certain ways.

"Yeah, I like it . . . I've never held hands with anyone before."

"Can I ask you a question?"

Peter laughs. "You just did."

"That's not fair." Eli smiles.

"What did you want to ask?"

"How many firsts am I?" Eli invites. It's a bold inquiry, bolder than even the hand-holding because this really isn't any of his business, but he's never been able to help his own curiosity. Besides, it'll help him get a better picture of what Peter's gone through. "You don't have to answer that if you don't want it to; I was just curious since I was . . . you know, your first date and all."

"No, it's okay." Peter lets his head hang. "I guess it's a reasonable thing to ask. You're writing an article after all."

He lets out a huff of air as they stop at an intersection, waiting for the light to give them permission to cross the street.

"I really haven't done much of anything before," Peter admits. "I've hooked up with someone. Tried to hook up with other guys, but it never amounted to anything."

"Really?"

"Is that a surprise?" Peter asks.

"No, no. Not at all." Eli tries to recover the moment. "Just . . . unexpected."

Peter hesitates, looking down at the sidewalk. Eli almost stops him, wondering if Peter actually wants to talk about this, article be damned.

But Peter keeps going. "My best friend in high school, Mark." Then Peter looks at Eli like he's suddenly remembered something. "Uh . . . don't put his name in the article, please."

"Of course not. This story won't make it in if you don't want it to."

Peter's mouth becomes a fine line, as if he's still thinking. "Our families grew up next door to each other in Comer. We were actually born three days apart, so we always celebrated our birthdays together with our parents. Being two of the only Korean kids made it easy to be best friends."

"That sounds nice." Eli squeezes his hand softly.

"It was. High school wasn't the easiest time. I was bullied pretty hard my freshman year. But when I started to bulk up, the football coach pressured me into playing. My mom hated it, but Mark joined too, and for a few months there, we were actually the popular kids."

Eli holds his breath, waiting for the *but* to drop.

"I didn't even realize I'd fallen for him, how much I liked it when we'd lay in my bed and he threw his legs over mine, or when he'd play with my hair. Or when we'd hang out with our teammates, and they'd all leave the Walmart parking lot one by one until it was just the two of us in the bed of his pickup truck and we'd go to Cook Out and get milkshakes."

"The Walmart parking lot?" Eli tries to tease, seeing how much this story is bothering Peter.

"There aren't that many places to hang out in Comer," Peter says, smiling that soft smile that's already become so familiar. "Then, it just happened one day. We were watching a movie, he asked if I'd kissed anyone, I said no. He kept asking questions, the last of which was if I wanted him to kiss me, and I did."

"You know, I hear about that all the time in movies and books, but no one ever wanted to practice kissing with me in high school," Eli protests, still trying to add a bit of levity.

"Maybe I was cuter than you?"

The comment is such a surprise that Eli can't help but stare at Peter with his mouth open. "Hey!" Eli yanks his hand, pulling Peter toward him, but their steps never falter, and Peter laughs boldly.

"Sorry," he says, laughing along with Eli.

"No, it's probably true. God, my acne was out of control as a kid, and starting a film club certainly didn't help." Eli reactively touches the zit that's barely below the surface of his nose. "What happened to Mark?"

"We kissed a lot after that. And kissing turned into touching, that turned into hooking up. In our rooms, at school under the bleachers after games, behind the grocery store we got part-time jobs at. But his parents found Grindr on his phone one day, found the older guys that he was talking to."

Eli's heart sinks. "Oh, Jesus . . ."

"Yeah, then they found our texts and told my parents."

Eli's stomach sinks, his hand tight around Peter's. "You don't have to talk about this, Peter. It's okay."

"No, I mean . . ." His breath hitches. "I've unpacked parts of it. My parents didn't care. I mean, they *did*. My mom hated that I was keeping secrets from her, and my dad had a lot of questions. Things were really weird at first, but we figured it out. They're okay with it now, send me texts every June for Pride month, like it's my second birthday or something."

They walk for a minute in silence before Peter opens his mouth again.

"Mark's parents sent him to conversion therapy. My mom said it was just a different school, but I found a brochure that Mark's mom gave her. Then the rumors around school started to spread. And people would ask me what I thought; I was his best friend, after all . . . and I . . . I never knew what to say."

"Peter . . ." Eli pauses, his arm stretching out as Peter walks ahead as if nothing had happened.

"Is everything okay?"

"I feel like I should be asking *you* that."

"It's . . . I mean . . . it's fine."

"Is it?"

Peter shrugs. "I mean, can it be anything else? Besides, don't you need this stuff for your article?"

Eli struggles to come up with what to say.

"It's been years," he says to Eli. "I still think of him a lot. I don't know if I'll ever forget Mark. Like after he was gone, I couldn't play football anymore, not without him. And I realized he was the only reason I was still friends with the people who'd bullied me when I was a freshman. But . . . that whole . . . situation. It's over, in the past."

"Yeah, but he was your best friend. Did you ever see him again?"

"I did, once. I saw him in town one day after we were both supposed to have graduated, and we caught up for a bit. But . . . he wasn't the same. I gave him my number, but he never reached out, and then his parents moved the next week, and he went with them. And I never saw him again."

"I'm sorry, Peter."

"I bet that's good material, huh?" Peter's voice even sounds lighter now, at least to Eli's ears.

"Oh, yeah . . ." Eli stammers, caught off guard. "I won't write about that, though. Not all of it, at least. I'm sorry that you went through that."

"Thanks." Eli feels Peter squeeze his hand.

The remainder of their walk is taken in silence. Eli's too afraid to unearth any more of Peter's trauma, so he leaves it be. And Peter doesn't seem to mind. They make it to the bus stop just as Eli can see the bus approaching.

"Can I ask you something?" Peter peers down at Eli.

Eli smiles artfully. "You just did."

Peter smiles right back at him. "Tonight was better, right?"

"I think we're already seeing improvements," Eli tells him. "Though I want you to practice not logging in and responding to work messages when I'm not around."

"I have terrible news," Peter says. "I have to write a report over the weekend."

"Peter Park."

"I'll start on Monday," he says and holds his hand up. "Scout's honor."

"Were you really a Boy Scout?"

"Another Mark story, our dads thought it'd be good for us. But the other kids were just racist."

"Kids are assholes."

"Yeah." Peter nods. "I swear I have good memories."

"Can you tell me one?"

"Tonight is one," Peter offers before he cringes at his own words. "I'm sorry, that was cheesy. I always loved cooking with my mom— she'd always let me help, and we perfected our own little kimchi recipe."

"You'll have to share it with me sometime."

"And my dad, he loves his garden. He never got the chance to have one in Incheon; their apartment was too small. But they have a huge backyard in Comer, he grows all kinds of flowers and vegetables, and he let me help when he thought I was old enough. Eventually we started to take what we harvested to the farmers' market on weekends. Everyone loved his tomatoes; said they were the juiciest they'd ever had."

"Do you still cook? Or garden?"

"Nah, I wanted to when I moved into my apartment. There's a lot of good space in the backyard that the other tenants said I was free to use, but I never did. I guess gardening and cooking didn't have that same magic being away from them." Peter's voice is melancholic, as if he's imagining that he's right there with his parents in the garden or the kitchen.

The bus brakes at the intersection ahead of them, and Eli takes a leap. Metaphorical, of course. "Um . . . I have an idea."

"Yeah?"

"Can I kiss you good night?"

"You want to . . . to kiss me?" Peter stumbles through the question.

"Only if you want to," Eli says. "For practice?"

"Yeah . . . I mean, yes. Of course, that makes sense. We're supposed to be boyfriends, and boyfriends kiss. That's a normal thing for boyfriends to do, and I guess I should learn how to kiss, I think that—"

"Peter?"

"Hmm?" In an instant, Peter seems to snap out of whatever trance he worked himself into.

"It's okay if you don't want to," Eli promises. Perhaps the idea was a little far-fetched.

"No, I mean . . . I like kissing. And I think kissing you would be fun."

"Do you want me to lead?"

"If you don't mind?"

Eli takes Peter's other hand, just as his bus pulls up to the stop, the brakes hissing as their lips meet for a short, chaste kiss. It's simple, sweet, Eli lingering *just* long enough to taste whatever moisturizer is on Peter's lips. He even has to stand on his tiptoes to meet Peter, and that's barely enough to truly close the distance.

It's not much. But it's enough to turn Peter bright red again. From his cheeks to the very tips of his ears.

"How was that?" Eli asks.

And Peter smiles brighter than Eli's ever seen him smile. "I liked it."

"Good. Now." Eli lets him go, stepping onto the bus just as the doors open. "Do me a favor?"

"What?" Peter asks, still caught in a haze.

"Pick the next date," Eli says.

The confusion sets in immediately. "What?"

"Tell me something you want to do," Eli says as the doors close and his voice becomes muffled. "You have to pick what we do next!" Eli yells through the door.

"But I—" is all Peter gets out before the bus lurches out and speeds along the route. Eli scans the Clipper card on his phone, picking a spot at the back of the bus for his ride home.

His phone dings a second later.

PETER: I'm supposed to pick the date?

Eli smiles at his screen.

ELI: we did something i wanted to do

ELI: now we do something you want to do

PETER: What should I pick?

ELI: whatever you want

ELI: it's your date.

ELI: just make it interesting.

Peter doesn't respond until Eli gets home, walking into a dark apartment. Light is coming out from the crack at the bottom of Patricia's door, but he decides not to bother her. He can hear Rose snoring in her bed, so he can't talk to her. Which leaves him all on his own, falling face-first onto his bed and listening to the frame of the bed creak with his weight. He pulls out his phone, scrolling back through the texts to Peter, all the selfies he's sent, their first few awkward messages.

It's nice to feel like they've already made progress. Tonight Peter really shined, opening up to Eli in a way that he didn't really expect. Sure, the night began rocky and awkward, and it's not as if Peter's been magically fixed.

But progress has been made, and he's already got a few ideas for what to put in both articles he'll have to write. He thinks about Peter's story, how scary it must've been for the boy you liked to be there one day and totally gone the next.

Then for him to return, just to be a different person. He knows his conscience won't let him write about those exact circumstances, but he *has* to include them in some capacity; it's too interesting not to.

He jots down a few notes for Michael's article as well, how Peter is seeming to relax when he's with Eli, how they spoke about his addiction to his work. It doesn't feel like much, but like Eli's mother tells him often: "Any progress is good progress."

His phone vibrates while he brushes his teeth and washes his face, leaving Peter's final message of the night unchecked for a good few minutes before Eli grabs his phone again, diving under his comforter.

He smiles when he reads it.

> **PETER:** I have a few ideas.

> **PETER:** Also, I made it home.

Eli types a quick reply.

> **ELI:** glad you're home safe.

> **ELI:** and I can't wait to hear what your ideas are.

Chapter Six

To Wong Foo, Thanks for Everything!
Julie Newmar, dir. by Beeban Kidron

You know, my friend Amy, she has a son. And he's cute!" Eli's
mother stands at the sink, rinsing lettuce in a strainer.

"Mom . . ." Eli throws his head back, nearly hitting it against
the cabinets. "You don't have to set me up with anyone."

"I'm just saying! He's even interning at the press."

Eli's mother is a woman of prominence, the name Rue Clark
carrying weight in the art circles of the Bay Area as the longest-
serving director at Orion Press, one of the last publishing companies in the United States that creates their books completely from
scratch.

From the paper to the binding to the illustrations to the lead
they melt down to do the typesetting, it's all done in-house. Eli's
taken the tour of the foundry more times than he'd care to admit,
watching as the lead is melted down to form the individual letters,
how the ink printing and illustrations are made, how the books are
bound, glued, and sewn together with care.

There's a reason they do just two projects a year at *very* limited
print runs, and why the price tag for those books would cover Eli's
rent for several months.

"I'll pass."

"Eli, honey." She swats the water off her hands, putting the lettuce in a pretty comical device that she spins like a centrifuge in
order to dry it. "It's just one little date, and he's a nice boy."

"Then you go out with him." Eli turns away from her at his spot seated on her counter, playing with the magnets on the side of the fridge. The photos they hold up almost serve as a timeline of his life: baby pictures at Golden Gate Park or North Beach, Eli lined up with his childhood softball team, his first day of middle school. The few he'd been okay with keeping up.

Then there's Eli's mother on her second wedding day, him stuffed into an uncomfortable suit beside her as she stands next to John. His mother in her hospital bed just hours after giving birth to Eli's half sibling, Les.

"I'll give you his number," she continues, dumping the lettuce into a bowl and reaching over to hand Eli a block of Parmesan and a cheese grater. "I want you to call him, you'll like him."

She's been like this since Keith broke up with Eli—after she got over the pain of losing the man she'd considered a second son.

For a brief second, Eli considers telling her about Peter, just to get her off his back. But he knows that'll lead to a whole string of questions he isn't ready to answer just yet.

"You know, you don't have to do this," Eli tells her, leaping off the counter and setting the grater above an empty bowl. "I'm fine just how I am."

"Yes, you are," she tells him, pulling him in for an aggressive kiss on the cheek. "You're my perfect baby boy who I adore."

"Mom . . ."

"I just want you to be happy."

"I *am* happy," he tells her.

"Are you? You don't seem happy."

"Jeez, your confidence in me is inspiring," Eli mourns. "I'm fine. And I don't need a man."

"We all want love, Eli. It's the human condition."

"I have you, and Rose and Patricia, and Les. And I'm assuming John likes me."

His mother *tsks* at him with a long finger. "You hush, John *adores* you."

Eli hides his smile, handing her the bowl of grated Parmesan. "I'm fine. I promise you," he tells her, knowing that couldn't be further from the truth.

What's worse is that she knows it's a lie as well. Eli considers himself lucky, growing up in the house that he did, with parents who saw so clearly through the embarrassing teenage angst of everything feeling like the end of the world, navigating dysphoria and his mess of gender. They played it safe; they gave Eli the space to explore himself while also attempting to be as aware as they could of what was going on with him, silently promising that they'd be just around the corner when he wanted to talk about it.

Of course, those feelings had taken a back seat when his father got his diagnosis, when the X-rays showed his lower abdomen glowing like the Christmas tree in their living room. It took less than a month, Eli spending every second he could at St. Mary's when his holiday break began, sitting across the room from his mother, who slept on the uncomfortable cot that the hospital brought for her, Eli supplying her with clothes, toiletries, food.

He used to find it impossible to sleep on Christmas Eve, the excitement of the next morning looming over him, wondering just what he'd get if Santa had actually read the list of things he wanted. It was a normal thing for him to wake up when the sky was still dark, his parents asleep, and he'd sneak into the living room to look at everything laid out for him, unable to see his gifts through the wrapping paper but still doing his best to guess.

That year it was still dark, and he was still awake when his phone began to ring. He knew two seconds before, that feeling in his gut settling, that honest relief that came with knowing that his father was no longer in pain.

Then his mother said the words.

There was no crying, not until he got to the hospital, the staff bare bones so early on a holiday morning. Rue met John less than a year later in her group therapy session, the two of them becoming quick friends before things turned romantic.

Eli wasn't exactly pleased, and he remembers with shame how much he resented John when he was a dumb teenager. The worst part was that John never minded, not once. He identified with what Eli was going through, what it was like to lose someone. He simply gave Eli—and by extension Rue—his space, only making Eli feel more guilty because he knew how happy John made his mother. As he grew older, Eli promised them that everything was okay, that it would take time but that he thought John was a good guy. He stood beside them at their wedding, spent as much time with his mother as possible as she went into labor with Les, helped them pack up their things and move to Berkeley when he left for college.

"You know, it's not wrong to want to date someone," his mother continues. "It's not some . . . grand stance against cis-heteronormative standards to not want to date when you're gay." Her lips struggle around the words.

"Who taught you the word 'cis-heteronormative'?"

Eli's mother turns toward him, her eyebrows raised and a smile on her face. "I'm hip with the children! I watch *Drag Race*!"

That's when the back door opens and Eli's stepfather, John, walks in, leaving his keys on the counter, Eli's half sibling, Les, right behind him.

"Are we talking about RuPaul?" he asks loudly. "I love that Jaida Essence Hall, what a lady!" The name *Jaida Essence Hall* coming out of John's deep, straight, fifty-year-old New England mouth makes Eli laugh in a way that he's quick to hide.

Les, ever the embarrassed preteen, breezes right past their father, setting their cello case and backpack next to the counter before they speed off down the hall toward their bedroom.

"Les!" Eli's mother calls out as John comes up behind her and kisses her cheek. "Come and get your things and put them in your room, please!"

There's no answer, leaving Rue to look at her husband.

John gives her a sympathetic look. "Their teacher told me some of the girls in their class have been picking on them."

"Oh, God . . ."

"Do you want me to talk to them?" Eli asks.

"No, no. I'll do it." Rue sets the tomato she was about to slice down on the cutting board. "We can't go to you for everything."

"Just the trans stuff, right?" Eli prompts.

And Rue agrees. "John, honey, can you slice these? And, Eli, watch the bread in the oven."

"Can do!" John leaps right at it, taking the deep chestnut handle of the serrated knife and cutting into the tomatoes. "So, Eli!"

Despite growing more accustomed to John over the years and appreciating his company, Eli still finds it difficult to make small talk with the guy.

"So, John!" Eli mimics John's enthusiasm, opening the oven and peering in, earning a blast of hot air to the face before he shuts it.

"Rue told me she's gonna give you the number of that intern at the press."

"No," Eli assures him. "She is not."

"Yeah, I said it wasn't such a good idea."

"Really?" Eli hops back up to his old spot on the counter, watching John carefully cut the tomatoes.

"Of course! I told her, 'Rue, you've gotta let the man go at his own pace.' You don't just get over heartbreak. Trust me, I know."

"Oh, well . . . thank you," Eli says slowly.

"How's the job going? Did you get that writer spot that you wanted?"

"Oh, uh . . ." He hadn't yet broken the news to either of them about how poorly the interview had gone. "They went with someone else."

"Ah, they're idiots. I've read some of your stuff, they're stupid for not promoting you."

"You read my stuff?"

"Yeah! I mean . . ." John struggles for a bit. "It was just your high school and college writing that your mom found. I looked online and couldn't find your portfolio or anything. But it was still impressive."

"Well, when you only have a few articles to your name and they're for some San José State student newspaper, it's not exactly a point of pride."

"The stuff I read might've been old, but it was good. And it's clear you have a passion for it."

"Well, *Vent* doesn't want those kinds of articles; it goes 'against the brand.'"

"Then quit! We could always help support you?" John says these last few words very carefully, almost as if he's unsure.

"It's not about the money," Eli tells him, even though that couldn't be farther from the truth. The single perk of working at *Vent* is the slightly-above-average pay and the benefits that come with working for Michael. Eli can't imagine how expensive his wisdom teeth removal would've been without their dental plan.

Besides, he's taken enough money from both of them. Even before Rue met John, the hospital care for Eli's father had done a number on her savings. Then therapy and counseling for both of them, Eli's gender-affirming care, student loans, rent. At least in the early days.

So, borrowing more money isn't exactly something Eli wants to do right now.

"You could try freelancing, there's good money in it," John says, rinsing the knife and setting it on the drying rack. "You shouldn't be miserable in a job you hate. It eats away at you."

Eli appreciates the advice, but John is the director of the Museum of Fine Arts in Berkeley, with a résumé full of positions in galleries all over New York, Chicago, and Los Angeles, procuring artists and their work for exhibits. He's been doing the work that he loves for three decades now, so it's easy for him to just tell Eli to quit.

If Eli quits, that's five years of his life down the drain. Five years of learning nothing other than that he can barely tolerate the smell of coffee, how to do double-sided collated scans, and that he has to bring cash to the UPS office down the street because their card reader is always broken. He's gotten no experience in writing, is barely any better at self-editing, and has no audience of readers eager to follow him somewhere else.

He'll have nothing.

Then again, Michael might just fire him anyway for pulling this article stunt. But at least then he'd be going out swinging.

A moment later, Rue and Les both come back into the kitchen.

"Hey, kid." Eli snags a crouton from the bag on the counter. "How was cello practice?" There's a certain awkwardness that comes with being sixteen years older than your younger sibling. By the time Les was born, Eli was in his junior year of high school, and the last thing some dumb teenager wants to do is help raise their younger sibling. But through the years, the two of them have gotten more comfortable with one another, their odd friendship cemented when Les told Eli they're non-binary, asked for his help with their clothes, their hair, how they wanted to present.

Because nothing can bond two half siblings together like a little gender dysphoria.

"Fine." They wrap their arms around Eli, giving him an awkward hug. "Are you coming to the recital in January?"

"Wouldn't miss it, dude." Eli rakes his hands through their short hair. "John said there were some girls who were messing with you?"

"Yeah."

"We talked about it," Rue says, turning off the burners on the stove and grabbing her strainer for the pasta noodles. "I'm calling their instructor first thing in the morning. He is *not* going to take my money and sit there while my baby gets bullied."

"Mom . . . it's not that serious," Les protests.

"Hey," Eli whispers, pulling Les in closer. "Take some oranges and put them in a sock. It won't leave any bruises."

"Seriously?" Les asks.

"Eli!" Rue glares at her son. "Don't you dare."

"What did I say?" He feigns innocence. "Les, did I tell you to do anything?"

"Nope!" Les says quickly, their voice going higher at the lie.

"See?"

Rue eyes both of her children suspiciously, probably thanking God that the two of them didn't grow up together. She might have grayer hair if they had.

For the rest of the night, he's safe from any talk of a relationship. At least, that's what he thinks. It isn't brought up again until his mother offers to drive him across the bridge and back to his apartment. Eli claims it would be too out of the way, but eventually accepts a ride to the BART station because he knows his mother won't let it go.

"Are you sure you don't want Oliver's number?"

"Who is Oliver?" Eli asks, turning up the heat to warm his hands.

"Our intern, he's a very nice boy. Very handsome. Studied Latin in school!"

"Why? It's a dead language."

"Still, it's impressive!"

"Mom . . ."

"Don't 'mom' me, Eli. I'm just trying to help you out."

"By setting me up with guys I've never met?"

"I just want you to be happy. I feel like you're being held back by your inner saboteur."

"Is that another RuPaul thing?"

"He's a *very* smart man."

"Well, he does support trains rights."

"See?" Rue waves her son off, not getting the joke. "I'm just saying, you'll never move on past Keith unless you get back out there."

"It sounds like you've been talking to Patricia and Rose."

"I have! They're very nice girls." Rue flips on her turn signal. "But that's not the point—"

"Mom, I'm seeing someone."

Eli lurches forward as his mother slams on the brakes, his seat belt locking.

"You *are*?" she says, shock all over her face.

"You don't have to act surprised." He can't help himself. It's the only way that he can get his mother off his back.

"Well, you've spent the last six months turning down every boy I've wanted to introduce to you."

"Yeah, well . . . I didn't want to tell you just yet."

The car behind them honks loudly at where they've stopped in the middle of the street.

"Okay, okay, don't get your panties twisted." Rue fusses, accelerating to catch up with traffic. "So, tell me about him. What's his name? Does he live in the city? He doesn't work with you, right? I told you, Eli, you need to stay away from your coworkers, it only makes things messy—"

Eli has to stop her before she *truly* starts to rant. "He doesn't work at *Vent*, Mom. He works in tech."

"Oh, well . . ." Rue pretends to be happy to hear that. "That's wonderful."

"Yeah."

"Show me a picture."

Eli sighs, questioning whether this truly was worth it. He fishes in his pocket, pulling up his texts to Peter and the selfies that he sent.

"Oh, what a handsome young man."

"Mom!" Eli has to scream so she'll brake, avoiding a fender bender with the car in front of them.

"I'm sorry, I'm just . . . so happy for you, Eli." She smiles at him.

"Thanks."

"When do I get to meet him?"

What a good question, Eli thinks. He figures that introducing Peter to his family at some point will be a good test, a showcase for what Peter's learned. He's already gotten a head start on both articles, writing a bit about his and Peter's first two dates. And he's written a few paragraphs about the things Peter had shared with him.

"No idea," Eli tells her. "It's still new."

"We'll go out next weekend."

"Mom, I don't want to scare him."

"You're saying I'm scary?" she asks.

"Maybe a little bit," Eli teases. It's just that Peter was a nervous wreck meeting Eli for the second time. "I'm just taking things slow."

"Well, he seems nice."

"You don't know him," Eli says.

"I know, but I've got that sixth sense. A mother always knows." She points a finger. "And this Peter looks like a nice boy."

Eli's inclined to agree.

Peter's a very nice boy.

Maybe even too nice for his own good. Though Eli isn't sure he can say the same about himself. No, scratch that. He knows he isn't good. If he were, he wouldn't be lying to two different people about the intentions of his articles. But that's all these are, articles. That's it. That's what Eli tells himself at least.

And that's all they have to be.

Chapter Seven

Dog Day Afternoon, dir. by Sidney Lumet

"You'll just need to sign this waiver here," the gym instructor informs Eli as she slides the iPad across the counter.

"There's a waiver?" Eli glances over the pages-long document, swiping through paragraphs upon paragraphs of legal jargon.

"Yeah," the gym instructor, Helen, according to her nametag, says in a voice far too chipper over a document that includes the words *We are not liable for your death, accidental or otherwise.* "It's standard stuff, just acknowledging that you know the risks of rock climbing and using the equipment. Now, do you know if you'll be bouldering or rope climbing?"

"Umm . . . I don't actually know." His attention is now divided between the waiver in front of him and the odd harness that Helen is showing him. "My friend, he's the one who invited me."

A friend who is still nowhere to be seen.

Eli texted before he left, on the long bus ride from the Castro to the Presidio, and even waited outside to see if Peter would meet him there.

Nothing.

"Here, we'll get you a harness, just in case. And what size shoe are you?"

"I'm an eight." Eli signs the document with his finger without reading the rest of it. "Why?"

"Because you need climbing shoes." Helen dips below the counter before she springs back up with a pair of ugly white shoes with a red strip down the center.

"Is this Velcro?" Eli asks, inspecting them closely.

"Yeah, they're specifically made for climbing."

And for making grown adults look like five-year-olds, he thinks. "Thanks." Eli hands back the device to her in exchange for the shoes, climbing harness, and a locker key.

He steps away from the front desk, following the signs that lead him toward the locker rooms. It's been a little over a decade since he was in a gym, and he'd spent most of that time on the bleachers, lying about his period to get out of dodgeball.

All of a sudden, he feels out of his element, watching people lift, press, and lunge with little to no effort. He doesn't even own any proper workout clothes, just sweatpants that he only uses for lounging around the apartment, and Peter said he should wear shorts or tights to avoid snagging.

So he had to borrow clothes from Rose and Patricia, which is why he's currently sporting a tank top that drapes too loosely on his body and makes it look like he isn't wearing any shorts at all. Normally he might mind being thought of as a total pervert, but the shorts advertise the phrase PHOEBE BRIDGERS WAS ROBBED AT THE 63RD ANNUAL GRAMMYS written across his ass, so maybe it's for the best that they're hidden.

"Peter . . ." Eli sings softly. "Where are you?" He checks his phone again, typing a quick *i'm waiting for you* text before walking into the locker room.

Which is where he collides with a dense—yet oddly soft—wall of muscle, unable to stop himself from toppling back from the force generated by hitting a man square in his chest.

A chest that belongs to Peter.

At least the floor is padded.

"Oh, God, are you okay?" Eli hears Peter ask him. Eli can't help but laugh as Peter's face hangs over his, slightly hidden in shadow. "Eli?"

"That's me." Eli chuckles softly.

Peter raises an eyebrow. "Are you all right?"

"Yeah, yeah. Just my pride, but that was already in shambles anyway." Eli takes the strong hand offered to him, letting Peter hoist him up without any effort at all. For a moment, just a *fraction* of a second, he wonders if Peter is strong enough to carry him around.

Just a fraction, though.

"Good, okay!" Peter reaches into his ears, pulling out small earbuds.

"How long have you been here?" Eli takes Peter in, very visibly sweaty in his gym clothes, his tank top showing off the strong arms that Eli had imagined hidden under Peter's hoodies.

"I came right after work, did some warm-ups, lifting. I was getting my phone and saw that you'd texted me." Peter shows Eli the screen with his family photo and the missed texts, along with about a dozen missed calls and Slack messages. "Sorry."

"It's okay. I was just worried for a second." Eli smiles slyly. "Thought you might be late again."

"The alarms are doing their trick." Peter beams at Eli, like he's proud of himself.

"I'm more surprised that you left your phone someplace where you can't answer it."

"It makes it hard to concentrate if I'm getting all these notifications and messages."

"So . . ." Eli nudges, curious. "The gym is important enough to ignore your phone. But our date wasn't?"

"Well, you know." His ears go red. "I have to, uh . . ."

"No, I don't, Peter," Eli teases. "Tell me what I know."

"It's just that, well, it's like—" It's funny, seeing Peter so clearly worked up and bothered, but Eli also knows it's torture to the poor man.

"Peter, relax." He puts a hand on Peter's broad shoulder, hoping that'll ground him, but Peter's cheeks only turn more flushed. "I'm just messing with you."

"Right, yeah . . . Right."

"It's worth investigating, though," Eli continues. "Why do you think it's okay to put your phone away now when you're working out, but not on a date?"

"I guess it's like muscle memory in a way," Peter says. "I mean, I've been working out since I was in high school. So maybe force of habit? I don't know."

Eli nods, making a mental note to ask Peter more about his high school experiences for the article. "Makes sense. Kind of." Then Eli stops. "Wait, you had earbuds in, but your phone was in your locker?"

"I just use them for the noise cancellation." He hands them to Eli, both fitting in the palm of his hand. Sure enough, when Eli tests one of them, there's no sound. "Did you sign up already?"

"Yeah, actually, and I need to discuss with you how I might *die* doing this. Like that's an actual concern?"

"Don't worry about it, the floors are cushioned." Peter's straight line of a mouth finally cracks into a smile.

Eli does a soft bounce on the three-inch-thick black padding that covers the floor. "You're not inspiring any confidence in me."

"The climbing section has *extra* padding. It'll be fine!" Peter gives Eli a very heavy pat on the shoulder. "Go get ready, and I'll wait for you here."

Eli obeys, walking into the locker room, trying his best not to take notice of the gym showers that are just on the other side of the half-wall, the sound of what has to be *very* naked men laughing about something as Eli leaves his things in a random locker and fixes the Velcro shoes that pinch the tips of his toes.

Just as he promised, Peter is waiting for Eli near the entrance.

"So, what do you want to do first? Bouldering? Rope climbing?"

"Which one doesn't involve the harness?" Eli asks, showing Peter the straps that he can already imagine causing the wedgie of the century.

Peter smiles. "Bouldering it is, then."

And as Peter leads Eli through the gym, past the cardio machines and weight benches, past the front desk, Eli notices a very odd phenomenon.

Peter greets almost everyone.

Sometimes it's just a wave, or, to someone like Helen, it's an entire conversation where he asks about her cat's vet appointment before Eli returns the harness and she tells them to have a good climb. It's almost like there's a different man in front of Eli, a Peter that he doesn't entirely recognize.

"You seem very . . . comfortable here," Eli offers, stepping next to Peter as they walk past more machines.

"I guess you could say that," Peter replies. "I've been climbing every Wednesday since I moved into the city."

"So, you *do* have hobbies outside of work. Impressive."

"Huh . . ." Peter stares like he'd never actually considered it. "I guess I do?"

"When'd you start?"

"After I moved here for college. My first weeks were rough, to say the least. I went through a pretty bad depressive episode. I tried to tell my mom, but she didn't get it and just mailed food."

"But the rock climbing?"

"One of my classmates, a friend, I guess . . . he'd suggested that I do my best to be active again. So I went to the school's gym; they had a whole bouldering section, and I just fell in love with it."

Eli follows Peter, stepping up onto an elevated part of the floor and nearly falling again. It's only Peter who saves him from dropping to the floor.

"*That's* what you meant by cushioned floor?" Eli stares down at his feet, marveling at the way they sink in like he's five years old in a moon bounce. He even rocks up and down, grinning as Peter stares at him.

"As you can see, your chances of an untimely death are low."

"But not impossible," Eli corrects.

He follows Peter up a short flight of stairs, each step decorated with the colors of the Pride flag, right next to a steep cushioned incline meant to catch climbers who dared to take on the task of climbing upside down on the wall hovering above it.

"I think the newbie wall should be up here."

"Newbie wall?" Eli challenges. "What makes you think I'm new at this?"

Peter gives Eli a quick glance from head to toe and moves on without another word.

"I resent that."

"I didn't say anything!" Peter argues.

"You didn't have to." Eli laughs.

They come to the top of the stairs, an area that looks out onto the rest of the gym, giving Eli his first look at the entire building. Along with the novice wall, various other skill-level walls wrap their way around the gym, along with a tall tower situated in the middle. And that's only half of it; the other side of the gym is entirely dedicated to the rope-climbing mechanics with walls that seem so impossibly tall that Eli is confused as to how they actually fit in the converted warehouse.

"Here should be good." Peter stops in front of a set of bright yellow bricks marked N-0. "Try these out first."

"N-0?" Eli ponders.

"Novice zero. This is the most beginner wall you can climb."

"Okay, okay. Give me some space." Eli waits for Peter to take a step back, swatting his hands back and forth as if that's how he's choosing to warm up. After all, it's rock climbing; how complicated can it be?

Eli places his hand on the rough surface of the first rock, pulling himself into the air and then placing his left foot on a rock. But as Eli reaches to put his right foot underneath him, he falters, his shoes sliding against the wall.

His body short-circuits for a moment and he just lets go. There's a second where he tries to catch himself, waving his arms like a baby bird to try and get his balance back, but it doesn't help, and he drops a whole two feet back onto the floor.

And there's no Peter to catch him, so he just lands on his ass.

"I don't want to hear a word." Eli points in Peter's direction without even sparing him a glance.

"I didn't say anything," Peter protests once again.

"I heard snickering!" Eli proclaims.

"Here." Peter offers him a hand, getting Eli to his feet.

"I just have to get used to it, is all." Eli's pride is only slightly more wounded than before as he reaches for the same rocks, pulling himself up. This time, his foot doesn't miss the hold, so he lifts higher into the air, then dares to let go so that he can grab onto the next rock above him.

Eli grins as he climbs and climbs, his arms aching already, but still he carries himself higher and higher until he finally reaches the rock with the word FINISHED! etched into it.

"Ha-ha!" Eli boasts loudly. "See, told you I could do it!"

"That's great, Eli!" Peter calls to him, sounding further away than Eli anticipates. "Now jump down."

Eli looks underneath him to see just *how* far he is from the floor. In an instant, his blood runs cold.

"Oh, God . . ." He whispers, pulling himself as close to the wall as he can get, one rock digging too close to his crotch for comfort.

"What's wrong?" Peter asks, such an innocent question.

Eli peers down again, his vision going blurry for a moment. "Oh, you know . . . just wanted to enjoy the view."

"Are you stuck?"

"No!" Eli answers too quickly, showing his hand, grabbing onto the gray safety blocks with full grips to readjust. "I'm just . . . showing off. Look at how long I can stay up here!"

"The floor is padded, Eli. If you can't climb down, just fall."

"I don't wanna!" Eli hides his face like a child.

"It'll be okay, I promise," Peter tells him. "You'll survive."

Eli grips the fake rocks so tightly that he's afraid he might just pull them clear off the wall. He presses closer, hugging the wall, hoping and praying that his foot doesn't slip. But it does, and he flails wildly for a moment before he finds purchase again. "I'm fine staying up here, actually!" he shouts back.

He starts to imagine how he can make a living in the gym, work remotely, have his laptop fixed to the wall, type with one hand. Totally logical!

His eyes are closed so tight that Eli doesn't notice as Peter climbs the wall next to him, almost completely silent as he makes his way up.

"Eli?" Peter whispers.

"Ah!" Eli can't help the yelp that slips out, recovering his composure in an instant as he realizes that Peter is now *right* next to him. "Oh, Peter. Hello."

"Enjoying the view?" Peter looks up at the lights that hang from the ceiling.

"Yeah, yeah . . . totally."

"Okay, well . . . some people really want to use this part of the wall, and you're keeping them from doing that."

"Hurry up!" a kid shouts from the floor.

"Mind your business!" Eli yells right back.

"Hey, hey, eyes on me, okay?" Peter urges him to focus. "I'm going to guide you, all right?"

Eli nods quickly. "Okay, yeah."

"Okay."

Peter begins to climb down, and Eli feels the panic rise in his chest, a brewing in his stomach. He doesn't even want to think about what it might look like to vomit from his current predicament. Except he can't stop his mind from going there, and—

He swallows, determined to not make a fool out of himself.

Well, no more than he already has.

"Wait, where are you going?"

Peter says with a smile in his voice, "I'm going to get under you."

"That's smart. Good thinking."

Eli waits, his cheek chafing from where it's rubbing against the rough wall. Then he feels a hand on his right ankle.

"I'll lead you on where to go, okay?" Peter's voice arrives as a relief, even if it's only been a few seconds.

"Okay, okay."

"Put your foot here, just go down a bit." Eli lets Peter pick his foot up off the rock, trusting that he won't let him fall as he guides Eli to the next rock. "Now take your left hand down onto that smaller rock. Use the black or the purple ones if you need to."

Eli is embarrassed to admit that it's the first time he'd even noticed the other colors of rocks on either side of his body. In his mind, he supposes he thought using them meant he was cheating.

"Okay, now your left foot, down to here." Peter continues to lead him down the wall. "And your right hand down, just like that. You're almost there."

"You swear?"

"I swear."

Oh, he's never going to live this down, he knows that much.

"Now here, and left arm here." Peter guides him until, finally, Eli feels him release his ankles.

"Where'd you go?" Eli tries not to let the panic take control again.

"I'm on the floor," he says. "And so are you. Basically."

Eli looks down again out of squinted eyes, and instead of the miles from the floor that he'd imagined in his head, he's barely half a foot off the ground, and he finally breathes a sigh of relief.

"Oh my God . . ." Eli lets his forehead fall against the wall.

"Come on, let's get some water."

Eli finally lets go of the wall, his arms aching from keeping his weight up for so long. He tries his best not to meet the eyes of the ten-year-olds who are waiting for their turn, watching as they climb the same wall that he had, only to make it to the very top and then leap onto the padded floor as if it's all a playground.

"It's tougher than it looks, you know," Eli says.

"Oh, I'm aware," Peter tells him, and Eli ignores the patronizing tone. Instead, Eli lets Peter guide him to the benches that sit against the railing. "You okay?"

"Oh, yeah. Totally. You know." Eli does his best to wave him off, but his heart is still pounding. "Those kids make it look easy."

"We can leave, if you want," Peter offers.

"No way." Eli shakes his head. "This is your date. So, we're staying. Plus, that wasn't . . . the worst experience in the world."

"You could argue that me wanting to leave for you shows that I'm willing to sacrifice my own interests in order to make sure you're safe."

Eli straightens, staring at Peter. "Where'd you learn that?"

Peter flushes. "I read."

"Read what, exactly?"

"Don't worry about it," Peter tells him. "At the very least, we can break here for a bit."

"Thank you."

"By the way . . . who's Phoebe Bridgers?"

"Who's what?"

"Your, um . . . on your butt," Peter asks, stammering like he's afraid to say the word *butt* out loud. "You have the name Phoebe Bridgers. Something about a Grammy?"

"So, you were staring at my butt?" he teases.

"Well, it was in front of my face. I couldn't really help but notice."

Eli laughs at that. "She's a singer. Rose is a big fan; I borrowed the shorts from her."

"I take it you don't work out often?"

"What was your first clue?"

"Your form is pretty terrible, for one."

"Okay, what *form* can you have for rock climbing?" Eli asks.

But Peter ignores him. "And being afraid to fall."

"It's a long drop."

"You were eight feet up, max."

"I'd like to see how *you* climb."

Peter stands without a second thought, crouching for a bag that sits on the side of the mat. His hands come back white, caked in a chalk dust. He shakes off the excess before he rushes toward a wall marked M-10, grabbing on in a leap of sorts, earning him a head start.

The fake rocks are a color that's a near-perfect match for the wall, each of them only slightly bigger or smaller than Eli's balled-up fist, some of them sloped with no visible grips so that Peter has to hang on by the *very* tips of his fingers. For a moment, his tank top rides up when he reaches for the rock above him, and Eli can see the perfect shape of the man's ass and the strength being exerted in his calves and thighs as he braces against almost nothing at all with his feet.

In seconds, Peter's reached the top of the wall, climbing onto the edge to stand with his hands on his hips and a too-proud smile on his face.

"Okay, yeah. I get it."

Peter slips back off, hanging on the edge as he checks that no one's below him before he drops, falling into a perfect squat on the mat. Of course, the uneven flooring causes him to fall backward, but there's no fear in his eyes, only a little heaving in his chest and a thin coat of sweat on his skin. Eli stands, offering a hand to Peter to help him up, though he isn't sure what good it does.

"Thanks."

"You're a showoff, you know that?" Eli braces himself as best he can, hoping Peter doesn't take him to the floor as he hoists himself up.

Peter smiles at him, the corners of his mouth disappearing into his dimples. "You're okay at it. You just need to learn to fall."

"Yeah, I've never been the greatest at that," Eli tells him, wiping the fine layer of chalk now on his hand onto his black tank top, leaving faded white streaks. "I was too afraid to learn to ride a bike because of it."

"You can't ride a bike?" Peter seems genuinely amused by the information, a soft sound slipping past his lips.

"Okay, okay! You know, it's not *that* big of a deal. Plenty of people can't do things."

"No, I mean . . . I didn't mean to laugh at you."

"Yeah, yeah." Eli picks up his own water bottle. "You can laugh; it *is* pretty embarrassing. Every time my friends ask me if I want to go riding down to Crissy Field or the Great Highway, I have to fake a backache or say I'm too busy."

"You could still learn."

"Isn't there some statistic about it being harder to learn to ride a bike as an adult than it is as a kid?"

Peter's thick brows furrow. "I think that's ice-skating. Or the violin?"

"Either way, I think I'm safer on two legs. The people in this city can't drive anyway."

"Fair."

"Okay, so . . ." Eli sets the water bottle down, turning toward Peter once again. "If I'm going to learn to do this, be my teacher."

"Your teacher?"

Eli nods. "I'm your dating coach; be my climbing coach. Where do we start?"

Peter just stares down at Eli, smiling that smile that's already become so familiar. "Okay, okay . . . let's go over here."

***

Eli's body aches, his arms feel like jelly, his thighs are burning, he feels like he can't catch his breath, and he's so sweaty his hair has become permanently plastered to his forehead.

And it's been barely thirty minutes.

"I don't like this wall." They'd decided to let Eli stick to the N walls, though he'd managed to graduate from the N-0 to the N-4.

"You can't learn if you don't challenge yourself," Peter says from his spot *right* next to Eli. It's like he's deliberately showing off, the way he follows Eli's every step during his climbs with ease. "Make sure you're keeping your center of gravity closer to the wall, falling back only forces your body to work harder."

"That much I can do." Once again, Eli's cheek is rubbed red from just *how* close he rests while holding on to the wall.

"Okay, go for this one next." Peter taps on the blue rock that's *just* out of Eli's normal reach.

"I can't. I have short arms."

"Your arms are average," Peter tells him. "And you just have to go for it, lunge. Get some momentum going and grab it."

"What level did you say this wall was again?"

"Novice five."

"That doesn't seem accurate."

Peter shrugs. "Sometimes they're a little loose with the ratings. But you can do this, come on. Just brace your foot here, bend the knee, and go for it!" Peter's excitement somehow works its way through Eli's nerves.

"Okay, okay, yeah. I can do it," he says, mostly to himself.

Eli does exactly as he's told, bending his knees and lurching forward. It's not quite a jump, because there isn't enough room for that much force. But Eli still goes for it, feeling as inspired as he ever has.

Except he misses the hold.

Well, he doesn't miss it *exactly*. Eli grabs ahold of the blue rock, but there's not enough grip, or really any grip at all. And he makes the mistake of letting go with his other hand far too early, meaning there's nothing keeping him on the wall.

So he falls.

"Peter!" he calls out, yanking on Peter's shirt, but the fabric slips free of Eli's chalky hands, and he just falls and falls and falls.

A whole five feet, landing on the cushy floor and bouncing for a bit before he settles.

"Eli!" Peter yelps out, leaping effortlessly back to the floor as he crouches in front of Eli. "Are you okay?"

Eli can tell that Peter's totally caught off guard when he sees the smile on Eli's face, Eli picking his head up with a wide grin, laughter spilling past his lips.

"That was fun!" Eli does his best to bounce on the floor.

Peter smiles, letting out an exasperated sound. "I'm glad you're finally having a good time." Peter starts to sit beside Eli, then scoots back. "Come on, get away from the wall, we'll take a breather."

Eli looks back, following Peter's lead as they move toward where they set their things.

"So, I've been dying to ask," Peter starts, squeezing water into his open mouth.

"Shoot." Eli does the same, but not without spilling some all over his chin.

"Why did you let me choose the date night?" he asks. "I thought this entire experience was to teach *me* how to date? I don't see what this taught me."

"Well," Eli starts to say. "I wanted you to pick what we did tonight because dating is a partnership. Both parties have to be enthusiastic, they have to show interest in one another, in their hobbies. If I were a real date, I like to think tonight would've exposed me to a part of your personality."

"And that's a good thing?"

"Why wouldn't it be?"

"I don't know," Peter says, suddenly quiet. "When we got here, I was worried I'd picked the wrong thing. Rock climbing can be a lot for someone." He lets out a shaky breath. "And you've seen my personality."

"Do you care about rock climbing?" Eli asks.

Peter seems surprised, like he'd never expected anyone to ask him such a question. "Yeah, I guess I do. To a certain extent."

"You guess?" Eli pokes a little harder.

"Yeah, I mean it's fun. I've always liked working out, feeling strong. It's why I stuck around on the football team for so long, even when I hated it."

Peter looks away, like that isn't the whole answer. Eli can spy a *something* just below the surface.

"Then why push yourself?" Eli feels like he can see where this is going from a mile away, but he wants Peter to be the one to talk about it. Interviewing means asking the right questions, knowing *exactly* where to steer things in order to get the most information.

"I guess, I dunno, I was afraid."

"Why?"

Peter smiles for the briefest of moments. It's an uncomfortable expression, and Eli almost slams on the brakes.

"Growing up in Comer, it was scary. Being one of like four Asian kids at school already made me someone that people didn't like. If they knew I was queer, I can't imagine how they would've reacted. I guess I just wanted to be someone that others didn't mess with. I never wanted to give people a reason to think I was weak."

Eli sits in silence, suddenly regretting bringing this up at the gym of all places.

Then, Peter chuckles. It's a soft sound. "Sorry, shouldn't have gotten so dour out of nowhere."

"No, it's okay." Eli hopes that Peter believes him.

"Can I ask *you* a question?"

"Sure."

"Why me?"

"For the article?"

Peter nods. Because what else could he have been talking about?

"Well, why does a journalist write any article? I think that you have a unique perspective, and I'd like to write about it."

"But why *me*?" Peter asks.

Eli stares at him. He doesn't really know how to answer Peter's question. He isn't sure what it is about this disaster of a man that has drawn him in with such interest. "I don't really know," he finally says. "I just think that you're an interesting person. And I think you have a lot to share."

"Pfft, first time anyone's said that to me." Peter lies back on the padded floor, tucking his hands behind his head, giving Eli the full picture of his muscles flexing. "So why writing?"

"I started in high school. It's not even like I knew I wanted to do it since I was a kid or anything. My school had an extracurricular requirement, and the journalism club was the only one with an opening by the time the deadline to join clubs came around."

"So, you joined because you had to?"

Eli nods, laying his head down not too far from Peter's. "But I fell in love with it. I didn't want to at first; I resented the whole thing. But Mrs. Jackson kept challenging me, then eventually I got to write my own pieces, I was interviewing and reporting, breaking stories about what was happening at our school. I was even head editor in my senior year."

Peter smiles at him.

"What about you? Did you have to do any writing in college?" It occurs to Eli that he has zero clue what goes into earning a computer science major.

"Writing? Me?" Peter responds almost too quickly, turning his face away from Eli. "No, I've never had to do that."

Weird, Eli thinks to himself. But he decides to drop it. For the time being, at least.

There's never silence in a gym, not with people grunting and shouting and running and falling. The zip of the rope climbers rips through the gym, the sound of shoes falling onto the padded floor. The slam of weights. The pop song playing distantly over the speakers.

But silence is all Eli gets from Peter. He dares to turn his head toward the other man to see his eyes focused dead ahead at the ceiling. From where he lies, Eli can see the softer angles of Peter's face, the roundness of his cheeks, that sharpness of his nose, the brown of his eyes.

"Do you seriously think you're not interesting?" Eli asks.

"Why would I? You didn't like me on our first date."

"It wasn't you," Eli tells him. "That wasn't the real you. That was the nervous you, the you that was going on your first date."

"As opposed to the me that's been on two?"

"Three," Eli corrects. "And yeah, I'd say this Peter is an improvement over the first."

"It does feel easier," Peter says. "Like I'm already more comfortable around you."

"And you'll find that with another person," Eli promises. "You've just got to open up to them the way that you're opening up to me."

Peter doesn't say anything. He just gives Eli a sad expression that he tries to turn into a smile, but Eli can see through the pretense.

And when Peter asks Eli if he's ready to climb some more, he says yes and takes Peter's hand, letting the man help him to his feet. Eli mostly watches for the next hour and a half, letting Peter climb his heart out as he scales walls with a speed that Eli could never imagine.

He gives it an honest go a few times, managing to climb up the first three walls without much trouble by the end of the night. But his arms and legs start to ache like never before, and he has to bow out, watching Peter from the floor.

"You kind of are like Spider-Man," Eli says as Peter continues to show off for him.

"If only I could swing on webs," Peter tells him with a smile. "Are you ready to go?"

"Sure."

They walk to the locker room to grab their things and switch shoes.

"Did you drive here?" Peter asks him as they turn in the shoes and the locker keys.

"Oh, God, no. You think I can afford a car?"

Eli watches as Peter heads to a branded bright yellow refrigerator filled with energy teas all bearing the same logo as the fridge. "Do you want a ride?"

"I can wait for the bus, it won't be that long."

"But you live in the Castro—that's like an hour on the bus, plus it's late."

"I promise you"—Eli pushes on the bar for the door—"I've lived in this city my entire life. I'll be—" He pauses as they step outside, a gust of wind cutting through the both of them. Since the gym is in the Presidio and therefore *right* on the northern shore of the Bay, there's nothing to block the wind coming off the water. And without anything at all to cover himself with, Eli catches every small slice of freezing-cold air Mother Nature has to offer. "Actually, yeah, a ride would be nice."

Peter leads him to a black car parked around the corner from the gym.

Eli is shivering by the time he makes it to the door, Peter opening it for him. He gives Peter his address in the Castro, then relaxes as the seat underneath him begins to warm his butt. It's a nice car, something that he'd expect someone in the Bay Area who works a tech job to drive.

But more importantly, it's not a Tesla.

The real surprise comes when the music from Peter's phone begins to auto-play and the album artwork for a Miles Davis record comes up, the smooth sounds of a saxophone playing through the speakers.

"Jazz?" Eli stares.

"What? Is that . . . weird?"

"No, just . . . unexpected."

"What kind of music do I look like I listen to?" Peter asks.

Eli doesn't really have an answer for him. Partially because neither of them has brought up their taste in music before.

"I don't actually know."

"Jazz is nice, relaxing under the right circumstances."

Of course as Peter says that the song erupts into a fury of drums, saxophone, trumpets, and piano.

Peter lowers the volume a bit. "And other times it's chaotic and messy and just what I need."

"I bet you'd love *La La Land*."

"What's that?" Peter dares to ask.

"You haven't heard of *La La Land*?"

Peter shakes his head.

"Well . . . it's a love story about a jazz musician and an actress. There's a lot of love for the genre throughout."

"I'll bookmark it, then," Peter says, throwing on his turn signal. The darkness of the Presidio makes it difficult to see where they're going at times, but Peter seems familiar with the route. "You really like movies, huh?"

"Is that such a bad thing?" Eli asks him, feigning offense with his tone.

"No, no. Not at all, I didn't mean for it to—" Then Peter catches the look that Eli gives him out of the corner of his eye. "You're messing with me again, aren't you?"

"You're learning."

"You talk about them a lot. Movies."

"Yeah, I mean, I guess I love them. My dad used to take me to the theater at least once a week when I was growing up. We lived on Balboa, a block away from the theater, and they played a ton of classics, plus some bigger new stuff."

"That sounds really nice, actually."

"He thought it was important to see whatever we could on the big screen. He'd say, 'The TV is fine, but the theater is *really* where you want to be!' like an old Hollywood guy."

"Did he work in movies or something?"

"Nah, he taught at the college. English. He just always had a love for film."

"Do you still do the movie thing with him? Now that you're older?"

"Well, that'd be pretty hard since he's dead."

Peter brakes fast to avoid hitting the car in front of him, earning an aggressive honk from the car behind them. "Oh, God! Eli, I'm sorry, I'm so sorry!"

"Why?"

"Because I asked about your dad, and he's dead, and . . ." Peter pauses. "I don't know, I'm just sorry."

"But you couldn't have known—this is literally the first time I've brought my dad up."

"I know, but . . ."

"But . . ." Eli urges. He wants Peter to see the uselessness of constantly apologizing for something that couldn't possibly be his fault.

"B-but . . ." Peter stammers. "Nothing. I'm sorry."

"I'm going to have to start charging you for all these apologies. Only people *from* the Bay Area are allowed to say *sorry* as much as you do."

"I'll have to Venmo you," Peter says, changing lanes to avoid the bus ahead of them.

"Just buy dinner next time."

"Speaking of, do you have any ideas for our next 'date'?" Peter asks.

"That eager?"

"I mean, I like spending time with you," Peter admits. "And these dates have been pretty fun. In case you haven't noticed, I

don't get out very often. I don't have many friends. Actually . . .
I don't have any friends."

Eli can't help but smile at the man. There's something so earnest
about Peter, so . . . sweet.

"What about the people at the gym?" Eli asks. "They seemed to
like you."

"Yeah, but they aren't my friends. They're just being nice because
I go to the gym."

Eli wants to press, but he isn't quite sure how. Then he figures
maybe it's best to leave Peter alone, at least for the time being.

"Well, you know, if you'd like to be friends after this is done,
I wouldn't object," he says without thinking. It's not like it'd be a
conflict of interest, and the time he's spent with Peter has been fun.

"Yeah?"

"Yes, Peter. I would." Eli smiles at him.

"Thanks, Eli," Peter says just as they pull up in front of Eli's
building.

"And another thing?" Eli continues.

"Yes?"

"Let's start meeting for lunch."

"Why?"

"That's something that couples do. Just a few times a week.
But let's start tomorrow. You know where I work, and I take my
lunches at noon."

"Okay. I usually work through mine since I'm remote, but we
can try it."

"And . . ." Eli braces himself. "My mom wants to meet you."

Peter can't hide the shock in his voice. "Your mom?"

"I might've lied and said we're seeing each other to get her off
my back," Eli explains. "But I figured it might be good as a test of
sorts. Put the things you've learned into practice."

"I don't like how much sense that makes."

"Yeah, you're telling me." Eli unbuckles his seat belt.

"Actually, I have an idea," Peter begins. "It's not until Halloween, though."

"Give it to me."

"My office has these monthly outings where the SF and Oakland teams all hang out. I've never been because . . . well, you know."

Eli indeed does know.

"But . . . if you'd want to go with me, that might be fun?"

"Look at you, branching out." Eli beams.

"I think your lessons are working already."

"What can I say, I'm a great teacher." Eli dares to open the car door, letting the cold air hit his skin, goose bumps appearing in an instant. "We can go out this weekend if you're free?"

"Yeah, sounds good."

"Good night, Peter."

"Night, Eli."

Eli climbs out of the car and marches up the steps to his building, digging his keys out of his backpack to slip them into the front door. Through the glass of the front door, he can see Peter waiting for him. Eli waves at him, and Peter waves back before he drives off.

His body might ache, he's in desperate need of the longest shower of his life, *and* he embarrassed himself in front of half a dozen ten-year-olds, but Eli can't help but consider the night a success.

Bit by bit, he's peeling back Peter's layers. He can see the real man underneath blossoming into the person that he really is.

Slowly but surely, he's getting to know the real Peter Park.

And Eli likes what he sees.

Chapter Eight

My Own Private Idaho,
dir. by Gus Van Sant

"Eli, do you mind staying behind?" Michael asks as the rest of Eli's coworkers all gather their notebooks and tablets, leaving on the table rings of condensation from their iced coffees that Eli knows he's going to have to clean later.

It's hard to hide his annoyance. Thanks to the rock climbing, pretty much everything except his head aches, though Michael's doing his best to remedy that.

Gwen from IT shoots Eli a sly glance that seems to sing *You're in trouble . . .*

And Keith, well. He can't stand not being involved.

"Is there something that we forgot to talk about?" Keith asks, sidling close to Michael.

"No, no," Michael says, closing his laptop. "I just need to talk to Eli about a project he's doing."

"A project?" Keith can't hide his confusion, even daring to check his notebook. "I wasn't aware of any project Eli was assigned to."

"No, you weren't," Eli can't help but cut in.

Michael gives Keith a sympathetic look. "It's a private project, just between Eli and myself."

"Oh, are you *sure* I don't need to sit in on this one? Maybe I could offer some . . . advice?"

Eli isn't surprised. Keith has a habit of sticking his nose in where it isn't needed. There was a time when Eli thought of that as a helpful quality; sometimes Keith was able to offer sound advice, or he saw a typo or error that Eli hadn't. Other times Keith rewrote entire paragraphs of the articles Eli had given him to read through, even making the writing worse sometimes. Eli hates himself for how much he let Keith get away with.

"I appreciate it, Keith. But we don't need your input on this one." Eli feels a swell of pride at the disappointment on Keith's face.

"Okay, well . . ." Keith raps his knuckles on the table. "Just give me a call if I'm needed."

"You won't be," Eli says. Sure, maybe it's not the most professional reaction, but Michael sure doesn't care.

Keith shoots him a glare before he gathers his things, tucking his Apple Pencil into the pocket of his shirt as he walks out of the meeting room. For a moment, once the door is closed, he lingers, his eyes meeting Eli's again through the pane of glass.

"So, I've been reading what you have so far, and it's good stuff," Michael says, taking the seat at the head of the table once again. "You're selling me on how much of a loser this guy is."

Eli swallows. Working on two articles at the same time isn't exactly a walk in the park, especially when both are meant to be career defining.

"Don't call him a loser, Michael."

Sure, Eli had gone a little harsh in the fake article, knowing *exactly* what Michael would want to read. It'd felt awful, at first, lying about Peter, exaggerating their interactions, playing up his social and romantic incompetence. But the more Eli told himself that no one besides him and Michael would ever read it, the easier it became.

"Barks like a dog, looks like a dog, must be a dog." Michael smiles. "The guy is almost thirty and hasn't been on a single date yet? Pretty pathetic."

"Maybe you feel that way, but I think a fantastic angle for us to explore would be expectations in the queer community." Eli can't help himself. The sooner he wins over Michael for this better idea, the easier this whole scheme gets. "How a lack of experiences prevents you from learning anything about dating, intimacy, making connections. Peter comes from a really small town, so there was no one for him to have learned from. No community for him to find comfort in."

"Ah, Eli!" Michael throws his head back. "You're killing me."

"What?"

"You keep wanting to make this deep and meaningful. Just write the article, talk about how much of a dud this guy is, how you're fixing him, and we're good! We don't need *anything* more than that."

"But—" Eli tries to interject, and Michael stops him with a hand.

"Eli, I'm trying to help you here. I want you to learn," Michael waxes on. "You're writing about *dating*. Nothing else."

"Why can't dating be profound?" Eli asks.

"Because it's *dating*. Get over yourself and write the story. Okay?"

Eli swallows. "Okay, yeah. I've got it."

"When are you seeing him again?"

Eli pulls his phone out, double-checking his last messages from Peter. "Today, actually. We're having lunch."

"Good. And I like this note for him to meet your parents, that's a smart idea. See, that's what I'm looking for! Chase that lead, not whatever nonsense your journalistic integrity is pulling you toward."

"Understood, thanks . . ."

"You've got fantastic stuff here, just stop trying to make it something it's not. We're not highbrow, we're not looking to change the world."

All Eli can do is nod solemnly.

"Thank you!" Michael slaps his hand on the table. "Feel free to take your lunch whenever he gets here."

Eli tries his best to hide his frustration as he walks back to his desk, plugging his iPad back on the charging dock and opening his emails. He can see Keith walking toward him out of the corner of his eye.

"Hey, Eli!" Keith hovers behind Eli's monitor, like he's trying to play along with some joke that hasn't been made.

Eli deletes an email from the advertising department. "What can I do for you, Keith?"

"Nothing, I just wanted to talk."

"About the meeting?"

"No, I mean . . . I was just curious." Keith hesitates. "But it wasn't just about that."

"Yeah, right."

"How about lunch?" Keith asks. "We haven't gone out in a while."

"Because we're not dating, Keith. Or did you forget that?"

"I know, I know . . ." Keith tries his best to act ashamed. "And . . . I have regrets about how that went down. But just because I no longer felt romantic toward you, that doesn't mean we can't still be friends, right? I was thinking we could get some closure."

"No, Keith. Because I'm not interested in being friends with you."

Keith smirks that stupid dumb handsome smirk that he knows Eli fell hard for, gliding across the floor until he sits on the edge of Eli's desk. "Come on, let's just grab some lunch." Keith lets his hand drift closer and closer to Eli's keyboard, where Eli's hand rests. He's always been like this. Keith could never stand being out of the loop, unaware of what's going on.

Eli pulls away before Keith can even think about touching the skin between his thumb and pointer finger, a space that Keith seemed so fond of, his touch light when he traced invisible shapes there.

"Actually, I already have lunch plans."

Keith raises an eyebrow, staring at Eli like he doesn't believe him. "Oh, really?"

Eli can see the elevator doors opening, Peter strolling into the offices.

"Peter!" Eli calls out, waving. "Hey, baby."

Eli has to stop himself from cringing. Peter just smiles, waving back.

Keith doesn't dare move, like he wants Eli to be caught in some precarious position he'll have to explain.

"Hey . . . sweetie?" Peter can't say the word without it sounding like a question. Eli has to commend him for trying at least.

"You ready to go?"

Keith holds out his hand in front of Peter. "I'm Keith, nice to meet you."

"Oh, I'm Peter . . ." Peter takes the hand, obviously unsure.

Keith fakes a laugh, a familiar sound to Eli's ears, the laugh he used when they attended the fundraisers Eli's mother had to put on for the press, making the rounds in a room full of rich people. "So, you two are . . . together?" Keith looks at Peter, giving him a once-over as if Eli needs Keith's approval.

"Yep." Eli grabs his bag off the back of his chair, refusing to give Keith another pathetic moment of their time. "Let's head out, we'll go to the cafeteria."

"Sounds good." Peter tucks his hands into the pockets of his hoodie. "It was nice to meet you, Kevin!"

"It's Keith, actually!" he corrects.

Eli hides his smile.

"And likewise!"

He and Peter head toward the elevator, the door opening *just* in time for them to squeeze through without having to awkwardly wait for it to arrive.

"You know, he doesn't seem like *that* bad of a guy," Peter says once they're both behind the doors.

"Believe me, it's a point of shame that I gave him seven years of my life."

"Seven years?" Peter has every right to be shocked. "Wow . . ."

Eli shrugs. "Love makes you blind. You can't really see how big of a douchebag someone is until you've broken up."

"Was he really that bad?"

Eli pauses, staring at the ugly tiled floor. "No. Not while we were dating. But feelings like that, they have a way of hiding the worst parts of someone, even if they're right in front of you."

Peter's gaze follows Eli's. "That's a lot of time."

"Rub it in, why don't you?"

"No, I mean . . . I mean, I didn't mean—"

"Peter?" Eli eyes him.

"Yeah?"

Eli remains silent, waiting for Peter to catch on.

"You're messing with me?"

Eli nods.

"Right, right."

"You've got to get better at that."

"I have a problem with sarcasm sometimes."

"That's okay. That's why I'm here." Eli smiles, and Peter smiles back, the elevator doors finally opening.

* * *

"*Fargo?*"

"Nope."

"*Before Sunrise?*"

"No."

"*The King of Comedy*?"

Peter shakes his head.

"*The Devil Wears Prada*?"

"The one with Anne Hathaway, right?"

"Yes!" Eli exclaims.

"Haven't seen that one either."

"Most of those I can forgive," Eli tells him, pointing with a string-cut french fry. "But *The Devil Wears Prada*, come on."

Peter shrugs. "I haven't seen a lot of movies."

"Or any, it sounds like."

"I was just never a big movie guy. I saw *Spider-Man* with my dad; he found the DVD in a Walmart and my mom didn't want him to buy it but she knew how much he loves Spider-Man."

"Those are good. I like Sam Raimi."

"Who's that?" Peter asks, stealing a fry.

"The director . . . of *Spider-Man* . . . the first three, at least. *Darkman*, *A Simple Plan*, the *Evil Dead* trilogy?"

"Oh . . . yeah, he's okay, I guess."

Eli blinks in disbelief. "The guy's name is literally at the beginning of the movie."

"Yeah, but I was like five when I saw it. I hardly remember anything except how scary it was when those guys got turned into skeletons by that bomb."

"I can see how that'd be traumatizing to a young, impressionable Peter."

"What about you?" Peter prompts. "If you're going to sit there and critique my lack of movie literacy, let's hear about your favorite jazz musicians."

"I don't know anything about jazz," Eli admits.

"See! Not everyone knows everything about everything!"

"Yeah, but movies are . . . they're *movies*!"

"And jazz is probably the most influential style and genre of music that's ever existed," Peter swiftly elaborates. "Without jazz we don't have R & B, we don't get singers like Big Mama Thornton, who helped the formation of rock 'n' roll as a genre, we don't get Elvis, and without rock we don't get disco, eighties pop, the rise of grunge, modern pop music."

"Okay, okay, I get it." Eli nods, eating slowly.

"Can I ask you something?" Peter swiftly switches topics.

Eli smiles. "You just did."

Peter rolls his eyes, and Eli nods to let him know to ask his question.

"You gave Keith so much of your life."

Eli waits for Peter to finish his question, but he seems to have let it get away from him. "Yes?"

"I . . . I don't think I know what I was going to ask."

Eli can't help but laugh at that. "Well, what do you *think* you're trying to ask me?"

"I guess . . . I guess I'm wondering if you have any regrets about the relationship? Giving him that much of your time when it wound up to be for nothing."

"Wow . . . huh." Eli pauses, thinking.

"Iced Americano?" Peter offers.

Eli shakes his head. "No, just thinking. I mean, yes. There are regrets, things that I didn't realize were happening right in front of me until it was too late. Keith was controlling, telling me what to wear on date nights. And any argument we had . . . everything always seemed to be my fault. His mood swings could get pretty bad too, and I'd have to tell him to go take a walk and calm down before he came back to the apartment."

"Jesus. That sounds scary."

"Again, love can make you blind to a lot of things. And it wasn't all bad—those moments happened between the times when Keith and I loved one another, shared nights together, made dinner, went to North Beach to wait two hours in line for brunch. And I wasn't a perfect partner; I saw afterward how I ignored Keith, putting my needs before his own, how selfish I tend to be.

"But I don't regret the actual relationship, if that makes any sense. I learned a lot being with Keith—what I appreciated and wanted out of a relationship, what I expected. How I like to love other people, how I enjoy spending my time. It was messy, but I learned a lot about myself."

"I guess that makes it worth it, huh?"

"It's hard to rationalize that. Like you said, it's easy to think that, at the end of a relationship, there's nothing to hold on to. But my time with Keith changed me, taught me a lot, and I liked who I became after it ended. It took a few weeks, but I liked myself."

"What do you think you'll learn after we're done 'dating'?" Peter uses air quotes around *dating*.

Eli swallows, still keeping his smile. "You've certainly taught me about communication. The importance of giving second chances to the people who prove they're worth them. Oh, boundaries, you've really helped me there."

"You've gleaned all that from me?"

"Of course! Why wouldn't I?"

"I . . . I guess I didn't expect this to be a learning opportunity for you too."

"I think every relationship, platonic or romantic, gives someone the chance to learn more. About themselves, about other people. And that's valuable."

"I like the way you think about these things."

"What can I say?" Eli offers, trying to play off how deep he'd allowed the conversation to get. "I'm good at what I do."

Peter laughs, finishing the bottle of lemonade he'd had with his lunch. "Did you have any ideas for our next date?" Peter asks suddenly, and his boldness surprises Eli for a moment.

"Uh . . ." Eli chews his food. "Nothing yet. Why?"

"There's a jazz club I want to take you to. It's down the street from my apartment."

"I'd love that, actually."

"They're having a big show at the end of the week?"

"Sure."

"So . . ." Peter steals another fry. "If you love movies so much, have you thought about writing about them? Instead of being . . . you know, here?"

"I gave it some thought," Eli says. "It never really went any-where."

"Why?"

"I guess the writing got to be too personal." In the middle of what other people might call his more serious work, Eli has a whole slew of articles about queerness in horror films, particularly the trans history of horror. From the 1930s Hitchcock classic *Murder!* and Paul Bartel's *Private Parts* to more widely recognized exam-ples like *The Silence of the Lambs*, *Sleepaway Camp*, and *Dressed to Kill*. How the genre and history attempted to vilify trans people—especially trans women—for so long and yet trans people seem so drawn to horror because of how they're so often seen as the other.

He even wrote a full essay in college on how the *Child's Play* franchise, of all things, helped him come to terms with his gender identity by having the first non-binary main character he'd ever seen on the screen.

Of course, that character is a British doll that other characters call Shitface for most of the movie, but the point stood. Eli can re-call that character so clearly on his television as he watched through all the movies one by one, his mother objecting to them but his father sneaking them into the stack of VHS tapes and DVDs pro-cured from the rental place down the street from their apartment.

"*Shouldn't* writing be personal, though?" Peter asks.

"Maybe."

"I think so," he says. "One of my favorite authors says that some of their best writing is fact mixed with a little bit of fiction."

Eli can't help a smile. "Got that from all of your tech billionaire biographies?"

Peter looks away suddenly. "I feel like I should take that as an insult."

"Oh." Eli freezes, realizing how what he's just said sounds. "I'm sorry, Peter, I honestly didn't mean—"

It's Peter's arm, thrown casually over his mouth in an effort to hide his laughter, that so obviously gives him away.

"Oh, okay. I get it now."

"It's not fun, is it?"

"Yeah, now that you mention it—" Eli starts to say, but he doesn't bother to complete the thought when Peter's phone starts ringing.

"Hello?" A look of shock registers on his face before it sinks into frustrated disappointment. "Yeah, yeah. I stepped out for a minute for lunch. Let me get back to my computer. Give me ten. Yes. Yeah. Yeah. Send the data report and we'll go over it together. Okay. Bye."

"Speeding off?" Eli asks. He can't help but share in the defeat in Peter's expression.

"Yeah, I'm sorry."

"It's okay, I've taken enough of your time today. And you are *technically* on the clock. I'll text you tonight?"

"Sure. And we're okay with going to the club on Friday?"

"I can't think of a better way to spend a Friday night," he tells Peter.

"Okay. Bye, Eli."

"Ah-ah," Eli calls out to Peter just as he's sprinting away, barely catching himself on the slippery floor of the building cafeteria. "Forgetting something?"

"Um . . ." Peter gives himself a pat-down. "I don't think so."

Eli puckers his lips.

"Seriously?" Peter looks around at the other employees of the building's various offices, as if he's afraid of being caught.

"Don't you want to kiss your *boyfriend* goodbye?"

Peter beams shyly. "Yes."

"Iced Americano?" Eli asks him.

"No." Peter steps back toward his seat, his height making it easy for him to simply lean over the table and kiss Eli on the lips. It's longer than their first from so many nights ago, but only just barely. This one is so much more public than the last. Eli likes how it feels; he's always loved kissing for no real reason at all, how intimate it is, how easy it is to lose parts of himself in the best way possible.

It feels good to get to do it again.

"Get home safely," Eli tells him.

"I will."

Eli watches as Peter flashes his guest pass at the cafeteria door. Okay, so maybe he's watching Peter's ass more than anything, but can anyone fault him?

It's a *great* ass.

Eli hates himself for wondering what it'd be like to tease Peter with his strap-on, the vibrations of a short plug working its way inside of him while he makes a babbling mess out of Peter. Then he pushes his tray of half-eaten food away.

"God." He rakes a hand through his hair. "I need to get laid."

"Just the words I wanted to hear!" Patricia says as she slaps her hands down on the table, choosing the spot right across from Eli.

"Where'd you even come from?" Eli asks.

"Blame my parents."

"How long have you been here?"

"About ten minutes before the two of you walked in holding hands."

Eli groans. "So, you were watching me and—"

"And your boy toy?" Patricia finishes for him. "Yep, sure was." She steals a chicken tender, since Eli has the appetite of a six-year-old. "Figured I'd give you both your moment. Besides, I had edits to read through."

"So . . ." Eli dares to ask. "What do you think?"

"He's *very* cute." Patricia stares toward the door to the cafeteria, as if Peter is still standing there. "Nice ass too."

"I feel like this has to be some form of sexual harassment." His own guilt notwithstanding.

"You're telling me you don't want to take him to pound town?" Patricia asks him.

"Please don't call it that."

"Okay, you're telling me you don't want to *fornicate* with him?"

Eli shudders, covering his ears. "That's worse. Like you're *so* close to getting me to vomit."

Patricia's just laughing to herself. "But he's very cute."

"Yeah, he is."

"So, a complete three-sixty from your first date?"

"I think you mean one-eighty," Eli corrects.

"No . . ." Patricia chews the stolen food, nodding her head and pretending to think. "I think I'm right. So, when do Rose and I get to meet him?"

Another test that Eli figured he could put Peter through. If he can nail a dinner with Patricia and Rose, integrate himself into their circle without much effort, then he'd be that much closer to success. Besides, he could always take the feedback they were sure to offer, get a handle on any blind spots in Peter's rehabilitation.

"I don't know," Eli tells her.

"Come on, let us meet him!"

"I will, at some point."

"Don't make me pout."

"He's taking me to a jazz club on Friday," Eli tells her, breezing past the topic he'd rather not discuss. "He's a big jazz dude."

"In a sophisticated way? Or a pretentious way?"

"Leaning toward sophisticated."

"What about the rest of the weekend?" she asks.

"No idea."

"Okay, well, keep me updated," Patricia sings, tapping her fingers on the table before heading toward the exit.

"I will!" Eli sings back, watching his best friend exit the cafeteria, one of her coworkers grabbing onto her and handing her an iPad to maybe read over a piece before it's finalized. Eli sits there for a moment, staring at the space that Peter once occupied, and he can't help but smile to himself.

Chapter Nine

La La Land, dir. by Damien Chazelle

O h, this is like a legit lounge," Eli says, staring at the line that stretches down the block in front of the basement entrance. The rest of the building is dedicated to a closed bakery and apartments that sit above.

"Did you think that it wouldn't be?" Peter asks, his hand wrapped around Eli's as he bypasses the mile-long line of people.

Eli doesn't really know what he expected. He certainly didn't anticipate the long line and people dressed to the nines. He's never felt more self-conscious about his grandpa sweaters, especially with the nice-looking button-up that Peter has chosen to wear.

"A warning would've been appreciated," Eli tells him, desperate to not feel self-conscious.

"You look great," Peter promises.

"Where are we going? The line starts back there," Eli asks as he's pulled along to the door.

Peter glances over his shoulder, smiling at Eli. "I know the bouncer."

Eli feels like he's stumbled into a brand-new world, just like at the gym. Peter didn't even ask before he took Eli's hand. He simply took it, and they walked the three blocks from Peter's apartment. On the walk, Peter was beaming, grinning from ear to ear, and laughing at Eli's stories from the day.

It's not a *new* Peter, not at all.

It's the authentic Peter.

"Hey, Peter!" The bouncer at the door *looks* like she'd be a bouncer, with strong shoulders and biceps that seem to want to rip out of her shirt.

"Hey, Jaz."

"Your name is Jaz, and you work at a jazz club?" Eli can't help himself, but he's only met with a cold stare, and he feels his face go hot. "I'm sorry."

"This guy with you?" she asks.

"Uh, yeah . . ."

"Go on in." She nods toward the door. "We've got Harry Whitfield tonight."

"Why else do you think I'm here?" Peter asks, his smile bright in his voice. "I've been dying to hear him!"

"So has the rest of the city." Jaz peers back at the long line.

"I bet Meredith doesn't mind."

"Oh, not one bit." Jaz shakes her head. "Go ahead down, tables are filling up."

Eli feels like he just got whiplash from a conversation. *Who is this man?* he asks himself, his gaze focused on the back of Peter's head as they walk down the steps into the club proper. Peter just had a conversation, with a person that he clearly *knows.*

"What was that about?" Eli asks, leaning over the table as they take some seats near the stage.

"What?" Peter stares. "Did I do something wrong?"

"No! God, no. That was actually . . . impressive, really. You had a full conversation."

"She owns the club with her wife."

"Yeah, you talked like the two of you are friends."

"Oh, no way." Peter shakes his head. "She's just being nice. I see Jaz and Meredith all the time when I'm here."

"She didn't seem that nice to the people in front of us." Eli peers at him.

"She was just doing her job, that's all."

Eli lets out a *tsk tsk*, surveying the rest of the club's clientele. Most people seem to be on their own date nights, laughing at jokes, telling stories, clinking their glasses together while they eat from the small bowls of pretzels.

"What?" Peter asks.

"I don't think she was just doing her job," Eli tells him. But he decides to drop it. "Have you ever flirted with anyone?"

"I don't think that Jaz is flirting with me," he says. "I mean, she's a lesbian. And I don't think I'm her type."

Eli shakes his head, laughing. "No, I was just asking, I wasn't trying to imply that Jaz was flirting with you."

"Oh." Peter blushes. "I don't think I have, no. I mean, *maybe* with Mark? I don't know, there was never a lot of talking when we did what we did."

"Never a little playful banter between you and a guy on Hinge?"

"It's never really gotten that far."

"Can I see your profile?" Eli asks.

Peter hesitates, reaching for his phone. "You have to promise not to laugh."

"Why would I laugh?"

"Because it's embarrassing?" Peter pleads with the soft gaze of his eyes.

"I swear to you that I'm not going to laugh, Peter." Eli swallows, taking the phone after it's unlocked and offered to him slowly. Eli finds the Hinge app, but not before noticing that Peter's home screen is hectic, apps everywhere, completely disorganized. Though Peter seems to know exactly where everything is.

"Okay, okay, decent picture up top," Eli says, though it looks a little too much like a school photo for his comfort. Peter's very *face forward at a three-quarter angle* in the picture, an awkward smile on his lips.

It's unfortunate that that's the last good thing he has to say about Peter's profile.

The rest of the photos were obviously taken on the same day because Peter's in the same outfit. *They were probably taken minutes apart too*, Eli thinks. And they're all the same—all five pictures are nearly identical. Whatever hope Eli has that his answers to the prompts might save the profile are lost when he actually reads the answers.

"'We won't get along if . . .'" Eli begins to read. "'We don't have the same interests.'"

Eli looks at Peter.

"It's true."

"You got me there. 'I'm looking for . . . a boyfriend.'"

"Again, true."

"'My favorite dish is . . . mugs.' What does that even mean?"

"Mugs, they're good for hot things. You've got the handle there, they're comfortable in your hand."

"Oh, you sweet, sweet man."

"What?"

Eli feels his heart melt. "So . . . there's a lot to fix here."

"You think the pictures are that bad?"

"Only if you're not trying to attract a victim to murder."

"Okay, well . . ." The disappointment is obvious in Peter's voice. "Use the ones that we've taken."

Eli thinks for a moment. "Stay like that." He points the camera toward Peter. While it only lasts for a second, the image painted by Eli's phone is a gorgeous one. The cool dark blue lighting of the club contrasts with the lit candles decorating each table, painting Peter's face in the same warmer undertones of his skin.

He looks stunning.

"What? No. Please don't."

"Come on, you need decent pictures for your profile."

"Ugh." Peter pulls his jacket around his face.

"Okay, okay. I'm putting it away." Eli puts the phone under the table.

"Thank you."

"Psych!" Eli whips the phone back out, snapping a picture of Peter before he can hide himself again.

"Eli!"

"Relax, relax. I was too quick with it anyway." Eli shows him the screen before he deletes the blurry photo. "But if you want to do this, pictures are a necessity."

"I guess."

"Do you have pictures of you rock climbing? That'd get some of your hobbies across." And prove to any potential suitors that Peter doesn't just spend all day in his apartment.

"Who could've taken them?" Peter asks him, the pointed frustration in his tone abundantly clear.

"Are you okay?"

"Yeah, yeah. I'm sorry, I just . . ."

"Iced Americano?" Eli asks him.

"I don't want to use that every time I'm not feeling comfortable."

"That's the exact reason *to* use the signal, Peter. I don't want you to be uncomfortable." Eli pauses. "Fine. Iced Americano."

"Did I—?"

"No, Peter. You didn't do anything wrong. I just want you to communicate with me a little more."

"I guess I . . ." Peter hesitates, picking at the fabric of the tablecloth. "I guess I don't like having my picture taken."

"That's perfectly okay."

"I'm sorry."

"You don't have to apologize, Peter. If you're not comfortable with something, then it's okay. You're not comfortable. I'd consider not using Hinge if you don't want to post your picture, though.

Or any other dating app, for that matter." Eli knows the struggle all too well of anonymous profiles on Grindr and Tinder, most of whom loved making the bold demand that Eli send nudes before they even showed their faces.

"I guess I've just never liked looking at myself like that. I don't feel . . . attractive."

"Well, like I said, you don't *have* to be comfortable with anything. But speaking from an outside perspective, you're a very attractive man, Peter."

"It's just . . ." He continues to pick, this time at the skin on his finger. "Never mind."

Eli reaches forward, taking Peter's hand in his slowly. "I used to hate having my picture taken too, you know."

"Really?"

"My mom would take ones of me at family dinners or outings or whatever, and I just . . . I knew that person in the photos wasn't me. I mean, it was, obviously. But it wasn't at the same time. And they believed that it was, and that was enough for them. But I knew the truth." Eli lets out a careful breath. "Even after I started testosterone, even after I changed my clothes and my hair, even when my voice began to change and hair began to sprout up in places it didn't used to . . . Even after I started to feel a little more confident, I always wanted to hide my face. And the acne didn't help."

"Jeez, Eli . . . I'm . . ."

"No, no apologies." Eli tries to laugh it off. "I should apologize to you; I didn't mean for things to get that heavy. Ah, sorry . . ." Eli tucks his face away. "My point is that . . . I don't know exactly what you're feeling, but it's okay. We can work on it."

Peter smiles at that, and Eli feels a weight come off his shoulders. He's proud of Peter, at the very least, for verbalizing something that was making him uncomfortable. This entire experiment has been about forcing Peter into new social situations, testing him. And the last thing he wants to do is make Peter feel uneasy; Eli just wants to . . . challenge him.

It's the applause that pulls him from his trance, his gaze shooting right toward the stage as the spotlight shines on a group of older-looking Black men, each holding their instrument of choice, aside from the drummer, who only carries his sticks for obvious reasons.

"Hello, everyone." The man at the front takes the microphone. "I'm not sure if you know who I am, but my name is Harry Whit—"

An even louder round of applause interrupts Harry, and he waves gently to the crowd, requesting their attention again.

"I'm Harry Whitfield. Me and my friends here, some of the best people I've ever known, we were asked to come down to your lovely city and perform here at Jackie's. A club owned by one of my oldest and greatest friends in the world!"

More applause.

"Okay, okay. I won't bore anyone with stories. You're here to hear the music, and I'm dying to play it." He smiles brilliantly, raises his trumpet to his lips, and in a split second Harry and the rest of the band burst into song, the brass instruments blaring through the club before they cut out again almost immediately, the bass player plucking his strings thoughtfully.

Eli's eyes dare to glance toward Peter. Paying rapt attention to the band and their playing, he taps his fingers on the table along with the improvised beat, as if he can see what they're doing from a mile away. His smile brightens the dark room.

It's in that moment that Eli realizes just how jealous he is of Peter. He thinks of the silent confidence that Peter walks with, not even realizing it's there. Eli thinks about the gym, how at home Peter seemed there, and Peter's job, being a team leader, someone that his company seems to appreciate. He thinks about how, just a few moments ago, Peter so easily chatted with Jaz like the old friends they seem to be.

Without even realizing it, Peter has formed relationships, friendships. He's built his own world that he's allowed Eli to join.

And Eli's realizing just how much he appreciates that.

Peter taking the time to show Eli his world.

The rest of the club might've come here for Harry, and make no mistake, his playing is nothing short of amazing.

But as far as Eli's concerned, it might as well be Peter up there on that stage, just standing, smiling. Not doing anything at all.

Because that's all it would take for Peter to have the attention of the whole world.

* * *

For the next hour, the club is brought to life by the band and Harry, until he takes his final bow covered in a layer of sweat that glows under the stage lights. The rest of the band members take their bows as well, and the applause only grows louder.

"Okay, okay, everyone. Thank you," Harry says, taking the mic again. "We're done for the night, but keep this energy up for one of the greatest and most talented piano players I've had the privilege of knowing, my dear friend Sidra Carpenter!"

A woman walks up on stage. Harry gives her a soft kiss on each cheek before he takes her hand, raising it in the air. As she starts to play, the focus is pulled away from her, but only because that's what she's intending: the club fills with the soft sounds of piano meant to simply exist in the background rather than occupy the spotlight.

"So . . ." Peter leans forward, taking a pretzel from the bowl on the table. "What did you think?"

"Well, I have to say that I'm impressed. It was amazing to watch," Eli admits, and he's being honest—to watch the way the players moved, how they lost themselves in each of their instruments, clearly friends and yet still competing with one another to be the best player in a race that had no true winners or losers.

"Do you think I've converted you?" Peter asks. "Into a jazz lover?"

"Maybe. I'll certainly take more recommendations."

Peter smiles. "I'll make you a list."

"And now, we get to work."

Peter seems confused. "What does that mean?"

"I mean"—Eli smiles—"I'm going to teach you how to flirt."

In an instant, Peter is defensive. "I know how to flirt."

"Oh, yeah?" Eli sits back in his seat, crossing his arms. "Flirt with me right now."

Peter sits there for a moment. "Your . . . your sweater . . ."

Eli nods to keep him going.

"It's nice."

"Wow! I'm blushing, take my clothes off right now."

Peter hides his face. "Okay, so I don't know how to flirt."

"It's not that hard once you get the hang of things," Eli tells him. "You just have to get comfortable."

"Okay . . . so how *do* you flirt?"

"Well . . ." Eli has to think for a moment. It's one of those things that he's never given much thought to—explaining *how* you flirt. "You pretty much just have to find something that you like about a person, and be playful, loose. The most important thing, besides respecting boundaries, is that you're having fun."

"What does that mean?"

Eli doesn't even know how to answer that. You just know it when you see it. Like porn.

Then he gets an idea.

"Think of it like jazz." Eli sits up straight in his seat.

"Like jazz?"

"You know how jazz musicians play loose, they go with the flow of what they're playing, adapt to the other members of the band to make something great?"

"Yeah?"

"It's like that, being loose, going with the flow of the moment, responding to what other people around you are doing."

Peter stares at him, smiling.

"What?"

"When did you learn so much about jazz?"

"I might've watched a video or two," Eli says with an air of confidence. "Just trust yourself, you'll know if you've gone too far."

"So, what does 'going for it' look like? How will I know?"

Eli leans in closer. "You could be direct, say 'Your ass looks so juicy I'm dying to take a bite.'"

Peter almost chokes on his own spit.

"But that could delve into the territory of harassment if you're not careful."

"Okay, good. Yeah. Thank you."

"It's all very natural," Eli explains further. "Just be lighthearted, don't overthink it."

"Right, because I'm *so* good at that."

"Well, maybe a drink would loosen you up?"

Peter perks up. "Really?"

Eli taps on the table, motioning for Peter to follow him as he gets up. "What's your poison?" he asks once they're at the bar, grateful that it's slow enough that they can easily find seats.

"I don't know."

"You don't drink often?"

Peter shakes his head. "Not since college. It wasn't pretty."

"You, not pretty? I find that hard to believe."

"Oh . . . uh . . ." Peter's ears turn red again, and Eli's realizing just how cute that is.

"See, *that's* what flirting should sound like. Natural, a part of the conversation. Almost like you're slipping in a compliment." Eli peers over the bifold menu, trying not to react to the prices. "I don't think I'll bother asking them what's on draft. What about whiskey? Do you like that?"

"Don't know."

"There's a first time for everything." Eli smiles, waving down the bartender to order a whiskey sour. "So, is there anyone here who strikes your fancy?"

"Umm . . ." Peter spins around on the black leather stool. "I don't really know."

"What do you mean?" Eli asks. "There's *no* one here that you think is cute?"

"Well . . ." Peter's eyes find Eli's before he averts his gaze again, peering further down the bar. Eli glances over his shoulder. There are a few people that Peter could be looking at, but he has to figure it's the silver-daddy-looking gentleman, dressed in a deep gray button-up with the sleeves rolled to show off his strong-looking arms.

It dawns on Eli that he hasn't even considered what Peter's type might be. He went out with Eli, so he has to figure that bony little twinks who could be blown over by a stiff breeze are somewhere on Peter's radar.

But Peter also has that bigger kind of beefy twunk vibe to him, so maybe he's into stronger-looking guys as well?

"Him?" Eli turns back to Peter, nodding at the man.

"I guess."

"You guess?"

"I mean, he's handsome. Yeah."

Eli sneaks another look; the scruff that runs across the man's jawline paints a kind of maturity that even Eli has to admit is sexy. In fact, if he wasn't so focused on Peter, Eli might've asked the man for his number himself, if only for a quick one-night stand.

The bartender leaves Eli his drink, and Eli pulls the cherry speared on the toothpick free before he passes it to Peter. "Here, take a few sips, it'll help loosen you up."

"Okay . . ." Peter puts his lips to the glass, downing half the drink in a single gulp. Peter's face twists as he swallows, shaking his head. "Oh, ugh. I don't like that."

"That's because you chugged that thing. You *sip* whiskey, Peter." Eli takes the drink back, stealing his own taste. "Now, get over there and flirt your anxious little heart out."

"How?"

"Pretend that he wants you. That's all you need."

Peter swallows, standing at Eli's urging and walking slowly over to the older man at the other end of the bar, almost as if he's approaching a wild animal.

Bless his heart, Eli thinks as he goes back to the drink, trying to make it not so obvious that he's watching this unfurl.

The man smiles as Peter approaches, and Peter stands there awkwardly, looking for a place to fit into the conversation the guy was already having. Eli sees Peter jump in and say something to the man. At least, he tries; there's visible cringing. As the seconds drag along like hours, Peter begins to relax. His shoulders become less stern, his posture unravels, and he actually makes the other man laugh, leaning on the counter, subtly flexing his muscles.

Eli chuckles to himself. *He's better at this than I expected*. He watches, wishing that he could read lips so he knew what was going on, but sitting back will just have to do. Peter seems fine, maybe even great. The man laughs again, and there's a strong hand placed on Peter's shoulder, and Eli bites at his bottom lip. He wants to say he looks on with pride, but that's not what he's feeling, no . . . not with the way Peter looks at the older gentleman, his smile disappearing into adorable dimples.

No, pride isn't what he feels.

Is it . . . No, it couldn't be.

I'm not jealous, he reassures himself. *What do I have to be jealous about?*

He has to remember that he's here for Peter, not for himself. Sure, there are the articles, but tonight is about Peter, and Peter only.

Then something odd happens. Peter stumbles, catching himself on the man he's been talking to.

It's not in an "I tripped" flirty kind of way. But more in an "I'm so drunk I can't stand up straight" kind of way. Eli braces himself against the bar, standing slowly. Concern washes over the other man's face as well, and his friend tries to help Peter sit down on a stool.

Eli chooses that moment to intervene. "Hey, Peter, buddy. You okay?" he dares to ask.

The Peter he sees is a version of Peter that Eli's yet to have the chance to meet. His face is bright red, and not because he's embarrassed. His mouth is painted in what looks like a permanent smile as he giggles at a joke only he knows the punchline to.

"Eli!" Peter throws his arms out, wrapping them around Eli and pulling him in so tight that Eli thinks he might suffocate.

"I think your friend here can't handle his alcohol," the man Peter was flirting with says.

"I'm fine, I swear." Peter reaches for . . . something, Eli can't really tell, but he knocks over the silver daddy's glass, pouring the drink out onto the bar. "Oh, I'm sorry, let me get you some napkins." Peter reaches for the napkin dispenser on the bar.

"It's okay." The guy reacts quickly, picking up his glass before too much of a mess is made.

"I'm so sorry," Eli apologizes on Peter's behalf, taking him by the shoulder. "Come on, stand up slowly," Eli urges. "What could've happened? You didn't have *that* much to drink."

"If he's anything like my brother-in-law, he can't metabolize his alcohol," the silver-haired daddy says to Eli. "He's close to black-out after a single drink."

"Ding-ding-ding!" Peter sings, pointing to the man.

"Why didn't you say anything?" Eli asks.

"You wanted me loosey-goosey," Peter says proudly, the Georgia of his accent on full display now that he's good and intoxicated. "So, I'm loosey-goosey!"

"Oh, Jesus . . ." Eli tries not to feel guilty as he takes Peter by the hand again. "Okay, let's get you home."

"Okay!"

"Do you want help?" the silver-haired daddy asks.

"No—thank you, though. I'm really sorry about this."

"Get him some water and Tylenol and he'll be fine."

Eli loops Peter's arm over his shoulders, slowly leading the much heavier man through the lounge, avoiding the cutting gazes of people who want to judge Peter. Jaz asks about Peter as they make it outside, the night getting chillier. She helps Eli sit Peter at a bench on the corner before she returns to her job with Eli's promise that they'll be okay.

"I'm drunk!" Peter giggles.

"Yeah, that much is obvious." Eli sighs, doing his best to catch his breath.

Peter frowns, his drunken mood suddenly shifting.

"But it's not your fault," Eli admits. "I'm really sorry, Peter," he says, knowing that he'll want to make another apology when Peter is more sober. "I didn't realize this was a problem for you."

"No, I'm sorry . . ." Peter says, and there's no way for him to say the words without sounding like a child who did something wrong.

"It's okay," Eli stands, looking at the drunk man swaying in front of him, wondering what to do. *Obviously* he has to get Peter home, but how difficult is that going to be if Peter won't cooperate? "Do you think you can walk back to your apartment?"

"Mm-hmm . . . not that far," Peter says, his voice more tender, as if he's already on the other side of drunkenness where he's regretting his decisions.

"Okay, well. Let's go." Eli takes Peter's hand and helps him stand up. They barely make it around the corner before Eli has to stop because Peter keeps wobbling back and forth.

Eli leaves him for just a moment to buy a bottled water and a bag of Hawaiian rolls at a corner store, grateful that Peter hasn't run off by the time he makes it back outside.

"What's the bread for?" Peter asks, taking the rolls and resting his head against them.

"To soak up some of that whiskey," Eli tells him. Maybe it's not the most refined option, but he was in a rush. Plus the shop had a five-dollar card minimum.

"I'm sorry," Peter says.

Eli swears he can feel Peter's pulse, his heart thudding so heavy in his chest.

"It's okay, Peter."

"Are you mad at me?" His voice is so pitiful it nearly breaks Eli's heart.

"No, I'm not mad at you."

"You promise?"

"I swear, I'm not angry at you, Peter." Eli rubs circles into Peter's back. "You're fine."

"I'm sorry."

"I'm going to get serious about fining you for the apologies," Eli tells him.

Peter pauses at the intersection, not saying a word.

Eli sighs. "Go ahead. It's your last one."

"I'm sorry."

"I know."

Eli double-checks the traffic, deciding to jaywalk to get Peter home faster. "You really can't metabolize alcohol?"

Peter shakes his head too quickly, appearing to instantly regret it. "No. I can blame my parents for that one. It's *technically* an allergy, kind of. Just without the sneezing."

"So, like a single sip gets you drunk?"

"I'm usually fine with some beer, or things with low alcohol content." Peter nods, but once again, he does it too quickly. "This happened once in college. I sipped a friend's vodka and was throwing up ten minutes later."

"Jesus. Why didn't you tell me?"

"I thought maybe it would've gotten better the older I got?"

"I don't think that's how allergies work, Peter."

"Yeah . . ."

"Well, it's my turn to apologize to you," Eli tells him. "I shouldn't have pressured you like that."

"I could've said no," Peter says.

It's fair, Peter could have said no. But also Eli knows he shouldn't have defaulted to getting Peter intoxicated just so he could *talk* to someone.

"Still, I'm sorry, Peter. Do you remember how it was going?" Eli asks. "Before you got wasted?"

"It was fun. He was there with his boyfriend, the other guy."

"Oh, yikes."

"It's okay. They were nice and didn't mind when I said the guy had a nice butt."

"You couldn't even see his butt," Eli says. "He was sitting down."

Peter covers his eyes, smiling. "I imagined it."

Eli can't help a laugh. "Imagining other guys' butts, Peter? I'm impressed."

"You should see what else I can imagine," Peter says in a low, almost sultry voice. Or what he must believe is a sultry voice.

This time, it's Eli's turn to blush, his cheeks stinging against the sharp night. "Oh? Are you *flirting* with me, Peter Park?"

"Sorry, I didn't mean it like that." Peter's words slur a bit, making it clear that he's still drunk.

"How *did* you mean it, then?"

"I . . . don't know." And then, Peter starts to laugh, a soft sound that fills Eli's ears. Eli decides in that moment that he likes the sound of Peter's laugh. There's so much life in the sound.

The two of them walk for another three blocks, Eli keeping his hand around Peter's to make sure he doesn't wander off or stumble on the sidewalk. Eventually they approach a gated door, and Peter reaches into his pants pocket to pull out his keys, dropping them almost immediately.

"Sorry."

"It's okay," Eli promises, squatting down to get the keys. "What unit are you?"

"I'm the in-law," Peter says gently, leading Eli through the entrance before they step in front of an incredibly plain-looking door with a bronze *524 A* drilled into the wall beside it. "It's the silver key."

"Got it." Eli finds the correct key, slips it into the lock, and then walks Peter through the door, which leads into a garage.

"Back here," Peter mumbles. "The bronze key this time."

Eli slides the key into the lock, waiting for Peter to open the door first. "Do you want me to come in?"

"Oh . . ." Peter looks around, bracing himself against the doorframe. "Um . . ."

Eli hands Peter the keys. "I don't have to, but I'd like to make sure you at least make it to bed."

"Yeah . . . come in." Peter holds the door open wider. "But, um . . . take your shoes off, please."

"I'm not a monster, Peter."

He doesn't know what he expects when Peter turns on the light, drops his keys on the counter, and stumbles further into the apartment. Peter had seemed wary about showing Eli anything at all, so he thought that maybe it'd be a complete mess, like a tornado ripped right through it. Or that maybe Peter was self-conscious because the apartment is beautiful, and he's feeling insecure because for some reason men who live on their own shouldn't have nice apartments?

But no, it's neither of those things.

There's . . . nothing?

It's a one-bedroom, but barely. There's a wall separating the living room and bedroom; it's just that there's no door to be seen. The bed is a mattress on a basic metal frame, a simple IKEA table next to it. There's an L-shaped desk with what looks to be a pretty decked-out PC on it, as well as one of those budget black laptops, with a red mouse button nipple in the middle of the keyboard, right next to it with the Zelus logo as the background. A fancy-looking desk chair is parked in front. A wide television sits on what looks like a coffee table instead of the usual console.

Eli can't be sure, but among the sticky notes that decorate both of Peter's monitors, he swears he sees one with a list on it.

Fargo

Before Sunrise

The King of Comedy

The Devil Wears Prada

And a note next to it reads *La La Land*.

He can't help but smile.

There's no art, no pictures, no plants, no other furniture.

"Oh . . ." Eli pauses. "It's . . . nice?" he says at the same time as Peter says, "Unfurnished?"

"No, it's fine. It's a nice place," Eli reassures him, though he can't help but wonder how an apartment can truly be this bare after four years in the city.

"You can say it." Peter sits on the edge of the bed. "I guess I've just never cared about furnishing this place. Like who's going to . . ." Peter stops, staring straight at the wall ahead.

"Peter?"

"I think I'm going to vomit."

"Oh, uh . . ." Eli steps closer, taking Peter's hand. "Let's get you to the bathroom, come on." He hands Peter the last swallows of the bottled water, turning on the bathroom light and lifting the toilet seat. "Here, sit down."

Peter kneels in front of the toilet, bracing himself against the seat. "I'll get you more water," Eli says.

"Thank you." Peter's voice is quiet, but in the toilet bowl, it echoes plenty.

Eli steps into the kitchen and searches for any cups, finding only the red plastic kind with the Coke logo on the side that he's sure he's seen at pizza places. That's when he hears the first gag.

"Oh, God." Eli's stomach sinks. He grabs one of the cups and fills it up with tap water. He rushes back into the bathroom, leaving the water next to the sink, and sits on the edge of the tub, rubbing circles on the small of Peter's back. He doesn't let himself get too distracted, but he can't keep his eyes from wandering, noticing the skin-care items that litter the countertop. Eli even turns toward the shower, breathing a sigh of relief when he sees that Peter isn't one of those five-in-one Old Spice guys.

"Sorry," Peter moans.

Eli snorts. "Are you seriously apologizing right now?"

He swears he can hear Peter's smile. "Maybe."

Peter continues to choke, spitting a few times. Thankfully, when he finally pulls his head away from the toilet, the water is still clear.

"You okay?"

"Yeah," Peter promises. Eli watches as he brushes his teeth, gargling the entire glass of water.

"Here, go get ready for bed. I'll get you more water and some Advil."

Peter stands there, and for a moment, Eli thinks he might collapse when he starts to slowly fall forward. Instead, Peter remains upright, his head landing on Eli's shoulder. "Thank you."

Eli's taken aback, unsure of what to do before he finally wraps his arms around Peter's torso, scratching at his back lightly. "It's okay."

He lets Peter stay there for however long he needs, listening to the quiet breathing, feeling the rise and fall of Peter's back as Eli's nose fills with the soft, warm scent of Peter. They're silent, the sounds of the city so far away as to be barely audible.

"I think you're my best friend."

The words come out so soft, so sudden, that Eli's almost sure that he's hearing things. But he *knows* he felt Peter's warm breath on his neck, and he recognizes the sound of Peter's voice.

And his heart breaks.

He isn't sure what to say to that, and maybe he doesn't have to say anything. Maybe it's enough that Peter trusted him with that, maybe it's enough that Eli was here when he needed to be.

Maybe it's enough, and maybe it's not.

Eli almost doesn't want the moment to end, and when Peter steps back, Eli nearly pulls him back into the hug to hang on to him for just a moment longer.

But the urge passes, and Eli starts to mourn.

"Go get in bed," he says. "I'll be there in a second."

"Okay." Peter obeys, walking into the bedroom as Eli pauses at the bathroom sink, wondering just what went wrong in his life to lead him to this. He feels that thudding in his chest, that heat in his palms. He stares at the empty sink, focusing on the drain.

Eli takes a few deep breaths, forcing his tense shoulders to relax. He doesn't understand where all these feelings are coming from, and he doesn't like them.

He refills the glass and searches the medicine cabinet for a bottle of Advil, trying his best to loosen up before he strolls into the bedroom, averting his gaze when he sees Peter nearly naked, dressed only in his underwear.

"Oh! God, I'm sorry." Eli slaps his hand over his eyes.

"Hey, that's my line," Peter says hesitantly, pulling on a pair of gray sweatpants so quickly that he falls onto the edge of the bed.

"Here." Eli hands Peter the Advil and the water, watching as he gulps it down. "Now get under the covers."

"Thank you, again," Peter mumbles.

"It's okay."

"Can you just . . . sit here?" Peter asks him. "Until I'm asleep."

"Of course." Eli climbs onto the bed, sitting next to Peter with his back against the wall. Peter turns so he can look at Eli one last time before his eyes close, a smile on his lips, hands tucked under his pillow as he buries half his face in it.

It strikes Eli just how gorgeous Peter is, and he can't help himself from brushing a single lock of hair that escapes Peter's head, tucking it back. Eli wonders if Peter *knows* that he's beautiful. He hopes he does. Peter's the kind of person who deserves to know how bright his smile makes a room, how effortless it is to love a person like him.

And the inside of Eli's mouth turns sour.

He waits for Peter to wake up, but he's out like a light. For a while he lingers, watching Peter sleep. But he knows he can't hang around.

Eli feels his heart thudding in his chest as he slides off the bed, not realizing he left the Advil bottle right in his path.

"Shit," he whispers, waiting for Peter to wake up from the clattering of the pills. He kneels on the hardwood floor, gathering as many as he can from under the bed. It's when Eli pulls his hand free that he hits something and hears it topple over, something that sounds an awful lot like . . . books?

He yanks back the comforter carefully to peek under the bed. And just as he expects, he sees a floppy paperback. He carefully pulls it out and stares at it.

"*The Duke's Guide to Love and Lust*?" he reads quietly off the cover of the book, adorned with an illustration depicting two men in period-style clothing embracing one another. Well, *one* of them is clothed; the other has his shirt split open, showing off a perfectly oiled chest. A romance novel?

Eli grabs another book. This one is titled *Weather Man* and appears to be a meteorology-themed romance. Others with titles like *The Prince and His Pauper*, *Girlfriend Material*, *The Seven-Ten Split*, and *When Hairy Met Sally* have been hidden underneath Peter's bed for some odd reason.

Doing his best to hide the evidence that he snooped, even if it was accidental, Eli stacks the books back on top of each other and shoves them back under the bed, clueless about their order, hoping that Peter won't notice.

He wishes that he could watch Peter all night, keep an eye on him, but that'd be so very Edward Cullen of him, and Eli's not interested in being a stalker weirdo. So, instead, Eli slips his shoes back on, turning off most of the lights in the apartment before he steps back out into the garage, the gate automatically locking behind him.

He lingers there, in what little warmth the building entrance holds, before he walks to the bus stop, grateful that it's late enough at night that no one else is on the bus. The apartment is dark when he gets home, no lights under Rose's or Patricia's doors, so he decides not to bother them.

For a moment he considers starting a movie, putting on his headphones so he doesn't disturb his roommates, or grabbing his laptop to write about the night, but the former means he'd be going to bed far too late, and the latter just makes him feel guilty when he thinks about it. So, instead, Eli tiptoes to his bedroom, changing into sweatpants before he brushes his teeth then falls onto his bed, exhausted by the night.

He doesn't mean to dream about Peter, about the sweet honeysuckle sound of his laughter, or that barest hint of Georgia accent in his voice. He doesn't mean to dream about tracing his hand along that jawline, about feeling his hand in Peter's.

And he doesn't mean to dream about what it might be like to kiss him again, to taste his tongue, to feel his lips against Peter's and the heat of his breath, his teeth on Eli's throat, hands on his chest.

But he does.

And when he wakes up the next morning, he feels so much worse about himself.

Chapter Ten

Cruising, dir. by William Friedkin

"This is all you've got?" Michael asks, breezing through Eli's more recent notes. "There's nothing here."

"Well, I'm still finding it . . ." Eli starts to say, but the excuse dies on his tongue.

The dating article isn't nothing. He has a beginning, a good first chunk of writing that he's actually very proud of; the rest of the piece is less fine-tuned, a little rougher around the edges because he hadn't had the time to really string things together, make it cohesive.

It's just that it's fallen to the wayside. Both articles have, if he's being honest with himself. But at least his article about the queer South is looking close to readable.

"I like what I have, Michael," Eli tells him.

"You've had *two* weeks to deliver something more to me. Something beyond bullet points and boring nights at jazz clubs. I need details, Eli. The readers want the messiness, they want that *drive* to keep reading."

"I know."

"It doesn't seem like it. Maybe it's time to rethink this whole thing." Michael gnaws at the end of his thumb. "You're not as ready as I thought you might be, Eli."

"It's . . . it's tough. To write about," he tells Michael. "It's harder to quantify what's happening when there's nothing physical going on."

"I don't expect you to sleep with him. That'd be a conflict of interest."

Eli winces, breathing slowly. "No, I mean, there's no physical *change*. It's all mental, all happening in his head."

"That's bullshit." Michael stares at him.

Eli's used to Michael's directness, but this is new.

"Because I've read the emotion in your work, Eli. I've read your perspective, and you've never had a problem writing about something that you're passionate about."

Eli doesn't have the answer to a question Michael didn't ask. Though he's surprised to hear Michael speak so candidly about his writing. The most he ever heard in terms of feedback never stretched much further than *Our audience doesn't want to hear about this.*

"Well . . ." Eli begins to say. "What do you suggest?"

"You're not connecting."

Eli swallows. "I like to think that Peter and I are becoming friends."

"No, not with him." Michael points to his computer. "With the article. And right there, you just pointed out the biggest issue."

"That we're friends?"

"You're afraid to hurt his feelings." It's not a question, not a thought. Michael isn't wondering. It's a statement, a fact. Plain and simple.

Eli resents just how correct Michael is. God, it would be so much easier to hate Michael if he didn't actually have an eye for good editing and writing.

"The very nature of this article means that you're going to make an enemy of Peter, Eli. And you have to be okay with that."

"What if I don't want to be?"

"Well . . ." Michael hesitates. "Tough shit. I tell you what to write, and you write it. That's how things will work when you're a writer. And if you don't like it"—Michael nods to somewhere behind Eli, through the glass that surrounds his office—"the elevator is right there."

Eli rubs his hands on his knees.

It's complicated, hoping that this article will never make it to print, that Michael will miraculously see the error of his ways and publish the real article. Maybe this was a stupid idea, maybe Eli was ignorant to think that he could ever make a difference.

But Michael just said that he's read the emotion in Eli's voice, the perspective. Couldn't that be enough? If Eli just *showed* Michael what kind of difference they could make, then maybe he could convince Michael to let him run it.

"You have to be willing to offend people with the things that you write, Eli," Michael continues, and Eli listens. At the very least, this *is* sound advice. As a journalist, you can't ever be afraid whose feelings you might hurt, not when reporting the truth is the most important part of your job. "You can't be afraid."

"I'm not."

"This article says otherwise." Michael points with his pen to the monitor in front of him. "Prove to me that you're not afraid, and we can still put together something great here, Eli. You're a strong writer, with a strong voice. I just want what's best for you."

Another odd bout of sincerity where Eli expects it the least.

"Right." If only Eli could believe Michael's ever wanted what's best for him. "Okay."

"When are you seeing him again?" Michael asks.

A good question. It's been days since Eli and Peter have really spoken, let alone seen each other. Aside from a very awkward phone call where Peter apologized for getting too drunk, there have been text messages, but not much else.

Eli wonders if he's secretly been pushing Peter away.

Peter had apologized over FaceTime because a project at work was demanding attention that he couldn't give to Eli at the moment, even telling Eli all about a night where he'd been forced to sit in front of his computer for fourteen hours just to make sure nothing went wrong with one of his company's biggest—and confidential—clients.

And Eli accepted the excuse because the less time he spent with Peter, the less he had to write about, and the less time he had to think about what these new feelings mean.

"Three weeks," Eli says. "He has a Halloween thing with his coworkers—"

"Three weeks?"

"Nineteen days, really."

"No, see him this weekend. Make plans."

"Okay . . ." It's such a funny feeling, being told by your boss to go out on a date.

"Text him, see what he's doing, have fun. And write about it!"

"I will."

"Good, and call Fiorella's and try to get me a reservation, my wife wants to go there tonight."

"Understood." Eli nods. "Anything else?"

"You're good to go," Michael tells him, and Eli stands, eager to get out of the office. His eyes meet Keith's from across the office, but Eli does his best to ignore him. He pulls up the actual article.

LATE BLOOMING IN LAVENDER COUNTRY: GROWING UP QUEER IN THE SOUTHERN UNITED STATES

Growing up in a rural red state, in a small town of only 1,000 people, is in itself no easy feat. Coming of age as a queer teen in the same environment is even harder. An hour and a half outside of Atlanta, one of the few safe havens in Georgia, being openly queer in Athens is still considered taboo, a topic discussed in quick hushes and whispered gossip, as though the implication of being queer were comparable to the accusations of being a witch in the 1600s or a Communist in the 1950s.

In a town where no one is truly permitted to be their authentic self, queer children often grow up internalizing their own prejudices, hiding themselves and never finding the permission to live in a way that allows them to discover their true selves.

The adolescent years are so formative for teenagers, especially queer teens, who are so eager to find understanding and relatability. But what happens to those teens who are never given the chance to experience those moments? What do we do for those queer teenagers who grow into queer adults who have yet to craft these formative memories? What do we do for queer adults who have never dated, never been kissed, never had the opportunity to hold hands with their first crush? What are they supposed to do when the community meant to show support and welcome them with open arms shuns them for not having enough "experience"?

He has a handful of notes. Comments typed out, bullet points of things he wants to explore, questions that he wants to ask, his sources.

He thinks back to his conversations with Peter, when he talked about his friends and their late-night hangouts, about Mark and their memories with one another, about Peter's parents, how they craved the quieter life. These are the specifics he's done his best to work in, writing about Peter growing up in a town with a .01 percent Korean population. About how, even after moving to a larger city, Peter still felt uneasy about connecting to other Koreans or Korean Americans. How his queerness was a wall between them. How places believed to be safe havens for queer people can be so dangerous for people of color, queer or otherwise.

He does consider the weight of being a white man writing about the Asian experience. But Eli's done his hardest to present these parts of the article as strict fact, using the words that Peter himself has used to describe his terrible experiences meeting men whose dating profiles proudly proclaimed, "No fats, no fems, no Asians."

Not all of the pieces of the article are there, but it's shaping up nicely. Eli skims over paragraphs he's already reread, double-checking that he's changed the names of anyone he's written about.

Then he opens the other article about Peter.

THE BUILD-A-BOYFRIEND PROJECT

Over the last few years, it seems that dating apps have only gotten harder to use. These sites once meant to help users find the mythical "One" are now inundated with people searching for hook-ups or looking for thirds, and users who won't reply to a single message.

That was my experience. I tried every app I could find, even dedicated far too much time to the likes of Grindr and Scruff in the hopes of finding anyone worth my time.

I'd just about given up on my search, doomed to wander the streets of San Francisco single for the rest of my days.

Eli rolls his eyes at Michael's latest changes.

It was after a heinous string of bad conversations through apps that I agreed to be set up. I've never been one for blind dates, but I figured why not give this stranger a shot. So I did. To say that the night was a complete disaster is an understatement. He showed up an hour late, spilled food on me, and ignored me to take several phone calls. He even missed the movie we went to.

I left the date embarrassed and ashamed of myself.

"Laying it on a little thick, aren't we, Michael?" Eli mutters to himself.

He rereads what he has, cringing. Peter has gone from a socially awkward sweetheart to a douchebag with no common sense. Eli tried to slip in a few lines about Peter's experience growing up Korean in the South, the intersectionality of being a gay Korean man, having no one to learn the formative basics from, how he was never permitted to earn experience, never given the chance to mess up and learn until it was too late and everyone around him expected Peter to just know everything.

It's all struck through by Michael, the words a bright red as he tracks the changes to the document.

The article isn't even his anymore. There's nothing from him; even the voice is wrong. Michael's comments populate the margins, highlighting passages with notes like "I can feel the awkward" or "Clean this up, too clunky."

He looks at the Lavender Country article, trying to envision his own writing from Michael's perspective, wondering what might be too much, what might need refining. He spends an hour second-guessing his word choices, wondering if the introduction is too dated, if he needs to come up with something else.

At the very least, he can recognize that his writing is good. There's a connection there, a soul to the story. When he closes that window, going back to the Build-a-Boyfriend article, his stomach churns. He stares at the blinking cursor, almost as if the Google Doc is making fun of him. He holds the backspace key down, then switches to Ctrl+Z'ing when he goes a little too far and deletes some of the things that Michael actually likes.

His coworkers start filing out as the day reaches its end, gathering their things and muttering their goodbyes. Eli takes out his phone, staring at the last messages between him and Peter. Basic conversations about potential plans, more pictures of himself that Peter's taken.

Eli rereads their old conversations, and he begins to type.

> **ELI:** want to grab dinner tonight?

Eli stares at the message, hesitating. Then he deletes the text.

> **ELI:** hey, want to do something?

> **ELI:** the alamo in the mission is doing a horror marathon, want to see something?

> **ELI:** i don't think we should hang out anymore

> **ELI:** i'm an asshole, i'm sorry.

> **ELI:** it'd be better for both of us if we just stopped this whole thing.

He almost sends that last message.

Almost.

But then, a message from Peter comes in.

> **PETER:** I'm sorry, that big project is still going on, my boss has me working all weekend to make sure things go smoothly.

> **PETER:** Sorry

So there; it's decided for him.

ELI: it's okay.

ELI: i've been drowning in work too

ELI: we can hang out next week!

PETER: Yeah. I'll let you know how it looks.

He almost tells Peter what's going on, just to give Peter an out. But he can't bring himself to do it. Because he can't stand the thought of a world where Peter Park hates him, where he no longer has that smile to comfort him, where he no longer gets to hold Peter's hand, where he—

Oh.

Oh.

"Fuck me . . ." Eli almost throws his phone onto the desk before remembering just how little protection the rubber case grants him.

"Only if you buy me dinner first." Patricia sets down her purse, pulling up an empty chair like she always does.

"You know, despite us sharing the same plumbing, I'm not sure I'd be able to give you what you need," Eli says with his hands over his face.

"At least you know where the clit is. Not many men can say that."

"Fair enough."

"What's got you down, clown?" Patricia crosses her long legs, accentuated by the flared pants that she wears. Eli's always been jealous of just how effortless her style seems, how she bleeds confidence almost naturally, even though he knows better than anyone how long it takes her to get ready. "Boy problems?"

Eli thinks for a moment, hating how easy it is to see right through him. "Nothing, just . . . Michael . . ." Eli lies, almost daring to tell Patricia the truth, just to have someone, *anyone* who he could open up to about this. He almost does.

Almost.

But he can't bring himself to. "I don't wanna talk about it right now."

"So, it's Friday," Patricia says, leaning all the way back in the desk chair.

"That is a fact, yes." Eli types out a last-minute reply to an email from the marketing team before he shuts off his computer.

"We're doing something!"

Eli feels his mood sink further. "I don't know if I want to—"

"Come on, we've all been so busy this week. I'm cracking under this deadline and I've got a model demanding she renegotiate her contract, Rose had a kid lose their two front teeth thanks to a kick-ball to the face, and you . . . well."

Eli stares at his best friend, a blank expression on his face.

"Self-explanatory."

"Thanks," he grumbles. "I don't think I'm feeling tonight, though." It's the perfect night to sit on the couch, the window open, letting a nice breeze in while he bundles under a blanket with his heating pad, turning on a horrible horror movie while getting high, devouring the bag of Oreo-flavored popcorn in the pantry that's been calling his name all week.

"Come onnn!" Patricia whines, spinning back and forth in the chair. "We haven't gone out in *weeks*! Plus they're doing a Hallow-een thing at Mulholland Drive."

"I've never understood that place. Mulholland Drive is in LA, and whoever named it *definitely* didn't see the movie."

Patricia rolls her eyes so far back that Eli can see the whites fluttering. "God, you're such a dork."

"Why are they even doing a Halloween party?" Eli asks. He's

usually such a fan of the holiday, but it wasn't even on his radar this year. "It's not for weeks."

"What about gay people makes you think they'll only celebrate Halloween *on* Halloween?"

He has to give her that one. "I don't have a costume."

"Okay, I have angel wings you can borrow, you can be every basic white twink out tonight."

"I'm tired, Patricia," Eli tells her. That, and there's a twisting in his stomach that he can't escape, and the last thing he wants to do is go to a crowded club with pounding music that'll just make him feel worse tomorrow morning.

"For me?" She bats her eyelashes. "Just for a few hours, come on. We'll get Mickey's afterward."

Because the only thing that could make him feel worse than alcohol are boozy milkshakes. But Eli's never been able to turn down Patricia, no matter how hard he's tried. Back in college, she was constantly pulling him out of his dorm to go to parties and showcases that were far too cool for him. But if it wasn't for Patricia, he wouldn't have made any friends during those four years.

"Patricia . . ." Eli moans.

But she just keeps staring at him with those bright brown eyes of hers.

And eventually, he relents. "Fine."

"Yes!"

"But I'm not dressing up," he tells her.

And Patricia scoffs. "Neither am I. But I think Rose is doing something."

"Well, she's doing it alone."

* * *

"I still can't believe you made me do this," Eli mumbles as the three of them stand outside the entrance to Mulholland Drive. Despite his and Patricia's protests, Rose had three costumes laid out for them when they got back to the apartment.

Though given how Patricia had to dress as Annabelle, complete with pasty doll makeup that leaves lines painted on either side of her mouth and an awful pigtail wig, he figures he got off easy with his Freddy Krueger costume.

He already had the sweater after all; Rose just provided the glove.

"How long have you been planning this?" Patricia asks.

"A few weeks." Rose *sounds* like she's smiling, but the creepy Michael Myers mask she wears hides all expression on her face.

"How come Eli is the only one who gets a weapon?"

Eli peers at the knifed glove on his hand, the quintessential Krueger weapon with rounded plastic blades at the tips to avoid taking any eyes out. "You can have it if you want. It's too big for me."

"No!" Rose protests. "We're staying in costume."

At least she couldn't find a fedora, Eli thinks, grateful that his hair has been spared a flattening night.

The three of them stand in stark contrast to the sexier versions of characters that wait along with them for their turn to enter one of San Francisco's most popular queer bars.

"Plus, Annabelle doesn't have a weapon," Rose reminds Patricia.

"I could've been that other doll, the android thing."

Their IDs are checked at the door, the three of them pushing through the tight hallway at the front of the club, through the fake spider webs and past the stack of jack-o'-lanterns with scary faces carved into them.

The club, normally decked out in full rainbow regalia, has exchanged all of that for more spooky attire. Lights glow orange and purple, bats hang from the ceiling. Each cocktail served seems to pour out dry ice from the lip of the glass, and everyone is dressed up.

Eli passes by at least three Trixie Mattels and two sets of Sanderson Sisters before he, Rose, and Patricia find a tall bistro table where they can stand.

The last time he'd been here was with Keith, who'd dragged Eli along much as Patricia had tonight. But back then, Eli didn't mind doing things that made him uncomfortable. He didn't mind going on hikes, or trying new restaurants, because Keith was there next to him to reassure him. But now he can already feel his palms getting sweaty, though maybe that's because of the sweater and the too-large leather glove with fake knives attached to the fingertips.

"Smile!" Patricia shouts at Eli over the Lady Gaga B-side that shakes the very foundation of the club floor.

"I'm fine!" he says back. "I promise."

"Do you want a drink?" Rose asks.

"I can get them," he shouts. "What do you want?"

Armed with their orders minutes later, he navigates the perimeter of the sunken dance floor in an effort to get to the bar, walking past two women making out dressed in incredibly accurate costumes from the *League of Their Own* television show and a couple dressed like Daphne and Velma. He glances at the platform stage right in the center of the club where a local drag queen is lip-syncing to the song while dressed in an outfit made of sacrificed Kermit the Frog plushies.

"All right, time to change things up a bit," the DJ says, one song seamlessly blending into the next. "Everyone, I want you to please welcome to the stage your favorite drag triplets, Mary, Kate, and Ashley!"

Another Lady Gaga hit rocks the club just as Eli gets his drink order. He carefully does his best to balance the three cocktails in hand as he turns around. The rest of the club gets into the performance, throwing dollar bills at the trio, all of them dressed in bloody knitted sweaters and blonde bobs à la Drew Barrymore from her opening kill in *Scream*.

One twink rushes past Eli, angel wings knocking right into him, causing Eli to stumble into another person, and—more importantly—spill two of the drinks all over himself.

Only Patricia's is spared.

"Ah, dude . . ." he groans.

But the guy doesn't even notice. He just takes the hand of the man next to him and pulls him to the dance floor.

"You okay?" a voice asks, one that might normally sound low and mysterious but, thanks to the volume of the music, is booming. And yet, somehow, still sensual. A firm hand grips Eli's bicep in an effort to keep him from totally falling to the sticky floor.

"Yeah!" Eli shouts back. "Thanks. The glove makes it hard." He sets Patricia's drink on the counter and reorders Rose's, deciding he doesn't need that whiskey sour, pulling off the knife glove while he's at it and abandoning it on the bar.

"Do you need any help?" the mysterious man asks.

That's when Eli sees the man truly for the first time. Strong, taller than Eli by at least a foot, and dressed in a black jumpsuit, his cherub mask pushed to the top of his head so that Eli gets a full look at his handsome face, a line of scruff running along a jawline that Eli's sure would cut him if he traced it.

"Are you the killer from *Valentine*?" Eli can't help but ask.

"Oh, yeah!" The guy seems surprised. Eli swallows when he realizes just how pretty the man is. It seems so unfair, with his neat hair, eyes as sharp as his nose, plump lips. "You're the first person to get that."

"I love that movie."

"Me too. I mean . . . you probably could've guessed," he says with an awkward smile.

Eli feels that fluttering in his stomach. Despite the jumpsuit covering 90 percent of the man's body, there's no doubting that underneath he's strong. Almost as if the outfit would rip if he flexed the right way. And it's so easy for Eli to pictures the muscles, glistening with sweat from the heat of the packed club.

"So . . . do you need help carrying those?" The man nods to the two drinks. "Unless you don't want to share them."

"Oh, I mean . . . they're for my friends. Not for me." He puts out the feelers. Okay, so maybe he didn't want to come out tonight, but if it means he gets to leave with a beefy guy like the one in front of him, he certainly won't complain.

At the very least, that means he gets to leave the club early.

One eyebrow goes up. "Just friends?"

Eli nods, biting at his bottom lip. "Yep. Just friends."

"Well, let's go meet them."

The man takes the drinks for Eli, following as Eli navigates around the dance floor again, finding their table miraculously still free, which is impressive considering that Rose and Patricia are nowhere to be seen.

"Oh, well . . . they *were* here," Eli says, his voice a little softer now that they're further away from the speakers.

"That's okay," the stranger says. "Now I get you all to myself."

"Someone's a flirt." Eli sets his hand on the table.

And the man puts his on top of it, wrapping Eli in this safe web. "Only with guys as cute as you."

"Pfft, I bet you say that to everyone you meet."

"No, I don't," the man dares to say.

For a moment, Eli weighs his options. He hadn't even wanted to come out tonight, and yet, here he is, standing in front of a man who is *very* interested in him. And Eli's just as interested. He's always had a thing for men bigger than him, who look like they could throw him around given the opportunity. Hopefully in a sexual context. Though he's never gone on the internal journey to really parse out what that means exactly.

So why is there this voice at the back of his brain that he doesn't have the time to listen to, not when a strong hand is placed at the back of his neck, pulling him into a kiss? The stranger's lips taste like honey and whiskey, the flavor bitter on Eli's tongue as it slips so easily into his waiting mouth.

He leans against a nearby column, letting Eli fall forward, almost into his lap where he can feel the growing erection underneath the jumpsuit.

The same hand along his neck drifts up, tangling in Eli's curls, scratching at his scalp slowly, comfortably, luring Eli in as Beyoncé sings about a boy blowing up her phone, and the song pauses to play the call between Drew Barrymore and Ghostface. Eli barely has time to consider where the man's other hand is going as it leaves his cheek before he feels it firmly on his ass.

He also can't help the gasp that escapes past his lips.

"I wasn't lying," the man says, his voice warm in Eli's ear.

"What?"

"When I said I don't call just anyone 'cute.'"

Eli takes Rose's drink from the table, some melon liquor and lemon juice cocktail colored a toxic neon green, then he downs it in a single shot, cherry and all.

"Well, I've never met a serial killer I've wanted to sleep with before," Eli teases, pulling the cherub mask on top of the stranger's head down. "So I guess there's a first time for everything."

"Oh!" The man laughs, situating the mask more fully on his face. "Does this do something for you? The mask?"

"Maybe." Eli's head already feels fuzzy, and he remembers that he didn't even eat lunch today and none of them thought to grab dinner before they headed out, so the alcohol is rolling around in an empty stomach. "But we can leave it off for the time being."

"Agreed." The man takes the mask off with a single pull, discarding it on the table, totally forgotten. "Makes it easier to kiss you." He traces a finger along Eli's jaw until he reaches Eli's chin, putting forth *just* enough pressure to get Eli to tilt his head up toward him, giving the chance for their lips to meet again. This time there's a fever to the kiss, a heat that boils Eli's stomach. He moves his legs ever so slightly, doing his best to straddle the man despite their verticality, his thigh rubbing against the length in his pants.

Fuck me, Eli thinks, barely able to form a coherent thought.

He dares to let his hands find the stranger's chest, feeling the solid muscles underneath. He wants this stranger. It's been *months* since he last felt the touch of another man, and he's hornier than he wants to admit, even to himself.

He wants to go back to this man's apartment, let him do whatever he wants to Eli's body, painting him in harsh purple marks as his teeth graze his skin. He wants to follow him back to his bed, to walk home sore tomorrow. He wants to take him into the bar bathroom, eagerly locking the door behind them.

He wants it all.

So why does it feel so wrong? Why does his stomach twist and churn, why does he feel so . . .

Guilty.

That's the word.

"Come on." The stranger takes Eli's hand.

"Wait, I . . ." Eli tells him. "My friends."

The stranger smiles. "We don't have to leave the club to have a little fun." His voice is low. "I'm not sure I could make it back to my place anyway."

Going pliant in the man's grip, Eli allows himself to be led toward the exit, veering off into the tight hallway to enter one of the bar bathrooms. Eli's never been this type of person before. Sure, there were times that he and Keith hooked up when the setting was less than opportune. They'd had to keep their voices down while Eli was fucking Keith in his dorm once, another person on the other side of Keith's bedroom door during a party.

But he'd never done anything publicly; he's never thought of himself as an exhibitionist, and perhaps he'd never even consider this if the melon liquor wasn't working its way through his system.

The moment the door opens and he's pulled inside the single-person bathroom, his ass planted on the cool seat of the toilet, he feels himself sober up. Despite that ache in his thighs, that heat pooling in his stomach, despite how vulnerable he feels in this man's arms as he's pulled in for yet another kiss, only one name comes to his mind through his admittedly horny fog.

Peter.

What would he think about Eli if he walked in? Would he feel betrayed? Would he feel hurt?

And Eli has to ask himself why Peter would even care. They're not dating.

They're not.

It's all fake. It's all for Peter. It's all for those articles.

But that doesn't absolve the guilt.

The man huffs, unzipping his jumpsuit in one fluid motion, letting the top half fall to his waist. For a moment, Eli wants to run his tongue down the hairy trail that disappears below the zipper, and he can't ignore how obvious it is that this man came out to the club without an inch of underwear on, no waistband to be seen.

"Ah, fuck . . ." The man's hand goes to Eli's curls, urging his aching mouth further and further to wrap around him.

But even as Eli wants to lose himself in the moment, to become someone other than himself just so he can enjoy the experience, he just can't.

He can't bring himself to do it.

"I . . ." Eli lets his hands drop from the jumpsuit.

"What are you waiting for, cutie?" The man's voice is so much clearer in the privacy of the bathroom.

"I, uh . . . I'm trans," he whispers. Not what he meant to say, but it's—unfortunately—pertinent information. Normally he couldn't be bothered to out himself, to "warn" the guy, but he doesn't want to set an expectation that might lead to him getting hurt if it isn't met. He'd already taken the time to formulate an escape plan if one was needed, noting that the door would unlock from the inside with a simple turn of the handle, grateful that the bathrooms are *right* next to the entrance, that there seemed to be plenty of security and witnesses in the club.

"Okay?" The man stares down at him, his confusion obvious. It's never not funny to Eli how cis people never have to consider that something that should be as exciting and fun as sex is a potentially dangerous act for trans people.

"That's not a problem, right?" Eli asks.

"Only if it is for you," the stranger tells him, running his hand along Eli's cheek; it's such a tender expression, juxtaposed with the heavy thudding in his chest.

"So, it's okay that I have a vagina?"

"As long as you've got a hole for me to stick my cock in." The man grabs his dick through his jumpsuit, showing off the length. "Then I'm good."

Romantic, Eli thinks, wetting his lips, his hands on the jumpsuit, ready to do what he's been aching to do for months now.

But he can't.

The stranger stands above him, his hands worming their way into Eli's hair, almost as if he's pleading with Eli silently to *finally* grant him the release they're both chasing.

"I . . ." Eli begins to say, his words lost.

"You okay?" the guy asks.

"No, yeah . . ." Eli says, nodding. "Actually, no. I'm not."

The jolt of adrenaline that brought him to the bathroom in the first place is long gone, now replaced with a terrible cocktail made of embarrassment and self-loathing.

He *wants* this.

He wants to do this. He wants to taste this man, to hear the whispered curses because even if Eli wasn't confident in any of his abilities as they relate to the bedroom, he *knows* he can give a damn fine blowjob.

He wants that power, to hold this man in the palm of his hand as he takes in each and every inch of what a stranger he didn't know twenty minutes ago has to offer him.

But he can't.

And the pee on the toilet seat he accidentally sat on certainly isn't improving his mood. But he can't recall ever feeling worse about himself. He and Peter aren't a couple; it doesn't matter. The relationship that he shares with Peter isn't real, they aren't dating.

And yet he still feels like an asshole for doing this. Like he's somehow cheating.

How fucked is that? Eli asks himself, unable to keep a scoff from slipping out. "I'm sorry, dude . . . I can't do this."

"Oh, well . . . That's okay."

Eli feels an immediate relief that the man doesn't act like he's owed something.

"You can, uh . . . you can pull your jumpsuit back up now," he says, averting his eyes from the thick sprout of pubes still visible.

"Right, right." The man does exactly that, doing his best to adjust his erection.

"I'm sorry," Eli says.

"It's okay."

"There's just this guy, and I . . ." Eli doesn't understand why the words slip out the way they do. It's not like this complete stranger cares about whatever it is that he's battling.

"Oh, like a boyfriend?" the man asks, zipping the jumpsuit up finally, not that it makes his erection any less obvious.

"You don't have to listen to me," Eli says, shaking his head at the pure absurdity of the situation. "You can go or whatever."

"No, it's okay," he tells Eli. "Besides, I, uh . . . kinda have to wait for this to go down."

"Well . . ." Eli leans further onto the toilet, preparing himself in case he might have to throw up. "No, he's not my boyfriend; we weren't even friends until weeks ago. But I'm helping him learn to date."

"Oh, that seems . . ."

"Complicated?" Eli finishes for him. "Yeah."

"You've got feelings for him?"

"No! God, no!" Eli says, a little too quickly for his own comfort. "Well, I . . . I don't know."

"You think these feelings you were faking might've become real?"

Eli knows it's the truth; he's known this for days now. Maybe he's even known it since that first redo date with Peter, when they kissed that first time.

But knowing the truth and admitting it to yourself are two entirely different things.

"I'm going to take that as a yes," the man says.

Eli shakes his head slowly. "Am I that easy to read?"

"I have to have something to show for those eight years of medical school," he says. "You care about this dude?"

It's such a simple question, and yet, the answer is even simpler. "Yeah, I do. He's a good person, and I guess in another world . . . I'd want to be his friend." There's something left unsaid, though. Even to Eli's own ears, he can hear it.

"You could try telling him the truth."

"Right," Eli scoffs, the realization of just *how* ridiculous his current situation is dawning on him. "That's so easy."

"If you care about him, it should be," the stranger says.

If only life were so simple. Eli could have his cake and eat it too.

"Thanks . . ." Eli sighs, standing. "I'm sorry again, for the, uh . . ."

"It's fine, don't worry about it," the guy says. "I'm probably going to jerk off the second you leave."

"Oh, well . . ." Eli doesn't really know how to respond to that. "Enjoy?"

"Thanks."

"And if you haven't, check out *The Prowler*, it's a good slasher."

"Right, yeah." The man gives Eli an awkward nod.

Eli doesn't whisper a farewell or wave goodbye to the guy. He just opens the door as carefully as he can, as if he's afraid of being seen in the bathroom with another person, then closes the door once he's back in the hallway. A second later, the click of the lock makes him smile briefly, and then remorse settles into his stomach like a rock.

"What the fuck is wrong with me?" He pushes his hair out of his face, pulling out his phone and sending a text to the apartment group chat.

> **ELI:** i'm going to head back home

Eli weaves his way through the people still filing in, growing more and more desperate to get out the closer he gets to the door, his breathing becoming labored in a way that chills his throat, making it harder and harder for him to do anything at all besides push costumed people out of his way in a frantic attempt to reach the door tucked under the bright red EXIT sign.

Eventually, he breaks through, stepping out into the cold night, the rush of air coming as a relief to his warmed cheeks, grateful for the sweater of his costume. Eli takes his time, walking toward the bus stop down the block. The bus arrives just in time, the doors hissing open. Eli stands there, staring at the bright yellow rails and the blue plastic seats. Then he steps away from the door, back toward the stop so the driver knows that they can continue along their route.

Maybe he doesn't want to go home, not yet, at least. Of course, there's really no walking *all* the way home; the bus ride alone took half an hour.

A walk will be nice, though.

So that's what he decides on, tucking his cold hands into his pockets. But it's pleasant enough out, despite the breeze. He wishes that he knew what just happened, why the last twenty minutes feels like a total dream, why he feels like he needs to tell Peter the truth even though there's no reason for Peter to care about what Eli does with his free time. Or *who* he does.

It's fine, it's fine. It's not like any of it matters. In a few weeks, the article will be ready, it will be published, Peter will be "fixed," and Eli will have his staff job. They'll both have the things that they want.

The problem, he realizes, is that he never asked himself what happens after.

"Fuck . . ." Eli whispers to himself.

He walks and he walks and he walks. He considers dipping into a bar to grab a drink, or a nearby diner to get dinner. He even thinks about going into another club he walks by, the glowing red lights painting an image in Eli's head that might just lead to another bathroom rendezvous where he could fuck these feelings out of himself. He's depressingly horny enough to consider it for too long before he starts to feel sick again.

His eyes breeze past the still-open businesses until they start to peter out, Eli stumbling into a more residential area of the neighborhood until he realizes that he's just a few blocks away from Peter's apartment.

And then he sees an all-too-familiar face.

Well, an all-too-familiar back of the head.

He isn't sure at first, as he stops in front of a laundromat, but there's no mistaking those expansive shoulders and the way they slump forward. He considers walking away, finding the next bus stop. Peter's busy, reading a book with a bright orange cover while waiting for his laundry to finish.

But there's that pull, that urge. He *wants* to be around Peter.

And oh boy, does that feel so incredibly dangerous.

Eli walks around the corner, finding the open door, sliding right onto the bench that Peter's sitting on without much effort at all.

"Come here often?" Eli asks, trying to tease Peter.

"God!" Peter jumps, his book flopping to the floor with the cover on display. Eli doesn't look at it, not directly, but from the cover alone, he can tell it's one of Peter's hidden romance novels. "Eli! Holy crap . . . you scared me."

"I can tell."

"What are you even doing here?" Peter asks, snatching up the book and hiding it in his empty laundry bag.

"I was out with my roommates, but . . . I wasn't feeling it. So, I left the club to take a walk."

"Oh . . . where'd you go?"

"Mulholland Drive. They were doing a Halloween thing, as you can tell." Eli motions to his costume.

"Are you . . . dressed as someone?"

"Freddy Krueger? Hello?"

"Who's that?"

"You really haven't seen any movies, have you?"

"Guess not."

"It's okay," Eli promises. "Most of the *Nightmare* movies aren't that great. You're not missing out on much."

"Huh."

"I'd ask what you're doing here," Eli says, relaxing into the pretty uncomfortable bench, "but I guess it's obvious. Unless you're some kind of weirdo who gets off on camping out in laundromats."

"Yeah . . . right." Peter forces a laugh.

And Eli can't help but recognize that something is different; something's changed. Maybe that's fair, considering it's been a week since they had a real conversation.

"So . . ." Eli taps on his knees.

"So?"

Eli hates this, how quickly things have turned awkward. And any attempt he can think of to make things a little easier seems like the wrong move.

"How is your project going? At work."

"It's okay," Peter tells him, still not meeting Eli's eyes. "We're behind—my supervisor wants these tests done by February, which wouldn't be a problem except we have six hundred to run and they each take thirty minutes, and so far, none of them are going well, so . . . we're already behind."

"Yikes . . ."

"What about you?"

"Oh, you know. Getting coffee, making copies, going to meetings, resisting the urge to climb up to the roof and throw myself off the building."

"So, usual stuff?"

Eli cackles. "Pretty much."

Peter hums, focusing on his hands, clasped together. "I'm sorry," he says. "For being so distant."

"It's okay," Eli reassures him. "I owe you just as much of an apology. We've both been busy with work."

"It's that, and . . . I don't know, I think I was worried that you wouldn't want to see me after that whole thing at the lounge."

"Oh, that? Please, Peter. You're by no means the first drunken person I've ever had to take care of. Before I met you, I was spending my Friday nights wrestling bottles of pinot away from Rose."

Peter laughs at that, and Eli lets his guard down under the familiar sound.

"Besides, it was at least ninety-five percent my fault," he teases.

Eli dares to reach over, closing the distance between him and Peter. He almost risks going further than putting his hand on top of Peter's where it rests on the edge of the bench, but he stops himself.

"It's all right, I promise you," Eli says.

Peter smiles, and Eli melts, the warmth almost enough to negate the gust of wind that blows in through the open door.

"You okay?" Peter asks as Eli takes his hand back, tucking his arms under his armpits.

"I'm fine, I just always get cold. It probably doesn't help that I bought this sweater from Spirit Halloween." So it's basically paper-thin.

"Yeah, you have cold hands."

"Well, excuse me!" Eli feigns offense. "Not all of us are born with iron-rich bodies."

"Maybe if you ate more spinach," Peter teases him.

"Fine, make fun of me in my time of need," Eli whines. "I'll just sit here, brave enough to keep you company while I freeze to death."

"I didn't say you had to stay," Peter says.

"But you know you'd rather have me here."

Peter doesn't say anything, but the smile on his face is enough of a reply as he leans over to his other laundry bag where Eli's guessing he's stashed his clean whites because he hands a few T-shirts to Eli to hold while he digs.

"Here." He takes the shirts back and gives Eli a gray hoodie, still warm from the dryer.

It's cold enough that Eli can't even pretend to turn it down, slipping his arms through the sleeves easily. "Thank you."

"You should layer more," Peter says, pulling the drawstring on his bag closed. "You'll catch a cold."

"You sound like my mother."

"Well, she's right."

"Yeah, yeah." Eli buries himself in the hoodie, breathing in the warmth, but even that simple act is not without its costs as he inhales that familiar cedar scent. Here, lingering on the hoodie, it's concentrated, like a poison working its way into Eli's veins.

"Thank you."

Peter simply nods. "How's the article going?"

Eli blows a raspberry with his tongue. "I'm stuck." Rather than daring to explain himself, Eli pulls his phone out of his pocket, going to the article and handing it to Peter to read.

"'Lavender Country,'" he reads, his accent coming through softly.

"I thought it was a good title."

"I like it." Peter goes quiet as he begins to read, his thumb slowly scrolling to carry him down the page until he reaches the list of bullet points that Eli has yet to elaborate on. "Huh . . ."

"'Huh'?" He straightens. "What 'huh'? Is there something wrong?"

Peter opens his mouth again, and then closes it.

"Peter, please. I'm begging you. If you have feedback for me, *please* give it. This article is about you."

"I think . . . I think the article is sad."

Eli finally feels himself unclench.

"And maybe that was the point, for where you're coming from."

"No, you're right." Eli takes his phone back, speed-reading the article.

"Don't get me wrong, I mean, it's not like it was a utopia. But everyone thinks that the South is totally backward, full of nothing but homophobes and racists and transphobes. But . . . I have happy memories too."

"Why don't you tell me?" Eli offers, opening the voice memo app on his phone. "Can I record this?"

Peter nods. "How do you want me to do this?"

"Just like we've been doing. Tell me about the positive things you experienced growing up. Tell me how you feel about how others represent where you're from."

"Well . . . I mean . . ." Peter seems to think. "I know it's popular to shit on where I come from, especially deeper South states like Alabama or Mississippi. When I came here, I was so excited to know other Korean people, to feel like I had a community. And I had friends in my program at Berkeley, but sometimes . . . I don't know."

"Keep talking through it," Eli presses; he doesn't want Peter to let go of this.

"Sometimes, they'd surprise me by making fun of my accent, especially when it came through when I was speaking Korean. They'd call me a hick and laugh at me, ask if I'd just gotten back from the cornfields."

"Not Korean enough for the Korean community, not gay enough for the queer community."

Peter nods. "It was easy to feel . . . stuck. But it wasn't all bad in Comer; there were nice people too. Southern hospitality always has a way of coming through. And the food, the food was amazing. Y'all on the West Coast don't know a thing about pulled pork."

"I can't argue with you there."

"And there was this yearly jazz festival that my parents would take me to, that's where I fell in love with it for the first time. Country music too; some of it's ass, but classic country is so heartfelt. And there were plenty of kind people too. Our neighbors always loved me, they said I was such a cute kid. And things were . . .

I don't know, quiet. Everything here, or even in Berkeley, it's so loud. Everyone's going all the time, no one says hello to each other really."

Eli nods, not saying anything to let Peter get his thoughts out naturally.

"There's so much good about the South. The music, the people, the community. I spent so many years of my life feeling isolated, but I also remember the people. I never knew a stranger when I lived in Comer. Even when people were mean, it was like . . . I hate when people make fun of the South for being backward when here, people will do everything behind your back, under a veil of kindness, or like they're doing you a favor. At least back in Georgia, people would say that stuff to my face. I never had to second-guess their intention."

Peter peers ahead at the washing machines before his gaze finally settles back on Eli.

"Sorry, I feel like I ranted."

"No, don't apologize. That's what we're here for, right?" Eli hesitates, thinking about how amazing all of these details will be for the article. Then he has to pause, remembering that's not the most important thing right now.

"I love where I come from. It's not perfect, not by a *long* shot. But nowhere is. And I think it's important for anyone, for any community, to remember and appreciate where you've come from."

"That's beautiful, Peter."

"I just hate that the South gets such a bad rap. Like yeah, things are bad there, but things are bad literally everywhere else. Plus, we have Bojangles."

"I'll have to take your word for that, because I have no idea what a Bojangles is."

"I'll take you to try it one day." Peter grins, and Eli tries not to focus too hard on the fact that Peter is apparently planning vacations back home and he wants to take Eli with him.

Eli puts away his phone. "You know I'm going to have to ask what you're reading."

Peter's expression sinks. "You really don't have to."

"Well, considering how quickly you threw it in your laundry bag there, I'm going to guess it's some steamy erotica," Eli teases, because he can't ever help himself.

"It's not."

"Come on, we all have our vices. What is it, a dinosaur and a priest?"

"How would that even work?" Peter asks.

"Use your imagination," Eli tells him. "It's a powerful tool."

"No dinosaurs."

"So, there *are* priests, sexy. Is the father getting a little hot under the collar for Jesus?" Eli even pulls on the neckline of Peter's hoodie.

"No priests either."

"Okay, okay . . ." Eli hesitates. "Would you be mad at me if I said that I saw your romance collection?"

Peter pauses, clearly unsure of how to react to Eli knowing what he has to consider a deep, dark secret.

"How did you—"

"I dropped the Advil bottle in your room when you'd passed out, and some of them went under the bed and I know that sounds like a made-up excuse so I really hope you don't think that I'm just lying to prove that I didn't snoop around your apartment or something because I didn't," Eli says the words in one long breath, only realizing what he's done when he's finished speaking. "But I am sorry, for finding the books."

"It's okay, I guess."

"Can I ask *why* you hide them?"

"You know . . . I think about that every time I finish one of these and I reach for a new one." Peter dips down, pulling the book free of its smelly prison. "Or when I go to the bookstore and I buy two other books I don't care about just so I can hide the books I actually want to read."

"Please tell me you've never done that," Eli pleads.

Peter hesitates.

"Peter . . ."

"It only happened once—after that I learned to only buy books online or read them on my phone." Peter smiles, and Eli hopes he knows that he isn't making fun of Peter. "But if you ever need a book on World War I or a biography of James Buchanan, you can borrow them from me."

"I think I'm good."

Peter shrugs. "I donated them to the library already."

"You didn't answer my question, though," Eli continues. "Why do you hide them?"

"Because . . ." Peter lets his head hang low. "It's embarrassing."

"Why?"

"'Cause I'm a grown man reading romance novels. Isn't that reason enough?"

"No, I don't think it is. In fact, if you were interested in women, I'd go as far to say that'd be in your favor."

"It's cheesy, though." Peter takes the book, flipping through the worn pages. It's clear just from the spine that this is either used or a library copy, or one that Peter has read over and over again.

"Peter, honey. Lots of people don't read *at all*. Besides, you're allowed to read what you want. It's your money and your time. So long as you enjoy it, who cares?"

"You don't think it's weird?" he asks.

"Why would I?"

"I don't know." Peter shrugs, and he lets a nervous giggle out. "Actually, at one point in time I was using them to try and learn how to date. Before you came along."

"Seriously?"

Peter nods. "It's probably a good thing I stopped, or else I might've turned into some alpha male douchebag."

"Hey, come on. Sometimes douchey guys are hot."

"Seriously?"

"No, I was kidding."

Peter laughs again.

"Besides, there's no way that reading romance is any worse than what's going on up there." Eli dares to tap Peter's temple. "Romances are cool."

"Have you ever read any?" Peter asks.

"No, but I've watched plenty. The classics are classics for a reason. *When Harry Met Sally . . .*, *Mamma Mia!*, *Love & Basketball*, *In the Mood for Love*, *The Watermelon Woman*."

"I've heard of a few of those," Peter admits.

"Color me surprised!" Eli exclaims. "But you shouldn't hide the things that you're interested in. If someone doesn't like that you read romance, then they're not someone worth your time."

"No, I know. I guess . . . I don't know. It's a force of habit," Peter admits. "I hid the books I read when I was younger, at home with my parents."

"Can I ask why?"

"Well, for most of them it's because they were queer. Of course that ended up being for nothing, but I was so terrified to tell my parents about being gay, and I thought they'd know if they saw me reading those books even though they literally never cared about what I was reading."

Eli's heart breaks just a little more.

Peter shifts so that he can face Eli. "Can I tell you something without you laughing at me?"

"Of course. I'm not going to laugh at you, Peter."

"No, like . . ." Peter's eyes finally meet Eli's, and Eli can see something different there now. Something new. "I, uh . . ." He pauses, still so unsure of his words, clearly. Eli wishes that he knew the right words, the correct words that could convince Peter that everything is okay, that Eli's not here to judge him.

Then again, isn't that exactly what he's here to do? Isn't that the entire basis of their relationship? Eli judging Peter, "fixing" him.

"I always wanted to be a writer," he finally says. "A romance writer."

"Oh . . ." Eli's brows furrow, and his face betrays him without meaning to.

"See." Peter lets out a frustrated sigh. "I knew I shouldn't have—"

"No, no! Peter, I swear I wasn't judging you." Eli reaches for him again, the warmth of Peter's skin against his spreading slowly. "I was just surprised."

"Is it that weird?"

"No, I mean, Peter . . . I want to be a writer too," Eli tells him. "I just thought it'd be something more serious than that. Not like—not that it isn't serious if it's your dream. But I expected . . . I don't know, like a terminal-illness-diagnosis level of seriousness."

Way to go, Eli, he thinks. *Taste that foot in your mouth?*

"I'm sorry," he says. "That came out so wrong."

"No . . . I mean, yeah. Kinda." Peter chuckles. "My parents told me that I'd never make a living that way, that I needed to be practical and actually do something with myself. That's why I picked computer science in a tech city. I didn't think I had the argument skills to be a lawyer. And blood icks me out." Peter shudders.

"Why romance?" Eli asks, hoping that he doesn't sound judgmental. He stands, following Peter to the dryers, taking a few of the items and folding them carefully, even if they'll just be shoved into a laundry bag for their journey back to Peter's apartment.

"I guess . . . growing up, I never got a love story for myself, especially not in Comer. I always felt like I was looking over my shoulder. Afraid that someone could just sense that I was gay," Peter admits, his voice low, almost like he's ashamed. "I found these stories of people falling in love, sharing themselves with each other. Some of them were gay, some of them Korean, sometimes both, but more often than not, I couldn't find books that replicated my experience, the things I felt. It was just nice to read about something happy. I always knew what to expect. They meet each other, resist their feelings, one or both of them mess up before they reunite and have that big final moment where they admit their feelings for each other. They got the happily ever after. It made me feel safe."

He sighs, this time trying his best to laugh, to add levity. It doesn't work, not on Eli at least.

"Which sounds so stupid when I say it out loud."

"No," Eli tells him, folding a muted orange shirt. "It doesn't."

Peter shrugs. "It's okay."

"No, it's really not."

"I wouldn't have made money as a writer. My work is terrible, and most writers can barely scrape by with their advances. Plus, I'd have to like . . . the idea of even one person who isn't me reading my stuff scares the shit out of me, much less potentially thousands of them." Peter closes his eyes. "I guess I just got tired of having a dream I was too afraid to chase after."

Eli pauses, Peter's words hitting him hard, wondering just what he feels in this moment. Because it's not just sympathy . . . it's understanding. He remembers all too well those feelings that loved to creep their way to the forefront of his mind as he edited an essay or article, staring at his screen and wondering *just* what he's doing, if it's worth it, if anyone would ever actually read any of it.

It's oddly a relief to see so much of himself in Peter, at least in this moment. He knows the feeling of chasing a dream for so long only to be disappointed time and time again, the fear that builds, wondering if he's good enough or if everyone's been lying to him.

"Thousands of readers? Getting ahead of ourselves, aren't we?" Eli jokes.

"Yeah, maybe."

"I was teasing, Peter."

"You're right, though," he admits. "It's best to just . . . keep it to myself. At least we'll always need people to code stock in a warehouse."

"I don't think that's even close to true," Eli says. "But you know what people *will* always need?"

Peter looks at him. "What?"

"Happy stories about people falling in love," Eli tells him. "The world is desperate for them. Always has been, always will be. Story-telling is our oldest art form." That's what he's told himself, at least. What he had to say to keep himself moving forward.

Even when he didn't believe it all the time.

There's the most delicate hint of a smile. "Thanks, Eli. I appreci-ate it."

Eli feels that sinking in his stomach, wondering if he's given Peter false hope that he shouldn't have. Who is he to tell Peter to chase his own dreams when he can't even leave *Vent*?

"Tell me about it," Eli begs, scooting closer. "Your idea."

"You don't want to hear it."

"I do." Eli looks him right in the eye, so Peter absolutely knows that he's telling the truth. "You're my friend, Peter. I want to hear about what you're working on."

"You really don't."

"Okay, then . . ." Eli has to think for a moment. "Then this is a dating lesson. In sharing yourself, your vulnerabilities, dreams."

Peter looks so unsure.

"If you're going to date," Eli elaborates, making up his excuse on the spot, "you're going to have to share parts of yourself. Even the scary parts that you think are ugly. It's what it means to fall in love—getting to know someone and being brave enough to share the pieces of yourself that you'd want to hide."

"But that's . . . this is—"

"Am I not teaching you how to be a better boyfriend?"

"Yeah . . ."

"Then this is a lesson."

"What if it weirds that person out? Or like . . . they don't like it?"

"Well, firstly, I think your brain is being mean to you. People *want* to be writers, Peter. If someone thinks that you're weird for wanting to follow your dreams, no matter what they are, then they're the ones not worth your time. Not the other way around. You deserve people who like you for you."

The smile that Eli is looking for finally appears, and it's the first time all night that he feels warm again. "Thanks, Eli."

"You're welcome, Peter. Now—" Eli sets down the last of the folded clothes, leaping up to sit on the empty dryer he's been standing in front of. "Tell me this idea, I want to hear all about it."

"This Korean guy is fresh to the city, he's never dated anyone, never kissed anyone, wants to paint but works at a job he hates, never been in love before."

"Sounds very autobiographical," Eli tells him. "So, what's the romance? Who does he fall in love with?"

"A friend asks him to go to a family wedding. Both of them have felt the pressure from their families to date and to get married, so they arrange this whole situation just to get their parents off their backs. Of course, while they're faking, they start to have real-life feelings."

"A tale as old as time," Eli sings.

"You think it's interesting?"

"Yeah, I'd totally read it," Eli tells him. "Even though I don't read fiction, or much at all beyond things for research."

Peter nods. "I have a full manuscript. Ninety thousand words, but I just . . . can't really get myself to open the document again. To start editing it, send it to agents."

"There's a fear of rereading your own writing." One that Eli's all too familiar with.

"Yeah, it's like that."

"I know what you mean." Eli kicks his feet back and forth. "Back in college, when I actually got the chance to write, I was *terrified* to give my editors the articles I'd written. No matter how many times I did it, no matter how many times they told me my work was good, that I only needed to change a few things. It never got any easier."

"It's just . . . if I finish this, if I edit it and send it out to people . . . what if it's still not any good? What if people hate it? I could get an agent, a publisher could buy it, and readers could still hate me and the book."

"Well . . . just because you spent a lot of time on something doesn't mean that it'll be good, or that people have to appreciate it."

"Thanks . . ." Peter tries to laugh.

"Let me finish my point!" Eli tells him. "*But* . . . as long as you like what you've done, as long as you can stand by what you've written, that you can say you're proud of it, then that's all that has to matter. The people out there who want your writing will follow."

"You think so?"

"I know so," Eli tells him, doing his best to ignore his own words.

But now, maybe Peter will take that chance, maybe this conversation will convince him to chase after his dream, to edit his book.

To do the one thing that Eli's never been able to do.

Chapter Eleven

The Doom Generation, dir. by Gregg Araki

It feels irresponsible for Eli to follow Peter back to his apartment just a few blocks away, one of Peter's laundry bags thrown over his shoulder.

"I can carry both," Peter reminds Eli for the dozenth time.

"You know . . ." Eli grunts, readjusting the bag. Under any other circumstances, he might've passed it along to Peter. It's amazing how a man who seemingly only knows how to dress like a frat bro could own so many clothes. But Eli isn't going to give him the satisfaction. "I'm perfectly capable of carrying laundry. *My* laundromat is two whole blocks away."

"Okay . . ." Peter hums. "We're near my place, it's just up this hill."

"Hill?" Eli stops, readjusting the bag to get it off his back. "Why didn't you drive?"

"Because it's only five blocks," Peter says, maneuvering up the street without much effort at all. "Plus, I'd have to worry about parking. And walking is fun!"

"Says you."

Peter beams at him as he continues up the hill.

They make it back to the apartment after Eli takes a short break on the corner. Peter unlocks the door and flips on the lights, seemingly less embarrassed than he was the first time he showed Eli the apartment. Certainly less drunk.

Peter finally takes the bag, setting them both on his bed. They'd folded most of the clothes at the laundromat, but there's no doubt that the way Eli slung the bag from shoulder to shoulder has left them a little crumpled. He follows Peter into the bedroom, picking a spot for himself on the edge of the bed because there's literally nowhere else for him to sit other than Peter's desk chair in the other room. Peter huffs, pulling out a bundle of hangers from his closet. Eli takes a few for himself.

"I've been dying to ask. You've been here for four years; how can your apartment be *this* bare?"

Peter shrugs. "I guess I just never took the time to decorate."

"Peter, there's decorating, and then there's having basic human necessities. You don't even have a couch, or real nightstands, or a shelf for the books you're hiding under your bed."

"I have a nightstand." Peter steals a look at the IKEA table that isn't actually a nightstand, before he hangs a few of his shirts. A quick peek inside the closet tells Eli that he keeps his clothing organized by color. Starting with black and white and then properly getting into the ROYGBIV. Of course, most of the closet is black and gray. "And it's not like I'm bringing anyone here, so . . . I guess I never saw the point."

"Well, we'll have to fix this." Eli stands, gliding toward Peter's closet and adding his hangers, organized accordingly. "There's a lot of nice antique and thrift shops in the area. And you can always order stuff from IKEA if we can't find it there."

Eli doesn't realize just *how* close Peter is to him at the moment, a few precious inches away as he watches where Eli puts the clothing.

"You can't invite anyone over when you don't even have a real bed frame, Peter."

"It's real enough." Peter reaches, and for a moment . . . just a *moment*, he swears, Eli thinks that maybe Peter is about to press his hand to his chin, to tilt his face up and capture him in a kiss just like the masked stranger at the club.

But he doesn't; instead he reaches past Eli, moving one of his forest-green shirts down a few spots. "This one goes here."

"Sorry . . ." Eli breathes deeply.

"Do you want to look now? For furniture?" Peter asks, stepping back toward his empty laundry bags and lining the clothes hampers in the corner of the bedroom with them.

Eli falls forward onto the comfort of the bed. At the very least, Peter didn't skimp on a nice mattress and duvet set. The bed almost calls to Eli, singing some magical lullaby to pull him in. "No, I'm beat."

"Too much dancing?" Peter asks him, staring at Eli's shape on the bed.

"Not at all," Eli promises. "I, uh . . . There was this guy?"

He says the words slowly, waiting for Peter's reaction. Which he can't see because the man is currently bent over face-first in his laundry basket attaching the bag liner with Velcro.

"Oh, yeah?" Peter says, his voice calm. "Was he cute?"

Eli doesn't know what reaction he wanted.

Bullshit, he thinks.

He wants Peter to be pissed at him, annoyed that he'd make out with another man and follow him to the bathroom in the hopes of getting laid. If Peter gets angry enough, he might end this. Cut this all off for him, take the reins for once and decide that he's had enough of Eli for no real reason at all.

"Yeah, when he wasn't wearing a mask, at least."

"A *mask*?" That's what gets an actual response from Peter, his head whipping around.

"It was a Halloween party, remember?"

"Right, right," Peter says, standing up straight. Eli watches him carefully as he walks to the head of the bed, taking a spot with his back against the bare wall.

"My friends wanted to go out, and I thought maybe, just maybe, I could get laid or something."

"What happened?"

Eli swallows, wondering how Peter might react if he told him the truth. At least, one of the truths. "I just wasn't feeling it. He didn't want to go back to his place, he just pulled me into the bathroom."

"Really?"

Eli nods. "It's whatever, I can go back to my apartment and dig around in my toy box until I find something."

"Your toy box?" Peter smiles. "Why would you call it that?"

Eli can't hold back the cackle that escapes, holding his hand over his own mouth as tight as he can, but it doesn't work. "I mean, that's what it *is*!"

"But it's so . . ." Peter shudders. "Wrong." The two of them laugh together, but the sound dies quickly, their gazes meeting before Eli darts his away.

"Can I ask . . ." Eli rests his back on the wall. "Have you had sex with anyone since Mark?"

Peter shakes his head. "Like, I've masturbated, but yeah . . . with Mark, that's it. Sometimes I wonder about that inexperience, just like everything else I haven't done before, and if I'll know how to do it right again when the time comes."

Eli lets his head fall against the wall. "I get it. I mean, when you think about it, sex is really weird. There's so much preparation that goes into something that should be so simple."

"Right." Peter turns away, hiding his blush.

"I mean, is sex something that you're *interested* in?" Eli prompts. "You know, not everyone is; sometimes people are repulsed by just the idea of it, or totally indifferent."

"I am interested," Peter admits. "I get . . . aroused is the right word, I guess. And, like, I *want* to have sex with people. I'm just . . . I guess I'm scared, and what if I'm not good at it, you know? What if . . . what if I'm bad, and it turns someone off from me? I think that's been a whole other layer to . . . this."

Peter motions to himself.

"I've heard so many stories about sex and being intimate with someone going wrong. And the last time I had sex, I was sixteen, and I know it wasn't good. Neither of us knew what we were doing."

Eli doesn't like how his brain goes right to how good those details will be in his articles. That's not what this is about.

He hesitates for the briefest of moments before he decides to go for it. "You know," Eli starts to say, "the second time I had sex with Keith, I threw up on his dick."

Peter turns to him in surprise. "Are you lying?"

"God, I wish I was." Eli feels the heat along his cheeks. "I was on my knees, giving him a blowjob, and he got a little *too* into the face fucking, triggered my gag reflex after a bit. I'm grateful that it was just spit and slobber."

"What did he do?"

"Made sure I was okay, apologized, and then we both just sat there on the bathroom floor and laughed about it. We watched TV in bed after."

"I guess that's good."

"Keith would never let me live it down." Eli's own words haunt him, and he can't escape the bitterness that rushes through him, even if it's one of the happier memories he still has. "That's important with someone you get intimate with. To be able to laugh, to appreciate the awkwardness that can happen instead of letting it hinder the experience."

"I guess things just seem so serious in the porn I watch."

Eli's ears perk up at that. "You're watching porn? Well, now I *have* to see what gets your rocks off."

Peter smiles. "Please."

"Porn is all fake, even the kind that tries to be as real as possible. You shouldn't judge your experiences based on other people's anyway, porn or otherwise." There's a silence that stretches, and for a moment, Eli wonders if he said the wrong thing somehow.

"Do you . . . do you miss him?" Peter dares to ask him. "You don't have to answer that question if you don't want to." These words come a little hurriedly, as if Peter's realized he's crossed some invisible line.

Of course, he's surprised, to say the least. He wouldn't have expected Peter to ask such a personal question.

"No, it's okay. It's just . . . tough to answer." Eli lets out a low, soft sigh. "I do, and it hurts to feel like I still do."

Eli pauses, and out of the corner of his eye, he can see Peter staring expectantly. He doesn't say anything, though.

"He gave me seven years of himself. He gave me seven years of feeling as if I belonged, like I was wanted. He made me feel the way no other person did. And it still hurts that it's just gone, that I don't have one of my best friends anymore."

"I think that's what scares me the most, about all of this," Peter says, crossing his legs on the bed. "That someone could just decide to . . . end it all like that. It's scary."

"Yeah, it is," Eli says to him. "But, you know . . . that's just a part of life. Something that you have to get used to."

"How do you do that?" Peter asks.

Eli looks at him. "When I figure that out, I'll let you know."

Peter lets out a low, pitiful laugh, and Eli follows the lead to not make the situation awkward. But as the sounds die on their lips, the silence stretches before them, neither of them clear on what to do next.

"Is falling in love really as scary as it sounds, Eli?" Peter dares to ask.

"It's terrifying," Eli admits. Because it's the truth. And it might be one of the few times he gets to be truly and totally unbiased with Peter. Because he really does believe that. "But that's what makes it special, what makes it truly one of the greatest feelings in the world."

Peter dares to smile, if even just for a moment.

"I hope I get to experience it one day," he says.

And Eli has to look away. "Yeah . . . I hope you do too."

* * *

Eli closes the apartment door behind him, peeking out the window when he walks through the empty living room. Peter's still out there in his car, having offered Eli a ride home. The angle is *just* right for the two men to be able to see each other if Peter leans over into the passenger seat. Eli waves at him, and Peter waves back before he shifts into drive, pulling slowly down the street.

Despite how late it is, and how he feels exhaustion deep in his bones, Eli knows that he'll never get to sleep, not with the unease that rattles around in his brain, so he sheds his outfit, only then realizing that he still has Peter's hoodie.

He doesn't mind, though. He doesn't even bother putting on sweatpants, just undresses down to his underwear and puts the hoodie back on, wanting Peter around him as he walks through the silent apartment half naked, catching the scent of Peter every so often.

Eli busies himself, pulling up the John Carpenter classic *The Thing* for the Halloween ambience before he grabs his laptop and goes to Google Docs.

There, right at the top, are both articles about Peter, half completed. He has an entire night of details to add. The laundromat,

Peter's dreams of being a novelist, that shared fear of failure and your life's work amounting to nothing. He writes about Peter's empty apartment, the lack of interior decoration, how Peter felt trapped in a career he never wanted because he thought pursuing his dreams was too risky. He writes about expectations in the queer community and how people like Peter are rarely afforded grace for things entirely out of their control.

Then, knowing just what Michael will say . . . he deletes those last paragraphs.

He sits there on the couch, his laptop precariously perched on the arm, staring at his blinking cursor, at the little *M* icon in the corner that shows it's been shared with Michael.

He could delete this entire article.

He could. It'd be simple to wipe the entire project off his Google Drive, marching into the *Vent* offices and showing Michael what he's actually been working on. He goes back to his article on Peter.

The real article.

He reads through it again, and again, and again. And then the thoughts begin to appear, and he starts to question every single decision, every word. He wonders if the throughline is strong enough, if he's shifted the focus *just* enough away from Peter to make this an article that hundreds of people can relate to. And the more he reads it, the more he despises everything he's ever written.

Without meaning to, he puts his sleeve-covered hand to his mouth, chewing on his thumbnail softly. He breathes in the fresh scent of Peter's hoodie, and something coils in Eli's stomach. There's that heady aroma, that warm tonic scent, the earthiness. It reminds Eli so much of the approaching fall, the bright orange-and-red leaves of the trees straight out of a Hallmark movie crunching under his feet.

He closes the article, his eyes catching the list of things he's written, the pieces that he's poured his heart into only for Michael to reject them outright under the excuse of "not meeting the brand." And any chance of selling them elsewhere was gone with the non-compete clause he signed upon accepting the job at *Vent*. Hours upon hours, days, weeks, months of researching, writing, editing, all totally and completely useless.

He scrolls further, his fingers moving quickly as the tiles come across the screen the deeper he goes.

UNHOUSED NUMBERS ON THE RISE, MANY OF THEM QUEER YOUTHS

TAX INCREASES DOING NOTHING TO HELP CITY

SHELTERS ARE MEANT TO PROTECT THE UNHOUSED, SO
WHY DO MOST PEOPLE FEEL UNSAFE STAYING IN ONE?

CALIFORNIA GOVERNOR SIGNS TRANS PROTECTION BILL
AMIDST COUNTRY-WIDE ATTACKS ON TRANS YOUTH

Five years given to *Vent*, given to Michael, all under the promise that someday, he'd achieve his dreams. He'd get that chance he wanted, finally be able to prove to himself and to everyone around him that he accomplished something.

But how can he tell Peter to follow his dreams when he can't do the same for himself? It's so easy to tell Peter to go for it, to take that leap. Submit the book to agents, let them sell it, give the book the chance to find the readers that so desperately need it.

Why can't he do that for himself? Why can't he leave *Vent*? Why can't he take that leap, leave behind this place and this team that he knows is holding him back? If he left *Vent*, of course things would be rough for a while; he'd have to budget hardcore, make sure he had enough savings set aside, find a part-time job to work while he focused on sending out his articles and essays.

So why can't he do it? Why can't he leave this bubble? Why can't he follow the very advice that he gave to Peter?

Because he's afraid.

Because he's a hypocrite.

He considers the article for a moment, staring at it until the blue light starts to sting his eyes and he finally blinks. He exits the article, going to Google and typing in "what to do with my life?"

In an instant, he's faced with article upon article about "Finding the key to life!" How to find your passion, your friends, your perfect job. How to align your chakras, how your life is already decided depending on your zodiac sign or the time you were born. There are life-improvement classes where someone will take your money just to give you advice you could get for free, and thousands upon thousands of self-help and lifestyle books.

Eli just sighs, closing the laptop. He slips it between the couch cushions before he turns the movie off just at the scene where Charles Hallahan's chest opens up and rips off Richard Dysart's arms, walking into the bathroom and leaving his glasses on the back of the toilet so he can wash his face.

Just be happy.

That was what his father used to tell him when Eli was younger. He'd meant it not in a "just get over it" sense, but more that Eli should pursue the things that made him the happiest.

So long as you're happy, that's all that matters in this life.

It was a familiar mantra, one that Eli kept close to his heart. Because those were the last words that his dad had said to Eli, when he'd dared to come out to his father just hours before he finally passed away.

He couldn't live with himself, knowing that his father would die believing that Eli was someone he really wasn't. Of course both of his parents saw the writing on the wall for years.

He'd asked his mother to leave the room, just so he could tell him the truth.

Eli's father had smiled at him. A smile that Eli never wanted to recall ever again, not with the breathing tubes in his nose, not with the sickly pale yellow his once-golden skin had turned. But it stuck in his memory like the tumors that slowly sucked the life out of his father, cursing him with an image that he felt desperate to forget.

"My boy . . ." his father had said. "Do you have a name for me?"

"Eli," he said slowly. "Because of Elijah Wood."

It was embarrassing, but shame wasn't an emotion Eli was capable of at the moment. *The Fellowship of the Ring* was the first movie Eli's father had taken him to see in theaters, way back when he was far too young to understand even a fraction of what was happening. Elijah never felt right, but Eli . . . He'd loved that name for years before he'd chosen it.

His father looked at him. "I love it, my boy, my Eli . . ."

Eli had tried his best not to cry, but that was the moment that he broke, when he fell to the bed with his father, resting his head on the very same pillow.

"Promise me one thing, Eli?"

"Of course."

"Never settle for a life that you don't deserve, because a boy like you deserves everything he's ever wanted."

"I don't know if that's true, Dad." Eli had tried his best to wipe his tears away.

"It doesn't matter what you know. This is what *I* know." His father pointed to himself. "And I know that you're a brave boy. And you deserve to be happy."

"Dad . . ."

"Do that for me, Eli . . ." His father's voice was rough, scratchy. "Just live your life in a way that makes you happy. Please."

"I will, Dad."

If only he could see Eli now.

He'd be so disappointed in me. How had he lived his life happily? How had he made his dad proud? He's basically lived paycheck to paycheck, worked a job he hates, held on to the heart of a man who'd crushed his. All in exchange for helping another man find the person he's meant to be with.

In what world had Eli respected his father's dying wish?

He's not happy, that much he can admit to himself. He's not proud of the work that he does, he's not proud of how he lost himself in his relationship with Keith, he's not proud of how he's spent weeks misleading Peter. Even Michael, whom he's been lying to under the hope that he'll be given even a crumb of a chance to make something of himself. He can't even pretend to be brave enough to share the real article with Michael.

Eli keeps the hoodie on as he crawls into bed, that ache stirring in his stomach again. Eli pulls his thighs closer toward himself, his fingers slipping so easily past the waistline of his underwear.

He's not proud of how easy it is to imagine Peter on top of him, whispering sweet nothings into his ear as he works himself inside of Eli. He's not proud of how he imagines that it's Peter's fingers instead that find his clit, rubbing softly at first, his chest rising and falling slowly. He's not proud of the way he wants to taste Peter, to pull his hair tight, to run his hands along that strong back, his fingernails leaving crescent shapes on Peter's soft skin.

If nothing survives what they have together, Eli could only hope that the marks would remain, as a reminder of just how grateful he is. To have had the privilege to live alongside someone as honest and as kind as Peter is a luxury that few are afforded.

And as Eli's back arches off the bed, his hand wet with release, his nose buried in Peter's hoodie, breathing in the smell that he prays is etched into his memory, he mutters a name that does not belong to him.

One name. The name of the man who took his heart without permission.

"Peter . . ."

The euphoria of his climax washes over him before dissipating in an instant, the shame settling in as he realizes just what he's done. Eli stands and washes himself off in the bathroom before he hides underneath the covers once again, unable to let go of Peter's hoodie even in the spell of embarrassment that he feels dragging him down.

It's that scent that lulls him into an uneasy sleep.

One where he dreams too much about a sweetly shy Korean man who deserves more than Eli could ever give him.

Chapter Twelve

But I'm a Cheerleader,
dir. by Jamie Babbit

This is boringgg . . ." Les groans, rolling off the couch.

"*The Hunchback of Notre Dame* is a classic! The backgrounds and art direction, the voice acting, the *songs*!"

"You would've made an amazing theater kid."

Eli shakes his head, turning off the movie. It might've been a selfish decision to throw on one of his comfort films. Though he's not sure what it says about him that one of those movies is a historical animated drama about religious crusades through Paris. Or that his favorite song from the movie is about lust and Catholic guilt.

"What do you want to watch?" Eli asks.

"I don't want to watch anything," Les says.

"Okay, well . . . did you do your homework yet?"

Their silence is enough of an answer.

"Go get your books."

"It's algebra," they grumble, picking themselves up from the floor.

"Well, it's a good thing I'm excellent at math."

"Really?"

Eli snorts. "No, not one bit. But we can figure it out. Google is free."

Les sits at the coffee table, pulling out their notebook and flipping to the appropriate pages as Eli sinks onto the floor next to them. It's not the night he wants, stuck babysitting his little sibling while his parents have their own date night, but Les's typical baby-sitter had to pull out at the last minute, and Rue had been talking for weeks about the fashion exhibit at SFMOMA that Patricia had gotten tickets for.

Eli looks over Les's shoulder at the problems they're expected to work out, marveling at just how much he's managed to forget after not being in a math class for years.

"Do you think I did this right?" they ask.

"How the hell am I supposed to know?" He's talking to them as much as he's asking himself. "Isn't there an answer key in the back of the book?"

"Nope."

"Okay, give me a second," Eli tells them as he begins to copy the problem into Google on his laptop to see if anyone has solved the same problems.

"Isn't this cheating?" Les asks.

"Don't worry, chances are *very* high that you'll never be doing this kind of math as an adult."

"So, you're saying I shouldn't care about school?"

"No!" Eli sort of shouts without meaning to. "You should try in school, *always*. Give it one hundred percent of your effort."

Les smiles. "But you just said that—"

"And look at where not caring about math has gotten me," he says. "I'm an assistant. Do you want to be an assistant?"

"Not really, no offense."

He can't help but smile at them. "None taken. Do your home-work." Eli scrolls through the results on his search, thanking what-ever God might be up in the clouds when he finds an entire PDF of the textbook's answer keys. Despite Les's pleading to just let them copy all the answers, Eli remains firm, only using the answer key to check Les's work behind them.

"Okay, yeah . . ." Eli's eyes bounce back and forth from the textbook to the laptop. "I think you've got everything." Though the work that Les has shown is complete gibberish to him.

He doesn't even notice the text bubble that appears in the corner of his screen.

"Someone texted you," Les says, leaning forward. "Can I see it?"

"What?" Eli turns his screen away from them to read the text.

PETER: How's your night going?

Eli leaves it unanswered.

"Is that your boyfriend?"

"Why do you care?" Eli asks.

"Because Mom's been talking about how you haven't introduced us to him."

"Yeah, well . . ." Eli swallows, cutting himself off without a point to be made.

"Is he nice?"

Eli dares to spare his half sibling a glance before he turns back to their homework. "He's very nice."

"Are you in love with him?"

Eli doesn't reply. Because he can't.

He knows that he can't possibly be in love with Peter. It's only been a few weeks, and these aren't the kind of circumstances that deserve love.

He's here to write an article, and fix Peter. That's it.

"Why are you so curious about my love life?" he asks.

Les shrugs. "I dunno."

Eli eyes them, squinting carefully. "How much did Mom pay you to snoop?"

"Twenty bucks," Les says, quickly giving Rue up. "And I get to go to Andi's sleepover next weekend."

"Mm-hmm . . ." Eli hums, closing the PDF, his open Google Doc with Peter's article taking its place.

"What's that?" Les asks.

"Nothing." Eli minimizes the window. "Have you practiced tonight?"

"Not yet."

"Okay, well, go do that. Mom said at least an hour."

"Ughhh." Les rears their head back onto the couch cushion.

"Go, go!" Eli shoos them. "And I'll know if you just put on some YouTube video of someone else, so don't try it."

"How can you even tell?"

"Superhuman hearing." Eli taps his ears. Besides, Les's YouTube account is attached to the living room television, so he can always check the video history. "Now go. Scram."

"Are you going to talk to your boyfriend?" Les sings.

"Leave!" Eli shoos them away.

"Fine!" Les stands up, grabbing their things and stomping down the hallway toward their room. Before he sits back on the couch, Eli listens for the familiar sounds of Les unpacking their cello, the hum of the strings as they begin to play.

He'd never admit it to their face, mostly because the kid can't take a compliment to save their life, but they're good at what they do. Incredibly so. And Eli has to try and not feel jealous over his mother not pushing him into playing an instrument when he was younger; by now he could've been perfecting his skills for nearly two decades.

No, instead he's a writer who can't write, with an article he's been staring at for a week now with nothing new to write about. He's plateaued.

Michael's noticed too, sending Eli an email at the end of nearly every day asking for updates, waiting for Eli to respond to the comments and questions left lingering in the margins of the document.

He's nearing the end of both articles, reading through them again and again, becoming more and more familiar with the story arc that he's built. Even in the fake-dating article, he's done his best to paint a picture of growth, of Peter coming out of his shell, of adapting to Eli's advice. And soon Peter will meet his parents, and Peter will prepare himself for another first date.

And that'll be it.

Eli goes back to his Lavender Country article. He knows it's good; he may not believe that in the moment, but if he places himself outside of the article, looks at it with an objective perspective, the article is well written. It tells the story of growing up queer in the South, of the hardships faced just trying to be yourself, the violence and microaggressions that people like Peter deal with.

But Peter's words have now injected so much warmth, so much culture. Eli dove headfirst into researching the food that he and Peter had discussed, the jazz musicians that Peter had grown up listening to. Peter had been willing to share a few pictures from his long-abandoned Facebook page, and Eli had to avoid gushing over teenage Peter Park, with his full cheeks and awkwardly sweet smile.

There's a familiarity with the people around him, one that only comes from growing up in a town where everyone knows everyone else. Before this entire project started, Eli had a stereotypical view of the Southern United States, that it was a place of racism, homophobia, and bigotry.

And of course those things do exist there, just as they exist everywhere in this country. In this world, in fact. No place is a paradise, just as most issues in the South aren't the fault of the people who live there but those who represent them, who redraw election maps to get the results they want, who refuse to allow voting to be a necessary and accessible outlet for every citizen's voice.

The South has a dark history, just as every part of America, and there's no separating it from that. It's something Eli doesn't want to shy away from.

Yet the more Eli grows to understand where Peter came from, the more he can appreciate it.

Maybe the article will go live. And maybe it'll attract the hundreds of thousands of readers that Michael promised Eli. And maybe he'll get that staff writer position, and maybe he'll have reliable income. And maybe he'll be able to work his way up, build a portfolio. And maybe in a year, he can create a decent enough portfolio to move on from *Vent*, find a place for himself at a different publication. One where he can write about the things he's passionate about, the things that matter to him.

It's such a funny feeling, isn't it? Weeks ago, Eli rejected the simple idea of getting close to another person. Because he didn't think it was worth it anymore.

Now, without permission, Peter has found his way in, made a home in Eli's heart, trailing gasoline as he stepped inside.

If only he hadn't fallen in love with the match.

The soft smile, and the feeling of Peter's firm hand in his own, and the sound of Peter's laugh. How he gets lost in the music he listens to, and how he doesn't always get sarcasm. His dedication to what he does, even if he doesn't love it. The way he hides the most precious parts of himself, and how he dared to show them to Eli.

Eli buries his face in his arms, breathing slowly. He's not in love with Peter Park. He can't be.

But when he stands outside of himself, he knows the truth.

It's another two hours before his parents come home, both of them clearly just a touch tipsy as Rue wraps Eli in a tight hug.

"How was Les?" John asks.

"Usual; we worked on their homework. They practiced, went to sleep about twenty minutes ago."

"Thank you so much for doing this so last minute, honey," Rue says as she immediately goes to take her earrings out. "I owe you big time."

"It's okay, not like I was doing much else."

"Well, you and Peter could've had a nice night out." Rue gives Eli a sympathetic look.

"Right . . ." He averts his gaze from both of them, listening as John reaches into a cabinet to get a bottle of whiskey and three glasses out.

"You want a drink, Eli?" John offers.

"Oh, I'm good. Thanks, though."

"Come on! It's Weller, double barreled." John sets the glasses down, clearly not taking no for an answer.

"Speaking of Peter . . ." Rue pulls her hair free of the bun she'd walked out of the house in. "When am I meeting this boy?"

Eli swallows. "He's pretty busy."

"Oh, come on, how about this weekend? We're heading into the city, Les wants to go ice-skating!"

"I've got plans," Eli says.

"Cancel them," Rue sings, waving Eli off. "I want to meet him!"

"I just don't think it's such a good idea." Eli takes the whiskey, sipping on it slowly as he's directed by John. It's a good whiskey, he'll give John that, but he can't appreciate the full flavor, not with the sour taste that already lingers on his tongue.

"Why? Did something happen?" she asks.

"No, it's just that . . ." Eli lets his words drift off into the ether. "It's nothing. I just don't want to go."

The moment hangs, empty, before Rue turns to John. "Honey, can you give us a moment?"

"Yeah!" John says, like he's come to some large epiphany. "Of course. I'll go shower. Have a good night, Eli. And thank you again!"

"Of course," Eli says slowly. His eyes follow John as he exits the large kitchen, but Rue's gaze stays focused on her son's face.

"Mom . . ."

"What's wrong, Eli?"

"Nothing. Why do you have to assume that something's wrong?"

"Well, for one thing, I'm not assuming." Rue's glass clinks against the granite bar as she sets it down. "I know you think that you're impossible to read and all mysterious and private or whatever. But I've known you since the literal moment the doctor had to cut open my stomach to get your stubborn ass out after seventy-two hours of the worst pain of my life."

"You really don't have to remind me of that every single time."

Rue raises her eyebrows. "But I will."

At least with her dress on, she can't show him the C-section scar this time.

"Well, nothing's wrong," he repeats. "I'm fine."

"And years ago I might've believed that. Because I wanted to give you the space to tell me about yourself on your own time. But you're an adult now, Eli. And adults talk about their feelings."

He despises the way that his mother sees right through him. At least she'd given him the space to be invisible at one point or another, eventually admitting months after both of his coming-outs that she'd suspected something but she'd wanted to give Eli the space and time to figure out the pieces of himself that he wanted to find alone, doing her best to show him that she'd be there to help when he needed it.

Of course, the hospital visits, the medical bills, the funeral, the ongoing years of grief, they'd slowed things down.

But Rue never faltered in being there for her child. And he's so unendingly grateful for that.

"I . . ." he begins to say, wondering just which truth he might give her, which one might slip out without his permission. "How did you know that you were in love?" he dares to ask her. "After Dad died . . . how'd you know how to fall in love again?"

"Oh, wow . . . deep question . . ." Rue picks up Eli's whiskey and downs the rest of the drink in a single swallow.

"I'm sorry, I didn't mean to—"

"No, no. I mean . . ." She sets the glass down again. "I know that we never really discussed it."

"Right."

There were those messy weeks when Eli resented his mother for moving on "too quickly." At least, what he'd determined to be too quickly. He remembers the promises that John wasn't a replacement, that he wasn't out to get anything from Eli's mother, that he genuinely loved her.

But they'd never talked about it more than that, besides the apologies that Eli had offered in return when he realized it'd been so long since he'd seen his mother as happy as she was on her and John's wedding day.

"In all honesty, Eli . . . I didn't know." She lets out a long breath, moving around the counter toward her son, her hosed feet padding softly on the wooden floors. "I had no idea that I was 'ready to love' again, or however you want to phrase it."

"It just happened?"

"Maybe . . . It's hard to know. There's no sign, there's no sudden sensation, you just *know* when you're ready, even if you might not actually feel that way."

"But wasn't it tough, after Dad?"

"Oh." She lets out a sad laugh. "It was impossible. When you think that you have your person, when you think that you have the one that you're supposed to spend the rest of your life with and they're taken away from you in such a slow, cruel way . . . there's a feeling you can't explain. It's a nothingness, a void. You're just . . . you're numb, apathetic."

Eli doesn't know the feeling as well as his mother does. His father was his father, but that's just it.

He was his father.

To Rue, he was the man she adored, the man that she'd shared decades of her life with, the man that she'd built a home with, raised a child alongside. He was the man who encouraged her to pursue her dreams at the press, who listened to every complaint that she had, who bought her flowers even on her good days because he loved how she smiled when he gave them to her.

Whatever Eli's father was to him, it can only pale in comparison to the man he was to his mother.

"And after he died, everyone called me a fighter." Rue scoffs, rolling her eyes. "I was a fighter for dealing with it, for 'coming out the other side,' for surviving when all I ever had to do was sit at his bedside and make sure he never felt alone as life ate away at him. John mentioned once in the group sessions that he'd gone through the same thing. He was a 'fighter.' Because he's the one who survived, he was the one who was alive. He admitted that it bothered him, and a lot of us shared the sentiment, but then he said something. Something that's stuck with me for years, ever since he said it."

"What?"

"He said, 'There's more than one way to be a fighter.'" Rue smiles. "And I think about that almost every single day."

"Huh . . ."

"And if there's one thing I know about you, Eli . . . it's that you're a fighter."

"Mom."

"You are." She puts a soft hand on top of his. "I know that you doubt it, but you are. You're a fighter because of your smile, and because of your heart. The way you care about other people, and about yourself."

Eli balls his other hand into a fist under the counter.

"Maybe that means less to you coming from your mom, but I like to think I know you better than anyone." She rubs the small of Eli's back.

It's been years since she held him this closely, since he felt this protected by her warmth.

The last time he can remember was after the funeral, when they'd both returned to the apartment by themselves, and for the first time in a week, they were totally alone. None of Eli's aunts or uncles were racing around, freezing the surplus of food that people brought for them, no one was asking about funeral arrangements that hadn't been made yet, no one was asking Eli how he felt, promising that his father's suffering was over without admitting that Eli's had just begun.

They sat on the couch, his mother holding him close as they turned on *Who Framed Roger Rabbit*, his father's favorite.

For the first time in weeks, they both laughed.

And Eli felt like he was home.

Now, he tries to feel the same sense of comfort, the same sense of belonging. But he knows what's coming. What'll happen if Peter decides that he doesn't want to be around Eli anymore? Every part of Eli's being tells him that Peter would never do anything like that. But he never believed Keith would break his heart either.

"Now." Rue continues to rub the small of his back. "I forget, do you already own ice skates?"

Chapter Thirteen

The Watermelon Woman, dir. by Cheryl Dunye

"A re you okay?" Eli asks while he and Peter are on the bus, both standing because every seat on the bus is filled, the evening riders packing themselves in like sardines.

"Yeah, yeah . . . I'm okay," Peter says quickly enough to tell Eli that he is, in fact, not okay. "I'm fine. Are you?"

"You seem more nervous than the first time we went out. The *real* first time, when you spilled soup on me."

"I'm fine, I promise. Totally okay."

"Iced Americano," Eli says to him.

Peter flushes. "Is something wrong?"

"Yes, you're not telling me the truth."

"There's nothing to tell," Peter tries to assure him. But Eli likes to think that he knows Peter well enough by now to tell when Peter's lying.

"Peter," Eli whispers. The bus is one of the newer fully electric models the city has been rolling out slowly, meaning it's almost eerily quiet, despite the amount of riders, and it's all too easy for their conversation to be eavesdropped on by the other riders. "Please, tell me the truth."

"I . . ." Peter opens his mouth, staring down at Eli before he turns away in embarrassment. "Yeah, I guess it's your parents."

"We don't have to meet them," Eli tells him. "I can call and cancel; we can do this some other time. They'll understand."

"No, I don't want to do that. Besides, isn't this supposed to be some big test for me?"

"It doesn't have to be," Eli says. "Not if you feel like you're not ready."

"I just . . . What if they don't like me? Or what if I make a total ass out of myself like I did that first date with you? I don't . . . I don't want to mess this up."

"Well, I think you can rest easy. My mother has pretty much already adopted you."

Peter gives Eli a smile that he can tell is forced.

"But nerves don't have to be a bad thing. I think anyone in your position would feel the urge to impress, it's a normal feeling." Eli recounts Rose's own words.

"Yeah, maybe you're right." Eli sees Peter's shoulders relax for the first time since he showed up at Peter's door. "I just want them to like me."

"They will, trust me. Just be yourself." Eli lets his hand fall from the bright yellow railing that runs through the entire bus, reaching down to grab Peter's hand and give it a soft squeeze. Peter looks at their hands, and then back at Eli. "Tonight's going to be fun."

"Right, yeah."

"Besides, I'm the one who should be nervous with the way my mom likes to tell any stranger she meets the most embarrassing stories from when I was a baby."

"Oh, really?"

Eli rolls his eyes. "And if I hear you've been going around and repeating them, don't forget, I know where you live."

Peter smiles at him, and this time, Eli can tell it's the genuine article. "I'm shaking."

The bus suddenly brakes, the driver laying on the horn. Eli lurches forward before he's thrown back into Peter's chest. Peter's reaction is immediate, letting go of Eli's hand and instead wrapping a strong arm around his waist, pulling him in close.

Too close.

Eli looks up at Peter, his heart beating a little faster thanks to being whipped around like a toy.

"You okay?" Peter asks him.

"Yeah." Eli swallows. "Thanks."

The moment passes, but Peter keeps his grip around Eli's hips, holding Eli close to him. Eli knows he could say something, pull away, grab onto the railing for himself. But there's a safety here, a comfort that he isn't quite willing to compromise for the sake of his own sanity.

* * *

Starting in late October, the Union Square Ice Rink is open to anyone brave enough to stand outside long enough to get their turn.

Ice-skating is one of those traditions that started in the Francis family well before Eli was even born, his parents spending nearly all night on the ice together, spinning in front of the giant Christmas tree the city puts up in the middle of November.

Despite skating for nearly three decades, Eli is a total disaster on the ice. It was easier when he was a kid and he could always use an ice walker. But his balance and center of gravity never seemed to improve, and the older he got, the more embarrassing it was to skate with the assistance.

He'd even paid for private lessons once but left the rink when he realized the only other adults were parents there to watch their kids.

Patricia never let him live that one down.

"Have you ever skated?" Eli asks Peter as they grab a pair of rental skates from the kiosk at the front of the park.

"Nope, you?"

"Yes, though you wouldn't know it by watching me."

Peter grins. "Oh, I can't wait to see how this turns out."

"You think you're *so* funny, don't you?" Eli asks sarcastically, tapping his card on the reader to complete the transaction. "So, okay . . . I know that I told you not to be nervous on the bus."

"And now you're going to undo all the hard work I've done since we got off?"

"No, I swear. I just think I should warn you that my mother, she's very . . ."

Eli can't complete his sentence before there's a cry from the other side of the park somehow cutting through the mass of people between them and his parents.

"Eli!" His mother shouts, her hands high in the air.

"Excitable," Eli finally gets out.

Rue rushes ahead of John and Les, racing toward Eli and Peter at a speed that almost makes Eli believe she could knock the two of them over if she didn't slow down.

"Oh, it's so good to see you, my baby boy!" She wraps Eli in a tight hug.

"Yeah, Mom. It's not like we just saw one another last week."

"But this is different," she tells him. "Tonight's special!" Rue finally lets go of her son, all of her focus now intently fixated on Peter. "And you must be the Peter I've been hearing *so* much about."

"Oh, uh . . ." Peter stammers for a bit, wondering what to do with the skates in his hands. "Hi, Mrs. Francis . . . or, it's Clark, isn't it? I'm so sorry." Peter holds his hand out for her to take.

"Oh, honey. As far as I'm concerned you can call me 'Mom.'" Rue ignores the invitation for a handshake, instead wrapping her arms around Peter too, squeezing him even tighter than she'd squeezed Eli. He's almost convinced that his mother could lift Peter into the air if she wanted to.

"Mom, let him breathe, please," Eli begs her.

"I'm sorry, I'm just so excited!" Rue squeezes Peter one last time before she finally lets him go.

Eli steps closer to Peter. "Told you she'd love you."

Peter grunts, holding his side. "I think she broke a rib."

Eli takes his hand, leading Peter toward the rest of his family. "This is John, my stepfather. And Les, my little sibling."

"It's nice to meet you, Peter!" John says, though through his accent, it comes out more as *Peetah*. "Oh!" John exclaims when he takes Peter's free hand. "That's quite a handshake."

"Thank you, sir," Peter says a little too quickly, his nerves on quiet display. "Hi, Les!"

In typical preteen fashion, Les can't be bothered to acknowledge Peter.

Eli tightens his own grip on Peter's hand, just as a reminder that neither of them are alone here. "Don't take offense," he says.

Peter nods. "They'll warm up to me."

"You two already have your skates?" Rue asks.

"Yep." Eli shows his mother.

"You're going to skate?" Les snorts. "That'll be a riot."

"Hey, I don't remember asking for your opinion."

"Gave it anyway!" Les sticks their tongue out, and Eli, very maturely, sticks his out right back.

"We'll meet you two at the entrance; go ahead and get your skates on," Rue orders.

"Yes, ma'am!" Eli gives her a mock salute.

Rue gives her son a *pssh!* before waving him off. "You're not funny."

"See?" Eli sidles even closer to Peter, if that were possible. "Told you they aren't so bad."

"I guess so." Peter's shoulders seem to relax again, his pulse slowing.

"I promise, they're pretty much ready to adopt you already. I'll also apologize for any talk of marriage Mom brings up."

"You think she'll do that?" Peter's voice goes a touch higher.

"Well, she asked Keith if he was going to marry me the second time they met, so I wouldn't put it past her."

"What did he say?" Peter dares to ask.

"I didn't let him answer. I faked that my apartment burnt down."

"Seems reasonable." Peter laughs.

And Eli smiles at him, tugging Peter toward a row of benches that everyone has been using to switch out their shoes for their skates. "Come on, it's time for me to make a fool out of myself."

"You can't be that bad, can you?"

* * *

Eli is, in fact, that bad at ice-skating.

He can barely even make it from the bench to the actual rink, Peter having to offer a hand as they both slowly stumble toward the ice, nearly getting knocked over by a group of children. Eventually, the two make it onto the ice, and it takes all of five seconds before Eli falls hard on his ass.

"No laughing." Eli points at Peter without even looking at him. "You're not allowed to laugh."

"I wasn't going to," Peter swears.

"Uh-huh . . ." Eli allows himself to be pulled into the air and back onto two feet, careful of his balance. At the very least, he's been doing this enough to master the art of standing on the ice, but the gravity of his body is constantly pushing him forward.

And since Eli's never learned how to turn or steer, he pretty much is set on an incredibly slow collision course for the rink wall.

"Bend your knees, Eli!" John says as he skates by, his hand held in Rue's.

"Thanks, John!"

Peter giggles, taking Eli's hand and trying to lead him away from the wall. Peter doesn't seem to be any more of an expert than Eli is, but he at least knows how to steer.

"How long have you been doing this again?"

"I said no jokes!" Eli reminds him.

"You said no laughing," Peter corrects. "Not no jokes."

"Jokes imply there will be laughing."

"Not if you make a bad one."

"Touché, Park." Eli lets his grip tighten, allowing Peter to take the lead, their arms spread out. Eli watches as Les skates circles around them, gliding on the ice. There are too many people on the rink to risk any fancy spins or flips, but Eli knows exactly what they're capable of.

"You're *still* bad at this," Les adds helpfully.

"Thanks for the confidence, Les."

"You're welcome!" They skate around Eli one last time before calmly finding their way next to Peter. "So."

"Oh, um . . . hello?" Peter swallows.

"You're in love with my brother?"

"Les!" Eli shouts, almost lunging for them before they slip again. Thankfully, Peter's a lot closer this time, and they both spin twice before finding their footing again.

"I, uh . . ." Peter starts to say before Eli stops him.

"You don't have to answer that."

Les sings. "Are you two in looooove?"

"Les, I swear to God—"

"Eli and Peter sittin' in a tree." Les makes a point of quite literally skating circles around the two of them while they sing. "K-I-S-S-I-N-G!"

Eli almost goes for Les again before he hears a surprising sound. When he looks up, he sees Peter laughing. It's such a soft, honest sound that it catches Eli off guard for a moment.

Les ignores their brother, skating off to the other side of the rink in record time.

"I'm sorry about them," Eli tells Peter. "Les has never been one to care about my love life, so this is surprising." Despite Rue and John's love for Keith, he always felt their family dinners were more of an obligation than anything. There's no denying that Eli's family can be a bit . . . overbearing at times, but they're still his family, and it always bothered him that Keith never seemed to appreciate them.

There's something heartwarming about seeing that Peter actually likes his family.

"I like them, they seem feisty."

"That's one way of describing them."

"I was jealous of my friends who had siblings. I always wanted one."

"I'll sell you Les; I'll even let you low-ball. A hundred dollars and they're all yours."

Peter laughs again, drawing Eli in so that they can both keep their balance. And for the second time that night, Eli's pulled in close to Peter's chest. They skate like that for a while, holding their hands together, listening to the scratching of the blades along the ice. Eli looks at Peter, and he can't help the overwhelming urge he feels to reach up and kiss him.

So he does. Standing on the tiptoes of his skates to reach Peter.

It's a short, sweet thing. But just enough to torture Eli, to leave him wanting more. When they separate, Peter's smiling; Eli adores the slight overlap of his two front teeth.

"What was that for?"

"For . . . practice," Eli says, like of course that's what it was for.

"Right, yeah. Practice."

"PDA's an important part of the experience, Peter. You'll need to get used to kissing in front of other people."

"Then . . ." Peter starts to say, like he almost doesn't want to dare. "Maybe I need more practice?"

Eli smiles at him, his hand tracing Peter's cheek. "Maybe you do."

He lets Peter's hand find his chin, tilting Eli's face upward yet again to capture his lips.

* * *

Eli and Peter only make it around the rink twice. Which, given the size of it, shouldn't have taken them as long as it did, but Eli kept falling.

By the time they're outside the rink, unlacing their skates, they're both cold enough for hot chocolate.

"I'll get it," Peter says. "No reason both of us have to wait."

"Are you sure?" Eli asks.

"Yeah, of course." Peter surprises him with a soft kiss on the cheek. "I'll be right back."

Eli watches as Peter takes both of their pairs of skates to the counter to return them, watching that energetic stride, the way Peter's shoulders seem almost light, taking in how Peter seems more confident.

He doesn't even notice his mother at first.

"I like him," she says without any preamble, draping herself over the wall Eli sits against.

"Who?" Eli teases, kicking his feet back and forth.

Rue gives him a soft smack on the shoulder. "Who else could I be talking about?"

Eli breathes an exaggerated sigh of relief. "He was really nervous to meet you," he says, wondering if outing Peter is the right move. But he doesn't know who else to talk to about this.

"What did you tell him about us?"

"Nothing!"

"Then why was he scared?" Rue asks.

"He's nervous by nature."

"He's very sweet." Rue pauses, and Eli braces himself for the worst. "When's the wedding?"

"There it is." He throws his head back.

"You know that I'm joking." Rue laughs, grabbing onto her son's arm.

"I know."

"But he seems very sweet, and . . ." Rue lets her voice drift. It's a rare thing for Rue Clark to leave words unsaid. Being the director of her own press leaves her no room to beat around the bush. Every single year, she oversees each step of their production process. And while she's not the only one responsible for the making of the books that costs thousands of dollars, she's the face of the company.

"What?"

"Nothing." Rue shakes her head.

"Mom."

"It's nothing, you don't want to hear it."

"Just tell me."

Rue pauses, glancing toward her son before she turns back to the ice. "For months there, you seemed so lost after Keith broke your heart. And . . . a mother never likes to see her child that way. Between him and how stuck you are at that awful website, I was really worried about you."

"Mom," Eli starts to say, but he's silenced with a hand on top of his own. The breakup with Keith brought many conversations. Rue had a higher opinion of Keith than Patricia or Rose ever did, but she'd admitted to Eli one night, post breakup, that there was *something*. A "gut feeling," as she'd labeled it.

"You didn't seem happy with him," she says. "Even a few months before the breakup . . . I don't know. Things seemed different between the two of you. Like you were already mourning something."

Eli doesn't say a word.

THE BUILD-A-BOYFRIEND PROJECT

"But . . . you seem happy now. Happier than I've seen you in a very long time, Eli. And it's just . . . it's nice to see."

"Mom. Don't get all sappy on me, please."

"I'm just telling you the truth!" she says defensively. "He's a sweet boy, and I'm glad that you found him. Gives me hope for grandchildren after all."

"Pfft, yeah, right. I don't think I'm father material."

"Your father said the exact same thing. I was so scared to tell him I was pregnant. But when I worked up the courage, he just smiled at me and he started to cry, saying, 'I'm going to be a father!' over and over again."

"Yeah . . ." Eli's gaze drifts toward the hot chocolate line, where Peter has sped through in record time, carrying a drink tray with four cups, a fifth cup in his other hand. He feels his heart swell with joy, pride.

Happiness.

"I like it when you're happy, Eli. Makes me feel like I did my job right."

"I like him a lot, Mom," he says softly.

And he hates that it's not a lie.

For a moment, he considers the future. Eli will show Michael the *real* article about Peter, and he'll fall so in love with it and realize the error of his ways that he'll offer Eli a staff writer position at *Vent*. Peter will finally be brave enough to query an agent, and of course they'll sign him right away and sell his book.

Eli could tell him. He could tell Peter about his feelings, be just as honest with Peter as he's asked Peter to be with him. He thinks back to their pull-out clause, his heart aching at the idea that he once thought he couldn't love Peter Park.

Because anyone would be lucky to have that privilege.

Peter Park deserves someone better than Eli, he knows that. But what if he accepted Eli for who he is? What if they had a chance?

What if?

Eli watches Peter as he makes his way toward him and his mother. He smiles, accepting the hot chocolate with another kiss on the cheek from Peter, breathing in the sickly sweet smell of the melted chocolate, a dollop of whipped cream already melting on the surface.

He leans into Peter, appreciating that warmth, that comfort.

It's a feeling he could certainly get used to.

Chapter Fourteen

Imagine Me & You, dir. by Ol Parker

Eli feels his heart thudding in his chest, bouncing around like a bongo drum, like it might burst out like he's John Hurt in *Alien*.

He stares at Michael as he reads the article. Not the fake-dating article.

The article.

Lavender Country.

He knew today had to be the day, that he couldn't put this off any longer. He *has* to share what he's been doing with Michael, come clean about this whole scheme of his, to show his work and plead with Michael to believe in him.

Just this once.

Eli licks his lips, his throat impossibly dry, his tongue heavy.

"I know this isn't—" he starts to say. But Michael just holds up a hand, silencing Eli. He rubs his sweaty palms on his knees, watching as Michael's eyes carefully dart across the page, reading the article line by line.

The seconds count down like hours, Eli wondering if he'll make it out of the building alive. How could he think this would go well? Of course Michael won't go along with this plan, why would he?

For years, Michael has told him *exactly* what he's looking for. And for years, Eli has refused to give it to him. And for what? All because his pride told him he was above writing the kinds of low-effort "articles" that Michael was looking for. Because he never wanted to sink so low as to write listicles about some Marvel movie garbage or steal content from people online for their own benefit.

How could he possibly think that this would go well for him, how could he—

"I love it."

Eli stares at Michael for a moment. "Huh?"

"I love it." Michael scrolls back to the top of the article, rereading the first few lines. "This story of growing up so isolated and alone, with no one to learn from . . ." Michael pauses. "It's really good, Eli."

He wants to laugh, but he stops himself, figuring it probably wouldn't read as the best reaction.

"You're not serious."

Michael raises an eyebrow. "What? You think it's not up to snuff?"

"No, no, it's just, well . . ." Eli had expected anger. He expected Michael to laugh at him the moment Eli gave him the incorrect article. He'd also expected it to be Michael's final straw, for him to order Eli to pack his things and make his way out of the *Vent* offices, never to be seen again.

Eli expected to spend his night job hunting.

"It's not what you asked for." Eli swallows.

"No . . . no, it's not." Michael's voice is careful, calculated even. "And to be quite frank, I should fire you for wasting my time. Going behind my back, writing something that I didn't ask for. But I have to admire the balls it took to ignore me and do what you thought was right."

Then Michael pauses.

"That wasn't offensive, right? To say you have balls? I can't keep track of the language these days."

Eli stops himself from rolling his eyes.

"It's fine," he lies. Now's not the time to bring up Michael's gross transphobia. "You mean that? Really?"

"I thought I was looking for something more exciting, scandalous. But I can see that you've taken the lessons I've been trying to teach you to heart. Just not in the way I expected."

"I *am* sorry, Michael, I never—"

Another hand stops Eli. "You did the right thing. Well, not the right thing, but the interesting thing. And that's what I've been looking for from you."

"So . . ." Eli doesn't want to ask, but he's realizing that he hasn't *actually* gotten confirmation. "You're going to publish it?"

"Yes, we're going to publish your story," Michael tells him with a satisfied smirk.

Eli has to stop himself from leaping into the air.

"That's, ah, that's amazing!" He's at a total loss for words. His heart still pounds in his chest wildly, and his hands shake, almost like there's too much energy in his body that's itching to escape. "Thank you so much, Michael."

"We'll have to discuss some things. Obviously, I want more eyes on this to see if there are any edits that need to be made. I'll read through it a few more times. And then there's your pay. I think we'll have to do a freelance rate on this since you aren't officially one of our staff writers." Michael pauses, as if remembering something. "Which, speaking of."

Eli feels relief that he isn't the one who has to bring up the writing position.

"I promised you something," Michael says. "And I'm not reneging on that—"

Oh no.

"But we do have to wait until we see the reaction to the article before I can offer you anything."

Fair enough, Eli thinks to himself, though he'd love nothing more than to celebrate tonight with Patricia and Rose. "I understand."

"But don't feel down; I've got high hopes, Eli."

"Thank you so much for trusting me, Michael. It means the world."

"I know." Michael beams. "Now get back out there. I've got an article to edit," he says with a wink.

"Of course, yeah." Eli stands, gathering his bag. He hadn't even let the workday properly start before he'd marched into Michael's office to tell him the truth. "Thanks again."

Michael nods, and effectively shuts Eli out until he's made his quick exit from the office. Eli drops his bag at his desk before he makes a beeline for the bathroom. Once the door shuts, he can't stop himself.

"Fuck yes!" His words echo off the tiled walls, and his coworkers can probably—definitely—hear him, but he can't bring himself to care. He jumps, his hands balled into tight fists. "Yes, yes!" He feels . . .

He doesn't know what he feels exactly.

So many emotions run through his head all at once that he isn't sure what to face first. What he does know is that it's happening. *Finally.* After years of wanting this, of sitting in on meetings with Michael, being told his work is too highbrow or too tough to read, of being afraid to go somewhere else.

It's finally worth it.

Eli smiles at himself in the mirror, and he feels his chest rising with excitement.

"Finally," he says to himself.

Then a toilet flushes.

Eli's eyes shoot toward the pair of feet that he didn't notice before under a stall door. The door opens, and who else would step out besides Keith?

"You're excited," he says, eyeing Eli as he walks toward the sink.

"Yeah, I am." Eli turns, his eyes darting from Keith to the floor, then back again.

"Any particular reason?"

"I've finally been offered a writing position," Eli tells him. Not a total lie. Eli's refusing to believe in a world where the article flops and Michael withdraws the offer.

"That's amazing, Eli. Congratulations."

"Yeah, it is . . . amazing."

Keith smiles at him. "I'm so proud of you."

"I wasn't really looking for your approval," Eli tells him. "But thanks anyway."

"Come on, Eli. Don't be like that."

"Like what?"

"If we're going to work together again, we have to learn to respect one another."

"Like how you respected me when you told me you didn't love me out of the blue?"

Keith opens his mouth to say something, but the door to the bathroom opens again. This time it's Greg, another of the staff writers. And by the look on his face, it's obvious he knows he walked in on something. "Uh . . . sorry, Keith. Michael wanted to see you really quick."

"Did he say why?" Keith asks.

Greg shakes his head.

"Okay, thanks."

Greg nods and exits the bathroom as quickly as he arrived.

"You know, I *am* proud of you," Keith says. "I wasn't lying." He stares at Eli, that gaze familiar and comforting at one point in their relationship. But now Eli can see the frustration behind it. Keith heads out, and Eli watches as the door closes behind him.

Eli stands there for a moment longer, double-checking under each of the stall doors quickly before he goes back to his celebration.

Because he *refuses* to let Keith bring his mood down.

This has been five years in the making, and he won't let this slip away.

His phone vibrates in his pocket, and he fishes it out quickly to see a text from Peter.

> **PETER:** Are you still interested in my work Halloween party?

Eli smiles at his phone.

The article is done. At least, the writing of it is.

That means that his obligation to Peter is done, which means that they can be friends now. Not that they weren't friends before, but now, there's nothing to stop them, nothing to make Eli second-guess every single one of their interactions.

> **ELI:** of course

> **ELI:** we've got something else to celebrate too!

> **PETER:** Oh?

> **ELI:** i'll tell you later

> **PETER:** Can't wait.

> **PETER:** Meet at my place?

Eli stares at the messages, gnawing at his bottom lip as his heart continues to thud in his chest.

> **ELI:** do i need a costume?

Chapter Fifteen

Caravaggio, dir. by Derek Jarman

"C ome in, quick, please!" Peter rushes out of the door to the garage, propping open the front gate just enough for Eli to open it himself. Eli barely has enough time to register what's going on before he's being led into the building.

Then again, the answer is pretty obvious when he sees Peter dressed in a skintight Spider-Man costume with his hand cupping his crotch.

"I need your help," he tells Eli when he finally makes it into the apartment. "Close the door." Peter continues on to the bathroom and Eli follows after him.

"Peter . . ." Eli leans against the doorframe. "You don't have to hide your dick; I think I can figure out what's going on here."

Peter eyes Eli warily before he dares to slowly remove both of his hands. Eli's mouth goes dry at seeing just how *much* of Peter the costume shows off.

Not a detail left to the imagination.

"Wow, okay . . ."

"See?" Peter covers his groin again before Eli puts his hands around his wrists, pulling them away.

"You don't have to be embarrassed, Peter. We're adults here."

Peter finally stands straight. "I thought it'd be fun, and Spider-Man seemed like an easy enough costume."

"No, I get it." Eli laughs to himself. "You didn't realize that you'd need a cup? Or one of those dance belts."

"Dance belt? What's that?" He looks at Eli with panic and confusion. "I was told I *have* to dress up."

"I don't think it's the end of the world if you don't show up in a costume, Peter," Eli teases, but the look that Peter gives him tells Eli that now isn't the time to make fun of him.

Peter hesitates. "I just wanted to be a part of the team."

"Okay, well . . . there's a simple fix here."

"Whatever it takes."

Eli dips out of the bathroom, going to Peter's closet where a pair of gray sweatpants is thrown over a hanger. "You don't happen to have a green jacket, do you?"

"Green?" He hears Peter creep back into the bedroom. "I think I might have one. I haven't worn it in a while, though . . ." Peter stretches toward the back of the closet, and Eli takes the chance to sneak a peek at just how the costume accentuates the cup of Peter's ass.

"It won't be entirely accurate, but it should at least help."

"Since when does Spider-Man wear sweatpants?"

"You know, out of everything you've ever said to me, admitting that you've never seen *Into the Spider-Verse* might be the most egregious."

Peter winces. "I'll write it down."

"It's okay, we'll fix it. But now you can still be Peter Parker, just a sadder . . . more desperate version."

"So, it's not that much of a costume, is it?" Peter laughs softly.

Eli just gives him a sad smile. Gray sweatpants might defeat the whole objective of hiding Peter's dick, but they're baggy enough in the inseam that they do a decent enough job at disguising Peter's embarrassment.

"Can I ask what you are?" Peter throws the jacket onto the bed, stepping into the sweatpants as Eli gives him some room.

"You can't tell?" He spins around in his red nylon short-shorts that might show off a little too much of his ass, his calves costumed under bright white socks with black stripes near the top, and black Converse sneakers. He thought that the gray shirt, stained with red food dye and the words CAMP CRYSTAL LAKE COUNSELOR across it, would be self-explanatory.

He'd even bought a plastic machete meant to fit over his head like he'd been sliced, but wearing it would mean not fitting through most doorframes all night.

"Is that from a movie too?"

Eli nods. "Yes, but don't worry, I won't put you through all twelve of them."

"Thank you."

"So where are we going? The bowling alley in the Mission?"

"No," Peter says, pulling his arms through the jacket. "The one in the Presidio; apparently it's nicer?"

"Is now a good time to admit that I'm not a good bowler?"

"Only if you're okay with me being bad at it too."

"What was your last score?" Eli dares to ask, falling onto the bed and getting a full look at Peter in the new-ish costume. There shouldn't be something so attractive about gray sweatpants and a green jacket, and yet.

"Seventy-four?" Peter admits.

"I've got you beat," Eli tells him. "Fifty-three."

"So, I don't have to try and impress you?" Peter holds out his hand, offering it to Eli.

And Eli gladly takes it. "Not tonight at least."

* * *

"Fancy . . ." Eli says as he steps into the bowling alley, Peter right behind him. He's heard of this place before, when he, Patricia, and

Rose wanted to go bowling one night. They took one look at the hourly rate of two hundred dollars and stuck with bowling on Patricia's Wii.

It's a fairly small bowling alley, with only a dozen lanes. There's the counter where you exchange your shoes, and even a little area filled with claw games. The real draw seems to be the other half of the building where the adjoining bar is packed with people dressed in their own costumes; celebrating, shouting, watching some game on one of the huge televisions mounted to the wall.

"Do you know who we're looking for?" Eli asks.

"Uh . . ." Peter shoves his keys into his jacket. "Actually . . ."

"You don't know what your coworkers look like, do you?"

"I'd recognize their profile pictures on Slack," Peter admits. "But it can't be that hard to find them." He walks right up to the front desk. "Excuse me? Is the party for the Zelus company here?"

"I think so," the woman—dressed in goggles, blue overalls, and a yellow sweater—says, checking her computer. "Yep! They're lanes one through four. What size are you guys?"

With their shoes exchanged, Eli trails behind Peter as they walk toward the reserved lanes.

"You at least know Francine, right?"

"Yeah, yeah . . . she'll recognize me."

"And she's here tonight . . ." Eli pauses. "Right?"

"Yes! I think . . ."

And as if on cue, from the large group of three dozen people gathered at the first four lanes, a tall blonde woman dressed in what Eli can only describe as very normal clothes beams brightly when she sees Peter inching closer.

"Oh my God! Peter!"

The woman stands up from the table where she's been nursing a Pepsi cup, racing over to wrap Peter in a tight hug, her arms thrown over his shoulders.

"Hey, Francine." He hugs her back, the smile clear on his face.

"I was so worried that you were going to bail again."

"Yeah, well . . . I'm trying this new thing," he says.

"We're calling it socializing," Eli adds.

"Oh, you're Eli, right? Patricia's friend?"

"That's me." Eli holds out his hand, but she ignores it, wrapping him in a similar hug.

"Sorry, I'm a hugger!" she says with a smile when Eli makes a surprised noise.

"That's okay!" Eli tells her.

"We haven't been here for long, come on." She takes Peter by the hand. "Everyone's been dying to meet you, officially, of course. You too, Eli, Peter's been talking *all* about you."

Eli gives Peter a sly look.

To their credit, his coworkers are all excited to see Peter, a few of them meeting him for the first time, which is hilarious given how long he's worked at Zelus. He's forced to make the rounds, which means that Eli is right there beside him, holding Peter's hand through it all as he's introduced as "Peter's friend" over and over again.

"Oh! Spider-Man!" one of his coworkers, a man named Daniel, exclaims at Peter's costume.

Peter looks at Eli with a smile.

"Do you want a turn, Peter?" Francine asks.

"Oh, I'm okay." He takes a seat at the tall table near the back of the lane, where different sizes and colors of bowling balls that aren't being used are stored.

"Come on, you can take mine," Francine tells him. "Can't do much worse than I already have." One look at the screen that hangs from the ceiling is evidence enough of that, with a Jedi Knight nearing a perfect score save for a 7-10 split, and a woman dressed as Chappell Roan getting another strike.

"Oh, really, I, uh . . . I'm okay," Peter says, rubbing at the back of his neck.

"What about you, Eli?" Francine shifts her focus, as if she's aware of how nervous Peter is.

"Yeah, sure! I'll go!" Eli tells her, daring to let go of Peter's hand, though there's that lingering touch, the kind that tells him that Peter doesn't actually want him to leave. Eli looks back at him, silently promising that it will be okay.

He goes to the automated ball return, selecting a ball with holes that fit his fingers before he steps up to the line in front of the lane. Taking just a few paces back, he glides toward the lane again, letting the ball go a little too late, meaning that it lands on the polished wooden floor with a *thud* before it actually begins to roll, drifting left and left and left until it sinks right into the gutter.

Eli glances back, grateful that only a few people seem to have noticed the blunder. Then there's Peter; his gaze is focused solely on Eli, and he's got this precious smile on his face.

Eli takes his short stroll of shame back to the ball dispenser, waiting for the familiar neon green to make an appearance before he tries it again. This time he's a little more successful, managing to knock down exactly one pin before the rest of the pins are taken down with the bar of the pinsetter.

"One's not so bad," Francine says as Eli joins the two of them at the tall table with the extra bowling balls. "Better than I've been averaging all night."

"Are you guys thirsty?" Peter spouts out of nowhere. "I'm thirsty, so I'm going to get drinks; do you guys want anything?"

"I'm good." Francine grabs a near-empty cup and shakes the ice around.

Eli doesn't want anything, so he just watches as Peter very awkwardly shuffles over toward the concessions area, joining the short line there.

"So . . ." Francine sips what remains of her drink. "You're super cute together."

"Thanks, we're . . . figuring things out," Eli tells her, because he isn't sure what she knows, how Peter has spoken about them, who she thinks Eli is to Peter. "How do you know Peter? Like obviously you work at Zelus together, but how do you *know* him?"

"I was his supervisor for a bit before he got a promotion, and we became team leads on a project a while back. Now we're in two different divisions, but we go to one another when we're trouble-shooting a lot of the time. Lots of overlap."

"Oh, that's way more involved than I thought it'd be."

"We just wound up talking a lot, and he seemed friendly. It took a lot of prodding, a *lot* of one-sided conversations before we became friends. Though I'm not sure if he sees this as a friend-ship."

"I'm willing to bet he does; Peter just takes a little longer than most people would bother putting in, I think."

"Yeah, he's a sweet guy." Francine peers over Eli's shoulder, daring him to turn around and look at Peter as he gives his order to the cashier. "I was worried he wouldn't come tonight; I invite him every time we do one of these get-togethers. But I'm glad that he's here with you." Francine turns back to the bowling, clapping when one of her coworkers gets a spare. "Yeah!"

Eli keeps his gaze focused on Peter as he taps his card on the reader, stepping down to the end of the bar to wait for the drinks. He must notice the eyes on him, because Peter turns, looking at Eli. He smiles so gently, giving Eli a careful wave.

And Eli waves right back.

* * *

It takes a little longer to get Peter into the swing of things, to go beyond just talking to Francine to chatting with his other coworkers.

He meets his supervisor in person for the first time, though he assures Eli that he's seen her face before in meetings and one-on-ones.

The Jedi Knight is named Jackson, a team lead who actually asks Peter for help with his current project, except it's pretty late in the night when this happens and he's fairly drunk, so he asks Peter to message him on Slack when he realizes he's explaining things poorly.

Eli even gets Peter to bowl a full game where he just barely cracks a score of one hundred before he gets a strike on his very last ball, and Eli can't resist running up to him and giving Peter a soft kiss, Peter daring to wrap him in a hug and pick him up for half a second. Eli wants the kiss to last longer, to bury his hands in that short black hair and make a fool out of both himself and Peter while they make out in a very unprofessional way.

But Eli stops himself. They haven't had that conversation yet; he can't cross that boundary.

As the night goes on, the crowd begins to thin out until most of Peter's coworkers are gone. Francine waves goodbye as she begins her duties as the designated driver.

And soon enough, it's just the two of them, the current game left unfinished as the bowling alley has gone dark, neon paint and lights illuminating the building while increasingly random pop music videos play on the projection screens.

"How did I do?" Peter asks as the screen flashes with Jackson's name as a reminder that it's his turn, even though he's long gone.

"A little rough at the beginning, but I could see you getting comfortable."

"Yeah . . . yeah . . ." Peter lets out a low sigh. "I don't know why I shut down when I saw everyone here. I guess I wasn't expecting that many people."

"That's okay, I wasn't either."

"Were you nervous?" Peter asks.

"Oh, hell yeah."

His brows knit together. "Seriously?"

Eli nods, taking Peter's Pepsi cup filled with lemonade. "Absolutely. At least you'd talked to most of them before. I was the total oddball out." Not that many of the employees had seemed to bring dates, save for Peter's supervisor bringing her wife and Jackson bringing his partner. "And like you said, I wasn't expecting that many new faces in a single night."

"You didn't seem nervous."

Eli shrugs, sipping from the straw until he hears the empty sound of ice rattling in the cup. "I guess I'm better at hiding it."

"Is that the trick?" Peter asks. "Hiding it?"

"I prefer to think of it as fake it till you make it."

"Meaning?"

"Fake being socially capable until you actually start to trick yourself into believing that you are."

"Huh . . . I've never thought of it that way."

"I don't think it works for everyone, but I didn't have a choice. I had to get over my fear of public speaking in college when I had to present my papers."

"I like that." He looks toward the end of the nearest lane, watching whatever music video the bowling alley is playing on one of their huge screens. "Oh, what are we celebrating?"

"Celebrating?"

"You said in your texts?" Peter makes it sound like a question.

"Oh!" It hits Eli suddenly. "Sorry, I was so worried about your dick I forgot to tell you."

Peter blushes. "Sorry."

Eli grins at him. "I, uh . . . the article, the one I wrote about you. I turned it in."

"Yeah?" Peter smiles slowly as he realizes what Eli's about to say. "Your boss liked it?"

"Yep!"

"You're going to be a writer?"

"Professional, baby!"

"Eli, that's amazing!" Peter wraps him in a quick hug. It's a little awkward thanks to the angle they're both sitting at. "Wait, can I read it?"

"Of course, duh!" Eli reaches into his pocket to fish out his phone, going to the Google Docs app. Michael doesn't seem to have had the time to make any real substantial edits, so it's mostly untouched from the last draft. "Here."

Eli tries not to stare as Peter reads through the article. "'Alex'?" he asks.

"Well, I couldn't call you 'Peter' in the article. All the names were changed." Not that Eli even brought Peter up *that* often. His story was just the framing device for what Eli really wanted to write about.

Peter keeps reading, and Eli watches for any subtle movements in his face, the twitching of an eye, the sinking of a smile. Anything that might tell him what Peter really thinks about the article. He doesn't realize just how fast his heart is racing, how his right leg begins to bob up and down from the nerves.

Peter's fingers scroll all the way until he finally reaches the end.

"So . . ." Eli can't stop himself from blurting out. "What did you think?"

"It's wonderful, Eli," Peter says slowly. "I'll admit, when you first told me about it, I really wondered why you'd want to write about something like this. But actually reading it . . ." Peter pauses, grinning. "You got the jazz festival in there. And my parents. The garden."

Eli couldn't avoid *all* the personal details.

"Is it good, like truthfully? Do you really think that it's good?"

It's a moment he's been dreading. No matter what Michael thought of the article, Peter's opinion always mattered more to Eli.

"It's amazing. It really is, Eli." Peter's smile falters for the *briefest* of moments, just long enough for Eli to recognize it.

"What's wrong?"

"Nothing," Peter assures him. "It's nothing."

"Did I get something wrong? Because there's still some editing that needs to be done. This isn't going up tomorrow or anything."

"Nothing's wrong with the article." Peter smiles again, the uncomfortable kind, like when people laugh to fill a silence. "I think . . . I think I'm jealous of you."

"Jealous?"

"I guess reading the article, and seeing you finally go for something. I don't know . . ." Peter sinks into the seat. "I'm almost thirty and I don't really know what I'm doing at Zelus, let alone with my life."

"Well, you know life doesn't end at thirty, right?"

"It's not so much about life ending at thirty, it's just . . . it's more that . . . I've had this image of having things figured out by then, that I'd be confident in my career choice, my relationships, my dreams. And so far, it just . . . hasn't happened."

"Huh." Eli pauses. He's familiar with those desires, that specific brand of jealousy knowing that Patricia and Rose—and even his parents—are capable and confident in what they do, that they have actual careers they're—mostly—happy in. "All I can say is that you definitely aren't alone in those feelings."

"Yeah, I've tried to get over it, but it's like it's ingrained in my brain, and the thoughts always pop up at the worst time."

"This is about your writing, isn't it?" Eli asks.

Peter sighs, his gaze focused on the floor. "I just don't like thinking about it," he says. "It's scary. That's why I chose comp sci instead of a BFA program. Writing . . . there's no guarantee in it. I don't know if I can find an agent, get published. Hell, I don't even know if I'm any good at it."

"Have you ever shared your writing with anyone before?"

Peter shakes his head.

"What about with me?"

"You'd want to read it?"

"Duh."

"You said that you don't read romance."

"Then I must really think that you're talented if I'm willing to read fiction for once."

"You don't have to," Peter tells him.

"You're right, I don't have to," Eli says. "But I want to."

Peter closes his eyes, but he can't stop himself from smiling.

"Do you have any of it on your phone?" Eli asks.

"Yeah."

"Gimme."

"Eli . . ." Peter huffs.

And Eli huffs right back, mocking the tone of his voice. "Peter."

"You really don't have to do this."

"Feedback and critique partners are a key part of any writer's repertoire. My roommate Patricia reads all my stuff, even if it's never published. And when I get the staff job, then I'll have a whole team of people checking my work."

Peter must realize there's no getting out of this, since he digs his phone out of the pocket of his jacket, unlocking it and navigating to the bright white screen of the Google Docs app. He doesn't have to scroll far to tap on a document that he opens before handing the phone to Eli.

"'Untitled.' It doesn't have a title?"

"Not yet," Peter admits.

Eli goes back to the screen, scrolling to the next page where "Chapter One" sits proudly before he starts to read. There's something about Peter's prose, simple yet connective all at once; even just ten pages in he's laughed quietly, the smile never leaving his face as he scrolls and scrolls.

"You don't have to read the whole thing," he hears Peter say.

"I'm enjoying it," Eli says, but he hands the phone back to Peter because he can tell that Peter's getting uncomfortable. "I can stop, though."

"Do you really think that it's good?" Peter takes the phone, staring at the face reflected back from the empty screen.

"Yeah, maybe there were some grammar mistakes, but coming from someone who will literally toss a semicolon anywhere I feel like it, I'm certainly not the authority on punctuation," Eli says. "Will you let me read more one day?"

"Maybe . . ."

Eli stares at Peter, at the sharp features that still look so soft on him. He feels his heart thudding again, wondering if this is the moment to tell Peter. The article is done, at least the writing part.

There's no conflict of interest, not anymore.

He could tell Peter. Tell him the truth.

I think I have feelings for you.

It almost feels like he's admitting them to himself for the first time as well. He might as well be with how hard he's been fighting them. Peter was never an option. Hell, Eli never thought he'd *want* another option after Keith.

But he can't deny what he's feeling.

Peter finally turns, the wide line of his mouth breaking into a smile when he realizes just how long Eli's been looking at him. "Iced Americano." Eli says the words carefully.

"What?" Peter almost giggles.

"Can I kiss you? For real?" Eli asks him. Of all the words he could think of, he surprises even himself when those slip out.

Peter's ears turn red. "Um . . . yeah . . . yeah, you can."

"Do you *want* me to?" Eli asks, just to be sure.

"Yes," Peter says after a moment of silence.

And Eli closes the distance between them. His hand automatically goes to cup Peter's cheek, his skin soft under Eli's touch. The kiss is short, chaste, and Eli pulls away after just a second. But Peter shocks Eli when he goes in for a second kiss.

This one he lets linger, kissing Peter softly before he dares to prod at the seam of Peter's mouth with his tongue. Peter's response is automatic, letting Eli in. He's still so careful, not wanting to push Peter's boundaries, not now. But he can feel a desperate heat rising in his stomach. He wants this so bad, to taste Peter, to feel him come apart at Eli's touch.

And if the tenting in Peter's sweatpants is any indication, he wants this too.

"Sorry." Peter pulls the jacket into his lap, desperate to cover his shame. "Guess it's been a while."

"Don't be sorry." Eli laughs, his hand finding the jacket.

Eli still can't help but think it's so adorable the way that Peter stumbled through that sentence, how quick he is to embarrass, the blush showing through the neon darkness of the bowling alley.

"You don't have to do anything you don't want to—"

Eli silences Peter with a hand on his thigh. "I know that jacket covered it up all night, but I literally cannot get the image of how perfect your ass looks in that costume out of my head." Eli says the words low, close to Peter's ear, so he can make out each and every syllable.

He leans back, watching the words register on Peter's face, his throat bobbing as he tries to swallow nothing.

"What are you thinking about?" Eli asks him, leaning in to rest his chin on Peter's shoulder. "Tell me the truth, Peter."

"I, uh . . . I had to sit down earlier," Peter admits. "Because your shorts rode up when you were bowling, and your butt just looked so . . . perfect."

"Good." Eli rubs Peter's thigh, squeezing softly. Peter's reaction is immediate. "You mean you got all worked up in front of your coworkers like that?" He dips his toe in the water.

"I didn't mean to," Peter says. "I just . . . couldn't stop staring."

"Well." Eli's hand dares to drift further and further down. He's waiting to wake up from the dream, to realize that he's still in bed, having one of the most visceral fantasies he's ever experienced. For Peter to utter the two-word coffee order that would put an end to this endeavor so that he can offer to take Peter out for a late-night dinner that isn't the curly fries they inhaled an hour ago.

But Peter remains silent, even as Eli wraps his hands around the half-hard length still obvious through the sweatpants. He should probably reflect and think about why Peter dressed in a Spider-Man costume paired with loungewear is enough to drive him up the wall, but he doesn't have the time or the energy. He'd rather lean in, nibbling on the lobe of Peter's ear, grateful that the tall back of their booth hides them from everyone in the now nearly deserted bowling alley.

"Ohh . . ." Peter lets out a low, guttural whine, and it's music to Eli's ears.

"Come on."

"I have to, uh . . . I have to wait a bit."

Eli can't help but laugh. "Just hide it with your jacket."

"R-right, yeah," Peter stutters. "Let's, uh . . . let's go."

* * *

The drive back to the apartment is torture, mostly because Eli doesn't want to take his hands off Peter, but Peter's driving, and Eli's not nearly horny enough for his libido to outweigh his will to live.

He's *close*, but not that close.

Peter and Eli both settle for a hand on Peter's thigh, massaging the muscle there. Eli even dares to let his fingers trace the outline of Peter's growing erection, but Peter slams on the brakes in the middle of a deserted intersection.

"Sorry."

"It's okay," Peter says through a nervous laugh. "Just wasn't, uh . . . expecting it."

Eli's grateful for the parking spot that's right in front of Peter's building, following Peter closely as he tries his best to get into the apartment as quickly as possible. Peter's shaking with what Eli hopes is anticipation, even dropping his keys as he tries to unlock the gate before he finally gets through, and they race through the garage.

They've barely made it inside before Peter turns, taking Eli's cheeks in his hands and pulling him in for another kiss. It's surprising for Peter to take the lead, but Eli loves how demanding the kiss is, how desperate Peter already sounds.

"Jacket off, tiger," Eli begs, giving Peter just enough breathing room to slip out of the coat and for both of them to step out of their shoes before Eli takes Peter's hand and leads him to the bedroom. "Sweatpants next."

"Right, yeah!" Peter says through heavy breaths as Eli falls onto the edge of the bed, once again the perfect height to be eye to eye with Peter's crotch.

In one fluid motion he peels out of the sweatpants, his erection on full display through the stretched spandex. And just as Peter goes to reach for the carefully hidden zipper of the Spider-Man costume, Eli stops him.

"Leave it on, just for a bit." He swallows, actually nervous.

Peter can't help but smirk at him. "Right, I forgot you have a costume kink."

"Not a kink," Eli says. "Just . . . an interest." Eli dares to reach down, to grip Peter's clothed crotch in his hand, giving his dick a soft squeeze. It's always amazed him just *how* sensitive it can be; he loved teasing Keith about it as they were getting out of bed, ready for the day, the yelp that Keith would let out as he avoided Eli's prying hands. Peter doesn't disappoint as he shudders when Eli presses his hand to the aching cock, hissing despite how tender the touch is.

Eli dares to lick the length through the stretched material; it's an odd taste, a bit too spandex-y, but Eli can't bring himself to care. It's been months since he felt the touch of another human, minus his one adventure in the public bathroom. It's only now, faced with the natural way Peter's hand finds his hair, that he realizes just how hungry he is for it.

Peter's whines are music to his ears, soft sounds that he drinks in as he continues to run his tongue along Peter's erection where his precum has formed a dark stain.

"Eli . . . please."

"Please what, Peter?" Peter sucks in a hard breath as Eli kisses the tip.

"Please, suck my dick." There's a desperation in his voice that Eli drinks up.

Eli presses a sly smile against Peter's crotch. "I am."

"No, I mean please let me take this costume off."

Eli continues, the sweet taste of Peter's precum on his tongue. "But I'm having fun," he teases. "You know what they say. With great power *comes* great responsibility."

Peter pauses. "You didn't just say that."

Eli laughs with him, ignoring the question. "You can take this off under one condition."

"Anything, please," Peter begs. "I'll give you whatever you want."

"Don't you dare throw this costume away."

"Fine, yeah. I'll keep it—now please let me take it off?"

"Okay." Eli reclines back on the bed, watching Peter stretch, the costume lacking the give it once did as he reaches for the zipper and pulls it down in a single move. Eli grabs onto Peter's hands, freeing his fingers from the sewn-in gloves and watches as Peter yanks the top half of the costume free. He's even sexier with his chest and arms naked, his soft belly poking out over his waist, broad chest on full display, nipples hard. Eli has to resist the urge to reach up, to cup Peter's tits, desperate to feel the pillowy, unflexed flesh in his hands.

But he has a job to do, and he reaches out to help Peter slide down the rest of the costume before Peter stops.

"Wait." Peter tells him, hands on top of Eli's. "I, uh . . . the costume wouldn't fit with my underwear."

"You went commando?"

"It kept bunching up." Peter's nervousness comes back in an instant. "And it was uncomfortable. That's why my dick kept showing through."

"You weren't wearing any underwear? All night long?"

"I . . ." Peter stares down to where Eli sits in front of his crotch. "Yeah?"

"I hate how hot that is."

"Really?"

Eli nods, biting his lip.

"Right, yeah." Peter lets Eli's hands go, allowing Eli to peel the costume further down. First there's Peter's belly, the skin below his navel coated in a sparse trail of black hair.

I guess it's called a "happy trail" for a reason, Eli thinks, letting the costume fall further and further. He's faced with the bush of Peter's pubic hair, before he finally lays eyes on the base of Peter's erection, tucked into the right leg of the costume until it eventually springs forward.

He takes him slowly, opening his mouth wider and wider, careful of the graze of his teeth while also desperately trying not to overthink it. Eli wants to lose himself in the action, inviting Peter to put his hands back in his curls, pushing him further and further down, inch by careful inch.

"Fuck." Peter sighs as Eli takes half of Peter's cock. "Eli . . . you're perfect."

"Haven't heard that one before." Eli lets a laugh slip past his smile as he takes a breath. His lips go to Peter's tip, licking at the precum there before he dares to go deeper and deeper and deeper with each swallow.

He hates how good Peter tastes; how he smells after being stuck in a spandex costume for the last four hours.

Peter pulls, urging Eli on until Eli is met with his bush of pubic hair. He has to stop there, his gag reflex triggering. He's careful, though, pulling away from Peter's cock slowly, his tongue running down the hard length.

"We could do more. If you want," Eli offers.

"I, uh . . ." Peter's fingers trace Eli's cheek, tucking a strand of hair behind Eli's ear. "I don't have lube, or condoms."

Eli grins. "There are other ways to get off, Peter."

"Right, yeah."

"Have you ever had sex with a vagina?" Eli already knows the answer to the question before Peter shakes his head. "Right, I can show you."

"Please," he begs.

Eli scoots back onto the bed, unlacing his shorts and pulling his T-shirt over his head to throw in the corner. For a moment he considers being self-conscious about the jockstrap that he wore all night, but there was literally no pair of underwear that he owns that wouldn't show through the leg of the shorts. And unlike Peter, he wasn't willing to go commando in front of a bunch of strangers.

Peter climbs onto the bed, helping Eli pull down his shorts. "Oh . . ." Peter whispers when he sees what Eli's wearing.

"Not a problem, right?"

"You know how you definitely don't have a costume kink?" Peter says to him.

Eli smiles. "Yeah?"

"I *definitely* don't have a thing for jockstraps."

"You meatheads and your jockstraps. Maybe I'll wear a football jersey next time or something?" Eli reaches for Peter, ignoring that he's presuming there will be a "next time." He urges Peter forward and captures him in another kiss, maneuvering himself carefully so that Peter can continue to pull his shorts down and toss them into a random corner of the bedroom, totally forgotten. There was a time where Eli was embarrassed of his body, of the changes that came as a result of his testosterone, his clitoris growing to be almost like a penis. His gynecologist had assured him that nothing abnormal was happening, that bottom growth was a normal reaction, just that Eli might be more sensitive than usual.

Eli takes Peter's free hand as they continue to kiss. Peter's fingers find the fabric crotch of the jockstrap, damp with Eli's arousal, pulling it down just enough to give him the space to maneuver while Eli still has it on.

"I don't, uh . . ." Peter says with bated breath. "I don't really know what to—"

"It's okay," Eli promises him, his grip on Peter's wrist firm. "Can I show you?"

Peter nods enthusiastically. Eli bites at his bottom lip as he feels Peter's fingers trace his folds carefully. It's been too long since fingers that weren't his own played with the shape of his vagina, tracing the fine line of skin there as Eli slowly begins to open for him.

There's no stopping the hitch in his breath, the way his body wants to pull away at rediscovering the sensation.

"This is okay?" Peter asks, an adorable concern washing over his face.

"Yes." Eli can't hide the wanting in his voice. "Peter . . ." Eli gasps, urging Peter's fingers deeper and deeper.

"Eli." Peter's breath is warm against Eli's neck, his teeth grazing the skin and sending a shudder down Eli's spine.

Eli isn't sure when he lets go of Peter's hand, his body going so pliant and loose that he can't even keep a hold on Peter's wrists, his hands gripping the sheets instead; it doesn't matter, though, it's easy enough for Peter to figure out, to follow the subtle movements of Eli's body underneath him, to listen to the sweet mewls that slip from Eli's lips as he urges Peter's fingers further inside, pulling Peter in for a kiss as he traces along Eli's clit and rubs softly in a way that Eli deems torturous.

And when Eli dares to open his eyes as Peter's fingers hit him just right, he can see the focus on Peter's face, that wanton determination, and it's so obvious to Eli that Peter only has a single goal in mind.

To make Eli come.

He's so close to saying the words, begging Peter to just fuck him, condom be damned, but he resists. It's a line they can't cross, not without testing, not without actually talking about it first, not without Eli spending an hour shooting water up his ass.

Not yet.

But he can't stop himself from taking Peter's cheeks in his hands, from kissing him over and over again as he lets his body fall onto Peter's fingers, urging as he feels a puddle of Peter's precum gather on his calf.

"Are you close, Eli?"

"Yeah, yes." Eli nods, chasing that relief that seems to slip just past his fingers.

"You can come, Eli."

Eli pleads with Peter silently, wanting nothing more than to give him exactly what he says. So . . .

He does.

With one final, only mildly embarrassing broken groan, Eli's knees knit together almost automatically, like he can't handle the release that comes, that wets Peter's waiting hand, Eli's back arching off the bed as Peter steals one final kiss.

"God . . ." Eli feels himself being pulled back to Earth, fully expecting regret to slap him across the face.

But it never arrives.

Even as he stares at Peter's face and waits for the realization that they crossed a line they can't come back from, he only sees Peter's smile, the man out of breath as he looks at the mess in his hand.

"Sorry about that."

"No, no. That was . . ." Peter looks at Eli again. "Amazing. Thank you." He reaches up with his other hand, tucking a strand of Eli's hair behind his ears and leaning down to steal one more kiss, this one just as slow, just as calm as their first all those weeks ago. "I guess I should get you a towel."

"Well . . . you didn't get to finish." Eli doesn't have to look down to feel Peter hard against him, leaking precum on Eli's thigh.

"Yeah, but . . . I mean, you don't have to, it—"

"Peter?"

"Mm-hmm?"

Eli captures Peter's cheek, pulling him down once more. "I want to make you come."

Peter grins like an idiot. "Yeah, okay!"

"What do you want me to do?"

"Well, you can . . . I mean, if you want, you could jerk me off?"

"Now say that like it's not a question."

"Jerk me off."

"Now say it like you're not some closeted frat bro."

"I'm not sure how to respond to that," Peter says, and Eli can't resist a laugh.

"Can I try something with you?"

Peter swallows, his voice quiet. "I think I'd let you do whatever you wanted to me."

Eli can't even begin to explain how dangerous that is. He thinks of wearing a strap-on, fucking deep into Peter until he's a whimpering mess. Of riding Peter within an inch of his life, controlling his movements carefully enough to keep Peter from coming until he's begging for it. Eli imagines eating Peter out while he edges him, his back arched, skin sweaty as he begs for release. He wonders if Peter would like to be tied to the bed so he can't touch himself. If he might like being spanked or degraded, or if Peter would want to try being more demanding, more in control. He pictures a thousand different ways to make Peter come undone underneath him, and he wants to explore all of them.

But for now, he picks himself up, his legs still feeling like jelly as he sits closer to the wall Peter's bed rests against, propping himself up with one of the discarded pillows. "Sit between my legs, here, with your back to me." He rubs his hand on the sheets, and Peter does exactly as he's told.

It's an odd feeling. Being the big spoon was never Eli's preferred role. He likes having that warmth, that comfort around him, almost as if he could suffocate underneath another person at any given moment. And with Peter's wider frame, it's a little tough to find the position he wants, but they both manage.

"Now . . ." Eli's able to whisper in Peter's ear, the angle right when Peter finally relaxes. "I think I want to go a little slower."

Peter hisses when Eli touches his leaking cock, the precum providing enough lubrication for what he has planned.

"Is that okay?"

Peter bites at his bottom lip, almost letting it go white. But he still nods.

"Say it, Peter. Tell me if it feels good."

"It feels so good, Eli."

"And you tell me if you don't like what I'm doing, okay?"

"Okay."

"Mm-hmm . . . good." Eli continues to stroke. "You know who follows rules, Peter?"

"Hng, I—"

Eli doesn't give him a chance to answer. "Good boys follow rules."

Peter swallows.

"You're a good boy, right, Peter?" Eli whispers, unable to stop himself from nibbling at the skin of Peter's neck. "I saw the way you blushed when I called you that before. I meant it as a joke, but . . ." Eli twists his wrist carefully, pulling his hand to the tip and rubbing his thumb along the wet slit of Peter's leaking cock. "You like being called a good boy, don't you?"

Peter bites at his bottom lip. "Mm-hmm . . ."

"Say it," Eli pleads. "Tell me."

"I like it."

"Like what?"

"Being a good boy."

"That's it, that's my good boy." Eli continues his motion, up and down Peter's length, drinking in the whines that spill from Peter's lips. "Now, I want to try something else, okay?"

Peter nods, and Eli can feel his own arousal peeking back up at just how badly Peter wants this. He wonders if Peter can feel him against the small of his back, feel the wetness there.

"And you're going to keep being my good boy, right?"

He nods again, his eyes closed.

"Say it, Peter."

"I'm going to be a good boy."

"Good." Eli traces his nails along Peter's thigh, running his fingers along the faint stretch marks, kissing Peter's shoulders where he's tattooed in much the same way. He moves his free hand up, cupping Peter's breast, his fingers ghosting one of Peter's erect nipples, encountering the rushing thud of Peter's heart as it beats wildly underneath the soft flesh. He traces Peter's neck, his jawline, feeling that slight chafe from where Peter recently shaved, before he holds his fingers up to Peter's lips.

"Suck," Eli orders. And Peter obeys.

He takes just one at first, working his way down Eli's index finger, licking at the space between before he takes the middle finger, and then Eli's ring finger.

Eli feels powerful at the way Peter shudders underneath him.

"Are you ready?"

"For what?" Peter dares to ask.

"I want to finger you," Eli says simply. He knows better than to mince words when the situation could turn uncomfortable at the drop of a pin. "Is that okay?"

Peter seems to hesitate, and Eli hopes that he doesn't feel pressured to say yes. But he finally nods. "Yes, please."

"Okay." Eli maneuvers, his wet fingers tracing Peter's back. The angle is still awkward, given the height Peter has on him. "I'm going to go in slowly." Eli's lips are right against Peter's ear. "You'll be a good boy and tell me if you want me to stop, right?"

"I'll be a good boy," Peter repeats. "I promise."

"You're learning well." Eli can't help but smile. "Try your best to relax, okay?"

Eli slides his index finger into Peter, past the firm ring of muscle. He goes slowly.

"How does that feel?" Eli asks.

"A little weird . . ." Peter winces, the words coming out in hushed gasps as Eli continues to play with Peter's cock, pumping slower and slower, second by second. He just wants this to last for as long as it can.

"Do you want me to stop?"

"No, no," Peter says, impatient. "It's a good weird, I promise."

"Okay." Eli kisses Peter's neck, biting softly as he adds another finger, twisting carefully inside Peter, searching desperately for the thing he knows is there.

"Ohhh . . ." Peter gasps, his whines a song to Eli's ears as he crooks his fingers inside. "Oh, God . . . Eli."

"Close already?"

"Mm-hmm!" Peter nods feverishly.

"I don't know if you deserve to come yet, Peter." Eli slows his pace. He wants to edge him in just the right way, to leave Peter desperate. Wanting.

Hungry.

"Please, Eli . . ." Peter gasps, letting out a high-pitched whine as his back arches, Eli's fingers reaching in deep.

"No, I don't think so," Eli whispers, applying pressure to the head of Peter's wet cock.

Peter humps the air, thrusting his cock into Eli's hand, his pre-cum leaking like a faucet. "Please," Peter whines, as if *please* is the only word he can possibly think of. "Please."

He doesn't dare to add a third finger; he doesn't want to overload Peter, no more than he already has. Eli knows he's already addicted to watching Peter melt into a puddle of absolute pleasure, left as nothing but a bumbling mess as Eli works his way inside.

Eli drinks in Peter's mewls and whimpers, searching for *that* spot.

And when he finds it, it's magical.

Peter's eyes go wide in shock as his back arches off the bed, continuing to fuck into Eli's hand as he desperately gasps for air, like he can't get enough of it. "Oh my God!" His words slur as he sinks into bliss, and Eli smiles.

"I'm going to show you the magic of a prostate orgasm, Peter."

"God, fuck . . ." Peter murmurs against Eli's skin, drooling just a bit as Eli continues to press against that precious bundle of nerves. "Okay."

"Are you my good boy, Peter?"

"Yes, yes, yes," Peter babbles, turning his face toward Eli, the two of them so close that Eli almost meets Peter with a kiss.

"Say it."

"I'm a good boy," he cries, his voice cracking.

"You are," Eli promises. "That's right, Peter. Now . . . come for me."

Peter continues to fuck into Eli's hand, chasing a release. Eli bites his neck.

"Eli!" Peter calls out as he climaxes, his hand reaching for Eli's bicep, chest heaving like he can't possibly get enough air.

He does just that. It's marvelous to watch Peter as his orgasm ruts through him, his eyes going wide, his legs shaking, hole twitching with Eli still inside him as he shoots far enough to decorate both his and Eli's faces. Eli doesn't mind; he needed to wash his hair anyway.

"I'm here," Eli coos softly, running his hand through Peter's soft hair, scratching softly at his scalp.

"Oh, God!"

"Was that good?"

"It was . . ." Peter huffs. "You were . . . perfect . . ."

Eli can't help but laugh.

Peter lets out a low, exhausted laugh. "I think we made a mess?" He looks down at the milky streaks on his chest.

"Yeah . . . I'd say so." Eli tries to catch his breath. "We should get cleaned up."

Peter laughs and readjusts, a gasp slipping past his lips unexpectantly. "I, uh . . . I think your fingers are still inside me."

Eli smiles, burying his face in Peter's shoulder, listening to the sweet song of his laughter.

*   *   *

"I almost forgot what it was like to have hot water," Eli says, stepping out of the bathroom dressed in the clothes that Peter offered him. He assured Peter that he could survive in the short-shorts of his costume, but the moment he slipped into the oversize sweatpants and matching hoodie, he was grateful.

"Do you not get hot water?" Peter asks, still sitting on the edge of the bed mostly naked.

"Well, I'm living with two other people, and there's like eleven of us in the building, you have to find the perfect time. Which usually means showering at two in the morning."

"Eleven people in a building? How many units are there?"

"Three. There's a family of seven that lives below us, don't ask me how they manage to fit. I'd go crazy if I had to share our apartment with one more person."

Peter smiles, but he just as quickly averts his gaze, staring down at his phone.

"You okay?" Eli dares to ask.

"Yeah, yeah."

"You had fun, right?"

Peter's gaze shoots toward him. "Of course, Eli!" he says a little too quickly. "That was . . . I mean, that was amazing. I just, uh . . . it's not the sex."

"Do you want to talk about it?" Eli falls next to Peter on the bed, resting his chin on Peter's shoulder. The reason for Peter's hesitance is immediate, an odd feeling washing over Eli as he sees the Hinge chat waiting on the screen. "Oh."

His heart sinks.

"We've been talking for a few days. But he messaged like an hour ago, when we were . . . you know . . ."

"Fucking?"

Peter's cheeks turn a soft pink. "Yeah. He wants to go on a date this weekend."

"Well . . ." Eli readjusts, pulling away from Peter, ignoring the feeling that stirs in his gut. "What are you going to say?"

"I have no idea," Peter admits.

"Can I see?"

Peter hands Eli the phone, standing. "I'm going to shower."

"Okay." Eli scrolls to the stranger's profile. Lucas is handsome, he loves his golden retriever, he works at a bookstore. He's six foot two, brown haired, and green eyed. There are a few too many pictures of him with IPAs for Eli to ever take an interest. Eli scrolls far enough up the chat log to see that Lucas liked one of Peter's photos first.

LUCAS: We should meet up this weekend!

That's it. Peter got a date.

Wasn't this the point? To help Peter get comfortable with going on dates on his own?

So why does it feel like the end of the world?

Eli's ears perk up at the sound of Peter's shower running. He can't help himself from swiping out of Lucas's profile, and he's faced with a page filled with matches. There are a handful of replies from Peter, a few one-sided conversations where Peter either never got or never sent a reply. Then there are a few where the chat began and ended with various versions of "Sorry, no Asians." Eli's stomach twists.

It's a breach of privacy, Eli knows that. He knows that and he can't help himself from closing the app, finding Bumble among the organized mess of Peter's home screen. It's much the same, a bunch of different matches stretching back a week or so. Anyone who's messaged has been met with no reply from Peter.

This pang slowly eats at his heart. He has to stop himself from swiping through all of these men and unmatching them. The phone vibrates a moment later, and then again, and Eli sees the screen light up with a text from Peter's mom, and another Hinge message from Lucas.

Eli swallows, tasting the bile on his tongue. He knows that it isn't too late, that he could tell Peter how he feels right now.

So why doesn't he?

He throws the phone onto the mattress and lets himself fall back, breathing in the mild scent that lingers on Peter's clothing. And to think he'd laughed when Peter said they should have some kind of clause in case one of them caught feelings for the other.

"Fuck's sake . . ." Eli murmurs.

He's not in love with Peter, he can't be. This entire situation is built off the idea that he's not in love with Peter.

He's *not* in love with Peter Park.

Eli can't do that to himself.

The shower shuts off, and Eli listens to the sounds of Peter drying himself off. The door opens, steam spilling from the bathroom as Peter walks back through to the bedroom with a towel wrapped around his waist.

"What do you think?" Peter asks.

"Hmm?" Eli can't look at him for longer than a brief second. "Oh, he's, uh . . . he's nice."

"Do you think I should go out with him?" Peter asks. "Do you think that I'm ready?"

"Yeah, you're ready." Eli can't keep the curt tone of his voice to himself, and he hates himself for it. Because none of this is Peter's fault.

Not an ounce of it.

"He's cute," Eli throws in, just to make it seem like he's actually interested.

"And he has a dog."

"Yeah . . ." Eli can't muster the energy to continue the conversation. "Well . . . I should get back home, I have to be up early tomorrow."

"I can give you a ride back, just let me get—" Peter starts to say, but Eli stops him.

"It's okay, I don't want to impose," Eli tells him, pulling himself up quickly, heading right for the door.

"Are you sure?" Peter asks. "I just have to get dressed."

"It's fine, Peter. I promise. I can take the bus." He doesn't like how short he's being with Peter. But the sooner he's out of here, the better.

"Oh, okay. Well . . . let me walk you out, at least."

"Yeah, sure," Eli relents, knowing that he's giving too much of himself away. He can't let Peter think that something's wrong.

Because nothing is wrong.

That's the lie he continues to tell himself as he waits for Peter to dress in sweats before he follows Eli out to the sidewalk.

"So . . . do you think you can help me get ready for this date?"

"Yeah, yeah . . ." Eli tells him, struggling to form words with just how quickly his brain is working against him. "Um, just text me the details."

"Okay, sounds good."

"Good night, Peter," Eli says quickly, ready to exit this entire night.

"Good night, Eli."

Chapter Sixteen

Little Miss Sunshine, dir. by Jonathan Dayton and Valerie Faris

Try as he might, Eli can't ignore his phone all weekend.

Peter keeps texting him, asking if he should really go on this date, what he should wear, where they should go for dinner, should they do anything afterward? What about kissing, is kissing on the first date okay? Should Peter hold his hand? What should they talk about? What topics are off limits?

It's as if the last two months hadn't happened.

Eli almost wishes they hadn't.

Almost.

He turns off the movie as the credits play, one of his favorite early aughts slasher movies coming to an end as he wallows on the couch.

Eli checks his phone again, annoyed at the irony that all day he'd begged for Peter to stop texting. And now, all he wants to do is talk to him. There's that absence in his heart, one that pulls on him, one that tells him all he wants is Peter here next to him on the couch, his larger body on top of Eli's to help ground him.

He misses Peter.

And he doesn't know what to do about it.

> **ELI:** soooooooooooooooo . . .
>
> how was the date?

He types out the text, praying that he comes off as more curious, rather than hoping the date was a disaster and Peter has no interest in Lucas.

He can't do this.

This was never supposed to happen. Eli was never supposed to develop feelings for Peter. This was never on the table. Hell, they'd even established a *clause* just in case. So why hadn't Eli pulled out?

Because he loves him.

He doesn't want to admit it.

But Eli Francis has fallen in love with Peter Park.

He loves the smell of him, that goofy smile, that curl to his hair as it's grown out. He loves the golden shade of Peter's brown skin, and the deep color of his brown eyes. He loves how Peter's two front teeth overlap in the smallest way. Eli loves his dimples, how large his hands are, how soft his skin is. Eli loves the mole on Peter's neck that he can't keep his eyes off of. He loves how brave Peter has been, how he always wants to care for others before he cares for himself, how he's never quite gotten the hang of sarcasm. He loves how Peter felt the need to hide the best parts of himself, and how he slowly allowed Eli to see all the things he was afraid to show.

He loves that he got the chance to know the real Peter Park.

Eli starts to delete the text message, knowing in his gut that it's the wrong thing to do, especially if Peter is still on the date.

The handle of their front door jiggles as the lock turns, and Patricia stumbles in, two bags strapped around her shoulders and holding another tote bag that she drops to the floor the *moment* the door closes behind her.

"Rough day?" Eli asks.

Patricia huffs, letting the other bags fall. "As if being called in on a Saturday wasn't enough, my editor suddenly decides that blue isn't the way to go for the new spread, so I had to rush new swatches, praying that she'd pick *something*. She didn't, so I had to visit three other fabric stores. Then I found out that our photographer from the last shoot suddenly thought he wasn't getting paid enough, so he's holding our photos hostage." Patricia strolls over to the couch, flopping down onto the cushions next to Eli. "Sidenote: his photos are *not* worth the extra grand that he's asking for."

"Didn't he sign a contract?" Eli asks her.

"Something I reminded him of before he *finally* sent the photos along. Then I added him to our blacklist." Patricia sighs, finally seeming to relax for the first time in days. "I need weed."

Eli hands her his pen.

"Thank you." She takes a careful hit. "What about you? It feels like it's been days since I've seen you."

"You saw me at lunch on Thursday."

"Which was basically three years ago our time." Patricia nudges him. "What'd I miss?"

"Well," Eli starts to say, sitting up straight on the couch. "I'm going to be published."

Patricia stares at him. "Shut the fuck up. Like . . . *published* published?"

Eli can't help his smile, despite all his nerves.

"By *Vent*? Or did you finally go somewhere else?"

"*Vent*."

"Eli!" Patricia almost leaps on him. "Why didn't you tell me?"

"You were busy," he tells her. That and he'd been busy with Peter.

"Wait, you've been writing something this entire time? What is it? What did you write about? Why didn't you let me read it?"

"This one was kind of a private project."

"Can you tell me about it now?"

He gives her the quick pitch, keeping out certain details, like the secret article about Peter. There's no reason he needs that judgment. Not tonight.

"That's amazing. Can I read it?"

"Yeah." Eli finds the article in his Drive. There are still no new updates from Michael, but Eli tells himself it's probably because he downloaded the article. Actual writers work in Word, not Google Docs. Patricia's eyes dart back and forth quickly as she scrolls through the article, her smile growing the longer she reads.

"Wow, this is great, Eli!"

"Thanks."

"I had no idea you were writing this."

"Like I said, it was kind of a secret thing I was working on with Michael."

She hands Eli's phone back to him. "I'm honestly surprised he wanted something like this. Something this serious deserves a better home than *Vent*."

Eli swallows. "Yeah, it was a shock to me too."

"And I'm guessing this 'Alex,' is that . . .'"

"Peter, yeah."

"So, you *haven't* been dating him this entire time?"

"No, yeah . . . about that. We came to an agreement, after he came to the office to apologize for how awful that first date was. That's when I pitched the idea to Michael, and afterward, when Peter and I were talking, I agreed to help teach him how to date in exchange for the article."

"So, you fake-dated for an article? What in the romance novel . . ."

"We didn't pretend to date. Until we did, but it was mostly about teaching him the things he'd never gotten the chance to learn; you know, growing up in such a small town."

"That's a great idea, Eli."

"Yeah . . ." He wishes it actually felt that way.

"So why am I getting the impression that you're not happy with things?"

"What makes you say that?"

"Well, first of all . . ." Patricia grabs the remote from the coffee table, exiting out of the movie. "You only watch *Cherry Falls* when you're depressed."

"Sometimes I just miss Brittany Murphy."

"Don't we all." Patricia sighs. "But you're also not giving me the energy of someone who's finally getting their big break after working on it for so long."

"Well . . . I don't know."

"This is *exciting*! You should've told me and Rose, we would've gone out!" Patricia peeks down the hallway. "Speaking of, where is Rose?"

"She went to Jolene's, had a hard week."

Patricia stands, grabbing Eli's hand and pulling. "Fair, but we can still go out. Come on, the milkshakes at Orphan Andy's are calling my name."

"I'm not in the mood."

Patricia sinks back to the couch as quickly as she stood. "What's going on with you? This is exciting, we should be celebrating!"

"It's not happening, sorry."

She pouts. "Come on, what's going on?"

"Nothing," he tells her.

He wants Patricia to know everything. He looks at his phone, staring at the half-deleted message before he holds down the backspace button, watching as it slowly disappears.

Then he makes a decision.

"You know what?" Eli looks at Patricia. "Fuck it."

She grins. "Milkshakes?"

* * *

PETER: Any chance you're still awake?

Eli wishes he wasn't. Between his stomach rolling from the milkshakes despite the Lactaid and the nerves of Peter's date, he's been stuck in bed, watching his phone slowly tick toward two in the morning.

ELI: unfortunately

ELI: what's up?

PETER: Can I call you, actually?

Eli sits up straight, turning on his lamp. He stares at the message, weighing the options in his head.

ELI: yeah, of course

The call comes in a second later. Eli braces himself before he swipes to answer it.

"Sorry, it was a lot to explain over text." Peter's voice is calm, tired almost.

"It's okay. Is everything all right?"

"Yeah, yeah. I just . . . I thought you'd want to know about the date, and how it went." He laughs low. "See what all your hard work accomplished."

"Oh, right. Yeah."

Silence.

"So?" Eli prompts.

"Oh, sorry. I thought you were going to say something else."

Eli can't help his laughter. "No, no. I'm waiting on you."

"Well . . . the date was . . . I mean, it was okay."

Eli feels his stomach unclench. "Oh? Just okay?"

"Yeah, he was nice. Talked a lot. Too much, actually." That explains why Peter is still up. "And you know me, I already don't talk a lot."

"No, no, you don't."

"But yeah . . . I don't know, it was nice, but there wasn't a . . . a spark, I guess is what the books would call it."

"A spark," Eli repeats.

"You know, that moment where you feel like someone might be 'the one' or whatever." Peter laughs. "I feel like an idiot, sorry."

"No, don't apologize. I'm familiar with the concept." Eli swallows. "You know, just because you don't feel this invisible spark on date number one doesn't mean that the person isn't the one for you."

"I know, I know. But still, I guess I was looking for . . . I guess some excitement. It sounds mean, but I don't think I'd look forward to another date with him."

"So, you decided not to see him again?" Eli cringes. *That's* what he took from Peter spilling his heart out?

"I don't think so. I mean, we both agreed that it was kind of a bust, which was mortifying at first, but I'm glad we had the conversation."

"Yeah, of course. Better to have that happen than to drag something out."

"That's what I was thinking." Peter's hesitation is pregnant, and the seconds between his words stretch on for so long that Eli's worried that the call might've dropped at first. "Do you think I did good?"

The question surprises Eli, though he's not sure why. "I mean, I wasn't there, so I can't be sure."

"Right, right." Peter laughs. "I wish you had been. I think I would've been more relaxed."

"Were you nervous?"

"Oh, hell yeah. I was so scared, and sweaty too. Thank God I was wearing a jacket."

"I think the real question here is, do *you* think you did good?"

"I think I did. I tried to keep in mind the things you taught me, being attentive, asking questions. We didn't kiss, and I didn't hold his hand or anything, but . . ." Peter pauses. "Never mind, that's stupid."

"What?"

Peter laughs nervously. "I'm not going to tell you."

"Oh, come on, you have to!"

"Nope, I actually decided that I don't."

Eli giggles. "Please," he begs. "It's just me, what harm could it do?"

"No, no way."

"What did we say about honesty, huh? Who else could you share this with other than me?"

More silence from Peter, though Eli can hear his careful breathing.

"I, uh . . . when I got too nervous, I'd picture he was you."

"Oh."

"See? It's embarrassing, who does that?"

"Plenty of people. Though they probably do the underwear trick. I'm not sure if I'd love thousands of people picturing me when they're nervous."

"I'm sorry."

"Why?"

"Because . . . I don't know. I just am."

"Well, I'm sorry too."

"Why?"

Eli swallows. *Why not?*

"I don't know." He tries to smile. "I just am."

He swears he can hear Peter's smile in his laugh. "Fine. We're both sorry."

"There, happy?"

"Yes," Peter says through a yawn.

"Do you want to get dinner on Monday?" Eli asks out of nowhere.

"Oh, uh . . . sure! Let's do it. We have to celebrate anyway."

"Celebrate?"

"Your article?"

"Right, right. Let's do it." Eli pulls his comforter closer around himself. "Let's do Doobu, first date round three?" He doesn't mean for it to be a question, but that's how it comes out.

"Sure," Peter tells him. "First date round three."

"Okay, go to bed. Please."

"I will," Peter says. "You go to bed too."

"I will."

"Good night, Eli."

"Night, Peter."

Eli ends the call first, setting his phone back on the charger. He lies back down, but try as he might, he can't fall asleep for another hour. Because he knows what he has to do.

And frankly, he can't wait.

Chapter Seventeen

Who Framed Roger Rabbit, dir. by Robert Zemeckis

Eli knows he should never wake up on a Monday feeling hopeful. But he can't help that rise in his chest as he opens his eyes just a few minutes before his alarm goes off. Sure, his body is fighting against him like it always does, and he lies there in bed scrolling on his phone until the absolute *last* possible second.

And it's raining, so his perfectly styled hair plasters itself to his forehead and the toes of his socks are soaked through thanks to a puddle he doesn't see.

And the first bus that comes Eli's way is out of service.

And the second bus is packed full of wet people who smell like sweat.

But he's *hopeful*.

He walks into the *Vent* offices still feeling like he's finally won, even as he sits down at his desk in front of Michael's empty office, the ever-constant reminder of where he's stuck. Except now he isn't.

Well, hopefully he isn't.

He resists the urge to email Michael, to walk around the office until he finds him, to ask him if there are any updates on the article. If the editorial team has gotten ahold of it, if the article is going to come out soon.

Eli has to stop himself, knowing he won't get anywhere rushing things.

He's waited five years for this.

He can wait a few more days.

Besides, he has bigger things on his mind. Like how this dinner with Peter is going to go. Maybe he should've given Peter a heads-up, told him that he wanted to have a serious conversation about where they're at, how things will be moving forward.

Because this doesn't feel fake anymore.

At least, not from Eli's perspective.

And Peter deserves to know that, just as he deserves to decide for himself. Whether or not he still wants Eli to be a part of his life knowing . . . knowing that Eli loves him. Eli pulls his phone out of his desk drawer, checking the last messages he sent to Peter the night before.

Eli had tried to stay up as late as he could, just to keep Peter company.

But he can see the moment he fell asleep, just as Peter was explaining his late-night dinner of peanut butter and Ritz crackers.

He stares at his phone, unable to help the smile that creeps up on him. It's so hard to believe that things finally feel . . . whole?

Maybe he's putting all his eggs in a single basket, something his mother always warned him about. But he can't stop the way his heart leaps in his chest.

Eli tries hard not to think about the fact that Michael's been missing all morning. But after several hours of fielding Michael's calls and telling his coworkers that he doesn't know where Michael is, he has to take a look around.

Michael's things are here, so he's been in the office. Eli checks the bathrooms and the meeting rooms, the private offices, and the lounge area.

And there's no Michael to be found.

He nearly goes to Keith to ask him if he knows anything, being the brownnoser he is. But Keith isn't in his office either.

"Gwen?" Eli calls for her just as she's passing his desk on her way to the elevators. "Have you seen Michael or Keith?"

"I think I saw them heading up to the cafeteria?" She looks at her watch. "That was first thing this morning, I'm not sure where—"

"Hey, Eli!" Owen, the hire who stole Eli's staff spot, decides to insert himself into the conversation, rapping his knuckles on Eli's desk.

"Oh, hey, Owen . . . Looking for Michael?"

"Oh no, no, I just wanted to give you my congratulations!"

Eli freezes. "Congratulations for what?"

"For the article? What a hilarious read."

Hilarious? Eli can think of a few jokes peppered throughout the Lavender Country article, but he wouldn't go so far as to describe it as hilarious. "Wait . . . does Michael have you editing it?"

"Editing?" Owen stares, stealing a piece of candy from the dish on Eli's desk. "No, it's on the site."

"It was posted?"

"Yeah, like half an hour ago, I think?" Owen opens the candy carefully, the wrapper crinkling in his hand. Gwen gives Eli a confused look. "What a ride, I couldn't stop reading. That disaster date, I don't think I would've given someone like that another chance. You're better than me for sure."

Eli's stomach sinks.

"What are you talking about?" His words come out slowly, careful, almost as if they aren't his own.

Owen just looks confused, because why wouldn't he be?

"What article are you talking about?" Eli asks him.

"The one about dating? That guy you fixed. What else could I be talking about?"

"Michael accepted a piece you wrote?" Gwen asks. "That's great, Eli!"

"No, no, it's not," he whispers under his breath. He doesn't bother looking it up on his computer; he doesn't want Owen or Gwen to see his reaction. So instead, he goes into the bathroom, hiding in one of the stalls. He pulls *Vent* up on his phone, hoping that he'll have to scroll pages to find the article.

"Building a Better Boyfriend" is all of the title that the trending page displays. Eli clicks on the link, redirected right to the page where the full headline reads "Building a Better Boyfriend: How I Molded a Walking Disaster into the Perfect Date."

By Eli Francis.

His vision goes blurry at the edges as he swipes through the article.

Because it's *his* article, the fake one he wrote to convince Michael that he was still going along with this idea, the one that was never meant to see the light of day.

It's his article. He desperately doesn't want it to be.

But it is.

"This doesn't make sense," Eli whispers to himself.

He never gave Michael permission to post the article; he didn't even write an ending. He never saw the need to. Yet there is one. Eli likes to think he's good at recognizing specific styles of writing. He's picked up on certain words or phrases or ways of weaving a story that some writers love to use. He's certainly familiar with his own writing.

After the first line, he can tell this isn't his.

He got someone else to finish it, Eli realizes.

He stands, shoving his phone into his pocket, letting the stall door slam behind him. Just as he exits the bathroom, who would finally make an appearance other than the two people he's desperate to find?

"What the fuck?" he says as loudly as he can without actually shouting. Keith's and Michael's gazes both shift toward him, finding Eli in an instant, as do the eyes of some of his other coworkers.

"Oh, Eli. I was just coming to find you," Michael says, continuing to his office as if nothing's wrong.

"What the *fuck* is wrong with you?" Eli asks again. "The both of you."

"Hey, what did I do?" Keith holds his hands up defensively.

"Don't fuck with me, Keith." Eli says the name with more malice than he ever has. "I edited and rewrote *how* many of your articles? I *know* how you write; I know you finished the piece."

"If you want to talk about this like a civilized person"—Michael stares at him—"then I suggest you come into my office, Eli. Otherwise, you're free to leave."

For a moment, Eli considers doing just that. He stares daggers at Michael, and then Keith, before he stomps into Michael's office.

"Give us a minute," Michael murmurs to Keith as he goes to close the door, and Keith nods, walking off, leaving Michael and Eli all alone. "Sit down."

"Fuck you, Michael," Eli sputters without thinking.

"Colorful language we're using today," Michael says as he takes his seat. "Will you give me a chance to explain myself, or are you going to continue acting like a child?"

"A child? *You* went behind my back and stole an article. You published my work without permission."

"Just like you went behind my back and wrote an article that I never told you to write?" Michael glares at Eli.

Eli opens his mouth to say something, but he stops himself.

"That's not the same."

"No, it's not. Because I *told* you what I wanted from you. And you've strung me along for weeks, showing me bits of what I needed from you. Then you come to me with . . . whatever that last thing was. And you expected me to just be fine with it? To be okay with you lying to me?"

Eli doesn't know what to say. A thousand things come to mind, at least half of them variations of "Fuck off." But he stops himself.

"You lied to me, Eli. And you thought you'd get away with it. But you didn't. This is me teaching you a lesson."

"What lesson?"

Michael types something on his keyboard before he turns his screen around toward Eli. "You're top of our trending page. Online, you're a hot button. It's been an hour and people have been talking all over about your article. Some TikToks have a few thousand views. Talking about *your* work."

The evidence speaks for itself. There are shares, posts, all discussing Eli's article. From just a few feet away, he can see some of the reactions.

They range from people calling "Alex" a loser and a freak, making fun of him for being almost thirty and never dating, to people telling Eli that he overstepped, that he's the asshole, wondering why a white man would write about a gay Korean man, asking how he sleeps at night after exploiting someone like Alex.

His stomach sinks.

"That's not what this was ever about," Eli tells him, his words desperate. "This isn't what I set out to do."

"The numbers are only growing, by the way." Michael ignores him. "The article is already the most popular this month."

"Doesn't it bother you?" Eli dares.

"Why would it? My paycheck is direct-deposited into my account every Friday, just like yours."

"Don't you give a shit? That I didn't want to do the original article? Doesn't it mean anything to you that I had to go behind your back to actually write something worth reading?"

"Like how you considered Peter's feelings?" Michael stares.

And suddenly, things go quiet.

"That's not—"

"Fair? Welcome to journalism. I thought that I could teach you something, I thought that you had the chops to prove yourself here at *Vent*. I wanted to mold you, Eli; you're a good kid, and a hard worker. But unless you're willing to adapt to what people *want* to read, you'll never make it anywhere in this industry."

"You held the writer position over me, you *promised* me—"

"Please, Eli. We're adults; promises don't mean anything. You can try to blame me all you want," Michael says. "But when I had this idea, I never held a gun to your head, Eli. *You* made the decision to work on the article. *You* decided to do this. Not me."

Eli stares, his chest heaving, fists balled together.

"And now you have to deal with the consequences."

He's right. Michael's right.

At any point, before this started, Eli could've said no, realized this was wrong, accepted that this was not how he wanted to make a name for himself. He could've said no, he could've quit *Vent* at any point and time. And he didn't.

He took on the responsibility. The duty.

The lie.

And at the end of the day, this is no one's fault save for his own.

"Take the article down."

"I can't," Michael says. "I'm not going to sacrifice clicks and ad revenue because you're in love with this guy."

"I'm not—"

"Please, Eli. I've read the articles. Both of them; so did Keith. It's clear that you have feelings for him."

"Just take it down, I didn't consent to you posting it."

"Doesn't matter," Michael tells him. "You wrote this for *Vent* as an employee of *Vent*, which means it belongs to *Vent*." He finally stands. "I'm trying to teach you something here, Eli. This chance, you can't let it go. The readership from this article, it's huge and it's only been an hour. You could have what it takes to be a real asset to *Vent* if you just let these personal feelings go. So, if you can just understand what I've been trying to teach you, if you can accept these lessons, then I'd love to offer you the staff writer position."

Eli snorts. "You're not serious."

"I am." Michael holds out a hand.

And for a second, just a *second*, Eli considers what it all means. More job security, the opportunity to write more, to make a larger name for himself, to build a career. *Vent* is only the first step to something larger. Once he has that platform, once he has a stronger portfolio, he can leave. He can go somewhere else, somewhere they'd let him write the harder-hitting, important pieces that he's been desperate to write for years.

And in exchange, all he has to do is give up Peter.

It's not like Peter will want to see him ever again, not with the article out there. So he should take the offer, right?

"You're right, this is my fault," Eli admits to him. "I could've said no to you, I could've come to you earlier and said that this is wrong. But I didn't, and I can't go back and fix that. Just like I can't make Peter forgive me. But at the very least, I can make a choice, right here, right now, to not be the person that you're asking me to be."

The frustration is apparent on Michael's face in an instant. "Well . . . I can't say I'm surprised, but I'm disappointed."

"I'll pack my desk up," Eli cuts in, walking toward the door.

"You've been a strength at *Vent*, Eli. You'll be missed."

"Thanks, Michael, can't say the same about you." Eli lets the door close behind him, then walks over and sinks into his desk chair. He doesn't quite know what to do with himself except start gathering his things and tossing them into his bag.

None of his coworkers bother to come up to him, none of them wondering just what happened in Michael's office. In fact, only one of his—now former—coworkers dares to look him in the eye.

From the comfort of his office too.

Eli stands, covering the distance to Keith's office in quick strides.

"Can I talk to you?" Eli asks, closing Keith's open door behind him.

"Sure, I have the time."

"Do you feel good about what you did? Worming your way into my article, turning around and finishing it for me after Michael told you what he was planning?"

"I did my job, Eli." Keith's voice is firm, unwavering. "I did what I was told to do because unlike you, I have what it takes to survive in this business."

"Oh, yeah . . . writing articles about TikTok trends by the time they're already outdated and some celebrity bleaching her hair blonde and how it gives you 'all the feels.' Real groundbreaking journalism, Keith."

"Did it ever occur to you that we don't have the same aspirations? That I don't want to wake up every morning and wonder how I can win the Pulitzer Prize as a secretary? That not everyone has the same level of self-important righteousness that you do?"

Eli pauses, not expecting the biting words.

"Yeah, at the end of the day I'm writing garbage, and I'm not always happy with myself. But at least I'm not a coward, Eli."

"What does that mean?"

"It means that you've been here for *five* years, and for four of those, you chewed my ear off about the lack of opportunities, never getting the chance to grow, when you could've left at any time. No one was stopping you."

"Michael was, he—"

"You could have *left*. And maybe things would've been rough, but at the very least you could've finally been working to make something of yourself instead of just talking about it."

Eli swallows.

"Is that why—"

Keith rolls his eyes, raking his hands through his hair. "Don't ask if that's why I broke up with you."

"Well, is it?" Eli begs anyway. "Is that the reason?"

Keith sighs before he asks, "Do you want the truth?"

And Eli nods.

"Yeah, it is. Part of it, at least," he finally says. "Because I'm an adult, and I had to move on with my life. And I couldn't be with someone who weighed himself down so badly to the point that he was afraid to move on. I want a future, Eli. I want a career, I want a home, and I want . . . I want. I want and so do you, but it was clear that we didn't want in the same way."

Now, it's Eli's turn to refuse to look at Keith.

"You're a coward," Keith continues. "And that was fine for a while because we're all afraid of something. I was afraid of breaking your heart. The difference between the two of us is that I'm not addicted to my own misery."

Eli has a thousand biting words on his tongue, ranging from the simple *Fuck you* to the lie that is *You're wrong*.

He knows Keith is right.

He's never wanted to admit it to himself before, but he's been afraid for a long time now.

"You're right," Eli tells him. "You're right. I was afraid. I *am* afraid."

Keith seems taken aback by the honesty.

"And I'm sorry for the things I put you through, for not listening more, for turning my problems into yours. That was selfish."

"Oh, well . . . thank you, Eli."

"And I'm sorry that things have been so uncomfortable here for so long. Maybe I should've taken that as a sign to get out of here earlier, to leave with a little more dignity."

"I can't fault you for that," Keith says. "I certainly didn't help."

"No . . . you didn't," Eli tells him. "Can I ask you something? You can say no, but I'd like your honesty if you choose to answer it."

"Okay." There's an exhausted tone to Keith's voice.

"Did you really fall out of love with me? Or was that just the excuse you gave me to spare my feelings?"

"No," Keith answers without hesitation. "I never fell out of love with you."

Eli swallows.

"But I could see that we're two different people, Eli. That we wanted different things out of life. And I knew that you'd never be brave enough to break my heart."

"So, you did it for me?"

Keith remains silent.

"Did it ever occur to you that that's not what I wanted?" Eli asks.

"No, because in that moment I needed to be selfish." Keith sighs. "Lots of things occurred to me, but I did what I thought was right. Because that's all any of us can do with what we have."

Eli doesn't know how to accept this odd truth.

"For what it's worth, Peter seems like a fantastic guy."

"You barely even met him," Eli says.

"Yeah, but I had to read all your notes and drafts to finish the article, and Michael gave me Lavender Country to look over. I know that the entire premise of this thing was for the two of you to fake everything, but . . . it seemed genuine."

"He taught me a lot," Eli admits. "Like going for the things that scare me."

"Have *you* talked to him?" Keith asks.

"Not yet."

"Well . . . you should."

"I know," Eli says, stepping toward the office door. "Thanks, Keith."

"Go, before Michael calls building security on you."

Eli can't stop himself from smiling, managing to forget for nearly a full second that the hardest part of the day isn't over yet. He strides back toward his desk, grabbing his bag off the back of his chair.

He nearly slips the company iPad and Apple Pencil into his bag as well. It wouldn't be the first time property isn't returned to IT, but he decides against it. He doesn't want anything of *Vent* to linger in his apartment. He's done with this chapter of his life. For better or for worse.

Now he has to come clean.

* * *

Eli calls Peter a total of twenty times.

Six times while he waits for the bus, eleven more times *on* the bus, and three times on the short four-block walk from the stop to the front of Peter's apartment. He only leaves one voicemail.

"Hey, Peter. Please call me when you get this. It's important."

It's all he knows how to say. He doesn't want Peter to hear anything else unless it's coming directly from him. Not even through his phone.

He rounds the block, soaked thanks to the rain that's now pouring down, seeing the gate to Peter's building out of the corner of his eye. He could turn around right now. Block Peter on everything, hide from him for the rest of his life and leave Peter with nothing.

But Keith was right. Eli is a coward. And he has been for a long time.

So it's time to fix that.

He presses on the doorbell again and again and again. He pulls out his phone, rain splattering the screen the same way it's covered his glasses, his hot breath fogging them up, hair hanging limp in his face.

There's still no answer, and Eli lets his head fall against the iron gate. If Peter isn't here, then he doesn't know where he could be. He doesn't know where to go to tell Peter the truth.

He doesn't know what to do.

"Eli?"

Eli hears the voice from behind, whipping around to face Peter dressed in his climbing clothes, an empty cup of iced coffee in hand.

"You're soaking wet."

"Hey . . ." Eli's voice manages to cut through the rain.

"Everything okay? I thought we were getting dinner?" Peter asks him, as if Eli's world hasn't been ending for the last hour.

"About that . . ." Eli starts to say.

"Come inside. You can shower and then we can head out if you want." Peter steps closer, pulling his keys free of his pocket. "Or we can eat here? I don't have many groceries, but maybe we could order something?"

"Peter, I came here because I need to talk to you."

"Okay, well, we can talk. Let's go inside." Peter swings the gate open, letting himself and Eli into the small apartment entrance. "Is everything okay?"

"No, it's not," Eli says, knowing that this can't wait, knowing that if he allows himself to step into Peter's apartment, he'll never want to admit the truth.

"Are you all right? Did something happen at work?" Peter asks over the echoes of the rain that's starting to fall again outside. Eli hates the careful nature of his voice.

"I fucked up," Eli tells him, plain and simple.

Except there's nothing simple about this.

Peter stares, obviously confused. "I'm sure it wasn't that bad, we can—"

"You know the article I was writing about you? It wasn't what I said it was. Well, it was, but it wasn't."

"Okay?" Peter stares, confused. A totally valid reaction.

"I wrote two articles. I wrote the article about you, about being gay in the South, about your experiences. But that's not what I told my editor, Michael, I was writing. I sprung that piece on him in the hopes that he'd want to publish it."

Eli can see Peter doing the math in his head. "So, what was the other article?"

"About dating you," Eli finally says, the words hurting as they leave his lips. "This entire thing, our fake relationship, me trying to fix you."

Peter doesn't say a word.

Eli pulls out his phone, opening his browser where the article sits. He hands Peter the phone, watching as he reads through it. Eli waits for the revelation, for the confusion to lift, the anger to settle in. He wants Peter to throw his phone down and smash it into a million tiny pieces; he wants Peter to yell at him, to call him every nasty, terrible name that he can think of. He wants Peter to hate him, because that would make things so much easier to understand. Instead, Peter gives him a numb look as he hands Eli back his phone.

His expression hasn't changed once.

"I don't understand what this is . . ." Peter says, hurt carrying his voice. Eli can't see how there's any room for misinterpreting what he's done. It's like he *wants* Eli to explain it to him, though Eli doubts Peter is that cruel. "'The naivete was a precious defense mechanism, but his lack of experience slowed him down.' What is this?"

"It's an article about fixing you," Eli admits. "I gave the idea to rehabilitate you to my editor. I thought that I could trick Michael into reading my other article about you and publishing that instead."

"My name isn't in it."

"I know, I changed it. To protect you." Which seems hilarious now.

"You wrote this about me?" Peter asks, his voice so soft the rain does its best to hide it.

"Yes. I did. And I'm so sorry, Peter. I don't have enough words to tell you how sorry I am—"

"So that's what this was really about? Is this why you wanted to help me? So I could be a subject for this article?" The hurt in Peter's voice twists into Eli like a knife. "So you could do this article and get your writer job?"

"No," Eli tells him. "I never meant for him to publish this article. Most of this isn't mine, in fact; Keith had to finish it."

"But you still wrote everything else?" Peter can only stare at Eli, his expression contorting with the hurt. "You wrote all of these cruel words, you lied to me, went behind my back, and still wrote this article."

"Peter, I'm sorry. No one was ever supposed to see it."

"But people did," Peter says plainly, with no anger in his voice. Eli hates that he almost wishes Peter would yell, then his feelings might be clearer.

"I don't want to talk about this," Peter says, turning, readying his keys for the door to the garage.

"Peter, please. I'm sorry."

"I don't want to talk to you, Eli. Please, just go home."

"Peter."

"You know what the worst part of this is?" Peter asks. "You're my friend. I knew that a part of this was fake, that this whole situation was weird, that we were only friends because you wanted something out of me, and I wanted something out of you. But I really thought . . ." He pauses. "I thought over these last few weeks that we'd actually become friends. I thought I finally had someone."

"You do, you're—"

"Is this all I am to you? A 'loser who seems incapable of forming a genuine social connection'?" Eli can't remember the words exactly, but he can recall seeing a similar string of them in the article. "I can't believe you'd play with my feelings like this. That you'd write these things about me."

"That wasn't me. My editor, he changed what I had, he—"

"Is that really what you think of me?"

"Peter, no! Please! Just let me talk to you." Eli reaches for Peter, but Peter yanks himself away, as if Eli's touch burns.

"And you thought you'd get away with it." Peter huffs, turning away. "Just leave, please."

"Peter . . ."

He slides his key into the lock, twisting it. "Go home, Eli," Peter says, his hand on the doorknob, face hidden in the corner. "I'm sorry that I ever agreed to this."

"Peter, please . . ." Eli feels the desperation rising in his throat. "I . . . I'm in love with you." He shouldn't say the words. It feels like a guilt trip, but they slip out without his permission.

Peter remains unmoving.

"I'm sorry. I know that I'm going to be saying that for the rest of my life, but I'm sorry. I wish that I could go back and change things, I wish that I didn't write this article, and I wish that I had the courage to tell you when I first started to feel this way, but I didn't. Just like I can't change how I feel about you, and how I'm glad that I got to spend time with you, that I gave you a second chance." Eli breathes so carefully, as if the world is truly that fragile.

Perhaps it is.

"I'm sorry, Peter. I have so, *so* many regrets, but you're not one of them."

Another long silence filled by the rain that continues to pour down in gallons just a few feet away. A car drives by, honking at another car, hitting a dip in the street that causes water to splash somewhere.

The seconds turn to minutes, turn to hours as Eli stands there, hoping for something.

For anything at all.

But he has to recognize that he isn't owed that. He hurt Peter, and whatever reaction he has is a valid one. Eli has to consider how he'd react if the tables were turned, if Peter had used him for clout, to further his career in a pathetic attempt to make something of his life.

No matter what, though, that's not what happened.

He hurt Peter, and no number of imaginary scenarios will ever change that Eli is the one at fault here.

No one else.

"Yeah, I was in love with you too," Peter finally says, turning the doorknob. "But I guess we both made the wrong choice." Peter opens the door, stepping into the garage. And Eli nearly follows him after it slams closed, nearly bangs on the door, pleads with Peter to hear him out.

But he doesn't do any of that, because Eli has to be okay with what just happened. He has to accept the truth of the matter.

Because there's no changing it. Only moving on.

So, with nothing else left to do, he does what Peter told him to. He goes home.

Chapter Eighteen

Star Wars: Episode III—Revenge of the Sith, dir. by George Lucas

Eli just wishes he could wallow in bed for a bit longer.

He gave himself exactly two days in bed. The first of which involved a lot of crying, Patricia and Rose bringing him water and snacks every few hours or so, like he's in bed with the flu. The second day was better, though he still didn't have the strength to crawl out from under his comforter.

By day three, he'd convinced himself to finally shower and wash his hair, hoping that it would help the emptiness that he felt in his chest, the pressure that rested there now and didn't seem to show any sign of going away. He rested against the atrociously pink tiled wall and sank to the ceramic of the tub, letting the water pour over him like the rain had just a few days ago.

Day four was the first that he dared to step out of his bedroom, and he only made it to the couch before he began to cry again. In fact, day five was the first day without any tears. But he made the mistake of watching *Happy Together*, which only made him feel worse about himself.

It was Patricia who picked up the remote, declaring, "Enough Wong Kar-Wai," before she found *Shrek 2*, which only made Eli cry harder.

He knew that he needed to give himself the space to grieve. Despite all of this being his fault, he'd still broken his own heart with what he'd chosen to do. It felt wrong to cry, but it also felt cathartic. When he cried, Eli didn't feel that pressure against his chest, the stack of boulders that grew steadily higher, making it impossible to breathe when he shot up straight in the middle of the night, looking around his bedroom at the once-familiar objects and posters that became foreign in the darkness.

By day six, he'd decided on his path.

He spends hours a day submitting applications everywhere he can think of. There's a blog-writing position with BART, an internship at Golden Bay Press, freelance gigs that he submits articles to, daring to send a few of his horror movie–related essays to places like *Fangoria* and *SplatterHouse*. He applies for food service, for a waiting job at a bar, to be a barista at several of the cafés he's been frequenting in an effort to get out of the house, a few of the bookstores in the city.

And three weeks into the search, he's only scored one interview.

Occasionally, he'll get an email, a confirmation that a résumé has been received or that the company has "decided to go in a different direction." But Eli starts to grow numb toward those as the weeks stretch on, deleting them the moment he's sure there's nothing important in the message.

Because there's only one notification he's looking for.

It's wrong of him to expect Peter to give him the time of day, he knows that. He knows there's probably no forgiving what he's done and no undoing it. Every few hours, he'll go to the *Vent* website, just to see his work there.

Of course, it doesn't end there. Eli's still—rightfully so—being taken down a peg or several in screenshots, TikToks, Instagram comments. At the very least, it's not as bad as it could've been, especially after he locks his Instagram. He breathes a sigh of relief when some TikTok influencer makes a thirty-part series about an ex-friend of hers, and the internet is quick to leap onto their drama, Eli forgotten just as swiftly as he'd become a target. He closes his laptop where it sits on the coffee table, then picks up his phone. No emails, no calls, no texts.

Not the one he wants, anyway.

He's considered calling Peter, asking him how he's feeling, if he'd dare to see Eli ever again.

But he doesn't.

He doesn't want to force Peter into that, to bring him back into a space that maybe he's finally worked his way out of.

Eli doesn't want to cause him any more trouble than he has already.

He just wants to know if Peter's okay, if he survived what Eli did to him, the hurt that he caused.

The doorknob turns, the lock clicking as both Rose and Patricia stroll into the apartment, bags hanging from their arms. Eli gets up quickly to help them before their bags fall to the floor.

"You two are late," he says.

"I met Rose at Grocery Outlet and we got some things for Friendsgiving," Patricia says, dropping the other bags in her hand on the floor and then dragging them into the kitchen.

"What are you making?"

"I'm going to do an apple pie," Patricia says, starting to organize things on the counter. "Rose is doing spring rolls and bún bò huế."

"Really?" Eli whines.

"It's not too late," Rose says with a smile, pulling the noodles out. "You can still come with us."

"Yeah, you try telling my mom that I'm not coming for Thanksgiving."

"Fair," Rose says, having only ever met Rue once, but knowing that she's a woman of tradition. "Can you steal some of her stuffing for me?"

"Me too?" Patricia implores.

"You guys act like she's not going to have an entire platter ready for me to take home for just the two of you."

"And some of her ham too," Patricia adds, letting out a satisfied sigh. "God, that woman knows how to bake a ham."

Eli winces in disgust. "Okay . . . I feel like we're veering dangerously close to you calling my mom hot."

"I mean . . ." Rose starts. "I'd hit it."

"God." Eli crams his head into the pantry.

"What? Rue's a *total* MILF, that streak of gray in her hair, and the whole boss lady thing? She's a total fox." Patricia lets out a purr.

"Shut up, shut up, shut up," Eli says, his voice muffled. But he can't help the smile on his face that steadily replaces the straight line of his mouth that he's had for weeks now, along with the same hoodie that belonged to Peter.

Because he just can't let some things go.

"Are you sure you don't want us to come with you?" Patricia asks. "I don't mind canceling. Harriet is going to be there."

"Harriet?" Rose groans, letting her head fall to the counter. "If she doesn't return my bowl she borrowed I'm ripping out her extensions."

"I wouldn't hold your breath," Patricia tells her before she looks at Eli again, scratching the back of his neck softly.

"I'm okay, it'll be nice to get out for a bit."

"M'kay, let me know if you change your mind."

"I will."

Eli helps them put away the groceries before he places an order at the pizzeria down the block. Rose and Patricia join him on the couch as they watch old episodes of *Top Model*, Rose and Patricia sending Eli whatever job applications they find online.

Patricia even sends a form for an internship at *InVogue*, though Eli isn't sure what he's supposed to do with an unpaid internship that doesn't even begin until the following spring. And Rose sends an application for the maintenance crew at her school that Eli happily fills out even though his experience with fixing things around the apartment begins and ends with putting duct tape on the slow leak in the kitchen sink.

At some point, the applications stop, and Rose breaks out her edibles. She takes a generous portion, leaving Eli and Patricia to nibble on the corners. Enough to relax the both of them as Janice Dickinson of all people shouts at some poor girl, and Rose snoozes from her impromptu pillow fort on the floor.

"How are you feeling?" Patricia asks, putting a hand on Eli's knee.

"I wish I knew how to answer that question," Eli says over the reality show, volume turned low. "It hurts. That's all I know for sure."

Worse than when things ended with Keith. Which is saying a lot considering Eli didn't feel human once everything was said and done with Keith.

"He hasn't contacted you at all?"

Eli shakes his head, though Peter hasn't blocked him on Instagram, so that has to count for something. Even thinking that makes him feel even more depressed, though.

"God . . ." Eli wipes at the corners of his eyes, his body feeling weighted down in a comfortable way. "I fucked up so hard, Patricia. And I wish I knew how to fix it."

"I know . . ." Her nails trace his skin as she lets him rest his curly head on her shoulder. "That's the awful part, though. Sometimes we can't fix it. Life isn't a movie."

"You mean I can't just wait for him to hop on a plane to go somewhere just so I can stop him at the gate and make some grand statement?"

"Don't I wish." Patricia takes a Nerds gummy candy from the

one-pound bag they broke out after dinner and passed around. "It'd make life a hell of a lot easier."

"I told him." Eli peers over at his best friend. "That I love him."

"What did he say?"

How could he forget the words, the way they'd taken ahold of his brain, absolutely refusing to let go of him?

"That he was in love with me too."

Past tense. *Was.*

How could he still be once he knew the truth?

"Eli?"

He buries himself deeper into her shoulder, desperate to hide his face in the sweatshirt that she's wearing. He hadn't expected the words. Hoped for them, yes. But to hear Peter say them out loud, to hear him admit that they could've had something together.

It stings.

Stings worse than anything else Peter could've possibly said to him.

Because that meant that Eli'd had Peter.

Eli had had Peter's heart in his hand in much the same way he'd offered his own to Peter. In another world, he and Peter could've been happy together, they could've worked things out. But then again, maybe they were never meant to. And maybe it's wrong of Eli to think that it could still work out.

"What do you want to do?" Patricia asks.

"I don't know, I can't talk to him, I—"

"Not what I asked." She straightens, reaching for the candy again, this time grabbing the entire bag. "Treat this as a hypothetical. If you could do what you *wanted* to do with Peter, what would it be?"

"I guess I'd . . . I'd sit him down, try to explain myself better, try to tell him that my feelings were real, that maybe this began as an act, but somewhere along the way, it turned into something real for me." Eli feels that familiar ache in his jawline, the pressure that builds slowly behind his eyes that's become like second nature to him over the last few weeks.

He remembers these same feelings after Keith.

"And I'd apologize for the article. I'd . . . I'd make sure he knew that there was nothing to fix about him. That he's perfect the way he is."

"Do you really believe that's true?" Patricia asks.

Eli wipes at his eyes with his sleeve. "Sure, maybe he needed help with social cues, understanding jokes, maybe he dresses like a frat bro and he's addicted to his work. But no, there's *nothing* wrong with Peter Park."

"You should tell him that."

She's right, and he knows it. There's no world where Peter takes him back, not after what he did. So maybe it's time that he stopped worrying about what he could do to win Peter back. Why bother trying to accomplish the impossible?

"Sometimes it helps to be selfish," she continues. "To do something for yourself. And maybe telling him that is what you need."

"So, what do I do?" Eli asks.

"Well, you could always write down your feelings," Patricia says. "But making a public spectacle of your apology might not be the way to go."

Eli thinks for a moment, recalling all the rom-coms that he's watched. Mark Ruffalo making Jennifer Garner a version of her dream home seems a little out of Eli's budget. Running onto a plane à la *Crazy Rich Asians* might end with Eli being on the No Fly List. Considering they're near the end of November, he seriously doubts there's some New Year's Eve party he could show up at like Harry did for Sally.

Then he has to wonder why his mind went instantly to using a movie to fix his problems, instead of just reaching out, asking Peter to talk. Of course, he knows already how that'll go. Peter doesn't owe him any of his time or energy. He doesn't owe Eli a chance to stand there and beg for forgiveness.

Peter doesn't owe him anything.

So maybe . . . maybe he should just leave Peter be. Maybe that's the best thing Eli can do for him, maybe that's the best way to prove how apologetic he is.

Just let Peter go.

Maybe that's the best gift Eli can give him.

Chapter Nineteen

Scream, dir. by Wes Craven

H i there, what can I get started for you?" Eli asks the woman on the other side of the counter, his fingers ready to tap on the screen for her order.

"I'll just do . . ." She peers at the menu on the wall behind Eli. "A large iced Americano, with whipped cream, please."

Eli can't stop the chuckle that slips out.

The woman stares at him. "Is something wrong with my order?"

"Huh? Oh!" Eli's gaze shoots up. "No, I promise, just, uh . . . thinking about a joke I heard."

"Oh, what joke? I love jokes!"

"It's nothing," he promises. "Is that all for you today?"

The woman nods, tapping her card when the amount for her coffee appears on the reader.

"Okay, it'll be ready for you at the end of the counter there."

"Thanks!" She drops a dollar in the tip jar on her way to the end of the bar where the rest of the customers are waiting for their drinks to be called out.

Mission Rise Coffee ended up being the only place Eli managed to get an interview at. And during the interview process, the manager had not-so-subtly hinted at how he'd been their second choice after the girl ahead of him took a job elsewhere.

But a job is a job.

Besides, Eli volunteered to work the morning shifts, which took some getting used to, but it pretty much means the day is his after noon. Most days, he takes off his apron and parks himself in a booth near the back of the shop with his laptop while he works on articles, essays, his résumé, and whatever ideas he'd come up with while he mindlessly cleaned the espresso machine.

And actually . . . it feels good.

Sure, most of his pieces have been rejected, but a few had thrown him into consideration, and some places had told him to resubmit with different material because they liked his voice but the subject matter didn't fit or they just weren't looking for freelance work at the time.

For the first time since college, Eli finally feels like he's *accomplishing* something, making strides toward a future he actually wants.

Now if only he hadn't had to lose Peter to get here.

"Eli! Back up front, we've got a line!" Corey, one of Eli's supervisors, calls to him.

"On it!" Eli hops back over to the counter, waking the screen up.

The rushes are easy enough to deal with; they pass the time, even if some customers can be more demanding than Michael ever was. Still, his feet always ache at the end of every shift. And the smell of coffee beans seems to linger on his clothes and hair no matter how many times he washes them.

The rush ends as quickly as it began, giving Eli a chance to help his coworkers with the backed-up orders, cleaning up behind them and reheating pastries before doing a walkthrough of the dining area, collecting plates, leftover cups, wiping down the tables.

It's easy . . . well, not *easy*.

More methodical. There's always something for Eli to do, never a moment of downtime besides his breaks.

It helps him not to think.

He still hopes, no matter how foolish he knows it to be, that Peter might call or text him, that when he checks his phone at the end of a shift, he'll see a missed-call notification, an unread text, Peter asking him to talk.

That's all he wants.

The chance to talk to him, one last time.

But maybe it's for the best that no text has arrived. Maybe it's better for Eli to give himself the space and time to move on from Peter. Eventually, he'll get back out there, find someone else to date, and this time . . . he won't lie to them, won't make them a laughingstock online.

"Eli!" Corey calls out again. "Counter!"

"Coming!" Eli leaves the dishes near the sink in the back to be cleaned later, rushing another influx of orders. It took him a week to really get down how the machines work; he still doesn't fully remember all the recipes, but he's close. He only has to consult the binder he'd been given on the first day for a handful of drinks, a fact he's pretty proud of.

It's during a slower moment, when Eli is setting a newly cleaned mug on the drying rack, that he hears the bell above the door ring, not thinking anything of it.

Because why would he? People have been coming in and out since they unlocked the doors at six in the morning.

He looks up instinctively, a greeting on his lips that dies the moment he sees who is at the door. Because of course Peter Park would come to *this* coffee shop. In a city full of hundreds, if not *thousands* of places to get coffee, Peter Park would walk into this establishment. Except, he isn't walking through the door.

No, instead he's holding it for another man, shorter than Peter, dressed in nice pants and a soft black button-up, a laptop bag thrown over his shoulder.

There's a clear look of familiarity between the two of them. They know one another. Once inside, Peter steps in behind this stranger.

They smile at one another; the other man whispers a joke and Peter laughs that warm sound.

Fuck.

Eli backs away without realizing what he's doing, slipping past the door to the kitchen area.

"Eli!" Corey calls out.

He's with another guy, Eli thinks to himself. And that's all he thinks. His palms turn clammy, and he tries to wipe the anxiety off onto his apron.

"Eli! Counter!"

"I'm taking my break," Eli whispers to the nearest coworker, Sam. Sam cleans most of the dishes and smokes weed behind the building on his breaks. And sometimes he'll share his joints.

Eli likes him a lot.

He pushes out the back door, squatting in the alleyway near a stack of pallets that the city never bothered to pick up. Eli's chest heaves slowly as he tries to take deep, heavy breaths, wondering how much air might be *too* much air. He buries his hands in his hair, slipping the cap off his head and letting it fall to the street.

He's with someone else, Eli thinks again.

And he has to be okay with that. That's what he tells himself. Because he *needs* to be okay with this. This was his mistake, and he has to reap the consequences of what he's done.

But he can't stop the way his heart thuds in his chest, how he wishes it would stop just so he wouldn't have to think of Peter anymore. He wants this to be over, the heartbreak to work its way out of his system.

But it still hurts.

It hurts worse than when Keith ended things. Back then, there was a pain, a sting to the words that Keith said to him, the way he said he didn't love Eli anymore. But it was so much easier to forgive in comparison.

Knowing that he'd once had Peter's heart, that he'd known Peter's true feelings—it wasn't a pain, it didn't burn.

It feels like nothing.

There's an absence in Eli's heart, a numbness. And now Peter's moved on. And Eli has to be okay with that.

Because what other option does he have?

Chapter Twenty

Monty Python and the Holy Grail, dir. by Terry Gilliam and Terry Jones

"Oh! My baby boy!" Rue pulls Eli into the house before he can even fully open the front door.

"Careful, I'm holding something." Eli holds the covered pie away from her.

"You baked?"

"Patricia did. She called it 'payment for the stuffing.' Which I'm hoping you have, otherwise you'll need to clear out the guest room for me to move in."

"I tripled the recipe this year. Those girls." Rue shakes her head, taking the pie. "God, this smells good. I love her baking."

"She's a wizard in the kitchen," Eli remarks, putting his jacket on the coat rack.

"So . . . you know I'm going to ask," she says, leading him into the kitchen.

Eli pauses at the door, watching as John steals a slice of ham from where it sits on the counter, as if he can't see what she's about to ask coming from a mile away.

"Where is Peter? I was looking forward to him coming."

Eli winces at the mention of Peter. His chronically offline mother had no reason to ever hunt down the article, but she'd managed to find it anyway, her coworkers "so proud" of Eli for making his debut at *Vent* before a phone call later that night when he explained he'd also quit. Even just her voice through the phone carried enough disappointment to still weigh on Eli.

"He's not coming," he tells her.

Her expression sinks. "I was hoping you would've made up by now."

"Yeah." Eli tries to hide his face. "I don't think that's happening, Mom."

"Well, I should say so." She sighs. "You really fucked the dog on this one, Eli."

"Fucked the dog?" He stares at her. "Do you mean 'screwed the pooch'?"

"Same thing." She waves her son off. "I'm sorry, Eli. But it's true. What you did was fucked up."

As if on cue, Les seemingly appears out of nowhere. "You have to put a dollar in the swear jar."

"Mommy's allowed one per month, and I haven't used it yet."

Eli winces. "Please don't call yourself 'Mommy.'"

"That's not the point here," Rue tells him. "I thought I raised you better than to do what you did."

"You did! I mean . . . I just . . ." Eli covers his face with his hands. "I was confused, and I felt desperate. Michael promised me that writer position and I just . . ."

"Honey, if you were that desperate, I could've talked to my friends on the board at the press, looked around to see if I could find you any work. Or you could come to them yourself—we have positions open, and there are apprenticeships in the foundry and bindery that we need to fill." She picks up her glass of red wine. "Turns out not a lot of people these days know how to operate printing presses built in the 1890s."

"Thanks, Mom, I appreciate it. But I don't want you to be the only reason I get a job. Besides, I'm not interested in commuting to Berkeley every single day."

"Self-made," John adds as he walks in at the tail end of the conversation. "I like it."

"All the more reason to move to this side of the bridge!" Rue adds, but Eli ignores her.

"More like I could never live with myself if I was so pathetic that one of my parents had to step in to get me what I want." Eli sighs. "I've got a job, anyway, and I'm working on essays. *Fangoria's* considering some of my horror writing."

"Honey, are you sure there's nothing I can do to help?"

"Mom, please!" Eli doesn't want her to think he's angry with her, but the exhaustion has been setting in the last few days. After what seems like a mountain of rejections for both his applications and his essays and articles, Eli can't help but start to wonder if there's something wrong with him.

Something that he'd never noticed, something that other people noticed and they'd just never taken the opportunity to tell him before. Eli's always tried to avoid being up his own ass about his writing, but at the very least he *knows* he has some eye for what he does. He wouldn't have survived the journalism program in school if he didn't.

Maybe he doesn't have what people are looking for.

Just like Michael said.

"I'm sorry, baby. I didn't mean to overstep." Rue slides her hand closer to Eli's.

"No, I'm sorry. I'm just . . . exhausted."

"I know." She reaches up, brushing his hair behind his ears. "Maybe a haircut would help?" she says with a smile, trying to break the tension. And Eli allows himself to smile for the first time in what feels like days.

"Maybe, yeah . . ." Perhaps it's a time for some changes.

Changes that Eli can make for himself.

* * *

It's in that post-Thanksgiving haze—after dinner has been eaten at three in the afternoon, and everyone's so full they fall asleep in whatever couch or recliner they land in—that Eli finds himself in the guest bedroom of his mother's house.

It's hardly used for what it was redecorated for, serving as more of an office for Rue and John with their desks and computers. There are boxes too, stacked in the corner near the large window that looks out onto the gorgeous back garden.

His mother's asked him a few times to come by and go through some of the boxes that Eli knows are his. And with everyone else in the house either asleep or sorting through the leftovers, Eli figures now's as good a time as any.

He cracks open the first box with his name written in black Sharpie on the top, pulling out piles and piles of the school newspapers that he'd saved. He can see the years pass before him, starting off when he was the page designer, printing out articles in various sizes and plotting where they'd go, making sure they fit and the margins looked good. There's the issue where he had to draw the weekly comic strip—a complete rip-off of a *Garfield* that he read somewhere—because the artist had a kidney infection.

He spies the first issue where he was made the secondary editor under Louise Davidson, effectively taking over the duties of an actual editor because she'd chosen to be part of nearly every club at school to boost her extracurriculars for college applications.

They'd made the story of his promotion front-page news.

Underneath the papers are some old clothes he should probably donate.

And in another box, there are his LEGO sets, the City sets because he thought those were the most fun, even though his father constantly tried to get him into the other "more interesting" characters.

"Look! These guys are pirates!" his dad had once said in the toy store.

Eli had just pointed to a bus set, complete with a little stop for the minifigures. "That one."

His father sighed with a smile on his face, and he bought Eli the LEGO bus. There are a few books, mostly ones he had to read for school. Worn copies of *Romeo and Juliet*, *Giovanni's Room*, *The Crucible*, *The Lord of the Rings*. There's a copy of a John Green book checked out from the school library that he never returned, and he tries to not feel guilty about that. Maybe he can mail it back without much consequence?

The boxes bring back loads of memories from Eli's time in high school and college, his yearbooks, his deadname scratched out of the first few because he hadn't yet decided on Eli, signed by people he hasn't spoken to in over ten years. People that he'd once thought of as friends he'd want to keep for his entire life, but the simple decision to go to different schools had led them down drastically different paths that had never intersected again. There's even a small locked box labeled ELI PRE-T PHOTOS. His mother had locked them away after Eli voiced his discomfort at seeing some of the old photos of himself around the house. She'd taken them down without out a second thought.

He reaches the last box, surprised to find a collection of used DVDs and VHS tapes. His father's collection, that much is obvious to him. He recognizes all the titles as ones that his father showed him. The animated movies that he tried to get Eli to watch instead of the more mature PG-13 films that he thought it was too early to show Eli. There are the original *Star Wars* VHS tapes and *Kill Bill: Volume 1*, which his father had showed Eli *far* too early in his preteen life but which he'd loved nonetheless. There's the DVD of *Who Framed Roger Rabbit* that his father bought when he was scared Eli would wear out the VHS. There's the 2005 *Pride*

& Prejudice, the movie that instilled a love of romances in Eli, and even convinced him to give the book a chance, leaving Jane Austen as the only author of fiction that Eli ever willingly gave his time to. There are also folded and rolled posters, movie magazines, old Oscar- or Golden Globe–themed issues that Eli had pored over despite the ceremonies having long passed by the time he was reading them.

Then, at the bottom, there's one last box. A cigar box, which is odd because Eli knows that his father never smoked a day in his life.

He grabs it, flipping open the cardboard lid with ease to stare at the pile of paper slips. Thicker than expected, yellowed because of their age, with ink that's nearly completely worn off in some places. But he can still read the information on the first ticket he picks up: *The Exorcist*, 9:30 p.m., Victoria Theater.

"Movie tickets?" Eli mutters to himself.

He finds the tickets with text that's still legible, which is more than he'd expect. Perhaps sitting in a dark box for decades helped preserve them?

There are titles that Eli recognizes: *American Graffiti*, *Paper Moon*, *Magnum Force*, the first two *Godfather* movies, *Young Frankenstein*, *Rocky*, *The Shining*, *The Empire Strikes Back*, Tim Burton's *Batman*. It's a tour through the decades of his father's trips to the movies, some of the films having multiple tickets from different days because his father just *had* to see them again.

"Eli? You in here?" A soft knock on the door pulls Eli's attention, and over his shoulder, he sees his mother standing there having long since changed into her sweatpants now that the holiday dinner has been cleaned up. "Whatcha got?"

"I was just going through some things," he tells her. "Found these movie tickets."

"Oh, your father's things." She smiles softly, sitting next to Eli on the floor. "The tickets." She smiles. "God, he always annoyed me with how he saved these things. I didn't understand him."

"Why did he?"

"He wanted the memory," she tells him. "He always said, 'Chances are one day my memory might fade, but at least I'll always have these. Even the crappiest movies are worth remembering!'" She laughs as Eli hands her a stack, letting her flip through it. It's strange watching how the tickets change, the thicker paper turning thinner and cheaper as the decades stretch on.

"There are more somewhere," she tells him. "These are maybe a quarter of the collection."

"At least I know where I get my hoarder tendencies from."

"Oh." Rue puts her hand over her mouth.

"What?"

She shows him a worn-out ticket with the title *Monty Python and the Holy Grail* printed in large block letters. "This was the movie he took me to for our first date."

"Seriously?"

"Yes. Lord, I hated it so much, nearly walked out. And then we had an argument about it afterward. I told him I just didn't think it was funny, and he acted like I'd spit on your grandmother or something."

"I've never heard that story before," Eli tells her. He's heard about other date nights, how they'd nearly driven all the way to Oregon to spend time in a cabin for their fifth anniversary, and how his father had proposed—he'd gotten chemical burns in a hot tub after a malfunction with the chlorine system and he proposed in the ER because he couldn't wait.

"I think he was embarrassed. The next day he came to my parents' place with his tail tucked between his legs, apologizing. I didn't even make him admit the movie wasn't really funny."

"You gave him a second chance?" Eli asks.

Rue nods, her mouth a firm line.

"Why?"

"I don't know." She continues to stare at the ticket. "I just . . . I had a feeling, in my gut. And I trusted it."

"You could've been wrong," Eli says.

And she turns to him. "But I wasn't. If we always focused on the what-ifs, we'd get nowhere in life, Eli."

He stares at the floor. "I really fucked up, Mom."

"Yeah," she tells him calmly. "You did."

"A little sympathy might be appreciated, you know."

"Oh, honey . . ." She takes Eli by the shoulder, pulling him in closer. "At least you know what you did."

"I really fell in love with him," Eli tells her. "That part wasn't a lie."

"And he knows this?"

Eli nods. "I told him when I showed him the article."

"And what did he say?"

"That he loves me too," Eli repeats the words so easily. There hasn't been a day since the blowup that he hasn't thought about them, echoing in his brain. Because he never wants to forget them, that last interaction where Peter promised Eli another world if things could've been different.

If Eli hadn't been so selfish.

If he hadn't been a coward.

"Have you spoken to him?"

"No." Eli shakes his head. "I doubt he wants to hear from me."

His mother's hand finds Eli's hair, playing with it softly. "I wish I knew the magic words," she says. "The fix I could give you to make things better."

"Thanks." Eli sniffles.

Rue lets out a low sigh. "If it's worth anything to you, I hope that you never give up on true love, Eli. I know this year has been tough for you, with Keith, with work, with . . ." Peter's name is left unsaid. "But I hope you know that you deserve to get the things you want."

"Thanks, Mom."

"You're a kind boy, you work hard, and you care a lot for others. And yes, you were selfish. And you made mistakes. You did something that you shouldn't have. But it's not a sin to want, Eli."

"I think it literally is," he tells her. "Isn't there some commandment about coveting or something?"

"Will you hush?" Rue hisses. "I'm trying to impart my wisdom."

"Okay! I'm sorry."

Rue smiles at her son. "Maybe it makes me a dreamer, and maybe it's childish, but I believe in true love."

It's like she's kicking him while he's down.

"I've listened to the way that you talk about him," Rue says. "The way you lit up. I don't want to bring him up, but . . . I never saw that in you with Keith."

"Then what do I do?" Eli can't help the tears that escape, sliding slowly down his cheeks before he can wipe them away with his sleeve.

"You could just try talking to him again."

"Do you think it'd be that easy?"

"No," she admits. "It's not going to be easy, and that's the point, Eli. If you want something badly enough, you have to fight for what you think is right, what you think will make you happiest."

"What if he doesn't accept it?"

Rue sighs. "At the very least, I think you owe him a *sincere* apology. One where you can take your time and explain yourself. You tell him in person—look him in the eyes and tell him what you did, and that you're truly apologetic."

"And if he doesn't want to see me?" Eli asks. "Or if he doesn't accept it?"

"Then . . . you must respect that. It's his decision. But if you love him, if you truly feel how you feel, then you've got to fight for him, Eli. Life is full of what-ifs, but you can't let that stop you from chasing after what you know you want. You should at least *try* to make things right. It's the least you owe him."

"Thanks, Mom . . ."

"We don't get to control who we fall in love with, Eli. It's a complicated, stupid, ugly thing sometimes. And yet, at the end of the day, it's really all we have. I wasn't lying when I said you seemed so happy when you were with him."

"It was never even supposed to happen. That first date was a disaster." It feels like so long ago. "I only helped him so he'd help me with my article."

"Maybe it started that way, but what I saw, between the two of you, that was real. I could feel it." Rue brushes her son's hair away from his face again. "Now, I'm begging you. Get a haircut."

He tries to laugh, and a strange sound escapes his lips, a mix between a giggle and a sob as he wraps his arms around her. "I will."

* * *

"Text me when you get back home so I know you're okay," Rue says from the driver's seat, watching as Eli hoists a tote bag with Patricia's and Rose's Tupperwares full of stuffing tucked inside.

"I will. Thanks, Mom."

"Love you, sweetie." She gives him a kiss on the cheek. "It was great to see you. Let me know when you and Peter are back together."

"Mom, please."

"I just want a son-in-law, is that so wrong?"

"Yes!"

"Fine." She blows Eli another kiss. "Bye, sweetie."

"Bye, love you." Eli steps out of the car, Rue not driving away until Eli is headed down the stairs of the BART station. He taps his phone at the ticket reader and then goes down another flight of stairs to reach the platform where he waits for the train.

With his phone in hand, he can't help himself from going to his last text messages with Peter, the reminder that it has been weeks staring at him in the face.

Echoes from the approaching train radiate through the tunnel, the gust of wind blowing past Eli as it comes to a stop, the door opening. Because of the late hour, the car that Eli picks is totally empty, leaving him to his choice of one of the lime-green seats toward the back of the car.

He knows that his mother is right.

He owes Peter an apology. Something more than just words whispered in panicked desperation. He taps Peter's name, then taps on the call button and presses the phone against his ear, knowing that if he doesn't do this now, he never will. He doubts that Peter will answer, and the longer the phone rings, the more reality starts to set in.

If Eli were Peter, he wouldn't want to hear from him either.

"Hello?" Peter's voice comes softly.

At first, Eli can't be sure that he isn't dreaming, that he hasn't stumbled into some alternate reality the moment he stepped into the empty train car.

"Eli?" Peter pauses, like he isn't sure how to say his name anymore. "Are you there?"

"Yes! Yeah." Eli straightens in his seat, grateful for the silence of the new BART trains. "Hey, Peter. How are you?"

"I'm fine." Peter's voice is solemn, and yet, oddly comforting. "How are you?"

"Been better, I guess."

"Yeah."

"Listen . . . I know that I'm probably the last person you want to hear from right now—"

The train moves again, cutting through the tunnel loud enough that even Eli knows Peter can't hear him. But he still gets the "Huh? Eli? Are you still there?"

"Can you hear me?" Eli shouts into the phone, hoping to cut through the noise. Even with his headphones in, the microphone pressed *right* up to his mouth, he feels like an idiot shouting in an empty train car.

"Hold on," Eli pleads. "We're stopping."

"Eli, are you there?" Peter asks.

Eli braces himself in front of the doors, urging them to open, seemingly waiting forever before he's able to step out onto the open platform of MacArthur Station.

"Can you hear me?" Eli asks again.

"Yeah, that's better," Peter says. "What was that?"

"I'm at the train station, coming back from my parents'."

"Oh, right, it's Thanksgiving."

"What are you doing?" Eli asks.

"Just got back from climbing. I was going to shower and go meet a friend."

"Seriously? The gym is open today?" Eli ignores the "meet a friend." Because he doesn't want to think about what that could possibly mean.

Peter lets out a quiet chuckle. "You'd be surprised how many people want to squeeze in a workout when they've got nowhere else to go."

Eli tries to laugh with him, but the sadness of Peter's words stings him.

"I wish you could've joined us today," Eli admits, even if it's the wrong thing to say. "My mom was wondering where you were."

A beat of silence.

"What did you tell her?"

"The truth." Eli sighs. "That I hurt you. That you're angry, and it's best that we don't see one another right now."

"I'm not angry at you, Eli." Peter's voice is firmer than Eli can ever recall it being.

Eli pauses, the words sinking in slowly. "You're . . . you're not?"

"I was, at first. Especially after I read the article. But . . . after a while, I don't know, I just . . . I stopped feeling angry. I'm just . . . I'm heartbroken."

"I know."

"What you did hurt me," Peter tells him. "A lot."

Eli doesn't know how to respond to hearing the words. Of course he *knew* he'd hurt Peter, but to hear him say it out loud . . . it's different.

"I know, Peter. And I wish . . . God, I wish that I could say I would take it back. Because I regret so much of what happened, and I regret lying to you. But if I hadn't taken Michael's stupid idea and done what he told me to, then . . . then I never would've given you that second chance. And I know that sounds fucked up, because it is. And it sounds selfish as hell, and it's because I'm being completely selfish right now." Eli takes a shaky breath. "I regret hurting you, I regret the article, both of them, and I regret lying to you for so long. But I don't regret getting to spend that time with you. Those weeks that we were together . . . they were the best time of my life, Peter. And no part of those feelings was a lie."

"They were good for me too," Peter tells him. "I wasn't lying either, when I said that I'd fallen in love with you too."

Eli can't stop himself from smiling, no matter how pained he feels.

"I didn't know what to do with those feelings at first, because I thought that you didn't feel the same way. And I was . . . I was afraid. Of letting you go. What our relationship would turn into."

Eli wishes that he could feel relief at the words; he wishes that he could feel like things are fixed, that everything is magical now. But he can't help but expect the ball to drop at any moment.

"And then you made the decision easy," Peter says.

There it is, Eli thinks.

"I wish you hadn't, but . . . what happened happened, I guess."

"Yeah, it did."

More silence stretches between them both; people walk past Eli, obviously annoyed with where he's chosen to stand as they make their way down the platform.

"I . . ." Eli starts. "I love you, Peter. And I wish that I'd been brave enough to know that sooner. Just like how I wish I'd been brave enough to leave *Vent*. I never should've agreed to write that article, even if I told myself it was never going to come out."

More silence.

"I've missed you," Eli admits to him. "I've missed eating dinner with you, having to explain my jokes because you don't get them. I've missed . . . I've missed hearing you mutter to yourself in Korean when you get frustrated, and I've missed hearing your laugh. I've missed how you're the only person I know under the age of fifty who likes jazz, and how you haven't seen any movies except for the Sam Raimi *Spider-Man*, and I've missed how you dress like a frat bro."

Eli swallows, the corners of his eyes burning.

"I miss how you smell, and I've missed the rough scrape of your hands against mine. And I've . . . I miss you, Peter."

No past tense here.

There's a pause, one that stretches on long enough to hold the entire universe. Eli stands there; hoping, *praying* that Peter heard him. And yet, at the same time, he hopes that Peter didn't. Because he doesn't want this to not work, he wants—no, he *needs* Peter to understand him. But he also knows that he can't control how Peter feels.

"I miss you too, Eli."

The words feel like they're holding the world together.

"And I wish I didn't. I wish that I could be angry with you. But I'm not, and I've been wondering what that means because I know I *should* be mad at you." Peter pauses. "Because what you did was shitty, what you did sucked. But I . . ."

Eli gives him the space to form his own words.

"I think the most important thing you taught me was that love never makes any sense at all."

"No, it never really does."

"And I know I love you," Peter tells him. "I like the person you helped me become."

"Is there *any* chance you'd be willing to see me?" Eli asks. "Even if it's just for a few minutes. I'd like to apologize to you in person. You don't have to say yes; please don't if you don't want to." Eli tries to stress this, though his focus on the words starts to sound like pressure to his own ears, so he stops talking.

It's Peter's turn to make the decisions. It's Peter's turn to take control of his own life, to make the choice to see Eli again.

And he has to be okay with whatever that choice ends up being.

"I wish I could, I'm busy with work tonight. Thanksgiving is only an American holiday."

"That's okay." Eli isn't sure where they'd even go. Tons of businesses no longer partake in celebrating or decorating for Thanksgiving, but most still take the opportunity to close up shop for Thursday at least.

"How about tomorrow? Is that okay?" Peter asks.

"Yeah, yes!" Eli says before he realizes that he sounds too eager. "I mean, yeah. I'd like that a lot."

"Okay . . . I'll see you tomorrow. Mission Rise Coffee okay?"

"Perfect." Eli stops himself from smiling. Because this isn't an acceptance of his apology, this isn't a second chance. But it *is* something.

What that something is, he doesn't really know. But it's more than he had before.

Chapter Twenty-One

Pride & Prejudice, dir. by Joe Wright

Eli puts a hand on his own thigh to stop his leg from shaking, but even that doesn't really work. He can only hope that the table is doing its job to hide his nerves. Every time the bell above the door dings he can't stop himself from looking up, hoping and praying that it's Peter who's walking through those double doors at the front of the café.

But it isn't.

Eli double-checks the time. Of course, he got here an hour early, just to make sure he was *on* time, but still . . . He sips the melted-ice-and-Americano cocktail at the bottom of his cup. One of his new coworkers comes by, collects his glass, asks him how he's doing. And Eli has to lie and say he's good, just here to see a friend.

Well, it's not a total lie, he supposes.

The door opens again.

Eli shoots up straight, ready to experience disappointment once again, but his heart swells when he sees Peter walking through the doors.

Followed by another man, the same man from the other day. He's dressed differently, save for the same laptop bag. He and Peter make small talk, followed by more laughter.

Eli's stomach sinks as they chat, the stranger laughing at whatever Peter was saying. And he wonders if this man is the same friend Peter mentioned on the phone call.

Peter's eyes glide over the café before they settle on Eli, smiling.

And Eli tries to force a smile back. Peter looks at the man, who's joined the long line near the door, and whispers something before he moves toward Eli, the world slowing down to an impossible spin as Eli takes in the scene.

Wasn't this the plan all along? To "fix" Peter, to work on him so that another man would want to date him?

Well . . . mission accomplished.

Eli stands too quickly as Peter approaches, nearly knocking the table over as he does so.

"Hey, hi!" Eli says.

"Hey." Peter's voice is quiet.

Eli tries to hug Peter, but Peter doesn't seem to want to reciprocate, so he drops it, awkwardly lingering there before he offers Peter the seat across from him.

"Sorry for not ordering you anything, I got here too early," Eli admits.

"It's okay, Ryan is getting me something." Peter peers over his shoulder, waving at the man he walked in with.

"Ryan."

"Yeah, sorry. He loves this place. Wanted to get some work done while we talk."

"Oh, well . . . okay."

"You don't mind, do you?"

"No, no," Eli promises. Even though he does—he'd been hoping to have Peter alone. Despite the public nature of the setting, he'd pictured getting Peter all to himself for at least an hour or two, hoping that they could . . . find something that remained.

"I'm glad that you called, actually," Peter begins. "I was . . . I wanted to call you, but I was afraid."

"You were?"

Peter nods, his body stiff. "I didn't really know what I wanted to say to you. And I was afraid that I might regret something if it came out in annoyance or anger. I didn't want that to happen."

"So, what changed your mind?" Eli dares to ask. "Why answer my call?"

"I guess I just . . . I had a feeling in my gut." Peter hesitates. "And it made me admit to myself that I missed your voice."

Eli pauses, unsure of what to say.

Peter smiles that lopsided grin at Eli, and Eli smiles right back. But as desperately as he wants to feel good about this, Eli can't help but see Ryan in the background, talking to the cashier.

No, he tells himself. He *cannot* be angry at Peter.

If Peter's moved on, then Eli has to accept it. At the very least, if he and Peter can become friends again, then everything will have been worth it.

"How have you been?" Peter asks him.

"Okay. Well . . . I've been better. I'm working here, actually. It's just my day off."

"I, uh . . . I thought you might be."

"Seriously?"

"The other day, Ryan and I were here. I heard a guy calling out for 'Eli,' and then he said, I think it was, 'Where is that frizzy-headed weirdo?' And . . . you're the only weirdo frizzy-haired Eli I know in the city."

"Oh, well. Yeah, that's me. But I've been writing more too, submitting essays and articles. To be honest, you kind of gave me that courage."

"I did?"

Eli nods. "The way you talked about your writing, and how you were scared of other people seeing it. I think I realized that was a real pot-calling-the-kettle-black moment for me. So, I took my own advice."

"That's . . ." Peter says with a soft expression on his face. "That's amazing, Eli. I'm really proud of you."

"What about you?" Eli asks. "How's the writing?"

"It's going great, actually." Peter smiles, hesitating like he doesn't want to say what comes next. "And . . . I have you to thank for that, funny enough. Your advice really helped."

Eli smiles back. "It's all you," he promises. "But I guess it was good for the both of us."

"Maybe, but I wouldn't have even tried if it wasn't for you, Eli. That's more than a push." Peter pauses. "I have a lot to thank you for. I wouldn't have met Ryan if it wasn't for you."

The knife twists deeper and deeper, and Eli has to bite back the emotions that want to escape. He's happy for Peter, he really and truly is. Ryan looks like a sweet guy, handsome, with dark hair. He certainly looks buffer than Eli.

Then again, it's not hard to be buffer than Eli.

But maybe he's what Peter needs. Someone clearly more put together. Someone who won't use Peter to benefit his own career, who'd never think of doing that in the first place. Maybe Eli just gets to be the natural step toward Peter being a more confident version of himself.

Ryan's name is called at the counter, and Eli watches as he grabs two drinks from the barista, walking over to bring Peter his.

"Here you go," he says. "I'll be at the other booth answering some emails."

"Thanks!" Peter smiles, and Eli half expects him to go in for a kiss or something. It feels so needlessly cruel, to have to watch this unfold. But maybe this is the universe teaching Eli his final lesson.

He fucked around, and now he's finding out.

Peter watches as Ryan goes to a booth on the opposite side of the café, pulling a laptop out of the messenger bag.

"He seems nice," Eli says.

"Yeah, Ryan's great. He's been helping me a *ton*."

"That's fantastic, Peter . . ." Eli has to bite back the crack in his voice. "The two of you are cute together."

"Yeah . . ." Peter pauses, turning swiftly back to Eli. "Wait . . . what?"

"You and Ryan . . . you're cute together. I'm glad that you found him."

"Well, thanks, Eli . . . but Ryan and I aren't dating."

Eli feels like the air's been sucked out of his lungs.

"Wait . . . what?"

And somehow, through all the confusion, Peter still smiles. "You thought Ryan and I were . . . dating?"

"Well, yeah. You walked in here together; he's buying you coffee. And I . . . well, I saw you here the other day, I thought that . . ."

Peter beams, shaking his head as he looks down at the table. "Oh, right, yeah. I guess I can see how you might've thought that."

Eli could sob at the relief he feels; ice-cold water that rushes over him in an instant. "Oh my God." Eli feels himself relax, finally, breathing easily for the first time in weeks.

Peter smiles. "If door-holding means you're dating someone, then I have some calls to make."

"No, no, it's my fault for assuming." Eli hides his face, feeling the heat along his cheeks. He starts to laugh at the ridiculousness of the situation, his shoulders heaving until he eventually brings himself down.

Then he feels a hand around his wrists, and the careful pressure as Peter pulls his hands away from his face.

"I'm sorry for the confusion."

"It's okay."

"Ryan's my agent," Peter explains.

"Your . . . agent?"

"After everything happened between us . . . I started to query my book. I guess I felt like I have something to prove now." Peter smiles carefully, almost like he's afraid to let himself be this happy. "He's usually in New York, but he has family in SF and came to visit them for the holiday. We thought it'd be the perfect chance to meet in person, discuss edits and going on submission to the publishers we want to try and sell to."

"That's amazing, Peter."

"Yeah, I'm still in shock, I think. All the blogs and authors I follow said that it took them years to get agents. And half the time those agents were either scammers or not a good fit, so they'd have to start all over again. But Ryan seems like the genuine article. He's the VP of his agency, which I didn't fully understand but seemed reputable enough. He even connected me with some of his other clients; they all adore him."

"I knew that you could do it."

"Not without you, I couldn't have." Peter stares into Eli's eyes, his hands still around Eli's wrists.

And Eli wants nothing more than to cry.

"You're so talented," Eli tells him. "I'm sure the publishers will be bidding for your book soon."

"Yeah, right. I can only dream."

"I'm serious, Peter."

There's a silence, this one more comfortable even as the wetness behind Eli's eyes grows.

"Can I ask you something?" Peter's voice is quiet.

"You just did," Eli says. Because he can't help himself. "But you can ask something else."

"If you thought that Ryan and I were together . . . why'd you even bother talking to me?"

"Because I'm not a child," Eli says. "Even though I act like one sometimes."

"But didn't you come here hoping that we'd get back together? Or . . . together for the first time? I'm not really sure what does and doesn't count. I know the lines got blurry somewhere."

Eli can't help a laugh. "I should've listened more when you said we needed a pull-out clause in case things got real." Peter chuckles along with him, and Eli can't help but want to drink in the sound of him. "I came because . . . because yes, it broke my heart to see you with another man. But the truth is that I did my best to not care, because no matter what capacity it's in, I want you in my life, Peter Park. I don't care if it's as a boyfriend, I don't care if it's platonically, I just . . . I want to be someone who gets to be around you.

"And more than that, I needed to explain myself. To sit across from you and say that what I did to you was too far, that it was awful. I lied, Peter. I used you for my own gain because I believed that was the only way I could advance my career. Because I was so used to shoving the blame onto Michael, onto *Vent*, instead of accepting that I never belonged there. I never took responsibility for the things that *I* chose to do. And I was in my own way." Eli lets out a short, shaky breath. "But more than anything, I needed to look you in the eye and apologize to you. For what I did, for hurting you, for betraying your trust the way that I did."

Eli pauses.

"I'm sorry, Peter. I'm so, so sorry for lying to you, for hiding the article from you. I never should've done that, even if I thought it'd never be released. And I can only hope that you'll give me the chance to be in your life, to prove how sorry I am, to try and work to earn the trust I lost."

Peter's expression sinks, and Eli's heart goes with it. Of course he'd entered this situation wanting the best outcome. For Peter to open his heart to Eli again, for Peter to forgive him in an instant, even though Eli hasn't earned it.

"I, uh . . . I don't know if I'm ready for that, Eli. The boyfriend thing."

Eli nods, accepting the words because he knows that his feelings aren't the ones that matter right now. Peter's do. Peter has to do what Eli taught him, to take control of this situation, to make his own boundaries, and be brave enough to make his own choices. "I completely understand."

"I wish it was that easy," Peter says. "But I guess . . . I don't know if I can trust you, not yet."

"I know, Peter."

"But . . ." Peter pauses, seeming to consider his words carefully. "I'd like to spend more time with you. Get to know the real you, give you a shot to know the real me," he tells Eli, his smile reappearing, this one sadder than the last. "I'd like to give you the opportunity to earn it again. My trust, that is," Peter adds.

"Are you sure you want to do that?" Eli asks. He wants this to be Peter's choice, and no one else's.

Then, after a beat, when Eli is given *just* enough time to consider Peter might actually say no, he nods. "You gave me a second chance. All those months ago. You deserve one too."

Eli's laugh is an exhausted, soft sound. "I don't think those situations are comparable, Peter."

He just smiles. "I think they are."

Maybe it's not the exact answer that Eli wants. Because he *wants* that movie magic. He wants Peter to declare his love for him, he wants Peter to lift him into the air, to kiss him, to forgive him for everything that he did. He wants the ending of Peter's favorite romance novels.

But life isn't a movie, it isn't a romance book, and it isn't full of such simple fixes.

That doesn't mean the opportunities never arise, though.

"I'd really love that second chance, Peter," Eli tells him.

And Peter smiles. "Are you free tonight?"

"You're not showing Ryan around?"

"He's visiting some relatives in Oakland with his parents. So I'm free. I thought . . . maybe we could get dinner, catch a movie? We never got that last date."

Eli stares into the eyes of the man that he's fallen in love with, the man he risked for everything he never realized he didn't want. The man who found a way into his heart even when Eli didn't want him to. Because love hits us at the most inopportune times. Especially when we aren't looking for it.

And Eli Francis knows, deep down, that he'll do whatever it takes to keep Peter Park as a piece of his life.

No matter the circumstances.

"Doobu?" Eli offers. "It's on me."

"Let's hope it's not this time." Peter chuckles. "I'd hate to ruin another pair of your shoes."

Chapter Twenty-Two

Spider-Man 2, dir. by Sam Raimi

Two Years Later

"We're late!" Patricia sings, power walking from the bus stop, her long legs carrying her along at a pace that neither Rose nor Eli can keep up with.

"We're fine," Rose tells her. "The event isn't for another"—she pulls back her jacket sleeve, checking her watch—"three minutes."

"And we're five from the store," Eli says, coming up behind her. He starts to jog to keep up with Patricia, Rose falling behind. Suddenly, he regrets the extra layer of his sweater as he begins to melt under the evening sun, catching brief escapes in the shade of the downtown buildings.

"I told you we should've taken a Lyft." Patricia adds insult to injury.

"And I told you it's rush hour, and all the rides were a hundred dollars minimum!" Eli takes several deep breaths, his lungs going cold despite the warm weather. "It's a good thing I'm gay," he whispers to himself, picking up the pace, pushing past a few pedestrians, and avoiding a bike as the rider zooms by the three of them.

"Use the bike lane, asshole!" Rose shouts at him, flipping him off before he turns the corner.

"Come on, he's not important." Patricia takes Rose's hand, nearly yanking it out of its socket as they jaywalk through a red light, Eli just *narrowly* avoiding being hit by a Waymo.

"How much time do we have?" he asks, trying to rid his body of the adrenaline that's now pumping through his veins after the near-death experience.

"Two minutes," Patricia says. "We're nearly there."

"Don't they have to introduce him or something? No event starts on time. Concerts start late, movies have like half an hour of previews," Rose adds.

"Yeah, well, Peter's book launch isn't a movie, Rose." Eli cuts through the traffic, not waiting for the light to give him the go-ahead to walk before crossing the street. "It should be just up here!" He can't hold himself back anymore; he just starts sprinting, his best friends trailing behind as they reach Hyde St. Books, one of the oldest, largest, and queerest bookstores in the city.

And the place where Peter's publisher planned his launch party.

Eli feels like he could rip the glass door off its hinges as he races to get inside, his heavy breathing that much more noticeable as the lady behind the counter stares daggers at him, pointing at a sign that reads QUIET PLEASE, EVENT IN PROGRESS.

And suddenly, Eli feels like a college student all over again, being stuck with his classmates in the library during a group study session.

"Sorry," he whispers. "Where is the event?"

"Down this aisle, to the left. There's a stage you can't miss," she tells him, and Eli notices the crowd of people who seem to be spilling over into the shelves. And distantly, he can hear a voice that doesn't sound like Peter's reading the script announcing future events at the store.

"It hasn't started, right?"

"Should begin any second now."

"Oh my God, cute!" Patricia whips out her phone, taking a photo of the flyer advertising the event with Peter's author photo plastered in the corner. "Did you take this?"

"Quiet, please," the lady reminds them, and Patricia gives her a silent apology as Eli motions for the two of them to follow him.

"Tonight, I have the pleasure of introducing a wonderful friend and fellow SF author." The voice echoes through the shelves. Eli recognizes Amber Thompson, another romance author represented by Ryan.

"Peter Park!" Amber smiles. There's an eclectic mix of readers, each of them holding copies of Peter's and Amber's books for the joint signing that will happen after the event. Eli even spies some of Peter's Zelus coworkers. "Peter was born in Incheon, South Korea, before his family moved to Georgia when he was young. And if I'm not mistaken, Mr. and Mrs. Park might just be in the audience tonight."

It's easy to pick out Peter's parents. They're seated right in the front row, pieces of printer paper with the word RESERVED typed in bold letters taped to their seats.

Eli can't help but smile. Peter had been so nervous to FaceTime them, to tell them he'd sold a book, that he was going to be a published author. Eli missed most of the conversation, Peter finding it much easier to find the words and explain his feelings in Korean. But Eli had sat across from him, just out of frame, totally silent. Not that he'd minded; Peter was already anxious for the book conversation—he didn't think he could handle having the Meet My Boyfriend conversation at the same time.

And that's when Eli had first witnessed Peter speaking Korean with a slight Southern twang to his voice.

It hadn't mattered, though. They were happy for their son, and they came to San Francisco to visit a month later and Eli was able to meet them officially for the first time.

"When he isn't writing books, he writes and tests code for a tech start-up, which Peter assured me is as boring as it sounds." A few laughs from the audience. "His debut novel, *What If I Love You?*, has earned acclaim from several publications, including starred reviews from *Booklist* and *Publishers Weekly*!"

Eli can't help but let out a "Whoo!" which earns him a few curt glances from some of the older people in the crowd. Peter had been even more scared to tell his coworkers about the book. Of course, once Francine knew, he didn't have to tell anyone else. They were all so excited for him, eagerly counting down the days until release.

Amber continues, "Everyone, please help me welcome to the stage Peter Park!"

Everyone begins to applaud as Peter comes out from behind a set of shelves marked PSYCHOLOGY. He'd asked for Eli's help in picking out his outfit, which meant that if he wanted to wear something that wasn't a hoodie and matching sweatpants—or a Spider-Man costume that showed off too much of Peter's crotch— they had to go shopping.

Peter's dressed as nicely as Eli's ever seen him, in a baby-blue button-up shirt, with black slacks that probably show off too much of his ass.

Not that Eli chose those pants on purpose.

Certainly not.

Peter blushes a soft pink as he walks onto the small stage, his ears red. He gives Amber a hug before he sits in one of the tall bistro chairs. It's obvious to Eli that Peter's nervous from the way that he takes the microphone and nearly drops it, wiping his free hand on his slacks.

But they've been preparing for this. Ever since Peter's team sent him the list of the Northern-to-Southern-California tour stops that he'd be going on to promote the book.

"Wow, uh . . . thank you all for coming out tonight." His voice shakes in a way that Eli can't help but find adorable. "I hope that you'll forgive me, I'm not used to speaking to big crowds. Or crowds at all, for that matter."

There are a few scattered chuckles, nothing gut busting, but the energy of the room is still electric.

At least Amber knows him well enough now too.

"Well, you should've expected this crowd with the kind of response you've been getting." She smiles, her voice relaxed. "Which leads me into my first question, actually. How has the response to *What If* differed from what you expected?"

"Well, I, uh . . ." There's a bit of microphone feedback and Peter pulls the microphone away, whispering apologies to the audience, but all with a smile on his face. Peter's charming enough that no one minds at all.

"I, uh . . . I don't really know how to answer that, because I never really had expectations. I mean, yes, I wanted people to read it. And I think a lot of us . . . we dream of that overnight success. Hitting the *New York Times* list, or having a movie adaptation announced. And those are nice, but I guess I knew as a gay Korean man writing romance, it'd be an uphill battle, you know? Frankly, I'm just glad that people are here, that there's been so much excitement online, from booksellers, librarians, and readers who've been waiting for release day."

Good answer, Eli thinks. Simple enough.

And Peter keeps that momentum through the rest of his conversation with Amber; he talks about how frustrating the editing process was but how his team trusted him to tell this story. All very standard stuff, the questions rehearsed for days as Peter tried to hype himself up.

"So, my next question"—Amber's eyes meet Eli's from across the room before she goes back to the cheat sheet she'd prepared for herself—"is one that I *love* to listen to my writer friends talk for hours about, so I'm hoping you've got a good answer for me."

"Depends on how good the question is," Peter teases, and Amber and the audience both chuckle.

"I want to hear about inspiration. Because—and if everyone will follow me, we need a little group participation—open your books to the dedication page." Amber picks up the copy of Peter's book that sits on the table between them. The cover is clearly for a romance, an illustration of two men, back-to-back, their arms folded, looking over their shoulders as they give the other a "Can you believe this guy?" expression. Peter laughed when he got the cover sketches in his email, then his eyes got wet and he started to cry, and Eli cried along with him.

"You've dedicated this book to 'the man who taught me to appreciate iced Americanos.' I was curious about that *very* mysterious expression; do you want to maybe elaborate on this mysterious man who inspired you?"

Peter gives her an awkward laugh, smiling as his eyes struggle to not meet Eli's.

He licks his lips slowly.

"Years after college, I found myself really isolated, unfamiliar with the city, scared to reach out and attempt to form connections. I worked from home, so I wasn't meeting people. There wasn't really a support system where I felt like I belonged; I was an actual adult for the first time, and I'd never been more alone.

"A coworker, Francine, who is here tonight, was the one person I felt like I had in my corner. And it wasn't anyone's fault, my other coworkers are here, and they're all great, and they've supported me in so many ways. But I was doing it to myself. And I didn't know how to fix it. Francine pushed me into a blind date. And to say that date was a disaster . . . it's an understatement."

A few more scattered laughs.

"No, I'm serious. I was late, stumbling over myself, I didn't know how to talk, I spilled food on him. I was a nervous wreck. It was a nightmare. I tried apologizing, and it just made things worse. But despite all of that, and despite a few . . . odd circumstances,

I got closer to another person. I was able to let my guard down, to let this person in as they guided me through the experience that I felt desperate for. And maybe it was wrong, to be *that* desperate for these things to happen, maybe I should've let them happen naturally, but . . . I don't think it's a crime to want things.

"Letting this person in, it was one of the scariest things I've ever done. But I haven't regretted doing it. Maybe there was a rough patch in there, and it took us a lot of time to fix it." Peter's eyes finally meet Eli's.

And Eli can't stop smiling at the man he loves.

"But having this person in my life is worth whatever trials we've gone through. And that's what I wanted to explore in this book. The things we go through for the ones we love."

"That was really sweet." Amber gives Peter a warm smile.

For the rest of the night, there are moments when Peter's eyes meet Eli's from across the store as he tries to answer the questions that Amber throws his way. His gaze has to break, of course; he has to give his attention to the other people in the crowd.

But never once, throughout the entire conversation, do Eli's eyes ever leave Peter.

* * *

"Do you need a sticky note?" the bookstore employee asks Eli.

"Yes, please. Thank you." Eli could've joked around, played the he-knows-me card, but decides against potentially embarrassing Peter. Patricia and Rose take one each as well.

"How many copies is this one?" Patricia asks, staring at the newly purchased book in Eli's hands.

"Just seven. Including the advance copy he gave me."

"The one you wouldn't let me read?" Rose grumbles.

"That one was just for me, you got your own!"

"Look at him, he gets one book dedicated to him and suddenly he's the most important person in the world." Patricia rolls her eyes.

Eli laughs. "And don't you forget it."

"Next up!" the employee calls for Eli, and Peter beams at him.

"I just have to say, I'm the *biggest* fan! I've read this book like ten times already," Eli teases, the employees clearly not sure how to react just yet.

"Only because I begged you to."

"Yeah, well, who else was going to copyedit it for you before you sent it to your editor?" Eli squats so that he's eye-to-eye with Peter, despite this being one of the few precious occasions when he'd get to be taller.

"I didn't want her to think I don't know basic grammar."

"But you know Java. And I'd like to remind you that checking your grammar is literally in your copyeditor's job description."

"So . . . let's see who I have to sign this to," Peter says, flipping open the paperback. "'Eli.' You know, my boyfriend has that name too."

Eli smiles. He doesn't ever think he'll get tired of hearing Peter say "my boyfriend."

"Good, it's an excellent one," Eli says. "I even picked it out myself."

"'Excellent' might be a stretch; I hear he's named after a hobbit."

"Oh!" Eli lets his mouth hang open in shock. "The author has *jokes*! That's the last time I tell you anything personal." Eli laughs along with Peter.

"Was I okay up there?" Peter eyes the stage. "Do you think I did all right?"

"You did amazing," Eli promises, reaching for Peter's hand across the table.

"You're not just saying that?"

"I *am* saying it," Eli tells him. "Which is how you know I'm telling you the truth."

Peter smiles at him. "Thanks."

"Also, my mother and John would like to pass along their congratulations, as well as an apology for not being here. They had a fundraiser they couldn't miss."

"That's okay, we'll see them this weekend, right? Before I leave for Sacramento."

"Definitely."

"Um, excuse me! Can you two stop flirting? We'd like to get our books signed," Rose shouts from behind Eli.

Peter chuckles. "I'm glad they could make it."

"They've been waiting all week." Eli taps on the book. "Now sign, so I can get out of here and back to my boyfriend."

Peter grins. "I'm sure he's a lovely guy."

Eli smiles back at him. "He is. Perfect, actually." Eli stands up straight.

"You didn't think that was too much?"

"I'm sure they appreciated the authenticity," Eli promises. "Besides, it was very sweet."

"Thank you."

Eli leans across the table, giving Peter a soft kiss on his forehead. "You're welcome, tiger."

"Hurry uuup!" Patricia groans, pretending to roll her eyes. "I've been waiting for *weeks* to meet my favorite author."

Eli and Peter continue to stare at one another. "I guess I should let the circus act have their turn."

"I guess you should."

"Do you have anything to do after us?"

"They want me to sign stock," Peter says. "But that shouldn't take too long."

"Okay, we can wait for you outside," Eli says, knowing the bookstore is just minutes from closing, and, given the preorder numbers that Peter already has to sign, it might be a while before he's done with all the extra copies the store ordered.

"Enough!" Patricia strolls up, stepping beside Eli. "You two can eye-fuck later."

"Hey, Patricia." Peter smiles.

"Hey, Peter." She opens the book to the title page where Peter has been signing all night. "Here's the sticky note."

"I'll see you in a bit." Eli leans over the table, kissing Peter once more before he steps away.

Rose and Patricia join Eli outside a moment later where Peter's parents are hanging out, their books freshly signed.

"We were worried you weren't going to make it," Mrs. Park tells Eli, wrapping him up in a hug.

"We almost didn't." Eli hugs her back before he gives Mr. Park a firm handshake. Despite how easily Eli had been welcomed into Peter's family, how he'd already gone to Georgia with Peter last year for Christmas, and for his mother's birthday before that, Mr. Park still intimidated Eli in an odd way. It certainly hadn't been helped by the awkward "I want to know your intentions with my son" conversation that'd happened the moment he and Mr. Park were alone for the first time.

"He's just trying to scare you," Peter had promised Eli afterward. "Trust me, Dad's a softie, and he likes you."

"My first autograph!" Rose does a little dance, showing off the way that Peter signed her name.

"This is so fucking cool, Eli." Patricia looks at her own name.

"I know," Eli says. "I'm so proud of him."

It takes another thirty minutes of waiting before Peter is done. Eventually, Peter makes his way back out, Amber right behind him. They whisper a few words to each other, hugging before Amber says goodbye to Eli.

"They gave me a free tote bag!" Peter shows off the store logo on the side.

Eli wants to hug his boyfriend, but lets Peter's parents get in first, whispering their congratulations to him. Peter has to wipe the red lipstick off his cheek when his mother is done. "Are you all finished up?" she asks.

"Yep, all done!"

"You did so good!" Eli throws his arms around Peter, kissing him gently.

"Ugh, gross . . ." Rose fakes a vomiting sound. "Come on, we're going out to celebrate."

"Actually, um . . . if it's okay, I'm pretty beat," Peter tells them. "And my hand hurts."

"Are you sure, Peter?" his father asks. "We have reservations."

"He gets all big and famous and suddenly he's too good for us," Patricia teases, rubbing Peter slowly on the back.

"We're gonna do our own celebration." Eli steps in, sensing Peter's discomfort. "Plus, he hasn't packed for Sacramento yet."

"It's okay," Mrs. Park assures him. "We'll go out with Patricia and Rose."

Rose crosses her arms, pretending to pout. "I guess the responsible thing to do would be to go home and grade those spelling tests from two weeks ago."

"Rose . . ." Eli stares. "Two weeks?"

"What? They're seven, they can wait. Priorities, Eli."

Peter goes in to give his parents a giant hug. "I'll see you tomorrow, Umma."

"See you tomorrow, adeul. Don't forget, we're getting breakfast in the morning. Then we're going to the bridge!"

"I won't forget."

The Parks hug Eli too before they join Patricia and Rose.

"I'll text you, Eli!" Patricia waves, as does Rose, and the four of them walk out of the store together.

"Good night!" Eli says to everyone, the bell above the door echoing.

"I'm almost sorry I'm missing that dinner." Peter looks down at Eli, wrapping his arm around Eli's waist and pulling him in. "So . . ."

"So!"

"Do you want to grab dinner somewhere? Maybe get takeout."

"Actually, I went to the grocery store for you earlier today, before work," Eli tells him.

"I had groceries; you didn't have to shop for me," Peter tells him.

"Peter, I hate to be the one to tell you this, but a carton of eggs and a box of baking soda are *not* groceries." Peter's refrigerator was already sparse on the good days, but over the last year and a half, Peter's days became consumed with both work for Zelus and edits and copyedits, plus the start of the second book in his two-book deal that was due in just a few months. So Eli had taken charge of making sure Peter fed himself.

"The eggs are groceries," Peter mutters. "But thank you, I appreciate it."

"I thought we could do breakfast for dinner."

"You want to do breakfast for dinner?" Peter asks with an air of uneasiness.

"Is that so wrong?"

"No, no." He laughs. "I'm just recalling what happened the last time you tried to make me breakfast for dinner."

"Hey, I was distracted. And that was *two* years ago."

"Okay, okay." Peter laughs, taking Eli's hand in his. "Breakfast for dinner."

"You can finally try my French toast."

Peter smiles at him. "I'd love that."

"Good, and if you hate it, you can't tell me." Eli pulls Peter out into the cool night, the wind blowing through his shorter hair.

"I promise I'll love it." Peter leans in. "But not as much as I love you." He takes Eli's cheek in his hand, pulling him in for a kiss.

"God." Eli winces. "That was so cheesy."

"Say it back!" Peter attacks Eli with smaller kisses, wrapping his arms tight around Eli so that he can't escape.

"Okay! Okay!" Eli can't help but giggle. "I love you!"

"What was that?" Peter pulls him in again, lifting him up in a hug. "I didn't hear you."

"I love you!" he says a little louder, Peter finally putting him back on his own two feet so that they can look at one another.

Eli glances up so that he can look at the man who shines brighter than the sun.

He leans in, smiling against Peter's lips. "I love you."

Peter smiles back, kissing Eli slowly. "I love you too."

Acknowledgments

Thank you to my agent, Lauren Abramo, who didn't know about this book at first. I wanted to surprise her with it, though we'd discussed the eventual move into adult romance. I think I wanted to prove to myself that I could do it before I shared it with anyone. But she loved the story; I remember the phone call after we first discussed where this story could go, and the ideas she had for changes. I left that conversation feeling the most accomplished I ever had.

To my editor, Shannon Plackis, without whom this book quite literally wouldn't exist in its current form. I don't think I've ever told her how nervous I was before we first met, but during my and Shannon's first phone call, every anxiety seemed to melt away. This book couldn't have found someone who understood it better than Shannon, and I'll forever be grateful for what she was able to bring out of it.

There's also the team at Avon, who've been championing this book behind the scenes. Marie Rossi, Hope Ellis, DJ DeSmyter, Danielle Bartlett, Kelsey Manning, Tess Day, Owen Corrigan, May Chen, Tessa Woodward, Jennifer Hart, and Liate Stehlik.

I also want to thank Victoria Cho, our sensitivity reader who helped me to make Peter more visible, for also helping me to inject so much love into his story.

Thank you to Sylvan Creekmore, who first gave this book a chance.

And an extra special thank-you to Ricardo Bessa, whose art I'd been following for years. Getting to have his work represent my own was so amazing and surreal to see come together.

Page Powars, Alicia Thompson, and Alison Cochrun all read this book before anyone else because I had no idea if I could successfully write an adult romance, so I want to thank them for all their help and advice, as well as their encouraging DMs.

To my other friends, the list of whom might get long, and I'm sure there's someone I'll forget, so please forgive me if I do: Jack, Ally, Leah, Adib, Camryn, Sina, Adriana, Becky, Julian, Misha, Ashley, Rachael, Jay, Karen, Sophie, Edward, and so many more people. Your support and friendship mean so much.

To my best friends Cam, Nguyen, Corey, and Huong, without whom I would've lost my mind a long time ago.

To Fede, who gave me my love story.

To my mother, who took me to the library as a child.

And lastly, I want to talk to us. Those of us who grew up like Peter, isolated from other queer people, who grew up without a community, without elders to look up to, without local queer history or heroes. Oftentimes, it feels like we've been left behind, like we're stunted almost. And even when we start to find our own space, even when we think we've found camaraderie among other queer people, we're faced with constant reminders about where we came from, mourning an experience that we never got to have. Through Peter's story, I hope readers get to find a piece of themselves in him—the understanding and the knowledge that life isn't about playing catch-up. In the middle of editing this book, I think just before we went on submission with it, an album by the title of *The Rise and Fall of a Midwest Princess* came out; a lot of you have no doubt heard of it. While I resonated with many of the songs, on my first listen, I was struck by one track in particular.

Hearing a lesbian artist sing such a heartfelt song about her small town and her dreams to dance on a stage, to experience a freedom she never had before despite knowing it'll upset her mother, that it may alienate her from everything she's ever known . . . her home.

It was the first time I'd ever heard what I didn't even know I had put into words. The song certainly unlocked something in me, an understanding, a perspective I wanted to put on this book that I didn't have before. And with Shannon's help, this book became far more personal than I ever really intended it to be.

So, lastly, I want to thank those of us who made it to the Pink Pony Club a little later in life, whatever that might look like for you. Like I said before, life isn't about catching up. What matters is you're here now.